Praise for
Miriam

"Mesu Andrews shines brilliant new light on the epic we only thought we knew, transforming the familiar biblical account of the Exodus with a narrative grounded in a deep love for God and his Word. *Miriam* illuminates the power and majesty of Yahweh, while weaving a story of real people waiting for deliverance from a God they have not yet learned to trust."

—STEPHANIE LANDSEM, author of *The Tomb: a Novel of Martha* (The Living Water Series)

"Mesu Andrews's novels have transformed my ability to hear the heartbeat of biblical figures like Job, Dinah, and Solomon. *Miriam* brings another cast of familiar characters to vibrant life—Miriam, Moses, Eleazar, Aaron, Hur—mingling them seamlessly with an imagined circle of loved ones that will have readers eagerly turning pages to witness God's stunning power at work for his people, both personally and nationally. With skillful prose, impeccable research, and a clear devotion to the biblical account of Israel's Exodus from Egypt, Mesu Andrews depicts these Old Testament men and women with a sparkling clarity, never shying away from what makes them relatable human beings—the failings, triumphs, and yearnings that are timeless."

—LORI BENTON, author of *Burning Sky, The Pursuit of Tamsen Littlejohn,* and *The Wood's Edge*

"Mesu Andrews's engaging novel, *Miriam,* gives us a new and vibrant appreciation for life in Egypt as the Lord visits the land with ten unforgettable plagues. With fascinating insight into biblical history as well as the human heart, this story will capture your attention until the last page."

— TESSA AFSHAR, award-winning author of *Land of Silence* and *Pearl in the Sand*

BOOKS BY MESU ANDREWS

The Pharaoh's Daughter

In the Shadow of Jezebel

Love in a Broken Vessel

Love's Sacred Song

Love Amid the Ashes

A TREASURES OF THE NILE NOVEL

MIRIAM

MESU ANDREWS

WATERBROOK
PRESS

MIRIAM
PUBLISHED BY WATERBROOK PRESS
12265 Oracle Boulevard, Suite 200
Colorado Springs, Colorado 80921

All Scripture quotations are taken from the Holy Bible, New International Version®, NIV®. Copyright © 1973, 1978, 1984, 2011 by Biblica Inc.® Used by permission. All rights reserved worldwide.

This book is a work of historical fiction based closely on real people and real events. Details that cannot be historically verified are purely products of the author's imagination.

Trade Paperback ISBN 978-1-60142-601-7
eBook ISBN 978-1-60142-602-4

Cover design by Kristopher K. Orr; cover photography by Kristopher K. Orr (Miriam) and Lightstock (background)

Published in the United States by WaterBrook Multnomah, an imprint of the Crown Publishing Group, a division of Penguin Random House LLC, New York.

WATERBROOK® and its deer colophon are registered trademarks of Penguin Random House LLC.

Library of Congress Cataloging-in-Publication Data
Names: Andrews, Mesu, 1963– author.
Title: Miriam / Mesu Andrews.
Description: First Edition. | Colorado Springs, Colorado : WaterBrook Press, 2016. | Series: A treasures of the nile novel
Identifiers: LCCN 2015043817 (print) | LCCN 2015046476 (ebook) | ISBN 9781601426017 (paperback) | ISBN 9781601426024 (ebook) | ISBN 9781601426024 (electronic)
Subjects: | BISAC: FICTION / Christian / Historical. | FICTION / Historical. | FICTION / Literary. | GSAFD: Bible fiction. | Christian fiction. Classification: LCC PS3601.N55274 M57 2016 (print) | LCC PS3601.N55274 (ebook) | DDC 813/.6—dc23
LC record available at http://lccn.loc.gov/2015043817

Printed in the United States of America
2016—First Edition

10 9 8 7 6 5 4 3 2 1

To Mary Cooley, my feisty eighty-six-year-old mama,
a woman with Miriam's strength, faith, and passion.

NOTE TO READER

Research for both *The Pharaoh's Daughter* and *Miriam* sent me into a different world. Historians and archaeologists disagree on many things about Egypt, but on one thing they're utterly united— ancient Egypt was unique, unlike any other nation on earth. Egyptians recorded their distinctiveness. They flaunted it, lauded it, and guarded it.

Until the Ramessid kings came to power.

The Ramessid kings were warriors, explorers, and builders who expanded Egypt's borders, brought the outside world in, and caused Egypt to lose a portion of its distinctiveness. However, under the Ramessid's *New Kingdom,* trade flourished and building projects surged, meaning the need for laborers in Egypt's Nile delta increased a hundredfold.

> So they put slave masters over [the Israelites] to oppress them with forced labor, and they built Pithom and Rameses as store cities for Pharaoh. But the more they were oppressed, the more they multiplied and spread; so the Egyptians came to dread the Israelites and worked them ruthlessly. They made their lives bitter with harsh labor in brick and mortar and with all kinds of work in the fields; in all their harsh labor the Egyptians worked them ruthlessly. (Exodus 1:11–14)

Bible stories mean so much more when we understand the culture and political climate in which the characters lived. I pray that as Miriam's story unfolds, you'll be driven back to God's Word to discover the truth behind the fiction.

PROLOGUE

I am Miriam, old but of use. I am a slave, a midwife, a healer with herbs. This is what I do, but El Shaddai makes me who I am.

The Hebrews call me prophetess; the Egyptians, a seer. But I am neither. I am simply a watcher of Israel and the messenger of El Shaddai. When He speaks to me in dreams, I interpret. When He whispers a melody, I sing.

During my eighty-six inundations, His presence has swelled within me like the Nile's waters, quenching my thirst, meeting every need. No relationship imprisons me. No task consumes me. No despair conquers me. I'm His alone, free to love others as He loves me.

But as I dab my parents' brows, creeping dread crawls up my arms like a living thing. Last night's dreams have shaken our divine union. *El Shaddai, Your messages have always been so clear. Why not give the meaning with the dreams?*

I know they portend death. But whose? Fear coils around my heart like a serpent. *Please don't take my parents, Shaddai.* A ridiculous request, I know. Abba Amram has seen 137 inundations and Ima Jochebed, 109. They are the wonder of the tribe of Levi, and even the Egyptians whisper rumors of a slave couple favored by the gods.

Abba's chest rises and falls with shallow breaths. Ima snores quietly. My heart will break when I must say good-bye.

A flash of light, and my mind grows dark . . . until Shaddai shows me a single soldier walking toward me. It's Eleazar. Last night's dream creatures dance around him, taunting, but he can't see them. My nephew walks quickly, calling my name. As suddenly as it came, the vision is gone.

Abba and Ima sleep peacefully while I lean into the constant presence of my Shaddai. Eleazar will arrive soon with our morning rations, but now I know last night's dreams have something to do with him. *Thank You, my Shaddai, for Your tender consolation.* For though the evil creatures tested and taunted, they could not destroy him. *But I know there's more to the dreams than that. Show me, Shaddai. Show me more.*

A warm breeze stirs the stifling air within our mud-brick house, and I know it's El Shaddai. *All right, I'll try to be patient.* New-found peace grapples with niggling angst. I'll sing. Singing always soothes me, lifts me, transports me deeper into His presence.

The tune is the same. Haunting, groaning, yearning. But something changes. The breeze dies. A strange chill races up my spine. I hum a familiar melody, waiting for new words of praise that never come—like the dream without a message.

Heart racing, eyes burning, my soul cries out, *El Shaddai, are You there?*

Silence.

I look out our window. The sun still shines. The birds still sing. But a chill breeze stirs in the hot sun, and I know. Change is coming. Change is here.

PART 1

The LORD said to Moses, "When you return to Egypt, see that you perform before Pharaoh all the wonders I have given you the power to do. But I will harden his heart so that he will not let the people go."

—EXODUS 4:21

1

[The Egyptians] made [the Israelites'] lives
bitter with harsh labor in brick and mortar
and with all kinds of work in the fields; in
all their harsh labor the Egyptians worked
them ruthlessly.

—EXODUS 1:14

Dawn's haze barely glowed over the eastern hills when the first injured slave leaned against Miriam's doorframe and peered around her curtain. "I've come from the plateau mud pits and have no way to pay you. Will you tend my wounds?" He averted his eyes, drew a breath, and held it. Was he waiting for rejection?

"Yes, yes, come in." Miriam rocked to her feet and hurried to welcome him before his courage failed.

He stepped over the threshold but hesitated after two steps onto her packed-dirt floor. "Others told me Israel's prophetess offered care for free, but I didn't believe it."

Miriam guided him to her sleeping mat, inspecting his wounds on the way. Besides the obvious cuts and bruises on his face, he bore deep whipping wounds on his mud-caked back. "I'm certainly not opposed to payment, but I can't turn away a child of Abraham in need."

He laughed without humor. "Well then, you'll likely meet several of Abraham's children today. The temperature is rising quickly, and the slave masters' tempers rise with it."

Miriam eased him down on her mat, giving him only partial attention while she listened for El Shaddai's guidance on proper treatment. *Shaddai, You know I can't minister to Your people without Your instruction.*

She'd been trained as a midwife by her friend Shiphrah, but treating injuries and wounds had come through years of experience—and revelations from God, who alone knew the intricacies of the human body.

The man must have noted her hesitation and pointed to his left side. "I think my ribs are broken. The guard hit me in the face and belly after he whipped me and then kicked my side when I doubled over. I need to get back to work before anyone notices I'm gone."

"Let's clean up your back first, and then I'll check your ribs and belly." She could apply honey to his cuts without a vision to direct her, but she needed Shaddai's wisdom to detect internal injuries. Working quickly, she pleaded with God to speak, but He remained silent. Her heart pounded wildly. *Shaddai, where are You? I feel like I've lost my right arm without Your breath on my spirit.*

"Lean back so I can check your belly." Hands shaking, she pressed on the man's abdomen and, though it was obviously sensitive, the tenderness seemed commensurate with a simple gut punch. "I don't think you're bleeding inside. I'll wrap your ribs for support so you can keep working."

Before she could turn to gather the strips of linen, he grabbed her arm. "Thank you, prophetess. I'm sorry I have no grain or milk to give for your services." He dropped his eyes in shame.

Miriam cupped his cheek, as she had hundreds of plateau slaves before him. "El Shaddai provides for my needs. He is the One True God, and one day He will deliver us all from bondage."

The man's look of shame turned quickly to a bitter smile. "I hope your healing talents are better than your prophetic skills. El Shaddai cast us aside when Joseph died."

"But He hasn't cast us aside," she said. "He speaks every day if we will only listen. We must never forget we're His chosen people."

The man winced, struggling to sit up. "If this is what it means to be *chosen* by your God, I'd rather serve Anubis and take my chances in Egypt's afterlife."

"Get out." A deep male voice intruded, and Miriam knew without looking that her nephew Eleazar had heard the slave's comment. "You came to my doda Miriam for help, but instead you insult her. Now, get out." His size and bearing were even more imposing in Miriam's small room.

"I'm sorry! I'll—" The slave tried to stand, but Miriam pressed on his shoulders, forcing him back on her mat.

"You'll sit there until I wrap your chest, and you'll listen—without interruption—about El Shaddai and His good plan for Israel." Miriam waved a finger at her nephew on her way to the basket of linen bandages. "And you will stop frightening my patients."

Eleazar crossed the small room in four strides. "Pharaoh has summoned you to the throne hall—immediately. You don't have time to help an ungrateful slave."

"Pharaoh can wait. There will be more wounded today because of this heat. I'm sure Pharaoh would rather see bricks made than talk to a simple midwife." She stepped around her towering nephew and began binding the slave's chest as tightly as he could bear. "Now, this is why we are called Shaddai's *chosen* people. When He chose to bless Abraham, He promised that all nations would be blessed through him and that Abraham's descendants would one day possess the land of Canaan. But our bondage isn't a surprise to El Shaddai. He warned Abraham that his descendants would become slaves for four hundred years in a country not their own before they inherited the Land of Promise."

"Doda, now." Eleazar tapped his sandal on the packed-dirt floor. "Pharaoh said you must come *now.*"

Miriam eyed her nephew beneath a scornful brow and returned her attention to the wayward slave. "If my abba Amram's calculations are correct, we will see the end of the four hundred years in our lifetimes." A shiver of excitement raced through her. "Can you imagine being free from this place?" She tied the last bandage and expected the slave to share her joy.

Instead, she saw only anger.

"Your family lives in Goshen, in the valley, which means long life and plenty of provisions. Not so with families on the plateau. My abba died when I was four, and no doubt I'll die before my son grows to manhood." He turned to Eleazar. "I mean no disrespect to the prophetess, but

I cannot trust a God who not only allows His people to suffer, but allows such disparity among us."

Miriam's heart plummeted. She knew Eleazar's response before he spoke it.

"I don't trust such a God either, friend. Now, get out."

2

Amram married his father's sister Jochebed,
who bore him Aaron and Moses. Amram
lived 137 years.

—Exodus 6:20

Eleazar's patience was wearing thin, but Doda refused to leave until he visited with Saba Amram and Savta Jochebed. "We appreciate that you share your palace rations with us each day," Doda said, "but your grandparents are more interested in seeing you than your food."

She was right, of course. Saba and Savta would be terribly disappointed if they woke and found both he and Doda gone, and Eleazar would rather face the Hittites in battle than disappoint his grandparents.

Slipping through the dividing curtain into the adjoining room, Doda knelt beside two sleeping forms. Saba Amram lay on his side, back facing the door, arm over the frail frame of his beloved Jochebed. They'd been married, as near as they could remember, almost ninety inundations.

Doda Miriam had lived in this two-room dwelling all her life—except for the time she'd served as handmaid to the pharaoh's daughter, the same woman who had saved Doda's brother Moses and raised him as a prince of Egypt. When Moses's heritage was discovered, the pharaoh's daughter was saved from execution by the king's merciful bodyguard and hidden among Hebrews. She was given a Hebrew name—Bithiah—and married the Chief Linen Keeper, a slave named Mered, who shared adjoining rooms with Doda, Saba, and Savta in this long house. Mered's family had grown and moved to another village, but Doda had remained here to care for Saba and Savta—and everyone else too poor to afford Egyptian physicians.

Eleazar ran his fingers over the marks on the doorway, lines drawn to measure his height as he grew up. His younger brother Ithamar's growth was measured on the opposite doorframe. They'd always been Doda's favorites—no doubt because Abba Aaron and Ima Elisheba were too busy doting on his older brothers, Nadab and Abihu. A sigh escaped before Eleazar could recapture it.

Doda jostled Saba Amram's shoulder. "Eleazar brought his rations for us. Your favorites, nabk-berry bread and boiled goose eggs." She waved the delights in front of his nose as he woke, and Eleazar chuckled at the sparkle in Saba's rheumy eyes.

The commotion woke Savta Jochebed, and her sweet smile welcomed Eleazar like a warm hug. "Good morning, our sweet boy."

Eleazar was forty-seven years old, bodyguard of Pharaoh's second firstborn, and as a war-seasoned military slave, had been given the position of slave commander at Rameses. Would he always be Savta's *sweet boy*? An unsanctioned grin assaulted him. He hoped so. "Good morning, Savta. Are you well?"

"Of course we are well." Saba bounced his eyebrows. "We have nabk-berry bread!"

Chuckles around their small circle released Eleazar from the shroud of Pharaoh's morning tantrum but reminded him of his duty. "I'm sorry I can't stay longer, but Ramesses has summoned Doda Miriam to the throne hall to interpret his nightmares."

"Nightmares." Doda whispered reverently. "Those must be the dreams El Shaddai showed me last night." With a wistful sigh, she set aside the food and reached for Saba and Savta. "Pharaoh can wait until we help your grandparents sit up against the wall to eat their fine meal."

Eleazar sprang into action, lifting them gently and stuffing straw behind their backs to make them more comfortable.

When he glanced around the room, Doda was returning with a bowl of water and cloths. "I'll just give them a quick bath before we go."

"Absolutely not!" His heated reply startled his elders, and the gentle rebuke in Saba Amram's knitted brow silenced him.

Saba searched Eleazar's face as if mining for copper. "You're frightened for Miriam to appear in front of Pharaoh. Why?" Saba Amram had always been able to read him like a scroll.

"I mentioned to Prince Ram months ago that Doda interpreted dreams. It was stupid of me to ever mention my family. Now he has a weapon to use against me." Eleazar held Doda Miriam's gaze. "Simply interpret the dreams and leave. Say nothing to antagonize Ramesses."

"If El Shaddai tells me the meaning, I'll give the interpretation."

The floor seemed to shift beneath him. "If? You always know the meanings of dreams. What do you mean *if*?"

Doda waved away his question like a fly from her stew. "Shaddai showed me the dreams, so we must believe He'll give the interpretation when I stand before Ramesses."

Eleazar opened his mouth, but no words came. Groping in the silence, he looked to Saba Amram for help. "I can't take her to Ramesses if she can't interpret the dreams. He'll kill her."

"Come here, daughter." Saba extended his blue-veined hand and pulled Doda close. "El Shaddai has been faithful to us our whole lives. But you must be careful. Egypt's kings once dealt shrewdly with the Hebrews, but Ramesses abandons all pretense. He needs no reason to kill a Hebrew."

Doda bowed on one knee and pressed her forehead against Saba's hand. "Pray for me, Abba. I don't feel El Shaddai's presence this morning."

Fear sucked the wind from Eleazar's chest as he watched his three elders bow their heads in prayer. He felt like an outsider—as he always did when they spoke of their God—but worse, he felt responsible for leading his doda into danger.

With a wink and a kiss, Doda received encouragement from Saba and Savta, rocked to her feet, and grabbed her walking stick on her way out of the long house. Barely a few steps outside, Eleazar could stand it no longer. "What do you mean you don't feel Shaddai's presence? He's invisible. How can an invisible God be any more present one day than another?"

She answered without slowing her pace or looking his direction. "El Shaddai's presence is more real to me than the Nile. He is the air I breathe. He is the beating of my heart. I converse with Him all day long, and He replies—in His own way. But this morning was different. He is silent."

Eleazar swallowed a growing lump in his throat and halted his doda. "I can't take you to Ramesses unless I *know* your God will give you the interpretation. I can't keep you safe when we're surrounded by Egyptian guards in the throne hall."

"*You* can't keep anyone safe, dear." She patted his cheek. "That's up to El Shaddai."

The look in her eyes was sincere, but sincerity wouldn't save her from Ramesses. "If I had left you and Saba and Savta in El Shaddai's care all these years, you would have starved by now." How many hundreds of times had they had this conversation?

With a snort, she began marching toward the city again, but Doda needed to face the glaring truth. "Half of my rations barely keep you, Saba, and Savta alive. Why don't you tend to the injuries of people who can pay you?"

"Sometimes the slaves bring me grain or a loaf of bread, and I have a small garden. El Shaddai always provides for us."

"Why can't Abba Aaron share a loaf of bread once in a while? Or my selfish ima give you some of her grain rations?"

Doda stopped and planted both fists on her hips. "You will not speak disrespectfully of your parents. Regardless of their shortcomings, you will honor them because they gave you life." She cocked her head, waiting for Eleazar's acknowledgement.

With his single nod, they resumed their walk. Eleazar reached inside his leather breast piece for his portion of rations and handed his bread to Doda. "You didn't have time to eat before we left. Eat."

She accepted, took her first bite, and lolled it to the side that still had a few teeth. "Why don't you talk while I eat?" Her smile was full of mischief.

He tried to maintain his stern bearing, but a chuckle betrayed him.

They walked on a narrow path between canals that had been swollen by the Nile's inundation. Slaves lined both sides, making mud bricks for the city's extensive building projects, while Egyptian slave drivers cracked their whips and shouted orders. Eleazar kept his voice low and his eyes averted. "These dreams have made Pharaoh even more unpredictable. You must be careful. Ramesses may tolerate some of your antics because he respects our family's longevity. Age means blessing even to Egyptians, but please, none of your impudence."

"I think that's more than I've heard you say since last year's inundation." She raised both eyebrows and took another bite of bread. "I'll interpret the dreams, and then we'll leave so you and I can talk about your marriage."

That grin of hers broke him every time. He laughed and squeezed her arm tight against his side. "I'm not getting married—ever. You're relentless."

"I learned it from your saba Amram. Why do you think he's 137 years old?"

The reminder both warmed and terrified Eleazar. Doda, Saba, and Savta were his life. The thought of losing them haunted him day and night. Why had he mentioned to Prince Ramesses that Doda Miriam interpreted one of his dreams years ago? He'd been so careful never to reveal family members' names. Too many Hebrew women were punished for a husband's or father's sins.

He pulled Doda closer as they walked. "Doda, just interpret his dream. Nothing else. No more words. Then I'll take you home."

Popping the last bite of bread into her mouth, she clapped breadcrumbs from her hands. "I promise I'll say only what my Shaddai tells me to say."

No matter how much he begged, she'd never promise anything else. *Her Shaddai,* as she called Him, had been the single light in her dark world. Since his first battlefield, Eleazar had seen the folly of trusting any god, but he would never begrudge Doda or his grandparents their archaic traditions. In fact, their beliefs were undoubtedly what had kept them alive through the changes they'd seen in their lifetimes.

He watched Doda's expression change to deep sadness as they left the canals and entered the thriving industrial section of the city of Rameses. She'd often told him of the single linen shop her friend Mered oversaw before the quiet Avaris estate grew to become the capital city of Rameses. Now this industrial section boasted multiple buildings, eight of which housed the finest byssus-linen production in the world.

The city of Rameses was the last stop on the Way of Horus—the world's most lucrative trade route. In addition to weaving the byssus linen, Hebrew slaves kept the king's brewery, winery, and metal shop producing other quality products that were traded in markets from Elam to Hatti.

Pharaoh Ramesses had built this namesake city on the backs of his Hebrew slaves. After using their blood for mortar and crushing their bones with its bricks, he made the city his home.

"Keep your head bowed as we go through the gates," Eleazar said as they approached the palace complex. "The guards know I'm Prince Ram's guard, but they'll use any excuse to beat us both."

She bowed her head and remained silent.

"How long since you've visited the palace complex?" He wasn't certain when she'd last served the king's harem as midwife.

Head still bowed, Doda spoke in barely a whisper. "I haven't left the slave village since Pharaoh Sety died, almost thirty years ago. When Ramesses became king, he wanted only Egyptian midwives attending his harem."

They passed through the gates unmolested, and Eleazar breathed easier. Doda tugged at the sleeve of her robe, and Eleazar tucked her under his arm. "No one will see your harem brand. They use a different symbol for Ramesses's concubines anyway."

Her eyes glistened. "Do you really believe people would think I'm Ramesses's concubine?" She shook her head with a derisive grin. "Women with a harem brand today could be concubines or simply slave girls, but when I bore this brand, it meant the master possessed a woman *completely*." Doda looked up to impress her meaning. "The master who owned me was my brother Moses—posing as an Egyptian prince."

Of course, everyone knew the story of Eleazar's uncle, Prince Mehy. Best friend and vizier to Ramesses's father, Pharaoh Sety, Mehy had been a Hebrew infant rescued from the Nile by King Tut's sister and raised as the Egyptian master of the Avaris estate. Tut's sister, Amira Anippe, had hidden his Hebrew parentage but secretly allowed Miriam to call him *Moses*. When Eleazar was a boy of seven, Prince Mehy had come knocking on Saba's long-house door in the night, begging help to flee. Pharaoh Sety had discovered his Hebrew heritage and ordered his execution. Prince Mehy stood at Saba's door, trembling in a filthy rough-spun robe flung over his pristine linen *shenti* and Gold of Praise collar. Eleazar recognized Hebrew fear on his Egyptian-looking uncle before the man ran into the night. *Good riddance, Prince Mehy.*

"Are you listening?" Doda Miriam shook his arm. "My brother Moses owned this estate before anyone knew he was a Hebrew."

"I know, Doda." Eleazar pointed toward the palace bathing room at the base of the entry ramp and steered her toward it, hoping to distract her from the rest of the oft-told story. It didn't work.

"Moses branded me so the estate guards would think I was his concubine. The mark made me untouchable. It protected me until I was past the age of the guards' interest."

Eleazar nodded but kept silent. Why did his elders insist on telling the same stories again and again? He drew her close and kissed the top of her head as he led her into the public bath chamber.

Ceremonial washing had become mandatory since the days when Doda visited the palace. Every slave, merchant, criminal, or king must now be cleansed before bowing to Egypt's god on his throne. Eleazar grabbed a clean robe and guided his doda toward a stone sink. "Splash your hands, arms, face, and neck." He kept his head bowed, but Doda gawked at the crowd of male and female bathers. Some disrobed completely in the open, while others stepped behind the curtained partitions lining the inner wall. Eleazar shook Doda gently from her trance. "Keep your eyes downcast and bathe quickly."

He waited as she took a stone wash basin behind one of the curtained partitions. Though he'd visited the bathing room a dozen times, even he found it hard not to stare. Nubians, wearing nothing but strings and feathers, splashed cool Nile water over their deep black skin. Merchants from the Far East carefully avoided getting water on their oiled and curled beards, and chained prisoners from Hatti winced as the water grazed open wounds.

Doda reappeared wearing the simple but luxurious white linen robe, her rough-spun robe draped over the brand on her forearm. After emptying her small basin into the gutter that funneled the dirty water back to the river, she nestled under his arm. "I'm ready."

Eleazar's chest constricted. He'd never realized how much the brand bothered her. "Doda, you must leave your old robe in the dressing room. You can't take it into the throne hall."

"The sleeves are too short." Her eyes pleaded, but her jaw was set like stone.

"Doda . . ." Eleazar glanced at the crowded bathing chamber and guided her to a secluded corner. "You're eighty-six. Everyone knows Prince Mehy's story—"

"But not everyone knows I was his sister," she said too loud, gaining the attention of several bathers. Doda took a deep breath and lowered her voice. "Those who do know I was Prince Mehy's sister may think the worst. The only Hebrews who knew the truth, other than your grandparents, are dead." Her eyes pooled with tears as she searched Eleazar's face. "Gossip and this brand made marriage impossible. But my devotion to Shaddai made marriage unnecessary."

Stunned, Eleazar had never realized the brand caused Hebrews to believe Doda was defiled by her own brother. He burned with new hatred for his dohd Moses—a man he vaguely remembered. "I didn't know you wanted to marry."

She wiped her eyes and waved off his answer. "Well, of course I didn't want to marry. What man could ever fill my heart like El Shaddai?" She poked his chest with her bony finger. "But it would have been nice to be asked, I tell you. Come now, Pharaoh is waiting."

Eleazar shook his head. Some things weren't worth the battle. As they began their march up the palace ramp, Eleazar contemplated the imminent confrontation. His seemingly undaunted doda would address Egypt's most capricious Pharaoh with a rough-spun robe draped over her arm. For the first time in years, Eleazar wished he believed in a god that heard his prayers.

3

Pharaoh gave Joseph the name Zaphenath-Paneah. . . . So Joseph died at the age of a hundred and ten. And after they embalmed him, he was placed in a coffin in Egypt.

—GENESIS 41:45; 50:26

When Miriam last visited the harem, it had been housed in what was then the larger of two palaces. Now there were three palaces in the royal complex, the grandest of which housed Pharaoh, his harem, and the throne hall in which she and Eleazar now stood. She'd seen Ramesses's extravagance evidenced in the massive statues of himself erected at the double gates of the palace complex, their inscriptions reading, "Ramesses, the god." His palace exceeded rumor, and the courtroom resembled a dream. Ivory and limestone washed the interior with the illusion of brightest hope, but the towering granite gods of Horus and Seth overshadowed the throne of Pharaoh's dark power.

Petitioners dressed in white nudged Miriam left then right, shoving forward to get a closer look at the king on his throne. Servants with ostrich-plume fans stirred tepid air over the golden chairs of Pharaoh's sons and officials, while noblemen and their women lined up with the giant pillars flanking the crimson carpet leading to Ramesses's throne.

Miriam adjusted her rough-spun robe to hide the brand on her arm. She'd borne the shame of gossip and wrongful accusations without regrets, but today's caution was about more than petty pride. What if Ramesses recognized the Avaris estate brand and realized her connection to the Hebrew who had betrayed his father, Sety? Did Ramesses still harbor the hatred for Moses that Pharaoh Sety had taken to his grave?

Miriam couldn't risk linking herself—or Eleazar—to the most despised Hebrew in Egyptian history.

She straightened her spine, took a deep breath, and stepped toward the throne, but was unceremoniously hauled back to the line of petitioners by Eleazar's giant hand.

He nodded and apologized to those with raised eyebrows. "Please, forgive us." He leaned close and whispered, "Doda, Hebrews are always last to be heard in Pharaoh's court. We must wait to be called forward."

"But I thought Pharaoh was in such a hurry to see me."

Eleazar's furrowed brow told her silence was preferred to promptness at this point.

She lifted her eyes to the king on his throne—thirty years older than the last time she'd seen him. More than age weighed on Ramesses's eyelids and wrinkled brow. Deep crevices lined his forehead and dark circles ringed his eyes. The double crown of Egypt rested on his shaved head, but his face was creased with years of worry, and his shoulders weren't the strong banner of youth they'd once been. He sighed and rested an elbow on his gilded throne, bending his forehead to his waiting palm. A droning dignitary draped in fur—during Egypt's hottest month—endorsed the visiting nation's fur trade.

"What would Egypt do with furs?" Miriam asked Eleazar a bit too loud. Two petitioners in front of her glanced back at her, sneering.

Her nephew pulled her closer and nodded toward the gallery of twenty young men sitting at Pharaoh's right hand in high-backed, embroidered chairs. "Those are Pharaoh's firstborn sons from each of his twenty wives." A knee-high gold wall etched with war scenes separated them from the nobles and petitioners. Ranging in age from midthirties to early teens, the twenty princes appeared as bored as their father and king. At the right shoulder of each royal stood an armor-bedecked guard—each shoulder but one.

"Is that your master, there?" Miriam pointed at the oldest of the princes, the one seated closest to the throne.

Eleazar nodded. "Yes, Prince Ramesses. Firstborn of Isetneferet—the Second Great Wife. I'll try to gain his attention. Perhaps he can alert

Pharaoh we've arrived." A head taller than most men in the room, Eleazar raised his hand slightly, waving in the direction of the princes.

A little pride warmed Miriam's heart knowing Prince Ramesses's personal guard stood at her side. "Does he know you call him *Prince Ram?*"

"Yes, Doda. Everyone calls him Ram because it would be heresy to call him by the name of the good god, Pharaoh Ramesses."

"I was harem midwife when Queen Sitre delivered Ramesses, and I can tell you he's not a—"

Eleazar's hand clamped over her mouth. Surrounding petitioners glared at her, and again Eleazar nodded and smiled. "I'm sorry if we've disturbed you." When all eyes had returned to Pharaoh and his throne, Eleazar removed his hand and whispered, "Doda, you can't say Pharaoh Ramesses isn't a god. That's treason."

Miriam wanted to say, *It's the truth,* but she crossed her arms and remained silent.

Eleazar nudged her forward as the next petitioner left his offering with the king's steward—two ostriches that squawked like trumpets. Miriam stretched up on her toes to catch a glimpse of Eleazar's younger brother, Ithamar. Pride swelled at the sight of him, personal slave of Pharaoh's chief scribe. Eleazar and Ithamar had done well as third- and fourth-born sons. In most Hebrew families, it was the first and second born who rose to the best positions. Not so with her brother Aaron's sons.

When Ramesses took Egypt's throne, his ambitious building projects demanded more Hebrew workmen, so he mandated only first- and second-born Hebrews be trained as skilled craftsmen while all others were put to work in fields, mud pits, the military, or some other harsh labor. Ithamar had begun serving in the military alongside Eleazar, but because of the younger boy's slight build and high intelligence, the palace scribes soon found better use for Ithamar's skills.

Miriam watched her youngest nephew's reed scribble across the papyrus scroll like a bird skimming the surface of the Nile. Concentration forced his tongue to the corner of his mouth as it had done since he was a small boy. Ithamar seldom visited the slave village of Goshen anymore, but when she'd seen him two years ago, he'd described his duties. *"I number the offerings brought by emissaries and tally the executions ordered by the king."* The sums, he'd said, were typically dead even.

While Eleazar continued to seek Prince Ram's attention, Miriam noted Pharaoh's demeanor change as two Egyptian guards brought in the next supplicant. A girl, who'd seen perhaps twenty inundations, stood trembling before the throne. Dressed in a simple white byssus robe, her sheer blue head covering distinguished her as Hebrew. She could have been a servant to any woman in the palace, but when the girl fell to her knees and stretched out her hands before her, Miriam saw the harem brand on her forearm.

Pharaoh shifted on his throne, his expression suddenly stony. "I will judge the woman who dared harm my ten-year-old son."

The throne hall became utterly still.

The girl pressed her forehead to the floor, her long hair coiled in a single braid beside her. "Please, mighty Pharaoh, Keeper of Harmony and Balance, Elect of Ra, it is with deep affection that I care for the young prince. I would never let harm come to him."

"And yet one of my fifty-six sons lies in his bed, leg broken, weeping in pain." Pharaoh let the silence draw out, repeatedly slapping the flail into his palm and trailing the horsehair through his fingers.

The girl's voice finally broke the tension. "My king, it was an accident. He slipped while climbing a palm tree—a tree he's climbed a hundred times. He's strong and agile as a gazelle. It was one missed step, and he was on the ground . . ." Her voice trailed off in a sob.

Miriam's feet propelled her forward, past the petitioners ahead of her and beyond Eleazar's grasp. "I seem to recall the same thing happening to you when you were a small boy, Mighty Pharaoh." Other noblemen parted as if she had leprosy, leaving Miriam standing in the middle of a starburst pattern of marble tile.

Pharaoh's guards advanced to protect the god on the throne from an eighty-six-year-old midwife. Eleazar shoved her behind him before they arrived. Bowing his head, he pleaded, "Forgive her, Son of Horus, Giver of Life, Strong in Right. This woman is my doda Miriam—I mentioned to my master, Prince Ram, that she interprets dreams for the Hebrews."

Miriam peered around Eleazar's right arm and saw only Ramesses's disdain. "I know your aunt. She tended my cuts and bruises when my divine father Sety ruled Egypt." He motioned her forward. "Stand before me, Midwife."

Miriam straightened, pleased to have Pharaoh's frustration aimed at her instead of the harem maid. Eleazar's arm circled her waist and he supported her elbow, leaning close. "Please, Doda, guard your words." They halted beside the harem maid, who was still sprawled on the floor, weeping quietly. Miriam bent to comfort her, but Eleazar pulled her upright with an iron grip, waiting before Pharaoh.

Ramesses's eyes narrowed, reminding Miriam of the haughty child he'd always been. "So you're the seer my son Ram told me about. I had no idea you were also the midwife from my childhood. Perhaps you are Isis in flesh, healing the Son of Horus as a child, then healing him again by interpreting the nightmares."

"I am no goddess, Ramesses. I only interpret that which the One True God allows." Gasps and whispers filled the room at the use of his familiar name. Eleazar's grip tightened around her waist, but Miriam felt no fear—only pity for this king lost in childish delusions.

Pharaoh raised his flail, securing instant quiet in the gallery. "And what sort of payment does your god require to interpret my dreams?"

"No payment, my king. When He speaks, I obey. When He is silent, I am silent." Miriam's heart now pounded like a hammer against her chest. *Oh my Shaddai, please don't be silent.*

Pharaoh slapped the flail into his palm again and tugged at the horsehair. A sinister smile creased his face, and he turned toward the harem maid, who had grown quiet. He motioned to two guards and pointed his flail at the girl. "Stand the girl between you."

They lifted her to her feet, and Eleazar breathed a name. "Taliah?"

Miriam turned to him in silent question, but Eleazar had no time to answer.

"You know her?" Pharaoh's delighted laugh sent a chill up Miriam's spine. He lifted his voice to the gathered crowd. "The midwife says she requires no payment, but every magician has a price. If she correctly interprets my dreams, I'll spare the girl's life. If she doesn't interpret them to my liking, the girl will lose her head right here, right now."

Miriam turned to Eleazar and spoke quietly. "How do you know this Taliah?"

He squeezed his eyes shut and whispered, "She's Putiel's youngest daughter. I promised I'd watch over her when he left with the crown prince to oversee the building project at Saqqara four years ago."

Miriam returned her attention to the girl, remembering the day Taliah's ima died birthing a fourth daughter. Taliah and two sisters had been left with a military abba and no ima. Putiel had found a husband for the oldest daughter, a kind man three-times her age. He'd given his second daughter to his uncle Ishbah to raise as a skilled weaver. But Taliah . . . she was third born and couldn't work as a skilled laborer. At five years old, she had already displayed her ima's beauty, which would make her prey for the guards in the fields or mud pits—dead before her twentieth inundation or wishing it was so. Putiel begged his master, Crown Prince Amenhirkopshef, to allow Taliah to serve in the harem. Though she was still just a child herself, she could entertain the toddlers and serve the king's young daughters. In a rare display of mercy, the crown prince agreed. Miriam hadn't seen the girl since.

"Doda?" Eleazar shook her and whispered, "Are you all right?"

She nodded and waved away her protective nephew. What a fuss he made over her. Turning to Ramesses, she noted again his puffy eyes and the dark shadows beneath them. Perhaps he would soften if shown some kindness. "Your eyes betray your sleepless nights, Great Pharaoh. Tell your physicians to combine rose paste with almond oil. Smear it on your lids and below your lashes, and then cover your eyes with cucumber slices while you sleep. Your eye paints will apply more smoothly the next morning."

Eleazar rolled his eyes, but Ramesses fought a grin. "I'll have it noted by the scribes. Now . . ." His humor disappeared. "My dreams, Midwife."

After a slight nod, Miriam met his gaze and spoke without hesitation. "In your first dream, you were trapped in the underground burial chamber of Zaphenath-Paneah—or, as we Hebrews know him, Joseph—the vizier who ushered in the Hyksos dynasty. There were ten wooden dolls standing guard around the tomb, east of the Great Wife's palace."

Ramesses scoffed. "Those wooden dolls, as you call them, are *shabtis*, and are buried with royalty in order to serve us in the next life. I wouldn't expect a slave to know our burial customs." Those in the audience laughed too, mocking Miriam's ignorance.

But she continued undaunted. "Then you realize it's only by God's revelation that I know Joseph's tomb is entirely underground."

The laughter died, and Pharaoh leaned forward. "Go on, but tread carefully. My dreams will not be soothed with almond oil and cucumbers."

Miriam bowed deeply, feeling real compassion for the fear on his features. The dreams replayed as vividly as she'd seen them as she slept the previous night. "Ten wooden *shabtis* sprang to life and opened Joseph's tomb. One by one, each succumbed to shocking destruction. The first was drowned in blood, the second eaten by frogs, the third—"

"Stop! I'll hear no more." Ramesses shouted, his face as white as his pleated *shenti*. "Tell me the second dream."

Miriam nodded and without preamble began her recounting. "You're in your abbi Sety's tomb, surrounded by the unspeakable wealth provided for his afterlife. He stands before you, arms outstretched, beckoning you to his embrace. But the Ramessid god Seth holds you captive as an invisible force cuts off Sety's ten toes, one at a time. When Sety's tenth toe is removed, he topples over like a great statue and shatters into a million pieces." The crowded throne hall inhaled as one, and Ramesses squeezed his eyes shut.

Miriam leaned heavily on Eleazar's arm and knelt before Pharaoh's throne. "These are the nightmares that have plagued Ramesses. Every detail. Nothing tempered."

Head bowed, Miriam felt Shaddai's warm breath across her heart and knew He had come to give her the meaning. The essence of the dreams filled her understanding, and though their message would incense Ramesses, her spirit rested in the truth.

On her left and right, magicians, noblemen, and officials averted their eyes from the throne. Had any of them the courage to speak such truth even if they knew the meanings of the dreams? Doubtful. But none of them had Shaddai on their side.

Miriam heard the king's unsteady breathing and could only guess what violence he would commit when he heard the rest of her message. *El Shaddai, I am Your servant. Be it unto me as You will.*

"Stand, Midwife."

Eleazar lifted her, setting her gently on her feet, and then replaced his arm around her. Her big, strong nephew was trembling. Dear boy.

Pharaoh's eyes narrowed, as if his stare could bore right through her. "If your god showed you my dreams, surely he can interpret their meaning."

Miriam tried to swallow but her mouth felt as dry as harvest season. She spoke in her gentlest voice. "In both dreams the number ten is significant, and both signify that Egypt's wealth will be ruined. The One God declares that with ten signs of His power He will ruin everything Pharaoh Sety worked to give you. Egypt will crumble before you, Mighty Ramesses." She sighed, relieved to be finished with the task, and dropped her head, waiting for her death sentence.

The king chuckled. Then laughed until the audience fell into hysteria with him. Only Miriam, Eleazar, and Taliah stood soberly. Perhaps they could hope for dismissal instead of death.

"The Hebrew god destroy Egypt?" Pharaoh's laughter ebbed through tears. "He can't even help pathetic slaves. How will he conquer the fiercest army in the world?"

Eleazar stiffened and answered before Miriam could catch her breath. "The Hebrew God is powerless against you, Great Ramesses. The Hebrews are your servants, committed to Egypt's glory."

The kohl-painted Eyes of Horus narrowed as Pharaoh examined

Eleazar. "You serve Prince Ram, second heir to Egypt's throne. He assures me you can be trusted." Pharaoh then turned to the gallery of princes. "Join me, Prince Ram, on the dais."

The well-muscled prince rose from his gilded chair. Only Crown Prince Amenhirkopshef held more power than Prince Ram, but Kopshef—as he was called—was in Saqqara, so Ram commanded Egypt's army and held his father's heart. The prince took his place at Pharaoh's right hand and waited to be addressed.

Pharaoh focused on Eleazar as he spoke. "We must trust those who serve us, my son. Do you still trust this Hebrew to oversee your military slaves?"

Miriam's mouth was as dry as Egypt's dust. *El Shaddai, I'm ready to endure whatever punishment comes to me, but please spare my dear Eleazar.*

"I trust him with my life, but I bow to your wisdom, mighty Pharaoh." Prince Ram's voice held no emotion.

Pharaoh nodded and rubbed his chin. "Very well. The Hebrew commander remains your servant, but I no longer trust the handmaid to care for my son."

Taliah whimpered, and Miriam stepped forward. "But you said—"

The guard on Taliah's right elbowed Miriam, doubling her over and ceasing her protest. Eleazar pulled Miriam aside, standing between her and the guard. He made no attempt to defend her. Smart boy.

Pharaoh cleared his throat. "You're still alive, Midwife, only because I know the gods have favored your family with long life. My son tells me your parents are well over 110—the age of perfection—and you yourself have lived more than eighty inundations. I dare not anger the gods by snuffing out your life, but I will not tolerate your insolence." Miriam straightened in the looming silence and found him smiling at her. "I will spare the handmaid as I promised, but her negligence must be punished. She must feel the pain my son felt."

He motioned Prince Ram closer for a private consult. The prince nodded and addressed Eleazar. "Break her right leg and remove her from the palace. She will live in the Hebrew village at the pleasure of the slave masters."

4

The LORD said to Aaron, "Go into the wilderness to meet Moses."

—EXODUS 4:27

Pharaoh had ordered the next petitioner to approach his throne before Taliah's agonized scream ebbed. She'd fainted when Eleazar lifted her into his arms, making her journey down the long hallway of the palace underground barracks bearable. Eleazar's small chamber was the nearest refuge to tend Taliah's broken leg before carrying her back to the slave village.

"It's that room, Doda." He nodded to a door on the right, halfway down. Miriam lifted the iron latch and entered. The smell of sweat-soaked leather and dirty feet greeted them. If he'd known Doda and an injured harem maid were coming, he would have asked his apprentice of four years, Hoshea, to tidy the room.

Hoshea's eyes widened at the intrusion. "Eleazar?"

Ignoring the question, Doda took charge. "Hoshea, clear off Eleazar's mat. Eleazar, set Taliah down gently. Easy, now."

Eleazar lowered the girl, and her eyes fluttered open. He moved away quickly as Doda crouched beside her. Taliah began to stir and then whimpered.

"Shh, it will be better soon," Doda cooed. "It will hurt for a while, but we'll get herbs at home, and you'll feel better." She looked over her shoulder at Hoshea. "Come here, boy. I need your help."

Hoshea and Eleazar shared quarters, and though Hoshea was only eighteen, he'd already learned to tend wounded soldiers on and off the battlefield. But the poor boy had never endured a commander like Doda.

"I'm going to straighten this broken bone," she said, holding his gaze. "You will lie across Taliah like a blanket to hold her still." Hoshea's cheeks bloomed red as poppies, but he squeezed his eyes shut and obeyed.

Doda Miriam said over her shoulder to Eleazar, "Get some leather for her to bite down on."

Eleazar tugged off the leather band securing his long hair at the nape of his neck. He knelt beside the girl's head and placed it gently between her teeth. She bit down hard, screaming through gritted teeth, while Doda straightened the bone.

Eleazar looked away, unable to watch Doda repair the break he'd inflicted. Prince Ram had descended the dais to ensure Pharaoh's order was carried out. He'd whispered to Eleazar, "Get her to the Hebrew village before Abbi changes his mind and kills her." Even Pharaoh's favored son walked a fine line between loyalty and morality. So Eleazar made the break as swift and clean as possible—one swing with his spear shaft below Taliah's knee.

Doda and Hoshea splinted her leg with Hoshea's broken spear shaft and torn bed linens. Both could easily be replaced.

Taliah's skin was the color of goat's milk, but who could blame her? Eleazar had seen soldiers faint from lesser ordeals. Without permission, his big, callused hand reached out to touch her cheek, but he stopped just in time. What was he doing?

Doda struggled to her feet. "All right, Eleazar. She's ready. You carry her." Hands on her hips, she tapped her toe and lifted an eyebrow.

He shot to his feet. "Why me? Hoshea can carry her while I gain clearance with the guards through the palace complex and beyond." It was a lame excuse, but Eleazar couldn't hold Taliah in his arms again. She was like a wounded lamb. And that perfume and soft skin made him dizzy.

Doda Miriam assessed Hoshea and then her nephew. "You're nearly twice the size of your apprentice. He's a fine boy, but Taliah needs strong arms and a steady gait to keep her leg stable." She lifted both eyebrows and tapped her toe—faster. Why could he never refuse his doda?

With a sigh, he knelt beside the mat and leaned in, but Taliah tried to scoot away.

"Wait!"

An instant sheen of sweat proved the pain of her effort.

Of course, she would be afraid of him. "I won't hurt you, Taliah." She nodded but wouldn't look up. His chest constricted. "I had to follow orders. Breaking your leg was the only way to save our lives."

"I understand. It's not that. I . . ." Her black eyes pooled with vulnerability more frightening than a Hittite's sword. "How did you know my name?"

Mouth suddenly dry, Eleazar tried to swallow but couldn't. His promise to Putiel had seemed so simple when Taliah didn't know. "I . . . um . . ."

Doda shoved him aside. "Your family and ours have been friends for as long as I can remember. Your great-saba Mered was the chief linen keeper who taught me to spin and weave as a girl, and your saba Jered—whose son Gedor is Pharaoh's current linen keeper—well, he used to play with my brother Moses when everyone believed Moses was Prince Mehy—"

Eleazar leaned close. "Doda, we must leave before Pharaoh finds her in the palace. You can explain family connections when we get her home."

"Home?" A tear spilled over Taliah's bottom lash. "The palace harem has been my only home. I've never seen any of you before, and I don't know where you're taking me." She pressed her palms against her eyes, enforcing a false calm, and then glared at Eleazar. "How does Prince Ram's personal guard know my name?"

Eleazar sighed, cursing his vow and his ignorance of women. But she deserved an explanation. "Your abba Putiel saved my life at the Battle of Kadesh, and I became his apprentice as Prince Ram's personal guard. When Prince Kopshef went to Saqqara, he demanded Putiel become his guard, so I now serve Prince Ram. Your abba asked me to look after you while he's away."

Taliah dropped her hands, a lovely V forming between her sculpted brows. "That was four years ago. Why have I never seen you before? How could you look after me when you were with Prince Ram and I was in the harem?"

"Before he left, your abba took me to the harem gate and pointed you out. Yours is not a face I could forget." His cheeks warmed at the inadvertent compliment, and he stared at his hands. "I bribed a eunuch. He keeps me informed."

When only silence met his confession, he looked up, finding Taliah's expression softened. "Thank you—Eleazar, is it?"

"Yes, well . . ." He cleared his throat and heard Hoshea snicker. A sharp glance silenced his young apprentice.

"My abba can't write, Eleazar, so I never expected correspondence, but I've had no word from him. Is he well?"

They were wasting time. He needed to get her out of the palace—and he didn't want to answer her question. "Why don't we talk on the way?"

He leaned toward her again, but she shoved him away, panic written on her features. "You know something about Abba. Tell me."

Spying his leather hair band on the floor, he reached for it with a sigh and pulled back his curly black hair. "I haven't seen Putiel since he left, but I've had no request for his replacement." Eleazar tried to smile in spite of the sick feeling in his gut. No Hebrew was safe with Prince Kopshef. "It's a hopeful sign. Now, we really must go."

Nodding, she wiped a tear and raised an arm around his neck, inviting him to lift her. He gently scooped her into his arms, but even the slightest jostle must have been excruciating. Taliah whimpered and buried her face against his chest, sending a terrible sensation through him. Surely, it was only compassion, perhaps regret, but—by the gods—he refused to feel anything else for this woman.

Doda retrieved Eleazar's lamb's wool headrest. "Hoshea, cradle this under Taliah's splinted leg, and I'll open the door."

Hoshea supported her leg as Eleazar glided into the deserted hallway. He didn't pause as Doda closed the door behind them, but kept his gait steady while trying not to look down at the beautiful woman in his arms.

His disciplined training offered a smooth ride for Taliah but failed miserably in keeping his eyes from her.

The realization of her allure burned in his belly when he considered how the slave masters might treat her. Eleazar leaned down so only she could hear. "Keep your face turned toward my chest." As they neared the end of the dark hallway, he whispered to Doda, "Hide her hair and throw your robe over her while we walk." The guards and slave drivers might question an injured harem maid leaving the palace, but they wouldn't think twice about a slave girl draped in rough-spun.

The midday sun burned hot by the time they cleared the colossal gates of the palace complex, and the dual statues of Ramesses bade them good-bye. Prince Ram expected Eleazar's return after his meal, but Eleazar couldn't hurry Doda or run with Taliah in his arms. He'd have to take the beating for tardiness.

Taliah peered up from beneath Doda's robe. "Pharaoh said I'd live in the slave village at the pleasure of the slave masters. Does that mean the slave masters will decide whose children I teach? It's all I'm trained to do."

Her innocence struck him like a blow. Was she really unaware of what the slave masters would do to a lovely maiden like her? "I'm taking you to Doda Miriam's long house. She'll care for you until your leg heals."

"I can still teach in spite of a broken leg, but I'll need scrolls. Where might I get those?"

Doda must have noted his distress and sidled up to them. "Life in Goshen will be quite different from what you're used to. You'll need to rest for a few weeks while your leg heals, and then I'll introduce you to your family. Mered and Bithiah belonged to the tribe of Judah, and their village is a bit farther west of ours." Then she patted Eleazar's shoulder. "You have nothing to worry about, dear. If my nephew promised Putiel he'd care for you, then you can be sure he'll provide a safe and happy home."

An invisible fist drove the wind from Eleazar's chest. A simple promise made four years ago suddenly felt like a life sentence.

They'd just passed the industrial section of Rameses when Eleazar noticed two slave drivers approaching. He leaned close to Taliah and whispered, "Turn away so they don't see your beauty." He curled her toward his chest, and Taliah cried out at the sudden shift in position. Eleazar shouted, "Shut up, girl, or I'll break your other leg."

The slave drivers laughed and nodded as they passed, satisfied that Eleazar was an overseer sufficiently abusive to his own people.

"There's no need to act like a barbarian just because they've trained you to fight like one." Taliah's sudden venom startled them all.

Eleazar considered dropping her in the dust. Doda drew a breath to speak but shook her head and kept walking. Hoshea's eyes were the size of ostrich eggs, but he dutifully held the lamb's wool under the girl's splinted leg.

Taliah seemed ready for a fight, but silence had served Eleazar well for forty-seven inundations. He ignored her, which seemed to cause her greater discomfort than her broken leg.

"If my abba had learned a trade, or even worked the mud pits, he wouldn't have left us when Ima died."

Eleazar stared down at her and lifted a single brow. He refused to acknowledge the untested opinions of one who had been sheltered in the palace all her life.

Doda, however, stroked Taliah's forehead as they walked, drawing the girl's attention. "I was there when your ima died giving birth to your little sister, dear, and your abba moved heaven and earth to secure a safe place for you to serve in the harem. I was the one entrusted to deliver you to the palace that day."

"You?" Taliah twisted in Eleazar's arms to search Doda's face. The little band halted on the road, while Taliah's fingers traced the wrinkles on Doda's forehead and cheeks. A tear slipped from the girl's eye. "I remember. Yes."

Doda trapped the girl's hand against her cheek. "You were very young, and we only met a few times. Your abba chose the best life for you, and El Shaddai has protected you all these years."

Taliah pulled her hand away. "I protect myself. Those who wait on men or gods to help are always disappointed." Doda winced as if she'd been slapped. If Putiel were here, Eleazar would suggest a good spanking for his daughter.

"Let's get home." Eleazar resumed their walk, nodding toward the Hebrew village now in sight. When they rounded the corner of the first row of long houses, they saw Abba Aaron waiting outside Miriam's doorway. Gasping, Eleazar nearly broke into a run even with the fragile girl in his arms. "Are Saba and Savta well?"

Hoshea lunged to keep up.

Taliah cried out, "You big ox! My leg!" But Eleazar was focused on his abba's drawn features.

"I must speak with you inside, Miriam."

He offered no answer to Eleazar. Not even a *Shalom*. Eleazar should be accustomed to Abba's disregard by now. The absence of mourners implied Saba and Savta were still alive. He would concentrate on that and be thankful for Doda, Saba, and Savta—and expect nothing from his parents or two older brothers.

Abba Aaron held the curtain aside for Doda Miriam and then barged in after her. Eleazar stood at the covered doorway with Taliah and Hoshea. Doda Miriam returned to pull aside the curtain, her eyes communicating an apology that wasn't hers to give. Eleazar ducked through the door sideways while Hoshea continued supporting Taliah's leg with the lamb's wool.

"Miriam, did you hear me?" Abba Aaron shouted. "I've had a dream."

Doda tugged at Eleazar's arm. "You can lay her on my mat. I'll get reeds from the river to weave another mat later today."

"Miriam, I must leave immediately—"

"Calm down, Aaron." Doda shuffled baskets and emerged with mortar and pestle and a few poppy seeds. "I'll listen after I ease Taliah's pain."

"You'll listen now!" he shouted, halting everyone where they stood. Eleazar had never heard Abba raise his voice—only Ima Elisheba shouted orders in their family.

"What is so urgent, Aaron?" Doda Miriam set aside the mortar and pestle and folded her hands, annoyed.

"El Shaddai spoke to me in a dream, Miriam—as He speaks to you. I'm to find our brother in Midian and bring him back to Egypt."

Eleazar needed to shake some sense into Abba. Hurriedly, he set Taliah on Doda's mat, and she cried out. "I'm sorry," he said, rushing back to Abba. "You've lived eighty-three inundations. You're a Hebrew slave. You can't leave Rameses. You don't even know if Mehy is alive."

"*Moses* is alive." Doda Miriam spoke in a whisper, tears pooling on her lashes. She and Abba stared at each other, communicating years of yearning for a brother they'd never truly known. "Shaddai has repeatedly shown Moses to me in dreams. He no longer wears the armor of Pharaoh's army but carries a shepherd's staff and walks among a flock of sheep. He sings the songs I sang to him as a child when I served his Egyptian mother as her handmaid."

"You see, he's a shepherd in Midian!" Abba Aaron was more excited than Eleazar had ever seen him.

"If El Shaddai gave you this dream, Aaron, He will make a way. You must go."

"This is nonsense!" Eleazar glared at his elders and finally focused on Abba. "You've never left Rameses. You have no idea what Sinai is like. You'll die before the first encampment."

"Send Hoshea with him." Doda stood calmly at Eleazar's right shoulder. "Hoshea accompanied you with Prince Ram's troops along the Way of Horus on your last march to Kadesh. Aaron and Hoshea will travel with the same ruse we suggested to Moses forty years ago. He'll pose as a rich merchant traveling with the next caravan. Hoshea will act as Aaron's personal guard."

"No, no, no!" Eleazar looked at his wide-eyed apprentice and back at Doda. "It won't work. Abba looks nothing like a merchant."

"His hands look like merchant hands." Taliah spoke from Doda's mat, pointing as Abba smiled and inspected his uncallused hands.

If Eleazar wasn't so angry, he might have been impressed by her sharp observation. "My abba is a metal crafter. He sits at a bench all day making jewelry." He offered the rest of his protest to Abba Aaron. "You have no merchant's robe, no gold or silver for travel, and you're too old to wander the desert."

Abba held his gaze. "Everything you say is true, Eleazar, but if El Shaddai calls, I'm going." How long had it been since he'd actually looked at Eleazar? Abba narrowed his eyes and tilted his head, a sign that he was pondering. "You didn't mention Hoshea's part in the journey—whether you would send him with me or not. Why?"

Eleazar hadn't mentioned Hoshea because it was the only part of the plan that could work. As Hoshea's commander, Eleazar could easily cover his absence. "I won't send him because you're not going." He stared un-flinching at his abba. Why must their first words in years be cross?

"Eleazar, listen." Doda's hand rested on his forearm.

He shrugged off her hand. *No, I'm not giving in this time.*

Abba Aaron drew nearer, his countenance brightening with hope. "El Shaddai will provide a merchant's robe, gold, and strength for the journey, my son. I need only provide the faith."

"He's already provided the robe." Doda held out her arms, displaying the fine linen she'd worn for her audience with Pharaoh. "We can com-bine the cloth from my robe and Taliah's harem robe to provide enough to make one for Aaron."

"But . . ." Eleazar looked at Taliah, his mind racing.

"We'll cover her with rough-spun, dear," Doda said, grinning. She left Eleazar's side and stepped into Abba Aaron's embrace. They held each other as if the other were a lifeline. "If you're sure El Shaddai gave you this dream, He will indeed provide all you need for the journey."

Eleazar grabbed Doda's arm, pulling the siblings apart. "You said, 'If El Shaddai gave him this dream.' Why can't you ask Him? You should be able to know for sure if this is from your God."

The sadness in her eyes made him regret his rash demands. "Shaddai has spoken through no one but me since the days of Joseph, but today has been a day of changes. Even now, I don't feel His presence as I always have." She returned her attention to her brother. "If Shaddai has chosen to include you in His counsel, Aaron, it is both a blessing and a burden. Bear it well—and bring our brother home."

Eleazar's heart leapt to his throat. *Please don't go, Abba.* But the words died in his mind as Abba left the small room without a backward glance.

Hoshea touched Eleazar's shoulder. "Will I accompany him then?" A spark of adventure danced in the boy's eyes.

Eleazar looked first at Doda, then at Taliah, and then back at his eager young apprentice. "Yes, you'll go, Hoshea. And if my abba dies, don't come back."

5

The season of *Akhet* was both blessing and curse. The Nile would reach its peak, and grain stores would wane. Pharaoh's tax collectors had measured the rising Nile the previous week, forecasting the highest inundation in forty years—as if anyone could trust tax collectors. The Nile's blessing meant better harvest and higher taxation of Pharaoh's people, from the noblemen in the city of Rameses to the peasants and slaves of Goshen. Miriam had no idea what noblemen were taxed, but Egyptian peasants returned to Pharaoh one-fifth of their annual produce from gardens and flocks. Hebrews surrendered three-fifths.

The peasants lived in mud-brick houses, little more than huts, interspersed among the slaves' long houses. Though some peasants owned Hebrews—and worked them like cattle—an Egyptian's belly rumbled as loud as a slave's when their grain stores ran low.

In the two weeks since Taliah had come to live with Miriam, supplies had dwindled considerably. Not because the opinionated beauty ate so much, but because everyone's provisions were running low. The few patients Miriam treated that might have been able to pay a few months ago, now had no herbs, food, or linen to spare. And she refused to turn anyone away.

"I need to contribute." Taliah hobbled toward the back room on the crutch she'd made, carrying a bowl of warm water and towels. "At least I can help tend Amram and Jochebed. I can't stand being idle while you do all the work and Eleazar provides the food from his and Hoshea's rations."

Miriam hung a few more herbs from the rafters. "I'm sure Abba and Ima would be happy to see more of you. They love your knowledge of Egyptian history—especially the stories that involve my brother Mehy."

Taliah halted at the dividing curtain. "I still can't believe you're *General Mehy's* sister." She shook her head and disappeared into the adjoining room.

Sometimes Miriam couldn't believe it either. The days of Mehy and Anippe and Mered seemed like a dream. Miriam's childhood had been idyllic—for a slave. From the time she was six years old, she'd lived in the estate's grand villa, serving the Amira Anippe and helping to raise Moses as Anippe's Egyptian son, Prince Mehy. Miriam was eighteen when Pharaoh discovered Moses's true heritage and Anippe's deception. After that, Miriam saw Moses only occasionally, usually to calm his troubled spirit with the ancient Hebrew songs she'd taught him as a child. Even as Egypt's general, he often sent a house servant to retrieve her from the slave village so she could sing to him on lonely nights. El Shaddai's presence was palpable when she sang—even for Moses. Fear of the unseen God was most often his response, and he'd abruptly send Miriam away, only to recall her when he felt alone or in need of comfort again. *Please, Shaddai, it is I who need the comfort of Your presence now.*

"Where is she?" A burly slave driver slapped aside the curtain and filled her doorway.

"Who are you looking for?" Miriam swallowed the lump in her throat.

He stepped inside, uninvited. "Pharaoh's concubine. I've heard the king discarded a Hebrew from his harem and she's staying here." He smiled, revealing three missing front teeth. "I want a woman fit for a king."

"I'm sorry, but you've been misinformed." Miriam breathed deeply, steadying her voice. "There is no concubine here, only the old nursemaid of one of Pharaoh's sons. I've placed her in the back room with my elderly parents while her broken leg heals." She pointed to the adjoining curtain. "See for yourself."

The guard's eyes narrowed as he studied Miriam and then the curtain. "Bah, I've got an old wife at home. Why would I want an old Hebrew?" He stormed out of the room as rudely as he'd come, and Miriam sagged with relief.

"Miriam?" Taliah peeked around the curtain, eyes round as the moon. "Who was he?"

"Someone I hope you'll never meet." She tried to smile. "You should stay in the room with Abba and Ima today."

Taliah disappeared, leaving Miriam to wrestle with the bigger issue. It was bad enough that Taliah was a lovely, single woman, but now that the slave masters imagined Taliah a castoff of the king, she was even more of a prize. They wouldn't stop pursuing her until she was dead or defiled by a common husband. *Shaddai, what should I do with this girl?*

Only silence answered, but she didn't need a vision to know. Eleazar must marry Taliah.

Hoshea had been gone only two weeks, and already Eleazar felt the sting of loneliness. Hoshea's absence had been easily masked, since he worked solely under Eleazar's direction. This meant Hoshea's rations were still delivered outside their chamber door morning, midday, and evening. The added provisions blessed Doda's household, but Eleazar sorely missed the camaraderie he and Hoshea shared. Late night games drawn in the dust, reminiscing about days gone by, planning for the months and years ahead—no one understood a soldier like another soldier.

He hurried his jog toward Goshen, anticipating the evening's visit with Saba and Savta. He'd ignore Taliah, who seemed intent on flaunting her intellectual superiority whenever he visited. *Youthful exuberance,* he told himself. But she wasn't a child. She was a woman who stirred an unwelcome desire in him. He'd known plenty of women—gifts from

Prince Ram for service well done—but Eleazar never allowed his emotions to cloud his judgment.

Taliah was different. She was dangerous. His mind melted like hog fat on a hot day when she looked at him.

As he approached Doda's doorway, he noted the closed wooden shutters and darkened doorway. Why were no lamps lit in the main room? The small hairs on the back of his neck stood at attention as he slowly pulled back the curtain. Empty. He slipped in quietly and saw low lights in the back room, heard pleasant conversation in low tones. *Odd.*

He shoved the curtain aside. "What are you doing in here?"

"Shhhhhh!" Four smiling faces motioned him into the room.

Doda patted the packed dirt beside her. "Come. Sit. I thought we'd eat in here tonight." Something in her voice betrayed her wavering grin.

Eleazar began unpacking the small bundle he'd thrown over his shoulder: olives, bread, cheese, dates, roast lamb. Pharaoh's soldier slaves often ate leftovers from the royal tables, and tonight's feast came from the queen's afternoon banquet. Saba giggled like a groom at his wedding feast, and Savta fed him from her own hand. How could two people love each other so long and well? Eleazar's parents certainly learned nothing from them.

"I think it's time I began earning my own rations," Taliah declared.

Doda stopped an olive before it reached her lips. "How do you propose to do that, dear?"

"I can teach peasant children when they're finished helping their parents in the market booths."

Eleazar grunted his disapproval and smeared goat cheese on a piece of bread.

Taliah snorted in his direction. "I knew a man of violence would see no need for a child's education, but I'll convince their parents that an educated child can barter more quickly, know the customs of other nations, and be able to converse with merchants in their native languages. An education will make their children invaluable at the market booths."

Eleazar rolled his eyes.

Doda set aside her wooden plate and gently cradled Taliah's hand. "It sounds wonderful, dear, but the Egyptians need their children's help in the booths from dawn until dark. I'm afraid you'll have difficulty convincing anyone to pay you for something they can't hold in their hand or put in their mouths."

Taliah ripped her hand away. "That's the kind of small-minded thinking that keeps peasants poor. If they would listen—"

"No, you listen," Eleazar interrupted, tired of her condescension. "You know useless facts that won't help you survive in Goshen. You must learn a trade like Doda's midwifery or Savta's basket weaving and hope that a man will marry you."

Eleazar looked to Saba Amram—the only other male in the room—for support but found only pity in his eyes. Saba squeezed his eyes shut and shook his head. Doda and Savta stared at him as if he'd squashed a puppy.

"You barbarian pig!" Taliah's face was the color of rubies, and her whole body shook. "You play with wooden swords and wallow in the mud all day but have the audacity to call my education useless? I could take a deben of gold and turn it into a king's ransom. You would spend it on prostitutes and beer since you've found no woman fool enough to marry you."

Eleazar hopped to his feet. "Mind your tongue woman or lose it." Taliah skittered toward Savta Jochebed.

Doda swatted his leg. "Eleazar, you will apologize!"

This is why he preferred silence. And yet, he spoke. "Taking her tongue may be the only way we find her a husband."

Taliah untangled herself from Savta's embrace and stood with her crutch, meeting Eleazar, nose to chest. "I resigned myself to never marry when I was in the harem, and I'd rather die alone than be bound to a man like you—or the slave driver who came for me today."

"Slave driver?" The declaration robbed him of breath. He turned on Doda. "Who came for her? Why didn't you tell me?"

"He'd heard one of Pharaoh's concubines had been discarded in our village and was staying with me." Doda lifted a brow. "I told him she was an old nursemaid of Pharaoh's sons with a broken leg, staying with my parents. I invited him to look in my back room for himself."

"You did what?"

"She used her brain instead of brawn." Taliah's smug expression was more than he could stomach.

He ignored the arrogant girl and knelt before his doda. "I vow that I will get a message to Putiel, but you must try to find her a husband. She needs to leave this house before her ignorance gets you all killed." He glanced back at the stubborn, stunning girl. "Until then, don't leave this house, and by the gods, don't let the guards see you."

6

One of Mered's wives gave birth to Miriam,
Shammai and Ishbah. . . . (His wife from
the tribe of Judah gave birth to Jered . . .
Heber . . . and Jekuthiel. . . .) These were
the children of Pharaoh's daughter Bithiah,
whom Mered had married.

—1 CHRONICLES 4:17–18

Miriam tightened her grip on the small bag of barley and leaned heavily on her walking stick, praying her visit with Aaron's wife Elisheba would go well. More than Taliah's future depended on it.

In the two weeks since the first slave master sought out Taliah, two more guards had come looking. Thankfully, the girl's leg had healed sufficiently for her to hobble up the interior ladder and hide on the roof. Eleazar continued to share his and Hoshea's rations morning and night, but if Taliah was in the room, he often dropped the bundle and left.

His attempts to contact Putiel had been delayed by his added responsibilities in Hoshea's absence, and anytime Miriam mentioned finding a husband for Taliah, Eleazar made an excuse to leave or changed the subject. Miriam interpreted his avoidance as confirmation that he was attracted to the spirited girl. With El Shaddai still silent, Miriam was forced to her own scheming. Eleazar just needed a little push to realize how much he truly cared for Taliah.

The sun had descended into its late-afternoon haze when Miriam reached the edge of the waste dump and heard a black kite caw overhead. The winged scavenger landed on the mound of waste to forage its evening meal from the scant remains of the land of Goshen. Hebrews had dwelt here since the days of Joseph—over four hundred years—but now shared the most fertile banks of the Nile with the new city of Rameses. The king's palace complex, industrial buildings, and noblemen's villas perched along the curved Pelusiac branch of the Nile. His fine, glittering city beckoned those sailing along the Nile, while the humble dwellings, waste dumps, and brick yards of Goshen were hidden along the straight base of the desert plateau behind his glitz and glory.

Miriam leaned on her walking stick to rest, scanning what was once a quiet Delta estate. Her long house was among those in the southern-most corner of Goshen where the Nile and plateau met. Her neighbors, like Miriam, had inherited their homes from what used to be Avaris's village for skilled craftsmen.

She set off again with a sigh. Now skilled workers from the Israelite tribes of Levi, Manasseh, and Ephraim settled together northeast of Mir-iam's village, beyond three large dikes and planting fields. "Why must everything change?" she asked no one in particular.

After crossing the first dike, she saw a young ima with her baby strapped to her chest. Miriam had delivered that babe a few weeks ago. Shovel in hand, the weary woman worked with other slaves to widen a canal for the swelling waters of inundation. She lifted her eyes and smiled at Miriam. They dared not wave for fear of the slave master's whip.

Miriam hurried her pace, anxious to see her sister-in-law. Elisheba and Aaron lived with their older sons, Nadab and Abihu. Their oldest boys had been trained in Aaron's skill. They walked to and from the metal shop each day, creating jewelry, goblets, and trinkets for the king and for trade. Elisheba worked as a house slave for a peasant's wife in their village, a shrew of a woman who thought herself as noble as Queen Iset-neferet. Miriam hoped to bribe the grouchy peasant with the barley she carried and speak to Elisheba long enough to force her answer. *Taliah needs a husband.*

On the day after the first slave driver sought out Taliah, Miriam had sought out Elisheba to suggest a betrothal for Taliah with one of Aaron's older sons. She knew she needn't wait for Aaron's return or his approval since Elisheba had been making all the important decisions in that household since she and Aaron were betrothed nearly seventy years ago. As expected, Elisheba had an immediate answer. "Nadab and Abihu are important men among the tribe of Levi, Miriam. I must have time to contemplate your request."

Important men? Contemplate? Nadab and Abihu were spoiled old men whom Elisheba had coddled to revulsion. No abba in Israel would offer his daughter as a bride to either of Aaron's preening sons. Miriam had given Elisheba two weeks to *contemplate* the betrothal—not that Miriam was anxious for Taliah to marry either of her oldest nephews. She really hoped Eleazar would discover one of his brothers had agreed to marry Taliah and would be so overcome with jealousy that he'd marry the girl himself. It was a risk, but Miriam could think of no other way to press Eleazar into declaring his true feelings.

As Miriam neared the village, she saw Elisheba bent over a new basket, weaving a final braid of papyrus around the top. Ima Jochebed had taught both her daughter and daughter-in-law the art of basketry before her hands and body had become too frail.

With a deep breath and renewed determination, Miriam closed the distance between them. "Shalom, Elisheba."

The woman shaded her eyes from the evening sun. "Shalom, Miriam. Do you bring word of my husband's return?"

"I'm sorry, no. Eleazar hasn't heard anything from Aaron or Hoshea."

"Then I have no time to talk." Elisheba returned to her basket weaving.

"I brought barley for your lady. Surely, she'll allow us a few moments to conclude our betrothal business."

"There is no betrothal business." She continued braiding papyrus without further explanation.

Miriam steadied her breathing, determined not to lose her temper. "Did you even consult Nadab and Abihu, or did you make this decision for them—as usual?"

She set aside the basket, eyes blazing. "You have no idea what it takes to raise children, Miriam."

The words wounded—as intended—but Miriam gritted her teeth to keep silent.

Elisheba tilted her head, assuming an air of instruction. "You see, Miriam, as an ima it's my responsibility to ensure my sons' future happiness."

"You've stolen enough of your sons' future to secure your own happiness, Elisheba."

Miriam's words hit her sister-in-law like a slap, bringing Elisheba to her feet. "My sons will never marry a filthy harem concubine."

"Taliah was not a concubine!" Miriam shouted, turning the heads of others working outside their homes. "Taliah was handmaid to a ten-year-old son of Pharaoh. She was tutored by the finest minds of Egypt to help a prince with his lessons. She is bright and beautiful and far too competent for my oldest nephews." Miriam turned and left Elisheba to her basket making, noting women's shielded whispers and stolen glances as she walked away.

Elisheba's *harrumph* propelled Miriam toward the next village. She'd wasted valuable time on a silly plan that might not have worked anyway. If only she'd felt El Shaddai's leading. She ached for His presence, His warm breath across her spirit. *El Shaddai, why have You been silent since giving me Pharaoh's dreams?* Four weeks felt like a lifetime when His presence had been life and breath to her. "Please, El Shaddai, I need to know You're here," she whispered to the dust.

Silence answered.

Her feet carried her to the only other people who might help Taliah, but a nagging dread had become reality. The Egyptians weren't the only ones who'd believed the lie about Taliah. Had all the Hebrew gossips labeled the girl a concubine, or was it just an excuse Elisheba used to keep her precious sons under her thumb? Surely, Taliah's extended family would either take her in or find a husband for her when Miriam explained the girl's predicament.

Miriam hurried past more slaves and their task masters, pressed by the sinking sun. She'd barely taken two steps into the next village, when several young women bowed low with respect.

"Welcome, Miriam," one girl said.

The other kissed her hand. "We are honored by your presence, prophetess."

Such a fuss. Miriam touched their heads and spoke a short blessing over each one. Most residents in this village followed El Shaddai faithfully and had come to Miriam for dream interpretations or advice from the God of Abraham, Isaac, and Jacob. They were descendants of the tribes of Judah, Issachar, and Naphtali—leaders of Israel, servants among the brethren, and preservers of the ancient songs.

Miriam lifted her hand over her brow to shield the sun, peering down the alley between two long houses and inspecting each doorway. Her dearest friends, Mered and Bithiah, had once lived here. Now their legacy filled the long houses to bursting. When Mered had dared hide the pharaoh's daughter in his home, change her name, and take her as his wife, building a life and family had seemed impossible. Now, as Miriam watched rows of families at work and play, she stood in awe of El Shaddai's marvelous plans and gained hope for Taliah's future.

"Miriam, my friend. Welcome!" The greeting came from behind her. She turned to find her old friend, Ednah, pushing herself from a stool outside her curtained doorway. "What brings you to our side of Goshen?"

Miriam fell into the woman's open arms, years of shared memories stripping away time between their visits. With a little squeeze, Miriam released Mered's daughter, now a great-grandmother. "You look well. How's your family?"

Ednah's once-bright eyes were now hooded with wrinkled lids, but the same genuine care shone through them. "The two oldest boys learned Ephraim's craft, of course, and are teaching their sons to weave as well. We've lost a few to field beatings and one in the brick lines, but the remaining children and grandchildren are healthy and strong. Our family has grown to thirty-two, but somehow El Shaddai provides for our daily needs. Ephraim would have been proud if he'd lived to see his family grow."

"Your abba Mered would have been proud too," Miriam said, hoping to remind Ednah of her family tie to Taliah. "Do you have much contact with your brother Jered's children?"

Ednah tilted her head, puzzled. "Of course. His family fills most of those three long houses," she said, pointing. "Jered's son, Gedor, is chief linen keeper and one of the elders with your brother Aaron. But, of course, you know that." Concern furrowed her brow. "What's this about, Miriam?"

"It's about Jered's fourth-born son, Putiel." Miriam paused, fretting about how to present her request. "Actually, it's about Putiel's youngest daughter. Who should I speak to about making a match for her?"

Ednah's demeanor suddenly cooled. "I heard she was sent to the palace as a harem girl."

"She was tutor to a ten-year-old prince." Miriam heard the venom in her voice and regretted it when Ednah stepped back.

"You know our village is the most committed to El Shaddai of all."

Miriam placed a calming hand on her arm. "I know, Ednah, I didn't mean—"

"Ten of Israel's fifty elders are men of Judah," she said, pulling her arm away. "The women of Issachar gather spare cloth and deliver it to your door for bandages, and the men of Naphtali have maintained our ancestors' stories for generations. Miriam, we cannot defile our village with a woman of questionable virtue."

"Questionable virtue like the pharaoh's daughter—my friend Bithiah, whom your abba married?"

Ednah threw back her shoulders and lifted her chin, stretching her neck like a strutting goose. "Ima Bithiah shunned Egyptian gods. She loved Abba Mered and loved his children."

"Putiel's daughter is hungry for knowledge, and she loves children. Isn't there someone in this village who—"

"No." Ednah's features grew hard. "There is no parent in this village who would join his son to a harem girl, nor a single man who would expose his children to a woman who worshiped idols."

Miriam shivered at the cold-hearted righteousness of her friend. "You would let Taliah suffer the plateau? A woman alone?"

Ednah's hard exterior faltered only slightly. "Why not make her your assistant if she's so eager to learn?"

"How long before one of the slave masters ruins her? She needs a husband and a home so she can become a common Hebrew slave, not a prize to be vied for by the slave masters." Miriam feared she might claw this woman's eyes out. "She has no idea what it means to be Hebrew, Ednah. Like Bithiah, she needs the love and patience of a man to teach her of El Shaddai's love. She doesn't need to be shunned by a family too busy being righteous to be compassionate."

"If she's still of birthing age, perhaps the Reubenites and Simeonites would take her to bolster their decreasing numbers. Most of their men are field and brick slaves. They die quicker."

Appalled at her friend's coldness, Miriam turned to go before she said something she'd regret. "Good-bye, Ednah."

"Miriam, wait!" Ednah reached for her robe, tugging her back. "I know I sound harsh, but . . ." She twisted her hands and stared at the ground. "We have no wish to anger El Shaddai—or His prophetess. If our God reveals in a dream or vision that one of our men is to marry Taliah, we'll compel him to obey."

Miriam didn't know whether to laugh or cry. Why must they wait to be compelled? Why couldn't compassion compel them? Miriam nodded and left the village saddened. The tribes she'd once thought the best place for Taliah now seemed worse than others. At least Elisheba hadn't tried to hide her bigotry under a finely woven veil of good deeds.

The sun glowed round and orange just above the hills across the Nile. So close, she might reach out and touch it. Brick makers and field slaves still labored as she made the long trek back to her village. Slave drivers paced impatiently, waiting for the last glimpse of the sun to disappear behind the hills so they could return to the city of Rameses, to their wives and children, their white linen robes, and their finely carved tables and chairs.

Miriam wiped sweat from her brow, still clutching the small sack of barley. At least they'd have barley for bread tonight. It was perhaps the only positive thing about her day.

"Maybe You don't want her to marry, Shaddai," she said aloud, not caring who heard. "Is that what You're trying to tell me?" Somehow hearing the words made the One God feel nearer. The audible conversation garnered a few puzzled stares from field workers, brick makers, and slave drivers, but most shook their heads and smiled. Did they accept it as an oddity of her calling? Or perhaps they simply thought her senile.

As she approached her long house, she felt the color drain from her face. How would she tell Taliah that not only had Miriam's nephews rejected the betrothal but her own family had shunned her? Miriam had spent the past two weeks convincing Taliah that marriage was the answer to her dilemma and recounting the romantic story of Mered and Bithiah, their children, and their children's children.

The bigger concern was the widespread perception that Taliah had been defiled in the harem. Miriam knew the damage such a rumor could cause.

Miriam arrived home as the last glow of dusk faded. She pushed aside the curtain and found Taliah in her usual spot, seated on Miriam's sleeping mat, leaning against the wall, splinted leg outstretched. She was grinding fennel seeds in the mortar and pestle.

"You're back," she said, eyes hopeful. "What did Elisheba say?" Miriam's face must have betrayed her discouragement. Before she could answer, Taliah returned her attention to the task. "Well, it doesn't matter. I can always stay with Abba Putiel's family. Surely they can find a husband for me among all the tribes of Israel." She tried to keep her voice light, but Miriam heard the quaver.

"I wouldn't have let you marry Nadab or Abihu anyway." Miriam joined her on the mat. "You deserve a man who will appreciate your wit and beauty, my dear. Now pass me a hand mill, and I'll grind this barley for tonight's bread."

They worked together in silence for a time, Miriam silently pleading for Shaddai's wisdom. She heard Taliah sniff and glanced in her direction.

Her cheeks were wet with tears. "Abba Putiel's family refused me as well, didn't they?"

Miriam set aside the hand mill and gathered Taliah into her arms. "I wouldn't let you live with them either. They're as false as an Egyptian's wig."

The comparison wrested a chuckle from the heartbroken girl. She wiped away her tears and sat up. "Miriam, I need to get out of these rooms. It's been four weeks. Please. It's past dusk. The slave masters have gone home. I'll walk down to the river and get fresh water. Just to the river and back." Her eyes filled with tears again. "Please."

How could she refuse? The poor girl had been cooped up far too long. "All right, but stay on the path and watch for crocodiles. They begin feeding at dusk."

"I will!" She pushed herself up and grabbed her crutch in one hand and the water jug in the other before Miriam could change her mind.

7

With cunning they conspire against your people;
they plot against those you cherish.

—PSALM 83:3

Late again. Eleazar hurried his pace, jogging on the dark, dusty path between Rameses and Goshen. At least he'd remembered a torch to stave off hyenas or jackals that might smell the rations he carried. Adding Hoshea's duties to his own made Eleazar's days longer and his nights shorter. He'd garnered a few puzzled stares from young slaves while polishing leather breast pieces and sharpening swords—tasks he hadn't done since he'd been Putiel's apprentice. Thankfully, no one had inquired about Hoshea. If anyone did, Eleazar held a dozen lies at the ready.

He swiped aside Doda's curtain, panting, and found the main room empty again, but the smell of fresh-baked bread was a welcome greeting. "Doda!" He moved through the small room into the adjoining chamber and found his three favorite people. Relieved that Taliah was hidden on the roof this evening, he kissed both Saba's and Savta's heads and sat down beside Doda Miriam.

They greeted him with halfhearted smiles that didn't reach their eyes. Eleazar unwrapped the bundle of rations and waited for someone to explain.

Doda reached for his hand, cradling it gently. "You must marry Taliah."

Heat spread up his neck and into his cheeks, but he kept silent, head bowed.

Saba cleared his throat. "You made a promise to protect her, son."

Eleazar's head shot up, and he looked into the rheumy eyes of the man who had loved him, chastised him, and guided him his whole life. "How can you ask me to marry her when doing so would put her in more danger? You know what happens to slave soldiers' wives and children. She would be tortured for my mistakes. She would be beaten and killed to punish me!" His voice broke with emotion, and he jumped to his feet. "Why do you think I've worked so hard to hide you three? I was stupid to mention Doda to Ram a few months ago, and now Pharaoh knows we're connected. That means you're all in danger. I can't do that to Taliah. I won't. She deserves a man more like her—smart, skilled, refined."

Doda reached for his hand and pulled herself to her feet, looking him sternly in the eye. "Taliah went to get water at the river. Go talk to her."

"How could you let her leave?" Not waiting for a response, Eleazar sprinted through the curtains and into the cooler night air, down the alley between long houses toward the river. He dared not cry out for fear of rousing predators—human or animal. His pace slowed as he reached the bank where women used the *shaduf* to fill their jars. There, at the edge of the water, lay Taliah's crutch and a broken jug. Eleazar had gone only a few steps when he heard a heart-piercing scream. *Taliah.*

He clenched his fists and rent the air with a war cry. "Aahh!" In the subsequent stillness, he heard a commotion in the bulrushes on his left, saw a man's silhouette in the moonlight. The man ducked back into the reeds.

"You there! Show yourself, or you'll wish a crocodile had found you first."

The man jumped up and started running, dagger in hand. Eleazar stood less than a stone's throw from the battered-down reeds, but his knees had turned to water. Though Taliah's cries beckoned him, dread cautioned his pace. What if that degenerate had ruined her—not her body alone, but her spirit and vibrancy? What could he say to her?

He approached the trembling bulrushes slowly so as not to frighten her more. "Taliah, I'm here. It's me, Eleazar." Her crying calmed to whimpers as he drew nearer, and he saw only a huddled form in the moonlight when he parted the reeds. She was curled into a ball, robe torn but pulled modestly around her. "He's gone. I'm here to take you home." He knelt beside her but didn't try to touch her. "Are you all right?"

She shook her head. Of course, she wasn't all right, but she had moved her arms and legs, so no bones were broken.

"May I carry you home?"

A low whine began in her throat. She shook violently.

He stroked her hair, and she calmed slightly. "I must get you out of the reeds. We're easy prey for crocodiles here." He gently slipped his arms under her back and legs.

She turned into his chest, trying to hide her battered face. "Your war cry stopped him before . . . before. . . ." Sobs choked off the words, but he knew.

Eleazar squeezed his eyes shut, grateful to whatever god might be listening that she need not fear carrying a child. He'd caught a glimpse of leather and a glint of bronze, suggesting the attacker was a slave master. A soldier would have stayed to fight. A peasant would have cowered in fear. Perhaps the man would lie, boast of a conquest that never happened, and save Taliah from future attempts.

She wept quietly in his arms, still shaking, and he wanted nothing more than to hold her forever, to protect her from the chaos surrounding them. But none of them were safe. Doda was right. He couldn't protect anyone. He had failed Putiel. Worse, he'd failed Taliah, and he could do nothing to keep it from happening again. "I'll send a message to your abba tomorrow. He'll know what to do."

After he'd left Taliah safe with Doda Miriam, he stood outside her long house in the moonlight, thankful that darkness hid his silent tears.

8

*The wisdom of the prudent is to give thought
to their ways,
but the folly of fools is deception.*

—PROVERBS 14:8

The night watchman pounded on Eleazar's door, providing his daily alert that dawn's glow tinged the eastern sky. Eleazar rolled onto his stomach and pulled his lamb's wool over his head. Surely it couldn't be dawn already. He'd left Doda's when the moon was well past its zenith without having exchanged another word with Taliah. Doda had been inconsolable for letting Taliah leave the long house. He'd tried to comfort her, but his words grew jumbled and awkward, again proving silence was his best course of action. He'd run like a madman back to the palace, chest heaving, and fallen onto his sleeping mat what seemed like only moments ago.

The image of Taliah's trembling, huddled form flashed through his mind, and he felt ill. If he thought he could bring her justice by finding the attacker, he'd hunt him down like the jackal he was. But no Egyptian cared that a Hebrew maiden had *almost* been defiled. Eleazar's best hope—and Taliah's—was Putiel. Perhaps he could give some direction for his daughter's future. The problem was getting a message to him without alerting Prince Ram—or any other Egyptian—to Taliah's whereabouts.

Eleazar sighed, rolled onto his back, and stared into the pitch-black void. He was exhausted. Between Taliah's care and covering for Hoshea's absence, the past month had been a nightmare. And it was getting harder and harder to cover Hoshea's duties. If Ithamar hadn't helped falsify armory records yesterday, Hoshea's absence would have been discovered. Eleazar had never been so glad his little brother was a scribe.

A scribe! My brother is a scribe! Ithamar could write a message to Putiel. Eleazar would dictate it, filling it with official-sounding business but including a veiled message about Taliah. Ram's messenger would read it aloud to Putiel, who would understand Eleazar's hidden meaning and dictate his reply to the waiting courier. Eleazar rubbed his forehead. Could it work? Surely, Putiel would appreciate the caution. What if Kopshef discovered the correspondence? Its contents must be innocuous enough not to arouse suspicion. Eleazar's teeth were set on edge at the thought of the crown prince. Yes, Eleazar must be very careful what he included in the message.

He rolled to his knees in his windowless chamber and patted the ground to find his flint stones. The stones lay precisely where he'd left them, beside his belt, sandals, and weapons. He struck them together and lit his single oil lamp, casting a meager glow in the small chamber. His first duty this morning would be to lay out the warriors' weapons on the sparring field. Then take morning rations to Doda Miriam. Rush back to the palace stables to groom Prince Ram's stallion before his morning ride—all before the prince broke his fast. Surely, he could think of a veiled message for Putiel by then. After that, he would find Ithamar.

He reached for his jug of beer, rinsed out his mouth, and spit into his waste pot. Lifting his arms overhead, he stretched high and then roared as he bent to touch his toes. He strapped on his cudgel and breast piece, then slipped his spear at an angle through the leather straps across his back. Upon opening his chamber door, he found his rations waiting as usual. Four small loaves of bread, two rounds of cheese, figs, dates, olives, and a variety of nuts. Hoshea's rations were the same, and the same quantity would be delivered at midday. A third, smaller delivery would appear after sunset which included a steaming hot meat of some kind and usually a fine jug of beer, sometimes wine. He stuffed a few dates in his mouth and chewed on a loaf of bread, wrapping the rest of his rations and Hoshea's in a cloth for Doda Miriam and the others. If he thought a god would listen, he'd pray that Taliah would eat something and maybe argue with him when he arrived this morning. He'd rather have her venom than her tears.

The morning progressed unremarkably until he arrived at Doda Miriam's. She was waiting outside, arms folded across her chest, a frown affixed firmly in place.

"We need to discuss Taliah." She kept her voice low, implying those inside were still sleeping.

Eleazar was both disappointed and grateful he wouldn't speak to Taliah this morning. "I know I failed to protect her, but Putiel will know what to do." He handed Doda the rations and kissed her cheek. "I must get back." He started back toward the palace, his mind already forming a message to Putiel.

"Your brothers won't marry her."

Eleazar stopped, turned, and tried to remain calm. He hadn't known this was even a possibility. "Lucky for her."

"Putiel's family won't help her either."

Anger rising, Eleazar raised a brow. "You've been busy."

"You need to marry her."

"We're not having this conversation again, Doda."

"Good. It's settled then. Your saba Amram can pronounce the wedding blessing tonight."

"No!" Eleazar shouted, startling birds into flight from the roofs above them. He breathed deeply, calming himself. "I'm not getting married. To anyone. I've told you already. Pharaoh uses close family members to torture high-ranking slaves. I won't put a woman's life in danger by marrying her. Good-bye."

"Please, Eleazar," she whispered. "I can't hear El Shaddai. I don't know what else to do."

A cold chill worked up his spine as he walked back toward Doda Miriam. Her head was bent, but he could tell she was crying. What could he say? He didn't believe in her God anymore, and this was partly why. If El Shaddai did exist, He'd proven to be vengeful and capricious, uncaring and unreliable, but it wouldn't help Doda to hear that now.

Eleazar gathered her into his arms and laid his cheek atop her head.

"If you could hear El Shaddai right now, believe me, He'd say I'm not the answer to Taliah's problems. She doesn't even like me."

But you will marry her.

Eleazar heard the pronouncement from someplace deep within him, not audibly, but it might as well have echoed in Pharaoh's throne hall. Surely, he was merely tired and imagined it.

"I'll send a message to Putiel today and ask what's best for Taliah." Putiel understood a soldier's caution. He knew the atrocities against wives and children of military slaves when Pharaoh sought to punish a man beyond a beating. He would never let his daughter marry a soldier slave.

Doda reached up to pat his cheek. "You're a good boy, Eleazar. I know you'll do the right thing."

He was trying to do the right thing, but she refused to see it. "I'll see you tonight with more rations." He walked away before she could say more.

The sun was already well above the eastern hills. If Eleazar believed in the gods, he could pray that Prince Ram had slept late. It was his only hope of readying the stallion for the prince's morning ride. Eleazar broke into a jog, hoping the morning air would clear his head so he could craft Putiel's message.

Eleazar hated deceiving his master, first about Hoshea's escape and now sending this message, but he simply couldn't confide in Prince Ram. Though the firstborn of Isetneferet was the best of Pharaoh's sons, he was still Egyptian, and Eleazar merely his slave.

The waters of the Nile rose ever higher during these months of Akhet, and the paths between the canals grew narrower. Eleazar sidestepped a slave driver who was dragging an injured—or dead—Hebrew away from a brick pile. Glancing back, Eleazar noted four Hebrews stacked in a pile awaiting burial and wondered fleetingly how many of his brethren died each day.

The sad realization spurred the idea for his message to Putiel. Eleazar, as slave commander at Rameses, was within his authority to send a census request asking how many Hebrews remained in Saqqara. Putiel, as Prince Kopshef's personal guard, would receive the request and order the counting. A slow, mischievous smile crept across Eleazar's lips. He would simply add a personal note within the scroll asking Putiel for direction on the obstinate she-camel he left in Eleazar's care.

Eleazar felt the weight of three chariots lift from his shoulders. He could even gain Prince Ram's permission to send the census request. One less deception made life a little less complicated.

Miriam watched Eleazar jog away and replayed his words in her mind. *If you could hear El Shaddai right now, believe me, He'd say I'm not the answer to Taliah's problems.* But she couldn't hear Him, and Taliah bore the pain of it. If El Shaddai had warned Miriam—as He would have a month ago—she never would have let Taliah go to the river. *Please, Shaddai, speak to me again. If it's me You want to punish, so be it, but please give me counsel to help those around me.*

Still she felt nothing but the dry, stale air of another unbearably hot day. Ducking around the curtain, she entered the main room of her long house, poured a bowl of water, and grabbed some towels.

As she moved past Taliah's mat, the girl stirred. "Has Eleazar come yet? I wanted to thank him."

Miriam paused, considering how much of the truth to divulge. Setting aside the bowl, she knelt across from Taliah and decided to tell her everything. "I didn't want Eleazar to come inside this morning."

Taliah's right eye blinked her confusion, but her left eye was too swollen from the beating to blink at all.

"You told me last night that you recognized your attacker as a slave driver. I was afraid if Eleazar saw how badly the man had beaten you, he would have hunted the Egyptian down. He wouldn't have listened to reason—that the beating you took when you struggled probably saved your innocence."

"Are you saying I should be thankful I was beaten?" The girl's voice rose in pitch and volume, and she pushed herself up to meet Miriam's gaze. "I don't think I can marshal that kind of gratitude."

Miriam pursed her lips into a knowing grin. This bold, beautiful young woman hadn't lost her spunk. "No, my girl. Never be grateful for tragedy, but always trust that God can use it in His good plan for you." She knew she sounded so wise, so sure of God. But how could she tell a girl who already doubted El Shaddai that even His prophetess now struggled to understand Him?

Taliah pulled her hand away. "If this is your God's plan, I don't like it."

"Our God always has a plan. We just don't always know it." Miriam started to get up, but Taliah tugged at her sleeve.

"Did Eleazar ask about me this morning?"

"I didn't give him a chance." Miriam saw a glimmer of hope for her wedding plans. "In order to keep him from coming inside, I confronted him at the doorway with a topic I knew would put him off."

"What topic was that?"

"I tried to convince him he should marry you."

"Marry me?" Taliah was on her feet in an instant, towering over Miriam. "I don't want to be married—especially to Eleazar. I mean, I appreciate his help and all, but . . ."

Miriam offered her hand, a plea to help her stand, and Taliah obliged. Once on her feet, Miriam gave her the bowl of water and towels. "Not to worry. He feels the same about you. He's not interested in marriage—yet. Now, let's go wash and feed Abba and Ima."

Taliah followed without a word. Miriam grinned. If this girl was silent, her mind was whirring.

9

I seek you with all my heart;
do not let me stray from your commands.

—PSALM 119:10

As the last shades of pink faded to gray in the western sky, Miriam said good-bye to the women of Judah who had delivered strips of linen for bandages. The linen keeper, Gedor, had heard about Ednah's crass rebuff of Taliah and wanted to make amends to Israel's prophetess. As a result, his donations of medical supplies during the past month had nearly doubled. Miriam wished Gedor's gifts had been motivated by his deep concern for his brother Putiel's daughter, but she knew he cared only about maintaining the favor of El Shaddai and His prophetess.

She examined the tight rolls of linen, the jars of honey lining the shelf, and various herbs stacked in baskets to the ceiling. However, even a hypocrite's gifts were welcome.

She set aside the basket just as Taliah emerged from the back room. Her injuries from the beating had healed completely, and she barely limped from the broken leg. The girl had remained in the long house of her own accord. She'd spent most days captivating Abba and Ima with stories of faraway lands and foreign cultures—things Miriam would never have guessed might interest her parents—and Miriam spent most evenings sharing stories about Moses's childhood and his early days on the Avaris estate. As the memories poured out, one thought rang in her mind constantly. *Will my brother really come home?*

"Did Eleazar bring tonight's rations yet?" Taliah poured dirtied water into their gray-water jug for disposal. "I've finished Amram's and Jochebed's baths, and they're ready to eat. I also have a question for him."

Taliah and Eleazar had barely spoken since the attack. Whether it was the awkwardness of what *almost* happened or Miriam's push for their marriage, they'd become adept at avoiding each other. "What kind of question? Is it something I could help with?"

Taliah hesitated, offering that impish grin Miriam had come to love. "I want to know if it's safe for me to leave the long house now. No slave master has asked about me since the attack. Surely, I can go to the river for water and begin to move about the village freely now."

Miriam reached for a small, crusty barley loaf and four cups. She tried to keep her voice light. "Where's the first place you'll go when you leave the long house?"

"I'd like to visit some of the peasants' homes and ask if I might teach their children in the evenings."

Again Miriam waited before responding, not wanting to discourage or seem overly protective. "I could go with you, maybe introduce you to some of our neighbors."

"I need to do some things by myself, Miriam. If I'm going to be a woman on my own, I need to begin building a life."

A woman on her own? Miriam tried not to panic. Why was she in such a hurry to leave? "It's late, and Eleazar hasn't arrived with our meal. Let's share yesterday's barley bread with Abba and Ima." She placed the bread and four cups of the golden-hued beer on a tray, refusing to argue about something that would hopefully never happen. How could Taliah think any woman could live alone in Goshen? "Maybe Abba and Ima will have some ideas on which households you might visit to find students."

They exchanged a genial nod and headed toward the adjoining chamber where Abba and Ima lay facing each other, chatting quietly. "And what are you two conspiring about?" Miriam loved watching Ima's cheeks pink like a maiden when they were caught in these tender moments.

Abba doggedly pushed himself to a sitting position and lifted both hands in victory. Miriam applauded. "Look at you, showing off!"

Ima tried too but couldn't quite push herself up, so both Taliah and Abba helped her.

"Taliah has been working with us to make our arms stronger." Abba beamed as if he'd just built the palace single-handedly.

Miriam winked at the girl whose bright and bubbly countenance had breathed new life into her parents. *Shaddai, she is so capable yet so foolish. If she is to teach village children, please give her realistic expectations about where she'll live and the need for others to help her.*

As had become the custom, silence answered her prayer, and Miriam fought back tears. She busied herself by unwrapping the bread and breaking it into four pieces, the largest ones, of course, for Abba and Ima.

She offered Abba the first piece, but he held her hand instead of taking the bread, forcing her to look up. "Something's troubling you, my girl. What is it?"

"I'm so happy you're gaining strength. Let's focus on that." With all her will, she forced her lips into a smile.

Awkwardness blared in the silence, and Taliah rose to her feet. "I'll go in the other room and grind some turmeric root. Is there anything else I can do to help?"

"You don't need to leave, dear. I'm fine, really." She looked around their small circle. "I'm simply concerned about Aaron and Hoshea." It was true, though not the whole truth. "Eleazar said merchants make the journey to Midian in three weeks. It's been seven. They should have been home by now."

Abba stared into Miriam's eyes, penetrating the surface, digging deeply into her soul. "Perhaps the greater concern is that El Shaddai hasn't told you when they would return. Or maybe you're upset that no one has come to you for dream interpretations since Aaron left?" The small room fell silent, and Miriam had no glib reply.

How could she explain her abject emptiness when no one else had experienced her absolute fullness? Shaddai had been everything to her— Husband, Friend, Teacher, Guide, and Master.

"I feel as if I'm withering from the inside out," she said finally. "I don't feel hunger or thirst or a yearning to sleep. I feel only a yawning void that was once Miriam but now is an empty shell . . . because Shaddai has abandoned me." The last words came out on a sob as she buried her face in her hands.

Consoling hands patted her back. Kind but useless. The only thing that could bring comfort was the return of Shaddai's warm breath on her spirit.

"Miriam, look at me." Abba's voice was gentle but firm when he reached for her. "Look at me."

Wiping her tears, Miriam felt like a little girl, obeying her abba's command. "El Shaddai has not abandoned you any more than He's abandoned Israel. For reasons that only He knows, He has chosen to become silent, and you must trust His silence—as Israel has trusted His silence all these years. Your ima and I have never experienced Him the way you have, but we know Him and love Him." He lowered his chin, giving her a stern look from beneath wiry gray brows. "You can learn to know Him anew, but you must trust Him in the silence, daughter."

Learn to know Him anew. Miriam had never imagined that she could know Him any way other than the way she'd always known Him. "Can you teach me, Abba?"

Ima leaned forward and laid her hand across theirs. "We can tell you how El Shaddai makes Himself known to us, but only He can teach you—as you trust Him. It's like your garden, Miriam. We can plant the seeds, but only God can make them grow."

Taliah fidgeted behind them, and when Miriam turned, the girl halted a few steps from the doorway. "I'll leave you alone to talk about your God."

Miriam felt the crushing weight of guilt again. Had she pushed Taliah further from El Shaddai by revealing her doubts?

"Come and sit with us, child." Ima Jochebed patted the packed dirt beside her. "Surely, a bright mind like yours would be interested to know how our God distinguishes Himself from the gods of Egypt."

Taliah's sagging shoulders lifted. "I have been puzzled by a few of your claims about El Shaddai, but I've been hesitant to ask, afraid I might offend."

"Nonsense." Abba waved her over. "Ask your questions."

Miriam wondered at first if they'd forgotten her, but Abba's furtive wink assured her he hadn't.

Taliah sat down beside her and scooted close. "It's more than a little reassuring to know that even a prophetess has questions."

Warmth flooded Miriam's cheeks, not with shame or embarrassment, but with a deep sense of awe. Perhaps Shaddai's silence was nurturing seeds beyond Miriam's garden.

Taliah addressed Abba Amram first. "Why don't gods speak to everyone? The Egyptian gods only speak with the priests or through Pharaoh himself, who claims to be divine, and El Shaddai speaks only through Miriam. Why is that?"

"That's a very good question." Abba Amram combed his fingers through his long, white beard as he pondered. "I can't speak about the Egyptian gods because I believe they are false, merely frightening bedtime stories to make naughty children behave. However—"

"Isn't that why all the stories of gods were created by men," Taliah interjected, "to control the ignorant masses?"

Miriam felt her defenses rise, but she remained silent, deferring to her abba's calm and thoughtful reply. "Many gods have been created by men, but only one God created all men. It is that one God that Israel serves—El Shaddai, the Almighty—who chose to make a covenant with Abraham and to bless all nations through his descendants."

"But why Abraham?" Taliah said. "And why speak to only one man?"

Abba shrugged, maintaining his kind candor. "I don't know why He chose Abraham, but I'm grateful El Shaddai spoke to more than one man. He spoke to Melchizedek, Isaac, Jacob, and Joseph. He made His will clear to Abraham's servant, who went to find a wife for Isaac, and Shaddai spoke to women too. Sarah, Hagar, and Rebekah all heard from God."

Taliah mulled the information, giving Miriam a chance to reflect on the stories she'd known since she was a child. El Shaddai spoke in many ways to many people. Could she learn to hear Him differently? To experience His presence again but through new expressions?

"Ultimately, my dear," Ima Jochebed chimed in, "it is El Shaddai who must reveal Himself to us. We are but dust and could never climb to the heights of His holiness to reach Him." She squeezed both Miriam's and Taliah's hands. "But He is near to those who seek Him with their whole hearts. We've seen it proven repeatedly in our lifetime."

"But how do you know He's near, Ima, if you don't have dreams or visions to interpret?"

Taliah looked at Miriam, seemingly surprised at her question. "That's what I want to know. How can we common people know *any* god exists when we don't feel or see signs of their presence?"

Abba chuckled. "Anyone can develop a *God sense* similar to the way we use other senses to experience things. Though we can't taste, touch, see, hear, or smell our invisible God, He sometimes uses those experiences to communicate His nearness."

"Like the warm breeze I sometimes felt while inside this long house," Miriam said, "that proved Shaddai was near."

Taliah looked at her as if she'd grown a third eyeball. "A breeze inside?"

Ima nodded and added, "I sometimes wake in the middle of the night to the smell of fresh-baked bread. The oven is cold, so I know it's Shaddai providing the most common form of comfort I know."

"And sometimes it's simply a feeling." Abba reached for Taliah's hand, patting it gently. "You simply know He is. There's no magic or sign. He just *is*."

The girl examined his blue-veined hands in silence for several heartbeats. "I've never had such feelings or sensations. I suppose I'm not special enough to be chosen." Before anyone could comment, she hurried to her feet. "Thank you for answering my questions. No one has ever talked with me about such things." She bent down to kiss all three before rushing from the room.

Miriam wanted to call her back and give her better answers, but she had none. Instead, she returned her attention to her parents. "Thank you. I'll continue to seek Shaddai—and wait for Him to reveal Himself." She kissed both of their hands and forced a grin. "But I still wish He'd tell me when Aaron and Hoshea will return."

10

*Then Moses told Aaron everything the LORD
had sent him to say, and also about all the
signs he had commanded him to perform.*

—EXODUS 4:28

The sun had set on another grueling day, and Eleazar ached from head to toe—but perhaps his head ached most. He was tired of worrying about Abba and Hoshea. They'd been gone more than seven weeks, and he'd heard nothing. Tugging at the iron locks on the weapons cabinets, he made sure they were secure—and imagined they were Hoshea's ears. He'd give the boy a piece of his mind when he returned. *If* he returned. But surely, Hoshea would return even if something happened to Abba Aaron on the journey. Eleazar's threat had been bluster, his anger overpowering reason again.

After checking the last weapons cabinet, Eleazar surveyed the military complex. The training arena was empty. All Egyptian soldiers had gone home long ago. Only two young slaves remained to polish their masters' shields—no doubt punishment for substandard performance. Egypt's soldiers demanded perfection from their slaves. Lives in battle often depended on how well a slave had attached a spearhead to the shaft or how precisely the slave fletched the feathers to guide an arrow's flight.

"You there," Eleazar shouted, startling one of the boys. "Lock the gate as you leave." Eleazar would, of course, check the gate on his way to Doda's house with rations. These minor duties were Hoshea's responsibilities, but Eleazar would never trust others to do it right.

He looked at the moon high in the sky and realized Doda's household would surely be sleeping by now. Guilt weighted his feet like iron.

Halfway back to his barracks, a grave reality struck him for the first time. When would he cease doing Hoshea's responsibilities? To do so would mean admitting his friend wouldn't return. He'd have to concoct a story—a lie—about his death. More deception. If he admitted a subordinate slave's escape, it could mean his own death sentence. Eleazar wiped weary hands down his face. He wasn't ready to face that dilemma.

Eleazar sped his pace to a jog, passing the houses of soldiers and noblemen, where families had laughed and enjoyed their evening meals together. His mind wandered to Saba Amram and Savta Jochebed. He missed spending time with them. When had he last heard one of Saba's stories? Almost three weeks had gone by since he'd given his grandparents more than a kiss on the cheek. Why must Taliah's presence rob him of time with his family? Quickening his pace, he made a decision. This evening, he would ignore the beautiful, quick-witted girl and talk to Saba and Savta the way he used to.

Reaching the palace barracks breathless, he bent over to brace his hands on his knees. *Who am I kidding?* He'd been trying to ignore Taliah since the day he'd broken her leg, but he'd failed miserably. She was more than beautiful. More than intelligent and high-spirited. Something about her drew him. If only Putiel would reply to his message. The courier had delivered the scroll to Prince Kopshef's scribe, yet did not wait for a reply. Three weeks, and no word.

It seemed Eleazar was waiting on everyone in his life, and his patience had run out.

He walked down the long, deserted hallway lit by torches and littered with half-full trays of rations. Most of his men had already eaten their meals and were settled in for the night. Since Hoshea's departure, Eleazar was always the last to his chamber, his food cold and bread stale. As he approached his doorway, the absence of his tray surprised him—no, infuriated him. Had someone stolen his rations? Looking both ways down the hall, he considered scavenging leftovers, but why should he? Pharaoh's military slave commander forage for food? It was an outrage! He grabbed a torch from the wall and charged into his chamber.

He was met by a growling dog and three men devouring his rations—Hoshea, Abba Aaron, and a man who looked vaguely familiar.

Hoshea licked honey from his fingers and smiled. "I brought them back alive, Eleazar."

The dog bared its teeth and took a step toward Eleazar. "Sattar, leave it!" the stranger commanded. The dog retreated to the man's side, keeping a wary eye on Eleazar.

"This is your dohd Moses," Abba said awkwardly. "He left Egypt when you were seven."

Eleazar looked beyond his abba's shoulder to a silver-haired man seated on the floor with his legs outstretched, crossed at the ankles. He wore a lazy grin, and his back rested against the wall as if he hadn't a care in the world.

"I remember only the Egyptian master, Mehy."

The man offered his bowl of stew to the dog and stood. Eleazar considered making dog stew. That food was for Doda and the others. How could he carelessly feed it to that mangy beast?

Before Eleazar could protest, Moses was standing before him, Eleazar's equal in height and weight. His arms and chest were well muscled though he was nearly as old as Abba Aaron. He'd obviously been a soldier, but what had he done these forty years in Midian to keep him in such fine physical condition?

"I'll never forget the words you spoke the night I escaped Pharaoh Sety's assassins and fled Avaris." Moses offered his hand in truce to Eleazar, but Eleazar kept his hands at his sides.

"I don't remember," he lied.

"You said, 'Pharaoh can't stay mad forever. Come back to us.'"

Eleazar raised his chin, refusing to be drawn in by the play for emotion. "Touching story, but I was too young to understand your betrayal. Pharaoh Sety had trusted you since childhood. He'd made you vizier of Egypt, yet you never told him you were Hebrew."

Moses stepped forward, not a handbreadth between them. "And you felt sorry for Pharaoh Sety?"

"I felt sorry for the Hebrews who bore his wrath after you escaped. And I'm angry that we still bear the rage of his son because of your sins." They stared in silent combat before Eleazar asked the burning question. "Why did you come back?"

Moses's countenance sagged, and he moved away from his nephew. "I didn't want to."

Eleazar shot a silent question at Hoshea and Abba Aaron, who both avoided his gaze. "Then why . . ."

"The Hebrew God heard the cries of His people, Eleazar. He will deliver Israel from slavery, and He's chosen me to confront Ramesses." Moses lifted his chin and locked eyes with Eleazar again. "I didn't want to come back, but I want to see our people free."

Laughing, Eleazar backed away, looking from one insane man to the other. Surely, Abba and Hoshea didn't believe this Hebrew-turned-Egyptian-turned-Midianite. But no one laughed. "You can't be serious. You'll kill us all with this nonsense!"

"I begged Yahweh to send someone else—"

"Yahweh?" Eleazar said. "Who's Yahweh?"

Abba Aaron approached, as if he could soothe Eleazar's frustration. "Yahweh is the secret name of El Shaddai. He never revealed His name to our forefathers, but on the mountain of God in Sinai, the God of Abraham, Isaac, and Jacob appeared to Moses and said Yahweh is the name by which He is to be known to Israel for all generations to come."

Doda Miriam. Eleazar wondered what she would think of all this. "Why you? Why didn't the Hebrew God tell Doda Miriam—the prophetess of Israel—these things?"

At the mention of her name, Moses smiled, the hard lines of his face softening. "I wish He had, son. I'm just a shepherd. I was a soldier before that. I've never been good with words. I stutter. I recounted these weaknesses to Yahweh—as if He didn't know. He became angry, but still wouldn't relent. His solution was that I speak His words to your abba Aaron. Aaron will repeat my words to Pharaoh."

"Abba Aaron can't appear before Pharaoh," Eleazar said. "He's a slave, and slaves only appear in Pharaoh's court when they're summoned. Like when Doda interpreted Ramesses's nightmares. If you want to march into Pharaoh's throne hall and get yourself killed," he said, poking his uncle's chest, "go ahead, but don't drag Abba Aaron with you." He paused, crossed his arms, and glared at him. "I don't hear you stuttering."

"I stutter when I'm nervous, and I'm telling you—it's not my choice to appear before Pharaoh." He moved closer, intense but not unkind. "Surely, as a soldier, you can understand, Eleazar. I'm merely following orders. I must do as Yahweh commands."

Eleazar was unnerved by his transparency. "I understand that you've returned to Egypt in an attempt to regain power, but this is no longer Avaris. This is Rameses, the capital of Egypt and the trade center of the world. If Ramesses discovers you're here, every Hebrew will bear the consequences of your return."

"If we disobey Yahweh, we will bear far worse." Moses held his gaze, unflinching. "Aaron tells me our parents are still living. And Miriam. We were hoping you would take us to them. Aaron said I could stay there."

Eleazar's ire immediately shifted. "Oh, he did? That sounds like Abba Aaron—offering Doda's hospitality when he has four wage-earning adults in his own household."

"You know your ima would never allow it, Eleazar." Abba's brows drew together above his eyes. Pitiful. "She hates dogs, and . . ."

"It has nothing to do with the dog," Eleazar said, sneering. "Ima cares only for Nadab and Abihu. I'm surprised she lets you live there, Abba." An awkward silence filled the room, and Eleazar's eyes fell on the empty tray of rations. He had nothing to offer Doda and the others. The scraps on the trays outside suddenly looked inviting. "No one speaks until we clear the palace gates. Hoshea and I will guard you like two peasants from Goshen going home after a late audience with Pharaoh. As soon as we're off palace grounds, we'll be safe." All three men nodded. "Since you've eaten the evening meal that should have gone to Doda Miriam and my grandparents, you will pick up food from the trays in the hall, wrap it, and hide it under your robes."

Moses looked stricken. "Eleazar, I'm sorry. I didn't know—"

Eleazar silenced him with a lifted hand. "You can make up for it by not getting us killed."

Miriam glanced at the curtained doorway again, and Taliah reached over to still her hands on the pestle. She'd ground the dried henna leaves to dust.

"It's late," Taliah said. "Even your faithful nephew is sometimes unable to keep his promises." She released Miriam's hand and returned to spinning her wool. "I'm sure he'll be here in the morning as usual with rations."

"You know it's not the food I'm worried about." Miriam rocked to her feet to fetch a jar for the henna powder. "If El Shaddai were still with me, He would have told me Eleazar wasn't coming—and probably why he couldn't be here. Can you imagine losing your ability to see colors or taste the sweetness of honey? That's a shadowy glimpse of the loss I feel at El Shaddai's silence."

"So everything is about your God abandoning you." The furrows of her brow grew deeper. "Aren't you just a little concerned about Eleazar?"

Impudent little snip. Miriam set aside the henna and took several deep breaths before responding. "That's my point. I never needed to worry when I lived in Shaddai's presence. He gave me insights that helped me protect those I love, but now worry has replaced His presence."

Taliah halted her spindle and whorl, resting it on her lap. "I don't mean to offend you, Miriam, but it seems to me if you believed your God had a good plan—as you told me after my attack—then you wouldn't need to worry."

A slow grin robbed Miriam's irritation. "You know, it's going to be very difficult to keep living with you if you insist on listening to everything I say." She chuckled then and began pouring the henna powder into the jar, cautious not to spill any on their small square table.

"Perhaps I won't live with you much longer."

Miriam's heart nearly stopped, and the last bit of henna missed the jar completely. "What do you mean? Where would you go?"

"When I begin teaching peasant children, I might earn enough to have my own home. Perhaps even have an extra room where I can teach the students."

Miriam inhaled deeply. This conversation had to happen. "Taliah, dear, life in Goshen is very different than you experienced in the palace. You've been protected in the safety of my little rooms and—"

"Protected? I've felt the sting of my family's rejection and the shame of a ruthless man's touch. I will fight, Miriam, for power, respect, and status so that I never need to rely on anyone—human or a god—again." The girl swiped at tears that intruded on her strength.

The sound of footsteps outside their window stole their attention. Suddenly Eleazar filled the doorway wearing a strange expression evident in the moonlight.

Afraid to ask, but unable to remain silent, Miriam prepared for the worst. "Have you heard from Hoshea?"

Eleazar stepped inside, and Hoshea ducked around the curtain. Miriam gasped and jumped to her feet, covering a joyful sob, but nothing could have prepared her for the sight that followed. Two older men shoved aside the curtain and stood as tall as Eleazar. Aaron, the brother she knew, and Moses, a familiar stranger. Unable to decide which one to hug first, she ran to the middle and circled both their necks until they buried her between them. Tears ran freely, lost years forgotten.

"You're home. You're finally home," she whispered. Before either brother could answer, a menacing growl interrupted. Startled, she turned and found a black-and-white dog moving toward her, snarling, hair bristled.

"Sattar, leave it."

Moses's single command quieted the creature, but Eleazar and Hoshea huddled at the doorway, Eleazar looking like he'd eaten a bad fig. "That stupid creature threatens anyone who gets near Moses."

Moses turned his head slowly, irritation evident. "His name is Sattar, *protector*. It is his nature to protect his master and the flocks in his care."

Moses and Eleazar locked eyes in a silent battle as the dog growled at his master's side.

"Well, this will never do." Miriam marched between her brother and nephew, interrupting the dog's guttural rumble. She rummaged in a basket for a piece of dried fish and tore off bits for everyone, giving the largest serving to Eleazar. "Go on. Feed him, Hoshea. You too, Taliah."

Sattar made his way around the room, gathering morsels from the hands of each new friend, but shied away when Eleazar offered his piece of fish. Eleazar crossed his arms over his chest. "See, Doda? The dog hates me."

"And Sattar knows you hate him, so who's the master and who's the beast?" Miriam stood beside her nephew and demonstrated. "Now, hold out your piece of fish—and be nice."

Eleazar scowled but held out the morsel, keeping his hand close to his side. Sattar stood his ground but stretched as far as his mouth would reach to capture the proffered meat. Two stubborn males brandishing wills of iron.

When Sattar finally latched onto the fish, he curled up at Miriam's feet. Her heart nearly melted. She reached down to stroke his rough black coat and gave him her last piece of fish. "That's a good boy. You know who's really in charge, don't you?"

Moses and Eleazar laughed first and loudest, draining the tension from the room. Moses opened his arms toward Miriam, but Sattar grumbled a low protest. Wide eyes and more laughter framed Moses's words. "I believe my dog has chosen a new master."

11

Go, assemble the elders of Israel and say to them,
"The LORD, the God of your fathers—the God
of Abraham, Isaac and Jacob—appeared to me
and said: I have watched over you and have seen
what has been done to you in Egypt."

—EXODUS 3:16

Taliah heard it first. "Miriam, Amram is calling."

Miriam realized she hadn't introduced Taliah to Moses, but now wasn't the time. Everyone stilled, listening for Abba's weak voice. "Moses."

Moses's eyes welled with tears, and he tucked his bottom lip under his teeth. Pointing toward the curtain, he asked, "May I go?" Miriam bobbed her head, unable to speak past the lump in her throat.

Everyone else stood like pillars, but Moses turned like a frightened child. "Come with me, Miriam."

She fell in step beside him, the others close behind. She held aside the curtain and heard Moses's small gasp when he saw their parents' frail forms lying side by side. He hurried to them, knelt, and gathered their hands in his. Ima Jochebed touched his face, his hair, as if in a dream. Abba Amram patted his hand, whispering, "My son, my son, my son."

Miriam and the others lined the wall, watching the holy moment in silence. Surely, there could be no doubt in any mind that El Shaddai had done this. Who else could rescue a babe from certain death, educate him in Egypt, refine him in the wilderness, and return him to his family? *No one but You, Shaddai.*

"You will see freedom, Abba." Moses spoke through his tears, stroking Abba's brow. "You have lived to see Abraham's promise fulfilled."

"What are you saying?" Miriam hurried to the huddled trio, kneeling beside Ima's shoulder. Sattar followed her like a shadow.

Moses's expression was a mix of joy and sadness. "The God of Abraham, Isaac, and Jacob met with me on the mountain of God. He has heard the cry of the Israelites in bondage and has sent me to command Pharaoh, 'Let Yahweh's people go.'"

Miriam felt the blood drain from her face. How could the God of Abraham, Isaac, and Jacob *meet* with anyone? And . . . "Who is this Yahweh?" Her tone issued a challenge.

Moses sighed and dropped Abba's and Ima's hands. "It is the name by which the God of Abraham, the God of Isaac, and the God of Jacob is to be called for generations to come." He held Miriam's gaze, a slight grin replacing his weariness. "It is His secret name, Miriam, like the secret name of Ra in the story Ummi Anippe used to tell me—except Yahweh is real, and He will prove it in the days to come."

Miriam's chest ached, and tears came without permission. Was it true? Had El Shaddai truly met with her little brother on a mountain in Sinai—while He'd been silent toward Miriam? Had her God told Moses His secret name? If Moses was telling the truth, Israel could be free. If what he said was false, he would tear this family apart.

She stared into the pleading eyes of a man she'd known since he was a baby in a basket among the bulrushes. He looked like any other shepherd—strong, tanned, weary—but the brother she knew best was an Egyptian master. She lifted her sleeve to reveal the branding scar. "Do you remember this?"

Moses ran his fingers over her wrinkled scar. "Yes. I hurt you."

"You saved me," she said, bowing her head to hide the mounting confusion. "And hurt me. Pain and protection aren't exclusive, Brother, and I fear that's what you'll do again."

"Should I look elsewhere for shelter while Yahweh delivers His people?" She heard the tremor in his voice and looked up. His sun-leathered cheeks quaked with barely controlled emotion.

Abba and Ima awaited her reply too. Aaron, Eleazar, Hoshea, and

Taliah—all were standing over them, waiting for the prophetess of Israel to speak. But she had no word from El Shaddai. She was empty, dry, abandoned. "You'll stay with us, here, in Abba and Ima's room." Abba Amram squeezed her hand in approval, and Moses exhaled. Why were they worried about her approval? Ridiculous men. They do what they want anyway.

Moses, still kneeling between their parents, tilted his head to meet her gaze. "Aaron and I will need your help to speak with the elders."

The elders? A stab of fear cut through her emotions. The elders would never listen to *Prince Mehy* even if he looked like a Midianite shepherd. "What did *Yahweh* tell you to do?"

"Aaron and I are to assemble the elders of the tribes and tell them what I told you. Yahweh has seen their misery and is concerned about them. He will deliver them from Egypt with mighty acts of His power." He pointed to a walking stick in Aaron's hand. "Yahweh showed me signs of His power by using that staff. Aaron will be my spokesman, and we'll do everything God commanded to convince the elders before we confront Pharaoh."

Abba Amram placed his hand on Moses's forearm. "You are my son, Moses, and we love you, but many of our people still see you as Master Mehy, Egyptian prince, vizier of Egypt."

Miriam wasn't sure if she felt better or worse that Amram shared her concerns about the elders' response to Moses.

"No one finds it harder to believe than I," Moses said, "but I find myself feeling like a soldier again—Yahweh's soldier—and I must do as He commands." He locked his gaze on Eleazar, the two engaging in some silent battle.

What had transpired before they arrived? Sattar rose to his feet and began stalking Eleazar. "Leave it!" Miriam shouted, remembering Moses's command. The dog looked startled but begrudgingly obeyed her.

"I'd say he's definitely chosen a new master." Moses chuckled, relieving some tension.

"If you're going to meet with the elders, you'll need to understand the traits of the various tribes of Israel and the leaders among them." Miriam glanced at both brothers. "Did Aaron explain the nature of Israel's tribes and their characteristics on your journey to Egypt?"

"We spoke of other things." Aaron shrugged, giving Moses a knowing glance. It seemed her two brothers shared secrets, and again Miriam felt ostracized, near tears.

Ima Jochebed patted Miriam's knee, sensing her daughter needed encouragement. "It's probably best that Miriam describe the tribes to you, Moses. Aaron has strong relationships with many of the elders because most are skilled craftsman that he works with every day, but Miriam has been El Shaddai's prophetess all these years. She's dealt with all the elders—the meek, the harsh, and every disposition in between—and she's gained a sense for how the elders are reflected by their tribes." Ima winked at Miriam. "Your sister knows which tribes will help and which ones will hinder."

"I'd be grateful for your insights, Miriam." The sincerity on Moses's features was the same today as it was forty years ago. She could trust him. Could she also trust . . . Yahweh?

Miriam breathed deeply and started from the beginning. "How much do you remember of the Hebrew lessons Ima Jochebed taught you before you were weaned?"

"More than you might imagine." Moses grinned, his neck shading a subtle crimson. Perhaps men were discomfited at spending their first three years at a woman's breast. "But I've learned even more from my wife's abba, Jethro, the high priest of Midian."

"You're married?" Miriam and Jochebed asked at the same time.

His eyes grew sad. "Yes. We had some trouble on the journey to Egypt. I sent my wife and two sons back to Midian."

Miriam wanted to ask more, but the set of Moses's jaw told her the subject was closed. "I'm sure your father-in-law, as a Midianite priest, told you of Abraham's descendants from his wife Keturah."

"Yes, but he also told me of my heritage through Abraham's wife Sarah, whose son Isaac was given the firstborn's blessing. Isaac's wife gave birth to twins. The younger, Jacob, stole the firstborn's blessing from his older brother, Esau. Jacob—whose name was changed to Israel—had twelve sons. One of them, Joseph, was sold into slavery in Egypt by his brothers. When Jacob and his sons experienced a famine in Canaan, Joseph brought the whole family to Egypt. Israel's family grew quickly and has become a nation of twelve tribes."

Miriam raised her brows and glanced at Taliah. "Did you hear that, dear? I've been teaching you about Abraham for seven weeks, and Moses summed it up in one breath."

Taliah's cheeks bloomed like a rose. "I would be honored to learn more from your brother. I've taught Pharaoh's sons about the brave General Mehy for years. His life is fascinating."

Eleazar rolled his eyes and groaned. "More stories won't help you bake bread or make baskets."

"Goshen has enough baskets," she sneered. "Israel needs teachers and knowledge—especially if we're to be free."

Moses looked to Miriam for an explanation, but she simply shook her head and returned to the tribes. "Let's see if I can summarize the twelve tribes for you. The people of Reuben are forgiving. Simeon has dwindled but remains strong in faith. Judah is bossy and boasts many overseers. Zebulun always finds a way to win. Issachar works hard at serving others. Dan is harsh but logical. Gad *always* fights—and wins. Asher would rather dig in the dirt than breathe. Naphtali preserves the ancient stories of our people. Joseph's sons, Manasseh and Ephraim, received the firstborn's double blessing, so each has a tribe in Israel. Manasseh never holds a grudge. Ephraim is empowered by adversity. And the tribe of Benjamin is mean—but fiercely loyal if you can win them over." She paused, sadness pressing against her chest. "And many of our people have adopted the gods of Egypt—either combining them with worship of El Shaddai or replacing Him altogether."

A look of utter terror washed Moses's face. "How do we assemble them?" He looked at Aaron. "Will anyone come if we summon them?" If he'd returned to Egypt thinking Pharaoh his toughest audience, perhaps now he realized Israel might be the bigger challenge.

"They'll come," Aaron assured him. "I'm an elder myself, and we meet regularly under the new moon. Occasionally, when we have a special concern like this, we send a messenger to all the elders during the day and then meet that night at the moon's zenith. We'll send my messenger tomorrow and meet at the designated spot on the plateau tomorrow night."

Miriam considered Aaron's calm demeanor. Even as a child nothing rattled him, and as an adult he'd been steady to the cusp of tedium. Perhaps a little more emotion would have shown Eleazar and Ithamar they were loved—since their ima was too busy fawning over Nadab and Abihu to spare a kind word to her younger boys.

"Will you come?" Moses asked.

All eyes were focused on Miriam, and her cheeks warmed. "I'm sorry. Will I come where?"

"To the meeting. The elders will be more inclined to believe if you stand with us." Moses reached for her hand. "Maybe you could sing. Do you still sing, Miriam? Your songs were the only thing that could calm me before I went to war."

Her throat tightened, and the weathered Midian shepherd before her suddenly became the child she'd played with a lifetime ago in the Amira's bathhouse. He was the boy Amira Anippe sent to the noblemen's School of the Kap, the young man traumatized by King Horemheb's bloodthirsty reign. He was Prince Mehy, torn between his Egyptian pharaoh upbringing and his Hebrew heritage. "Yes, Moses. I still sing."

But could she sing here? Now? She dropped her gaze and let tears fall with it. Miriam felt betrayed by El Shaddai, but perhaps more troubling —she felt like a betrayer for her selfishness. Why couldn't she rejoice at God's promised deliverance? Why did it matter that the instrument of deliverance would be Moses and Aaron—and not her? A sob escaped before she could restrain it.

"Can't you see what you're doing to her?" Eleazar shouted, startling everyone, his gaze fixed on Moses. "Doda has been El Shaddai's prophetess her whole life. She served Israel while you lived in a palace. She's suffered in Egypt while you ran to safety in Midian. Doda should be the one to speak to the elders, not you, not Abba."

Moses was on his feet and in Eleazar's face before Miriam could stop him. "I've told you, this is not my choice. If it were up to me, I wouldn't even be here." The words were like cold water thrown in Abba and Ima's faces. Moses realized their effect and knelt again beside them. "The night you helped me escape from Egypt, I reconciled it in my heart that I would never see you again. I gained a wife and two sons in Midian, and I had planned to live out my life there quietly. But with Yahweh's command to return came the precious gift of seeing you again. For that I'm grateful."

Miriam watched in silence as Abba and Ima whispered tenderly to their youngest son. Moses seemed utterly transparent and candid. Any pretense of the Egyptian prince who fled forty years ago gone.

When she glanced at Eleazar, she found him still fuming. Her nephew was Moses—thirty-three years younger. Same height, same build, same stubborn nature, same protective instincts, but he would bite his tongue off before expressing any emotion but anger. *Yahweh, if You still hear my prayers, help my Eleazar to find You, love well, and learn to obey You as his uncle has.*

She nudged Moses. "I'd like to go to the elders' meeting, and Eleazar will accompany me."

Eleazar started to protest, but she lifted her hand and spoke directly to him. "I need your help climbing the plateau, and we both need to see why Yahweh has chosen your abba and Moses to deliver Israel. Perhaps then I'll understand why Yahweh has been silent toward me."

The fire in her nephew's eyes dwindled, and he nodded his surrender. "All right, Doda. I'll escort you."

"It's settled then," Aaron spoke from the doorway. "I should go home. If Elisheba discovers I've returned but didn't go straight home, I'll eat dried fish and nuts for a week."

Miriam shook her head but smiled. Aaron would never change—nor would Elisheba—and somehow they lived together. Miriam joined him at the curtain and kissed his cheek. "Thank you for obeying El-Shadd— for obeying Yahweh and bringing Moses home to us." Tears threatened again at the familiar name that must now be replaced by a silent God.

Aaron held her face and whispered against her forehead, "Yahweh is the same God you've known, Miriam. He's simply decided to let the rest of us enjoy the relationship you alone have experienced all these years."

12

Anxiety weighs down the heart,
but a kind word cheers it up.

—PROVERBS 12:25

Eleazar and Hoshea placed all the scraps of food they'd collected from the barracks' trays on Doda's small table. "It's all we could find for you tonight. I'm sorry."

"It was my fault," Moses offered. "I had no idea Eleazar saved his rations for this household." Moses turned to his nephew, and Eleazar prepared for another confrontation. "You're a fine man, Eleazar, and Prince Ram is lucky to have you at his side. No wonder your abba Aaron is so proud of you."

Eleazar felt the compliment like a blow. Abba proud of him? "You know nothing of my abba's—"

"Eleazar, walk with me." Taliah looped her arm around his, tugging him toward the doorway.

"We'll see you in the morning." Doda's forced happiness told him to go. "And thank you for the food, dear." Hoshea followed them outside.

Still boiling, Eleazar let Taliah lead him into the cool night air. Her hand on his arm felt like a hot coal, sending warmth radiating in all directions. "What is it, Taliah?"

"Don't bite my head off because you're angry at your uncle."

"I'm not angry at him. I simply don't like him."

She waved off his reply and turned to Hoshea. "I'm glad you're home safely." He blushed like a ten-year-old, and Taliah giggled. "Would you mind if I spoke with Eleazar alone for a moment?"

"Of course, yes. I mean, no. I mean . . ." Hoshea stumbled over a rock on his awkward retreat, lightening Eleazar's mood.

"I'm sorry," Eleazar said. "I shouldn't have been unkind to you because I'm upset about Moses returning."

Taliah's dark eyes sparkled in the moonlight. "I've never heard you apologize before, Commander. I'm impressed."

"It's not something I do often." He felt warmth creeping up his neck and into his cheeks. Hoshea wasn't the only one acting like an awkward ten-year-old. "What was it you wanted to say?"

"Now that my injuries have healed, I'd like to begin asking some of the parents in our village if I can teach their children. Since the Hebrews believe I was a harem concubine, I'm sure they won't allow me to teach their children, so I'll ask only the Egyptians. Can you recommend any of the families?"

Had everyone in Egypt lost their senses? "And will the peasants be any happier about a concubine teaching their children?"

The genial woman disappeared, and a chill wind blew between them. "I'll assume you have no recommendations then." She turned to go, but Eleazar caught her arm. Taliah wrenched it away with a wounded cry. "Don't! Don't touch me!" Her lips trembled, but she lifted her chin and fought tears. "Don't worry. I won't ask for your help again."

"Taliah, please listen. We should hear from your abba any day. I'm sure he'll have a plan or perhaps even convince Kopshef to let him return to Rameses."

"You can't know that," she cried, losing the battle with tears. "I can't hope, Eleazar. Give me truth, but don't be cruel and give me hope." She hurried through the curtain into Doda's long house.

Eleazar dragged his hands through his hair and pulled out the leather tie that bound it. The teeth marks Taliah made when Doda set her broken bone still scarred it. Putiel's daughter was strong but not as strong as she pretended. If Putiel didn't send word soon, Eleazar would have to make some hard decisions for the girl's future.

Putiel, why did I ever agree to care for your little she-camel?

13

Moses and Aaron brought together all the elders of the Israelites.

—EXODUS 4:29

Taliah had returned to the long house crying last night. Moses had excused himself immediately to Abba and Ima's room, leaving Miriam to ask about her tears. When Taliah waved her away, Miriam settled onto her sleeping mat with Sattar beside her.

It was the last thing she remembered until Moses emerged through the dividing curtain at dawn.

"Good morning," he offered, rubbing his eyes as he'd done when he was a child.

Miriam rolled to her feet to greet her little brother. "Good morning. I didn't get to introduce you to our new family member."

Taliah sat up and quickly stuffed riotous ebony curls under her head covering. Swollen eyes said she must have cried into the night, but a bright smile was firmly affixed now. "I'm not really a member of the family. I'm living with Miriam until I can support myself."

Moses looked distinctly uncomfortable, eyes darting from Miriam back to the girl. "Are you an artisan? A weaver or metal crafter perhaps?"

"No, I was a tutor for one of Pharaoh's sons, and I hope to begin a school for the peasant children so they can become more effective traders in the market booths."

"A lofty goal for one so young—and a woman. How many students do you have so far?"

She cleared her throat and scuffed her toe on the packed dirt. "As a prince of Egypt, you must have been trained at the School of the Kap.

I'd love to learn from you to gain more knowledge to pass along to my students."

Miriam hid a smile. Avoidance. Taliah was a skilled orator for sure.

Moses grinned at Miriam. He'd caught it too. "How many students did you say you had?"

Miriam jumped in to help. "Taliah was trained by the king's tutors. She's very gifted."

"I see." Moses returned his attention to Taliah. "I look forward to comparing hieroglyphs and maps of the world's kingdoms."

"But I have no scrolls." Panic replaced Taliah's cool confidence. "I was cast out of the palace when the prince broke his leg."

"We need no scrolls, Taliah. We have our fingers and the dust of Egypt to draw on. I am at your service when you recruit your first student." He furrowed his brow, however, seeming puzzled. "But why would you live alone? Is it safe? Things must have changed considerably for young girls since—"

"Things have changed," Miriam interrupted, "but for the worse. And no, it's not safe for Taliah to live alone, but she's stubborn like her Saba Jered."

"You belong to Jered's clan?" Moses embraced her like a long-lost daughter and then held her at arm's length. "Jered and I used to fight with wooden swords outside his abba Mered's linen shop. Tell me about your family."

A deep line appeared between Taliah's brows. "My father Putiel was Jered's fourth born, and the whole clan has turned their backs on me." She turned a piercing gaze on Miriam. "Safety is a lie told by the courageous to the fearful, and the gods are as inconsistent as the wind. Living on my own seems no more dangerous than entrusting my life to another."

Miriam felt largely responsible for Taliah's cynicism but didn't know how to help when she herself felt the sting of Shaddai's apparent inconsistency.

Moses reached for Taliah's hand, cradling it gently. "I was forty before I felt the kind of loneliness I hear in your words, Taliah. I'm sorry you've experienced it so young. My heart was mended when I let people love me." He kissed the back of her hand as if she were a princess and he a prince again in Pharaoh's court.

Taliah's lips formed a tremulous smile that softened her granite exterior. Prince Mehy had always known how to sway the hearts of men—and women. If only he could charm the elders of Israel so readily.

Moses glanced down and saw the harem brand peeking out from Taliah's rough-spun robe. "Does this have anything to do with your family's rejection?" When she nodded, he reached for Miriam's arm and shoved up her sleeve to reveal the mark he'd burned into her flesh. "Miriam's brand isn't as ornate as yours, Taliah."

Wrapping his arm around Miriam's shoulder, he held her tightly. "Did you know this brand kept Miriam from marrying? Though I'd hoped to protect her from estate guards, the brand made Hebrew gossips believe she was my . . . well . . ."

Taliah gasped. "The Hebrews thought you were defiled like me, Miriam?" Her eyes went wide. "But he's your brother!"

Taliah's horror coaxed a chuckle from the siblings. Moses looked a little squeamish, so Miriam explained. "When Prince Mehy branded me, he was still master of the estate, and only a few people knew he was my brother. The brand meant I was Mehy's concubine so no Egyptian would touch me."

"Did you ever dream of marrying, Miriam?" Taliah's voice was small, vulnerable.

"Once, when I was very young, but a dear friend married him, and they were happy together. It's all right, though. No other man could compete with my love for El Shaddai."

Moses looked surprised, but he wasn't as surprised as Miriam. She'd never told anyone of her love for Hur. He'd married the midwife Shiphrah when Miriam was a little girl, but she'd always loved him—as a lifelong friend.

Taliah kissed Moses's cheek. "Thank you."

"For what?"

"For hearing me." She pulled her sleeve over her brand and grabbed a water jug. "I'm going to the river for water this morning." She took a deep breath and exhaled slowly. "Will you come with me, Miriam?"

"I'd love to, dear." It was a small step, but a good one. If Taliah could learn to ask for help and rely on others, perhaps someday she could even trust El Shadd—Yahweh.

Miriam hurried to follow, mouthing a silent *thank you* to Moses as she left. How had he known the depth of Taliah's need for fatherly advice, for unconditional love? *Shaddai, thank You for bringing Moses to encourage my young friend.*

When they returned from the river, Taliah set about her morning chores. Miriam found Moses visiting with their parents and leaned close to whisper, "Well, you've certainly made a good first impression." She elbowed his ribs, and they laughed together. It felt good to laugh with him—a little strange, but good. They'd need to re-introduce themselves, but so far she liked this shepherd brother of hers.

Hoshea soon arrived with their morning rations, claiming Eleazar was "indisposed" but would come after dusk to accompany Miriam and Moses to the elders' meeting.

When the sun had risen over the eastern mountains and still no injured slaves had arrived, Taliah shooed Miriam and Moses off to spend some time alone. Miriam knew of only one place they could be alone, but dare she divulge her quiet, shady paradise south of Rameses? A lone palm stood beside a dry creek bed that had not yet been filled by the Nile's inundation. In a month, this lonely place would be under water, but it was her favorite place on earth—and she would share it with Moses.

Sattar frolicked in the tall grass, chasing a desert hare and disrupting a nightjar in its nest. "I wasn't sure he'd adjust from tending flocks in the wilderness to naps and crowds in the Delta." Sattar chose that moment to leap into the air, nearly catching a bird in flight. His two masters laughed at his antics.

"It feels good to laugh," Miriam said, settling under the palm. She drew up her knees, still able to circle her arms around them and clasp her hands. She'd hoped silence would soothe her but found stillness most troubling of all. "Why didn't El Shaddai tell me His secret name, Moses? Why did He not tell me about His deliverance?"

Moses lay on his side, chewing on a long blade of grass. He didn't answer right away, preferring it seemed to watch a hoopoe bird plunge its beak into the dust for insects. She'd nearly given up on his answer, when she heard a quiet whisper. "I was tending Jethro's flocks on the far side of the wilderness, and I'd climbed far up Mount Horeb, the mountain of God. I saw a bush on fire, but it didn't burn up. As I drew near, I saw the angel of the Lord within its flames, and I started to walk closer, but a Voice from the bush called my name."

"Yahweh said your name?" Miriam's question came out on a sob.

"I'm sorry, Miriam. I'll stop if hearing about my encounter upsets you."

"No, no! My tears are more wonder than jealousy. He said your name, Moses?" She shook her head, barely able to fathom it. "How marvelous to hear your name from the lips of God." She wiped her cheeks and tried to stem the tears. "Please, go on." The sadness on his face shamed her heart. Why had she allowed pettiness to cause him regret?

"The Voice from the bush said, 'Take off your sandals, for the place where you're standing is holy ground.' I hid my face because I knew I'd heard and seen God—the One True God you'd told me about when we were children. He told me He was sending me to Pharaoh to bring His people, the Israelites, out of Egypt, and I asked, 'Who am I that I should go to Pharaoh and bring the Israelites out of Egypt?'"

Miriam's breath caught. It's what she desperately wanted to know. Why Moses? Why not her? "What did He say?"

"He said, 'I will be with you; that will be your sign that it was I who sent you.'" Moses held her gaze. "This isn't about you or me, Miriam. This isn't even about Israel or its deliverance. What we're going to experience is about Yahweh showing the world He is the One True God."

14

Moses said to the LORD, "Pardon your servant,
Lord. . . . I am slow of speech and tongue."

—EXODUS 4:10

Eleazar was a coward. A brave man would admit that his aversion to Taliah's independence was rooted in his desire to make her his own. A courageous man would admit his bitterness toward Moses was because of the love and admiration Doda showered on her long-lost brother—love and admiration that until now had been reserved for Eleazar alone.

Eleazar knew he was a coward, but how many others were aware? Surely Moses could see it. He'd been regarded as one of the greatest military minds of Egypt, a warrior trained to recognize fear. He knew how to read people's actions and reactions. How long before he recognized that Eleazar's barbs and sharp comments were merely masking deeper feelings?

How long before you admit you love Taliah?

The silent voice inside his head was unmistakable, indescribable. Pulling at his hair with both hands, he growled in frustration. Perhaps he was going mad. Why couldn't he treat Taliah with the same indifference he'd treated the women Prince Ram had given him? That was easily answered. It was because Taliah was unlike any woman he'd ever met. The spirit of a warrior lived inside her. Infuriating as she was, the fire within her drew him like a moth to a flame.

If only Putiel would respond to his message. Then he'd be free of her, and Taliah could find a good man who could protect and love her as she deserved. Perhaps the first letter never reached Putiel. Should he send another? What if a second message stirred Kopshef's overly suspicious nature? He couldn't risk it.

He couldn't avoid her forever. He'd sent Hoshea with the morning and evening rations because he didn't want to face Taliah or Moses. Ridiculous. Would he spend the rest of his life hiding in his chamber?

Tell her you love her.

Eleazar marched out the door, slamming it behind him, refusing to acknowledge the treasonous voice inside. To care for Taliah would place her in danger and thereby betray his vow to Putiel. He may be a coward, but he was no traitor to his friends. He grabbed a torch from the wall and started for Goshen.

Before he realized it, he was running. Through the palace gates, past the industrial section, and too soon arriving at Doda's village. He rounded the corner of her long house and stopped dead in his tracks. Taliah sat huddled around a torch with three small children, drawing a horse and chariot with her finger in the dust.

"Pharaoh Ramesses took his first four sons to the battle of Kadesh as a part of their military training. One of them wasn't much older than you, Masud. Kadesh was the greatest battle ever won by the Egyptian army."

"Kopshef was twelve, the age of manhood." Eleazar stepped nearer, adding his torchlight to theirs. "Princes Ram and Wen were eleven, and Prince Khaem was nine."

Taliah looked up, torchlight dancing in her eyes. "You were there?"

"I was there with your abba. He saved Prince Kopshef's life."

"How?" Her face fairly glowed with wonder, but the story wasn't wondrous.

Eleazar looked into the wide, innocent eyes of the children and remembered the blood dripping from Prince Kopshef's sword. Some children weren't so innocent. "That's not a story for your students."

Her smile dimmed, but she recovered quickly. "Would you like to meet my new friends?" Without waiting for his reply, she began introductions. "This is Masud. He's eight. And this is his brother, Haji."

"I'm six!" the boy held up two chubby hands, showing all fingers on one and a thumb on the other.

"Yes, and this is Tuya," Taliah added, while the little girl hid behind her. "She's five and a little shy."

Eleazar felt crimson creeping up his neck and cheeks. The temperature had surely risen; it felt like noonday. "Very nice to meet you."

Masud reached for Eleazar's cudgel. "Can I play with your weapon?" Eleazar instinctively slapped his hand, frightening the boy. Masud's eyes went wide before releasing an ear-piercing howl.

Taliah hugged the boy tight. "It's all right. Eleazar was protecting you. He didn't want you to get hurt playing with weapons."

"I'm sorry. I . . . I'm . . ." Eleazar could command an army of slaves but had no idea how to manage a yowling child. He rammed his torch into the leather holster outside the doorway and hurried around the curtain. Doda, Moses, and Hoshea waited inside, and Sattar growled his greeting.

"You look like you're being chased by hyenas." Doda grinned.

"Worse—an eight-year-old boy." The room erupted in laughter. Even the dog stopped growling.

Doda offered him a cup of beer, but he declined. "We should start our climb up the plateau. I want to give ample time for a few respites."

Someone entered behind him, stirring the air with the scent of acacia and honey. *Taliah.* He closed his eyes and breathed her in.

"Eleazar?" When he opened his eyes, she was standing in front of him, concern etched on her features. "Are you well?"

"Fine." Again, heat prickled his cheeks, and he turned to Doda. "Let's go, let's go."

Doda Miriam raised her eyebrows but said nothing. She patted Taliah's cheek on the way out. Moses and Sattar followed. Eleazar tried to hurry behind them, but Taliah snagged his arm as he passed. "Miriam and I only had to visit three households to find my first three students." The pride in her eyes shone like the stars.

He wanted to take her in his arms. Instead, he rushed out the door without a word, the cool night air kissing the warmth on his arm where her hand had been.

Hoshea had grabbed the torch to lead the group out of Doda's village.

The last days of Akhet offered shorter days for field workers as more till-able soil slept beneath the Nile's silt-rich waters. Production slaves, how-ever, maintained the back-breaking quotas of bread, beer, wine, jewelry, and linen. Night workers had gone, and the day shift had returned to Goshen for their evening meal. The villagers had settled in for the eve-ning, families enjoying their fresh breads, stews, and fish over the cook fires. Eleazar's stomach growled as he savored the aromas wafting through the long house windows.

Hoshea marched as if leading young soldiers to war, and they soon reached the first waste dump. Doda was winded. She'd never be able to climb the plateau at this pace. "I'll take the torch," Eleazar said, jogging to the front. Hoshea willingly relinquished it and supported Doda's left side with Moses on her right. She offered no complaints, a sure sign of her fatigue. Sattar stayed near, never more than a few paces from Doda since he'd adopted her last night.

Moses had seemed preoccupied since they left the long house but fi-nally broke his silence. "Are we going to the plateau we called dead-man's land when I owned this estate?"

Doda tried to laugh but was breathless from the slight incline. Elea-zar answered for her. "It's still called dead-man's land, but like everything else since you left, it's grown bigger and crueler. More Hebrews. More work. More deaths."

Moses took a deep breath. "When these lands were the premiere Ra-messid estates of Qantir and Avaris, Pharaoh Sety invited Egypt's noble-men to visit the adjoining estates for a month of leisure each year. In preparation for their arrival, Sety ordered the estate foremen to take a census, recording the ages of all slaves on the plateau. On the first day of the noblemen's arrival, Sety took wagers from the noblemen on the aver-age life span of slaves in dead-man's land." Moses grew quiet, his jaw muscle dancing in the moonlight, eyes glistening. "It was a game to them."

"Thirty to forty," Eleazar said. Moses turned a furrowed brow his direction. "The life span of a plateau slave. Men live to be thirty or forty. Women die younger."

Moses was silent for several steps. Eleazar wondered if he'd decided to change the subject. "You're right," Moses whispered in the darkness. "Most years the men's average was thirty-six and the women, thirty. Some women couldn't bear the abuse and ended their own lives."

Eleazar's stomach rolled. "And what did you wager, *Prince Mehy*?"

"Eleazar!" Doda Miriam stopped. "I won't have you—"

"It's a fair question, Miriam." Moses met Eleazar face to face. "Sety and I had a standing agreement. If I won the wager, he promised to provide an additional basket of grain to each family on the plateau at harvest."

Eleazar held his gaze. "And if Sety won?"

"He had the right to treat my slaves as his slaves until the next wager." Moses leaned closer. "He never won. I bribed the guards." Moses turned and looped his arm with Miriam's and began the steep climb up the plateau.

Eleazar hurried ahead of them to provide torchlight along the winding path to the top. They climbed in silence, each pondering private thoughts. Eleazar, of course, thought of Taliah. How long before a slave driver saw her playing with village children instead of working in the fields or serving in a home? She needed a skilled husband or a mistress to serve. Hebrews serving in a skilled position or working as military, palace, or house slaves might live to be sixty or more. But what could Taliah do? She would never survive the plateau.

"Eleazar, I must rest." Doda Miriam reached for Eleazar's arm, shaking.

"Of course, of course." He knelt on one knee and created a stool with the other.

She sat down, wrapped an arm around his neck, and kissed his forehead. "Thank you, dear." Sattar nestled beside her, nudging her hand for a petting. She scratched behind his ears but rested her hand there, showing the extent of her fatigue.

"You should tell me when you are getting too tired."

Doda waved off his scolding but remained silent—another sign of fatigue.

Moses glanced around them uneasily. "Perhaps we should douse your torch and let the moon guide us the rest of the way so the guards don't notice our gathering."

Eleazar bit back a retort. Moses didn't know this land anymore. He didn't know the slaves or the slave drivers. The elders' meeting was at the farthest reaches from the palace, and no Egyptian would venture to the plateau at night. Doda Miriam squeezed Eleazar's shoulder, and even in the darkness, he could see her silent pleading. For reasons beyond his understanding, Doda needed him to be kind to Moses.

He shoved the flame into the sand without comment.

Doda pushed to her feet. "I'm rested. Let's go."

With the torch extinguished, their best weapon against jackals was gone. "Hoshea, you provide rear guard with the hot-pitch torch and give Moses your spear." Eleazar drew his own spear and marched on.

Finally, they crested the top of the plateau and saw the elders gathered in the distance. Eleazar noticed Moses combing his long gray beard with his fingers, and Doda spoke to him quietly. "Yahweh is with you. Remember?"

"I rrre-mmem-bbber."

Eleazar found it hard not to stare. The vulnerability on this man's face didn't match the quiet strength he'd witnessed last night. Doda Miriam had once told him that Moses began stuttering as a child after witnessing merciless violence at the hands of his pharaoh grandfather, but the man Eleazar met last night was more consistent with stories of Prince Mehy—top student in the School of the Kap, military commander, Egypt's vizier. How could Moses fear speaking to a crowd of slaves?

As they neared the last row of elders, Abba Aaron came from the front of the gathering, greeting them with arms open wide. "Moses, welcome!" They met in the middle of the crowd, and Abba embraced his brother, ignoring those accompanying him. Eleazar's older brothers, Nadab and Abihu, had trailed behind Abba and offered Eleazar a condescending sneer. Now in their sixties, they were too spoiled by Ima's pampering for any decent woman to marry them. If Eleazar had believed in a god, he would have thanked him that his brothers refused a betrothal to Taliah. She deserved better.

Aaron wrapped his arm around Moses's shoulders and ushered him through the crowd. Eleazar, refusing to let Doda be forgotten, wrapped his arm around her waist and fairly carried her through the crowd as Sattar cleared a path, baring his teeth at any who threatened to impede their progress. As they neared the front, Eleazar spotted Ima Elisheba and leaned close to Doda. "What's she doing here?"

"I don't know, but I'm sure she'll tell us."

15

*And Aaron told them everything the LORD
had said to Moses. He also performed the
signs before the people, and they believed.
And when they heard that the LORD was
concerned about them and had seen their
misery, they bowed down and worshiped.*

—EXODUS 4:30–31

Eleazar steered Doda Miriam toward Ima Elisheba, who was waiting in the front row of elders with a small pitcher in her hands—the only woman among Israel's leaders.

"It's about time you got here," Ima hissed. "I've been waiting since dusk. Aaron wanted to come up here alone—before Nadab and Abihu returned home from the metal shop—and I said, 'Indeed not! You'll not go to dead-man's land and wait alone for who knows how long.' So I came with him and told him the elders would just have to ignore me. I don't care if they think it unfitting that I've come with Aaron. Let them think it, I say. Aaron is the best man among them, and it's about time someone noticed. This Yahweh seems like He's finally going to do something about—"

"What's the pitcher for?" Doda Miriam interrupted, causing Ima Elisheba to sputter.

She shoved the pitcher into Doda's arms. "It's water from the Nile. Aaron says you must hold it. I don't know why I can't hold it, but he said it must be you." Ima lifted an eyebrow at Eleazar. "Hmm." At least she acknowledged his presence.

Doda received the pitcher and nodded politely. "Thank you, El-isheba. How nice to see you this evening."

Eleazar stifled a grin at these women who'd been carefully *not* fighting since Abba Aaron moved in with Ima's family when they married. Saba Amram and Savta Jochebed approved the marriage but had been hurt deeply when Abba Aaron seldom visited and chose to provide for his wife's family, leaving Saba Amram and Savta Jochebed to fend for themselves. In Eleazar's eyes, it was unforgivable—especially now that Ima Elisheba's parents were gone and Eleazar's brothers earned a wage and still lived at home, feeding on his parents' rations like crows on carrion.

Without warning, Ima jerked Eleazar's hair, pulling his head sideways. "I see you still haven't cut your hair." She flung his hair away and pointed to Nadab and Abihu, who stood three camel lengths away near Abba and Moses. "Your brothers have cut their hair to match the Egyptian-style wigs."

Eleazar held his tongue—as always. But Doda didn't—as usual. "I suppose if Eleazar did everything like Nadab and Abihu, my parents and I would starve."

Hoshea arrived in time to hear, and he shot a panicked glance at Eleazar. Eleazar simply closed his eyes, waiting for the real henpecking to begin.

A disgusted huff coaxed his eyes opened. Ima lifted a brow in challenge. "I suppose Miriam has convinced you to marry the harem girl. Your brothers, of course, are men of distinction and will wait for a respectable maiden, but you . . ."

"Me, Ima?" As soon as he spoke, he regretted breaking his silence.

"It's well known that Hebrew soldiers have no morals, so why not marry a concubine? What does it matter that other men have traveled that path before you?"

Had he been on a battlefield, Eleazar's rage would have meant blood, but this woman was his ima, whether she behaved like it or not.

Doda furtively reached for his hand. "Taliah was a tutor in the harem, Elisheba, and she's far too intelligent to marry my older nephews."

Ima rolled her eyes, but before she could spew more venom, Abba Aaron's voice rang out like a trumpet in the cool desert air.

"El Shaddai has heard our groaning and will deliver us from bondage." He had stepped onto a pile of dried-mud bricks and held Moses's staff high overhead. Moses stood on the ground at his right side and motioned him to bend closer. The brothers whispered, and the crowd stilled.

But Eleazar had heard it all before. His mind was consumed with Taliah. How many others thought she'd been Ramesses's concubine? Was this lie also the cause of Putiel's family shunning her? He couldn't let a rumor ruin her reputation, her life, her future.

"The God of Abraham, Isaac, and Jacob appeared to my brother, Moses, in a flaming bush atop Mount Horeb in the Sinai wilderness." Abba continued the story of Moses's encounter, grabbing Eleazar's attention with details he hadn't heard. "He has revealed His personal name, Yahweh, meaning *His nature will become evident by His actions.* In generations past, only one man at a time—or a woman"—he nodded at Doda Miriam—"was given the honor of knowing our God. But for generations to come, all Israelites have the chance to know Yahweh through His mighty works. Each of us will learn of God personally as He rescues us from Egypt."

Abba paused as if waiting for roaring applause, but when met with only skeptical stares, he cleared his throat and leaned down to consult with Moses again. The elders began to fidget, an unsettled buzz stirring the crowd. Nadab and Abihu, standing on Abba's left side, cast a questioning glance at Ima, as if she would direct Abba—as usual.

Without warning, Abba Aaron rose to full height and threw down Moses's staff. When it hit the ground, a slithering cobra rose in its place, hood extended and ready to strike. Nadab and Abihu shrieked like frightened maidens, and Ima shouted at Abba, "Kill it! Kill it!"

Sattar growled but kept his distance, making Eleazar chuckle. But Moses seemed unruffled, walking around the circle of terrified elders, capturing the attention of those who dared look at him instead of the snake. Ending his perusal of first-row elders, Moses grabbed the serpent's tail, instantly returning the slithering creature to his sturdy shepherd's staff. He resumed his position at Abba's right side.

Now came the roaring applause, but neither Aaron nor Moses took a bow. Doda Miriam stepped closer to Eleazar and slipped her hand around his elbow. Was she afraid? It wasn't like her to be timid.

"I've seen that trick before in the market," shouted Medad from Dan's tribe. "Did your Egyptian brother teach you that, Aaron?" Discontent rumbled through the crowd, but Moses remained silent, chin high. A storied soldier knew better than to engage the rabble.

Abba Aaron raised his voice above the grumbling. "Yahweh anticipated your doubt and told us to display a second sign." Abba slipped his right hand inside his robe for only a moment. When he removed it, he lifted it overhead and scaly white skin fairly glowed in the moonlight—leprosy.

The audience gasped, and Ima Elisheba fell into Hoshea's arms, wailing. Abba Aaron turned his face away, seeming as rattled as the rest to see his flesh eaten so thoroughly. Eleazar felt the same panic and turned to one he hoped could explain. "Doda, why would Yahweh destroy the hand of a metal worker? Abba will be expelled from the craftsmen's village and sent here to the plateau to work the mud pits."

Before she could reply, Abba Aaron hid his hand inside his robe again and then removed it—this time perfectly restored. The awe on Abba's face matched the flutter of wonder among the elders.

Hoshea shook Ima. "Look, Elisheba. He's healed. Look!" But she was too busy crying to see the miracle before her.

Eleazar leaned over, trying to read Doda's puzzling expression. "What do you think of that?" Eleazar expected a litany of praise, perhaps a list of *I told you so's,* or at least a short song overflowing from her heart.

But she shook her head and covered her quiet sobs, cradling the pitcher of water. What was happening inside his typically effusive Doda? Yahweh's miracles had obviously overwhelmed her, but were her tears happy or sad?

"Why didn't you let someone inspect your hand, Aaron?" A dissenting voice rose among the elders.

"How do we know you didn't dip your hand in yogurt to make it white, and then just wipe it off?"

"There are a dozen ways you could do that trick." More doubters raised their voices until Eleazar feared the noise would travel to the watchmen on guard in the valley. Sattar had taken a protective stance in front of Doda Miriam, the fur on his back rising with his growl.

Eleazar considered quieting the crowd himself, but Moses joined Abba on the pile of mud bricks, and stilled the elders with uplifted hands. "I'm not asking you to believe in m-m-me, men of Israel, but at least consider the f-f-facts before you." He pointed to Doda Miriam. "Yahweh has spoken to my sister, Miriam, since she was a young girl—the only prophetess in Israel since the days of Jacob and Joseph. But as the Nile waters flow through the banks of Egypt, so God's power flows through His messengers, and now Yahweh's power also flows through Aaron and me."

Moses extended his hand toward her. "Miriam, please give Aaron the pitcher."

As if in a trance, Doda raised her head and lifted the pitcher into Abba's hands. Eleazar cradled her shoulders. She seemed so frail, so small in that moment. He leaned close to whisper. "He didn't say they'd been chosen to replace you, Doda." Her face twisted with renewed pain, and she waved away his sympathy. He squeezed her to his side and watched for more proof of Yahweh's power.

Abba Aaron tipped the pitcher and poured a small stream of water at the base of the brick pile, sending a puff of dust into the air before a puddle formed.

"Can everyone attest that this pitcher contains water?" Moses asked. "Those in front, please testify to those who can't see it. Is there agreement before we proceed?" Nods and anxious stares gave Moses permission to proceed. "Pour the remainder of the pitcher's contents on the ground, Aaron."

Abba obeyed, and the stream ran clear at first but gradually became red and thick, sticky as it hit the ground. Soon the stench of blood filled the air. Ima Elisheba screamed as it splattered on her robe. Abba kept pouring, the contents far exceeding what the small pitcher could have contained.

Moses raised his voice over the stunned exclamations. "When Yahweh appeared to me on Mount Horeb, He said, 'I have indeed seen the misery of My people in Egypt. I have heard their cries, and I am concerned about their suffering. So I have come down to rescue My people Israel from the hand of the Egyptians and to bring them up out of that land into a good and spacious land, a land flowing with milk and honey—the home of the Canaanites, Hittites, Amorites, Perizzites, Hivites, and Jebusites.'"

One-by-one, the elders fell to their knees, stretching their arms out before them, foreheads on the dust. Even Ima Elisheba and her sons bowed the knee, humbled in the presence of such power. Moaning and cries rose to heaven—hearts broken in worship of the God who had remembered His promise and His people.

Eleazar knelt on one knee but rested his elbow on the other, watching. He'd known many of these men all his life, grown up with their children, served with some of their sons. How could they worship Doda Miriam's God tonight when they'd bowed before Egypt's gods most of their lives? Some of their children knew nothing of the Hebrew God. The stories of Adam and Eve, Noah, and Abraham had faded into obscurity. Their loyalty was fickle, their worship now aimed at a God they didn't know.

Even more convicting was the seed of faith growing in Eleazar's belly. How dare he hope in the God he'd cursed at Kadesh! Could the same God who'd allowed a twelve-year-old boy to murder dozens of innocent Hebrew soldiers at Kadesh now rescue the whole nation from that boy's father? It would take more than a few tricks to bring Eleazar to his knees.

From the corner of his eye, he saw Doda Miriam's serene smile mingled with tears. Sattar sat beside her, attentive but peaceful. Doda lifted her hands toward heaven and opened her mouth, releasing the sound Israel had come to know as most holy worship. Doda's songs, with their haunting beauty, had silenced even the Egyptians, but tonight the melody

blended with the fledgling praise of Israel's elders. Whatever inner turmoil she'd experienced was soothed by her song. How could she praise a
God she couldn't see or understand?

Abba Aaron had said each Israelite would experience God personally
as His nature was revealed during their rescue. *Experience Him personally.* El Shaddai had always been Doda's God, Saba and Savta's God, but
never Eleazar's God. He was too holy to fathom and too distant to trust.

If You're there, Yahweh, prove it to me.

Surrounded by worship late into the night, unexpected emotion
rumbled up from Eleazar's chest. Only one person came to mind who
might understand his conflicted thoughts. Only one person was intelligent, candid, and open-minded enough to really listen if he could gather
the courage to voice his deepest questions.

Only Taliah.

16

The LORD is my strength and my defense;
he has become my salvation.
He is my God, and I will praise him,
my father's God, and I will exalt him.

—EXODUS 15:2

M iriam's song carried on the night wind, her voice as strong as it had been when she was a child. "El Shaddai is my strength and my salvation." Her heart skipped a beat, and she repeated the refrain using His new name. "Yahweh is my strength and my salvation. He is my God, and I will praise Him, my father's God, and I will exalt Him." Emotion threatened to choke off the melody, but she resisted. Repeating Shaddai's new name was the only way to know Him anew as Abba Amram had suggested. "Yahweh is my strength and my salvation. He is my God . . ." Into the worship she sang, eyes closed, tears flowing. Her heart, mind, and hands lifted to the Giver of Life, the Sustainer of her soul.

I rejoice in the revelation of Your mighty power, O God, but please . . . please . . . don't take Your Spirit from me. When Moses had demanded the pitcher of water from her, she had clung to it as if to a lifeline. Surely, Yahweh would allow her to participate in one miracle before the elders. Surely, He would use her brothers *and* her in His deliverance. But no. Only Aaron and Moses had been used to display Yahweh's mighty power tonight.

"Yahweh is my strength and my salvation. He is my God, and I will praise Him, my father's God, and I will exalt Him." The familiar chorus washed over her spirit like healing balm, reminding her of Moses's words.

This isn't about you or me, Miriam . . . it's about Yahweh showing the world He is the One True God. If she could keep her focus on Yahweh, concentrate on His mighty works, His ultimate plan. . . .

"Doda, it's late. I should take you home." Eleazar cupped her elbow and helped her stand. Dear boy.

She nodded, leaning heavily on his arm. "Come, Sattar." She snapped her fingers, and he followed. Moses noticed their departure and joined them; Hoshea too. The moon lit their path, and exhaustion imposed silence.

When they reached the long house, Moses turned to Eleazar and Hoshea before going inside. "Aaron and I will appear before Pharaoh in the morning. We'll deliver Yahweh's command, 'Let My people go, so they may hold a festival to Me in the wilderness.'"

"A festival?" Miriam touched his arm, drawing his attention. "You told the elders Yahweh would free Israel completely."

"And He will, but first we must ask this reasonable request of Egypt's unreasonable king. Ramesses will refuse. Yahweh has told us He'll harden Pharaoh's heart repeatedly, but God will compel Pharaoh with His mighty hand." He sighed deeply and ran his hand through his long, white hair. "Eventually, Israel will be free." He looked up at Eleazar. "But it will not be a quick deliverance." He disappeared through the curtain, leaving Miriam as confused as Eleazar and Hoshea.

Eleazar shook his head. "If Ramesses recognizes Moses as the man who betrayed his father, he may kill both him and Abba before they speak a word."

PART 2

Afterward Moses and Aaron went to Pharaoh and said, "This is what the LORD, the God of Israel, says: 'Let my people go.'"

—EXODUS 5:1

17

Pharaoh said, "Who is the LORD, that I should obey him and let Israel go? I do not know the LORD and I will not let Israel go."

—EXODUS 5:2

Pharaoh began receiving supplicants when the morning sun shone through the tall, narrow throne-room windows and stretched to the farthest corner. Eleazar had been watching the progression of the sun's rays across the marble floor all morning, waiting for Abba Aaron and Dohd Moses to arrive. He'd declined to help them gain an audience; refused to help Moses commit suicide. If Pharaoh Ramesses knew Prince Mehy had returned to Rameses, it would mean death for Moses and anyone associated with him.

Moses had nodded and smiled. "Yahweh will make a way," he'd said.

If Yahweh planned to make a way for them to see Pharaoh today, He'd better hurry. Pharaoh ceased his morning hearings when the sun's rays touched the left arm of his gilded throne. The tip of daylight had now reached the royal dais.

Prince Ram lifted his right hand and glanced over his shoulder, summoning Eleazar for whispered instructions. "Let's use battle-axes for our sparring today."

"You can test the new ones the Hittites forged last week." Eleazar resumed his position while the prince feigned interest in political affairs. Both of them hated court. They much preferred their daily sparring match at the armory after midday, but Pharaoh's second firstborn knew the importance of pleasing his father. So he sat and Eleazar stood for what seemed like days every morning.

A commotion at the two-story ebony doors drew every eye toward two men being escorted by the king's guards. Eleazar's chest constricted. *Abba and Moses.* Abba was dressed in a white supplicant's robe. Moses remained in his shepherd's garb. Their long gray beards betrayed their Hebrew lineage. Both men's hands were tied. They'd been arrested. Moses must have revealed his identity.

Ramesses flicked the horsetail flail, ordering the current supplicant aside. He leaned forward, narrowing his kohl-outlined Eyes of Horus, and addressed his soldiers. "Guards who disrupt my throne hall put their lives in jeopardy."

The soldiers, nearly jogging, hurried the prisoners up the long crimson carpet. The guard on the right spoke breathlessly. "Keeper of Harmony and Balance, Strong in Right, Elect of Ra—the time for petitions is growing late, and we knew you would want to see these men today."

"You knew, did you?" Pharaoh relaxed against his throne with a grin.

Abba Aaron bowed, but Moses stood like the royal he once was. "Good m-m-morning, Ramesses. It's been a long time."

Indignation swept Pharaoh's features. What Hebrew would dare use Pharaoh's familiar name? He looked closer, and confusion settled on the royal brow. Disbelief came next with a gasp. "Mehy?"

"I'm called Moses now, and this is my brother, Aaron. I've been a Midianite shepherd these forty years."

Ramesses's eyes bulged, and a slight chuckle escaped instead of the anger Eleazar had feared. "You're wearing Midianite stripes and you smell of sheep. The once-great warrior who taught me to wield a sword is now a shepherd? The one-time vizier and honorary brother of Pharaoh Sety is now brother to a slave?" His chuckle bloomed into laughter. "The gods have punished you far worse than Abbi Sety's death squads could have."

Moses nodded gracefully and placed his hand on Abba's back, nudging him forward. Eleazar swallowed hard when he saw Abba's hands shaking on the staff he carried. Would he do the snake trick? Maybe give the staff to Moses and again show a leprous hand?

"This is what Yahweh, the God of Israel, says to you, Pharaoh Ramesses." Abba's voice echoed off the high ceilings and columns of Pharaoh's cavernous throne hall. "Let My people go, so they may hold a festival in the wilderness."

Ramesses still chuckled, shaking his head in disbelief. "Who is this *Yahweh* that the god on Egypt's throne should obey him?" He waved his flail again. "I've never heard of Yahweh, and I certainly will not let my slaves frolic in the desert."

"But Yahweh has met with us." Abba Aaron stepped forward, and two guards shoved their cudgels in his belly. Eleazar closed his eyes, feeling traitorous in his helplessness.

Pharaoh laughed again. "Oh, your god met with you? The Hebrew god I've heard of is invisible. Was this an invisible meeting?"

Eleazar opened his eyes and watched Moses step in front of Abba. "Please, let us take a three-day journey into the wilderness to offer sacrifices to Yahweh, or He may strike us with plagues or with the sword."

Plagues or sword? This was new. Moses had said nothing of plagues or war last night. Was it a trick, or had he heard more from Yahweh?

Ramesses stood, hands on hips, his humor gone. "I think you Hebrews are lazy. Since you've decided to return to Egypt, *Moses*"—he spat the word like a curse—"you will work the mud pits with your Hebrew brothers. This isn't Avaris anymore." He sat back on his throne and scoffed. "The Hebrews have grown quite numerous. A trip to the wilderness would stop all production. It's out of the question. Back to work—both of you!" He pointed his flail at the door through which they'd come, and the guards rushed them out. A nervous hum buzzed among the crowd, and Pharaoh slammed his flail on the armrest. "Silence!" The double ebony doors closed behind Abba and Moses, leaving Pharaoh sulking on his throne and the next supplicant shaking in his sandals.

Eleazar breathed a sigh of relief, marveling at the undeniable favor that allowed Abba and Moses to escape with their lives. Whether or not Yahweh was real didn't excuse the inhumanity Eleazar witnessed every day. How could any god watch men's cruelty and do nothing? And if Yahweh was real, how could He let Israel suffer the harsh bondage of Egypt all these years? No matter how many miracles Yahweh performed, these questions deserved answers before Eleazar could trust Him.

Thankfully, only three petitioners brought cases for Pharaoh's hearing before the sun's ray touched the armrest. He sentenced all of them to execution and continued pouting even as his scribes rolled up their scrolls and started dismantling their reeds and pigment. From across the room, Eleazar's little brother Ithamar captured his gaze and raised an eyebrow as if saying, *I'm glad this day is over.*

But before the last scroll was packed, Pharaoh slammed his flail on the armrest again. "Prince Ram, you will summon the slave drivers and Hebrew overseers to the private throne hall in Sety's palace." The smaller structure, at the northernmost corner of the palace complex, had been the king's primary residence until Ramesses's grander palace had been built.

Ram stood among the gallery of princes. "As you wish, great and mighty Son of Horus."

The king stared at the double ebony doors as if reliving his disturbing encounter. "If Moses and his brother have energy to complain, they have entirely too much time on their hands. You will issue this order to the slave drivers and Hebrew overseers." He pointed to the scribes to be sure they recorded every word. "You are no longer to supply the slaves with straw for making bricks. Let them gather their own straw, but require them to make the same number of bricks as before." A sinister smile curved his lips. "If the slaves work harder, they'll have no time to hear lies about meeting with an invisible god."

18

*So the people scattered all over Egypt to
gather stubble to use for straw. The slave
drivers kept pressing them, saying, "Complete
the work required of you for each day, just as
when you had straw." And Pharaoh's slave
drivers beat the Israelite overseers they had
appointed, demanding, "Why haven't you
met your quota of bricks yesterday or today,
as before?"*

—Exodus 5:12–14

Miriam felt the soft rumble of Sattar's growl under her hand and
rolled over on her sleeping mat. The odor of soiled bandages
and lingering herbs stirred memories of yesterday's wrath. The slave drivers and overseers had ordered Hebrew slaves to gather their own straw for
dusting their hands and brick molds. Slaves typically chopped any sort of
plant stubble into fine dust to keep the mud from sticking to their hands
and molds, but to collect the straw themselves would slow their process
considerably. Though the slave drivers and overseers understood the delay
such an order would cause, they still required the same quota of bricks. It
was ludicrous. Impossible. Unreasonable. So why had they ordered it?

Miriam had a gut-wrenching suspicion it had to do with Moses and
Aaron's audience with the king. So far, no one else had raised the possibility. The brick makers knew only that yesterday had brought more pain,
more brutality, and more death than anyone could remember. But how
long until someone accused Miriam's brothers?

While the slave drivers' whips feasted on Hebrew failure, Moses and Aaron joined every available slave to gather straw from the land. But when beaten and wounded slaves lined up around Miriam's long house, Moses returned to help her tend the hundreds who begged for relief through her herbs and honey. Even Taliah had postponed her lessons with Masud, Haji, and Tuya to help with the wounded.

Most of their supplies had been used up yesterday, but they could still assist those who brought their own honey. Miriam had sent word to Gedor, the linen keeper, that they needed as many linen scraps as possible to bandage the wounded.

Sattar's wet nose nudged Miriam's cheek, bringing her out of half consciousness. Then he was on his feet, growling like a sentry between her and the giant form of a man at her doorway.

"Will that dog ever accept me?" Eleazar asked in the predawn darkness.

"Leave it, Sattar." Miriam pointed to her mat. The dog left his protective stance and returned to her mat, circled twice, and then lay down beside her. "You're scary in the dark." She loved teasing her nephew.

Taliah sat up and pulled on her robe, combing her luxurious black hair with her fingers. Eleazar walked two steps and offered his fist to Miriam. She grabbed it and saw him wince as he hoisted her to her feet.

"What's wrong? Let me light a lamp." She hurried toward her small table and felt for two flint stones to strike together. Before she could strike a spark, she saw a flash in her mind. A vision, quick as a blink, of Prince Ram's whip slicing Eleazar's back. Then darkness again.

Miriam laid her hands on the flint stones but didn't light the lamp. "Why did Ram beat you, Eleazar?"

"You were beaten?" Taliah gasped.

Miriam struck the flint stones together over the oil-soaked lamp wick. The lamp offered a small circle of light that she carried toward Eleazar. "Turn around. Let me see."

"I'm fine," he said, backing away from her light. He held two bags in his hands. The smallest appeared to be their normal food rations. The larger he held aloft. "Prince Ram sent me with more herbs and honey. He said you should expect increased injuries today. I probably won't return tonight. I, um . . ."

"I've already seen it. Yahweh showed me. Now, come here, boy." Miriam held the lamp higher in her trembling hand. When Eleazar hesitated, she moved closer, giving light to her fears. His face was badly bruised and swollen, his lips cut from a beating. Taliah whimpered but covered her mouth when Miriam cast a reproving glance her way.

"Lie down on my mat so I can treat the whipping wounds on your back."

A single nod was his only response.

Miriam began checking through the new bag of supplies. "Taliah, take the rations and then help Eleazar take off his breast piece."

"Me?" The girl began her protest at the same time Eleazar made excuses.

"But I must return—"

Miriam lifted her hand, cutting off both their pleas. "Now is not the time to be bashful or stubborn." Miriam pinned Eleazar with her sternest gaze. "I need to organize these supplies, and you need to get that leather breast piece off. The wounds are probably already festering under the dirty leather." Her voice broke, and she turned away with the lamp, hurrying to unpack the large bundle of herbs, balms, seeds, and powders. Her hands shook as she retrieved some turmeric powder, a few henna leaves, and a jar of honey. *Thank You, Yahweh, for speaking to me, but why must it be my Eleazar? Why my boy?*

Sattar, sensing the need, moved off her mat as Eleazar sat down. Taliah knelt behind him and began untying the straps, gently pulling the blood-soaked leather from his back. Eleazar kept his head bowed, silent. He'd worked hard to keep her at a distance and seemed determined to continue. Stubborn man.

Miriam knelt beside them. "All right, boy, lie on your stomach and tell me what happened."

"Doda, I'm not a boy. I'm forty-seven years—"

"You're my boy. Now, on your stomach." Miriam pointed to the mat and waited for her gentle giant to position himself. Nearly twice as wide and long as her mat, he rested his chin on a fist and waited for her to begin. She turned to Taliah, who was standing over them twisting her hands. "I'll tend the wounds, dear, but you must sit beside his head and distract him from the pain."

Taliah took tentative steps on shaky legs. But instead of sitting by his head, she prostrated herself, matching his posture with chin on fist, placing her face a handbreadth from Eleazar's. "Is this close enough to be a distraction?" she whispered to him.

Miriam could hear Eleazar's gulp from where she sat and decided now was the time for the turmeric powder. She sprinkled a thin layer across the deepest wound that extended the length of his back. He sucked in a quick breath. "The more you talk, the less it will hurt," she said. "Why did Prince Ram beat you and send you to me with supplies? And why would he warn us of more wounded?"

"Mmm." The single noise through clenched teeth was the only sound Eleazar could make until Miriam moved to the other wounds on his back. Taliah reached out and combed a stray curl from his forehead. He stilled under her touch and began his explanation. "Prince Ram believes his father is being unreasonable. They gave the Nubians and peasants leave to worship their gods last year, so even the king's officials realize that Moses's request isn't excessive. But no one will challenge the king because he's blinded by hate for Moses, and his anger is mounting."

Miriam placed the first henna leaf across the deepest wound, and he clenched his teeth again.

"Look at me," Taliah said. "What do you see in my eyes, Eleazar?"

"Mmm," he groaned. "I see Putiel." He buried his face in his hands. "Telling me to protect you."

She stroked his hair, removing the leather tie that bound it at his neck, and then leaned close. "If I look like my abba, two months without harem lotions and paints has done more damage than I imagined." Miriam grinned as she began coating bandages with honey.

Even Eleazar chuckled, lifting his chin onto his fist again. "Your only resemblance to Putiel is your strength of spirit. Thankfully, you have your ima's beauty."

Miriam kept slathering honey on bandages and placing them on his wounds, but Eleazar seemed oblivious to everything but Taliah. The girl looked up at Miriam, and her cheeks pinked. "Here, let me help you with the bandages while Eleazar tells us more about what Prince Ram said."

When Miriam smoothed the final bandage over his deepest wound, Eleazar's words came out on a groan. "The brick makers haven't reached their quota since Pharaoh commanded them to haul their own straw."

Taliah glanced at Miriam. "You mean Pharaoh issued that command? Not the overseers?"

Miriam squeezed her eyes closed. Her fears were valid. "Go on, Eleazar."

"Pharaoh's building projects are falling behind. He woke Prince Ram in the middle of the night, ordering him to command all Hebrew overseers beaten." He looked over his shoulder at Miriam. "Ram started with me to make a point."

Miriam's heart was in her throat. "Does he know you're Moses's nephew?"

"I don't think Prince Ram or the king has made that connection yet." Eleazar pillowed his hands and laid his head down, keeping his focus on Miriam. "The greatest proof of Yahweh's existence isn't my uncle's return or the miracles he and Abba performed in front of the elders. It's the fact that Ramesses hasn't killed Moses yet—because I know how much he hates Sety's betrayer." He paused and then shifted his eyes to Taliah. "I see worse than beatings if Pharaoh discovers any of us are connected with Abba and Moses. I won't be able to protect anyone in this house."

Miriam helped him sit up, and Eleazar held his hair out of the way while she and Taliah wrapped a single cloth around his torso to hold the treated bandages in place. Miriam gathered the new supplies and began categorizing them. "I know you try to protect us, and I'm grateful, boy. Really." She set aside her jars and baskets and cupped his face. "But consider for a moment that the God you're so angry with has protected *you* all these years and might have placed you in Pharaoh's palace for a reason

you can't imagine." She rolled to her knees and then stood, looking down
at two puzzled faces.

Let them wonder—it's how faith grows.

Within the bag of Prince Ram's supplies were more than rolls of
linen and dried herbs. Six jars of poppy seeds would provide anesthetic
and strong pain relief, and eight jars of turmeric powder were meant to
treat open wounds like Eleazar's. Prince Ram was telling her that injuries
would not only increase in number but also in severity. It was a warning
clearer than a courier with a scroll. Prince Ram often tried to moderate
his father's excesses—he was a good boy as Egyptian princes go—but he
was telling her that even he couldn't forestall Pharaoh's wrath this time.

19

When [the Israelite overseers] left Pharaoh,
they found Moses and Aaron waiting to meet
them, and they said, "May the LORD look
on you and judge you! You have made us
obnoxious to Pharaoh and his officials and
have put a sword in their hand to kill us."

—EXODUS 5:20–21

Injured overseers began arriving as Miriam and Taliah helped Eleazar
replace his leather breast piece.

"The Egyptian physicians won't treat us anymore," one man said,
offering her a jar of honey to treat his wounds. "They're afraid Pharaoh's
wrath will fall on them if they help us."

Miriam received his payment, but the amount he offered wouldn't
even cover his own wounds, let alone the wounds of those in the line of
slaves forming outside her door. She caught Eleazar's arm before he
slipped outside. "Ask Prince Ram to make arrangements with the Egyptian physicians. If they won't treat the slaves, they can at least share their
supplies with us."

By midday, Prince Ram's supply of bandages and treatments was
nearly gone, and Miriam had received no word from the Egyptian physicians. Thankfully, most of the overseers were better compensated than
plateau slaves and brought their own bandages and honey.

Now almost dusk, Miriam's back ached. She wiped sweat from her
brow, stretched her arms overhead, and returned to debriding the wound
of an overseer from the tribe of Reuben. A pair of brick makers carried in

an injured man. He was barely conscious. "He's an elder and overseer of Judah. Stop what you're doing and help him."

Taliah intercepted the demanding newcomers. "Let's take him into the adjoining chamber to wait. It's quieter, and he'll be more comfortable with Amram and Jochebed."

"No!" one of the weavers shouted. "The Judeans have donated more supplies than any other tribe. You will help him now!"

Calmly, Miriam left the Reubenite and inspected the Judean's injuries. Though no doubt painful, the whipping wounds on his unscarred back were neither life threatening nor urgent. "I am grateful to the tribe of Judah for their donations, but I decide who is treated first based on need, not bluster." She turned to Taliah. "He can wait outside if he refuses the quiet company of my parents."

The injured Judean lifted a weak hand toward the curtain and the adjoining room. His companions hadn't been the first of their tribe to demand preferential treatment. Judeans had been blessed with thirty overseers' positions—a distinction of honor any day but today.

Miriam returned to the Reubenite on her mat and finished her work with a prayer, "May Yahweh make Himself known to you by His mighty works on your behalf." She had prayed aloud over each patient, mentioning the name *Yahweh* so the nation of Israel would recognize their coming deliverance. Some of them thanked her without question. Some responded with growing faith, while others spewed cynicism that had grown from generations of buried hope. Some were inquisitive at the mention of *Yahweh* and asked why El Shaddai's prophetess would serve another god. "*Yahweh* is the new name by which every Hebrew can know El Shadd— Yahweh, the I AM. His mighty works will soon reveal the nature of the God of Abraham, Isaac, and Jacob as we've never seen before."

Somehow, the confidence of her declarations made Yahweh's silence to her more bearable.

Taliah returned from the adjoining room as the lavender hues of dusk shone through the window. "Our special guest is settled in the back room," she said, sarcasm dripping from her lips. "Amram is telling him a story to keep his mind off the pain."

Without warning, an image flashed in Miriam's mind—Moses and Aaron surrounded by jackals, and the snarling beasts were closing in on them.

"Miriam, are you all right?" Taliah steadied her arm, coaxing Miriam back to the moment.

Miriam assessed their three remaining patients. "Can you finish dressing this wound? The others can wait. I think Moses and Aaron are in danger."

Taliah nodded. "Of course. Go, Miriam."

Miriam hurried toward the door as the sound of shouting carried on the evening breeze.

"These stripes on my back are your fault!" a man roared.

"You put a sword in Pharaoh's hand to kill us!"

Miriam grabbed her walking stick and called for Sattar. The dog bolted from her parents' room and followed. In the distance, Miriam saw her vision being played out—Aaron and Moses were standing on the path connecting the city of Rameses to Goshen. The jackals closing in were angry Hebrew slaves and overseers.

Her brothers stood a head taller than the large crowd gathered around them. "Listen to us. Please!" Aaron lifted his hands high. "Let us explain." One of the Judean overseers pushed Moses, but her brother didn't retaliate.

Miriam hurried on aching legs and prayed she'd arrive before harsh words turned violent. "Wait! Wait!" she shouted.

Several faces turned her way, but most remained focused on Aaron and Moses. "You have made us a stench in Pharaoh's nostrils with your demand to worship in the wilderness."

"Who is this Yahweh? What has He ever done for us?" said another.

Miriam arrived at the edge of the growing crowd, and Sattar's vicious snarl cleared a path for her toward Aaron and Moses. She stood between her towering brothers and saw many of the men and women she'd treated earlier in the day. "I know you're in pain. I know it feels like Yahweh has failed us."

A Judean elder jabbed his finger in the air. "Moses and Aaron failed us. I expect nothing from your Hebrew God, Miriam." Rumbles of agreement surged through the gathering.

"Please, please," Miriam begged, "listen to me. For years, El Shaddai has interpreted your dreams through me. You know He is real. Now He has disclosed a new name—Yahweh—and has promised to reveal Himself to all of us through mighty acts of His power. After four hundred years of His silence, can we not be patient a little longer?"

Murmurs rippled through the gathering, but no angry dissenters raised their voices. Relieved, Miriam exchanged a hopeful glance with her brothers. "Yahweh told Moses that Pharaoh's heart is hard and we should expect refusals until he is compelled by Yahweh's powerful hand. Ramesses has issued unreasonable demands like gathering our own straw before. We must wait patiently for El-Shadd . . . for Yahweh's plan to unfold." How long would it take for God's new name to take root in her spirit?

"What if we don't like Yahweh's plan?" One of the elders stepped to the front of the crowd and pushed his daughter forward, pointing to her arm in a sling, her bruised and swollen face.

Miriam recognized her from this morning. She had not only been beaten but also defiled by a slave driver. This girl would bear lifelong scars. Only truth could offer hope to one so wounded.

"I don't like Yahweh's plan either." Miriam confessed, drawing a collective gasp. "But I choose to trust Him because only He can build a life on which the future fits perfectly."

Everyone fell silent. *Please, Yahweh, let my simple words be enough.* One by one, the crowd walked away. Some threw scowls over their shoulders, but at least they weren't throwing stones. No blood was spilled.

"Thank you, Miriam," Aaron said, hands trembling as he combed his long beard. "Moses and I heard that the overseers had gone to Pharaoh. We knew they would realize Pharaoh's edict was a result of our demand to worship in the wilderness. That's why we waited here on the road to address their fears . . ."

"Fears?" Miriam shot a blazing stare at Moses but his head was bowed. "It's more than fears I've been bandaging all day. It's more than fears that ruined that poor girl's hope of marriage."

Moses raised his head, tears streaming down his cheeks. "Why did Yahweh send me here? To bring more trouble on these people?" He stalked away, bumping Aaron's shoulder without apology.

Aaron rolled his eyes and pointed at Moses's retreating figure. "Behold our great deliverer." He turned in the opposite direction and marched toward home.

Miriam watched her departing brothers and turned her anger on the One who could receive it without offense. *So these are the men You've chosen to deliver Israel? At the first sign of trouble they run and hide.* With fists on her hips, she tapped her toe in the dust, fuming. Aaron would go home to Elisheba and get an ear full of criticism, but at least he had someone.

Though shadows lengthened and darkness loomed, she could see Moses headed in the direction of the private place she'd taken him to yesterday morning. "Come Sattar. Your first master needs our help tonight."

The dog nuzzled her hand, remaining close as she followed at a distance, keeping Moses in sight. As expected, he veered from the path leading to the city and walked along the narrow dike toward her palm tree.

The evening breeze cooled Miriam's temper, and she watched Moses settle himself under the palm. He hadn't seen her yet. He faced the Nile, his back against the palm. He drew up his knees, and laid his forehead on them—as agile as the little boy she remembered. Thunder rumbled in the sky.

Odd. No lightning preceded it. Before Miriam could ponder further, Moses raised his head and shouted, "Ever since I went to Pharaoh to speak in Your name, he's brought trouble on Your people, and You've done nothing to rescue them. Nothing!"

Miriam's breath caught. Was Moses shouting at Yahweh? And the thunder. *Could it have been Yah—*

A tremendous rumble shook the ground beneath her feet, and Miriam fell to her knees, face in the dust. Sattar yelped and cowered beside her. The thunder lessened to a gentle roll, and Miriam lifted her head to see Moses's face tilted toward heaven, eyes closed, expression pained. Was God speaking to him? Did it hurt?

She wanted to go sit with him, comfort him, ask him a million questions, but she remembered his account of the burning bush. *"Holy ground,"* God had said to Moses. Should she take off her sandals? Was her little palm tree holy ground now?

Just as suddenly as the rumble began, silence robbed the air of every sound, and Miriam heard only her own heart pounding in her ears. Sattar lifted his head, alert in the void of noise. Afraid to move, hesitant to breathe, Miriam waited.

Moses looked back, not startled but aware. "It's all right, Miriam. You can sit with me—if you're willing."

He sounded defeated. She shouldn't have chastised him after he'd already faced the elders' anger. Pushing herself to her feet with the walking stick, she approached her brother under the palm and nudged his shoulder until he looked up at her. "I once told Aaron that it was both a blessing and burden to be included in God's counsel. I do not envy your burden, Brother."

He looked at her, surprised. "Did you hear Yahweh's voice?"

She settled on the ground beside him and leaned against him. "I heard His voice thunder but no words. Can you tell me what He said?"

Moses remained focused on the Nile. "He wants me to assure the Hebrews that He will free them from Egypt's bondage and that He will give them the land He promised to Abraham, Isaac, and Jacob. But it's more than that, Miriam." He looked at her then, his brows knit together like the stubborn Prince Mehy of his youth. "Yahweh speaks of Israel as if we are His family, precious in His sight. On my journey from Midian, He called Israel His firstborn. A moment ago, He promised to take Israel *to Himself*—as if we were His bride. These are words of love, Miriam. I don't understand—"

"Yes, Moses, yes!" Miriam's heart leapt at his words. "It is love, and this is the El Shaddai I've known. He took me to Himself—like a bride— and has been my family, my everything, all these years." She gasped, wonder blooming like a rose in her soul. "He wants every Israelite to know Him as I have known Him? Truly?" It's what she'd been telling people all day, but had she really known it? Believed it?

Rather than the wonder she felt, only frustration showed on Moses's features. "How could a loving God let His people suffer four hundred years of injustice and continue to let them suffer now?"

For the first time, Miriam set aside her own offense and imagined the heartbreak of her Shaddai. "The bigger question is how could an all-powerful God let His people choose not to love Him? He lets us choose and then live with the consequences. He could force our obedience and impose His will, but instead He patiently treats us like wayward children. Only a God-sized love could restrain His power."

Moses nodded, but the crimson creeping up his neck testified to his dissent. They sat in silence watching the shadows lengthen. A heavy sigh escaped her brother's lips before he spoke. "Was that innocent girl a wayward child, the one ruined by the slave driver today? What about the hundreds who have died since I returned to Egypt? Were they all wayward—"

"I don't know," Miriam interrupted. "I don't know all the answers, Moses. I know only that I felt a rush of hope to think that others might realize El Shaddai's love as I've known it all these years." She laid her head on his shoulder. "Not since fellowship with God was broken in the Garden of Eden has Yahweh revealed His secret name—but He told it to you, Brother, and He's promised to reveal Himself to the whole nation of Israel. We can accuse Him or trust Him. It's a choice each of us must make for ourselves."

They sat in silence, watching the river teem with life. Finally, when Miriam's back ached from leaning too long, she sat up and focused on her brother. "I must apologize to you for my harsh words back in the village." He started to protest, but Miriam lifted her hand to silence him. "When I doubted you, I doubted God at work through you. I must ask you both for forgiveness."

Sattar growled, interrupting the tender moment. Miriam scooted closer to Moses and scanned the tall grass around them. "You know, we're too close to the Nile and too far from the city to be safe here in the dark."

Moses whistled and signaled to Sattar with his hand. The dog responded immediately, sniffing around the low-lying bushes and shoreline.

Miriam, thoroughly impressed, tried to lighten the mood. "He checks for danger? You'll have to teach me those signals."

Moses offered only a satisfied smile in reply. Sattar finished his inspection and returned to the tree. Moses scratched behind the dog's ears, his smile slowly fading. "I want my dog back."

Miriam's heart fell to her toes. She'd never intended to steal Sattar, but the dog had helped fill the emptiness of God's silence. "I want my God back."

Moses's brow furrowed, but he didn't answer. Miriam glimpsed his sadness before he began plucking the stray blades of grass between them. "I wish we could all go back . . . before . . . everything . . ."

Her brother was beaten. She sensed it. But he couldn't give up. He needed to understand his importance to the people—even if they didn't yet realize it. "El-Shadd—Yahweh speaks to me in pictures—dreams and visions that give me an inkling of what might happen, and then He gives me a sense of understanding." She turned to Moses, waiting for him to meet her gaze. "I was important to the Israelites because those dreams and visions gave them a sense of scope and wonder. That's not what they need now."

"But you're still import—"

"Yahweh speaks to you with words, Moses, not pictures. He tells you exactly what will happen and when. Don't you see?" A sense of resolve settled over her. "God is God, and He decides how He will speak and to whom. We must all be ready to acknowledge Him in whatever ways He reveals Himself."

Moses focused on the rising moon shimmering across the Nile. "I know only the Yahweh of miracles and the Voice from the fiery bush or thunderclap. So when I see Him do nothing—as has been the case in the past few days—it's hard to trust Him."

Miriam raised one eyebrow like a chastising big sister. "I agree. It's frustrating enough to shout at Him, right?"

"It did no good."

"Did He say anything else?"

"He told me what's next." He looked at her then. "Aaron and I are to return to Pharaoh's throne hall in the morning."

Miriam's blood ran cold. "Are you sure you heard Him correctly? Eleazar said Ramesses is very angry. He might kill you both if you return."

Moses closed his eyes and dropped his head into his hands. "I know. I told Yahweh it was fruitless. If the Israelites won't listen to me, why would Pharaoh listen to my faltering speech?"

She shoved him, barely budging her muscle-bound brother. "Stop it. Your stuttering has nothing to do with it. You said yourself that Pharaoh won't let the Hebrews go until he's seen God's mighty acts of judgment."

He lifted his head and turned a weary face her direction. "Aaron and I go to Pharaoh tomorrow. Yahweh said I'll be like God to Pharaoh and Aaron will be like my prophet. Ramesses will demand a miracle, and Aaron will throw down my staff as he did that night on the plateau. But—as you said—Ramesses won't be convinced to let us go. Who knows how long it will take, Miriam, but Yahweh said Pharaoh will ultimately *drive* Israel from Egypt." He grabbed her hands, squeezing them. "Aaron and I can't do this without your help. I saw how the elders listened to you. You must help us prepare the leaders and organize the tribes."

Miriam felt every day of her eighty-six years in that moment—every wrinkle, every ache, and every sleepless night. But when Moses had fled Egypt forty years ago, he had no faith in any god. Yahweh had changed him in the wilderness, and though he seemed as conflicted as she—one moment distraught, the next impassioned—it was obvious he truly believed Yahweh would deliver Israel.

Did she?

The magnitude of God's promise dawned in her spirit. Leaving Egypt meant more than simply embracing freedom. Israel would leave behind everything they'd ever known, everything familiar.

She nodded quickly before she lost her nerve. "Tell me how I can help."

20

So Moses and Aaron went to Pharaoh and did just
as the LORD commanded. Aaron threw his staff
down in front of Pharaoh and his officials, and it
became a snake. Pharaoh then summoned wise
men and sorcerers, and the Egyptian magicians
also did the same things by their secret arts.

—EXODUS 7:10–11

et's keep testing the new battle-axes." Prince Ram reached for a new
ax head, inspected its edge for sharpness, and then handed it to one
of Eleazar's men to be attached to a shaft. Eleazar reached for an ax head
as well, but the prince stayed his hand. "I think you'll spar with a wooden
sword today. Let's test your mettle."

Eleazar bowed. "As you wish, my prince." His heart pounded like a
battle drum. Was Ram using their sparring session to vent his anger on
all Hebrews, or had the prince discovered Eleazar's association with Abba
Aaron and Moses?

The men had returned to the throne hall this morning, repeating
Yahweh's demand that the Hebrews be released to worship Him in the
wilderness. To Eleazar's surprise and relief, Ramesses hadn't killed them
on sight. Instead, he'd challenged them to prove Yahweh's power with a
miracle. Abba Aaron threw down his staff, and Eleazar expected a snake
like he'd seen on the plateau, but the serpent that slithered sideways on
the marble floor was twice the size and astonishingly quick.

Pharaoh raised his sandaled feet off the floor and tucked them under
him on the throne. He called to the crowd, summoning his counselors
and chief sorcerers and magicians. Each nobleman stepped forward with

a smirk on his face, and assistants handed each one a multicolored rod. The snake trick was rudimentary, performed by street magicians in every city market. By pinching the nerve in the nape of the serpent's neck, the snake became rigid, appearing to be a finely decorated staff. Five magicians threw down their *rods,* and five slithering snakes came to life, hissing and writhing across the gleaming marble.

The circle around the serpents widened, while Pharaoh, feet still tucked safely beneath him, raised a single brow. "It would seem your god needs a new trick to gain our respect—"

Moses's serpent reared to the height of a jackal and in a single *swish!* devoured all five of the magicians' writhing rods. Women screamed. Men shuddered. Eleazar's knees felt like water. Pharaoh himself chirped like a hoopoe.

Abba Aaron merely reached for his serpent's tail, and the staff stiffened again. Moses nodded to Ramesses, and the two Hebrews retreated nobly through the double ebony doors. Pharaoh had adjourned court immediately.

"Choose your wooden sword wisely, Eleazar." Prince Ram grabbed his assembled battle-ax from the slave boy. "You'll reap my foul humor for all Hebrews today."

Eleazar breathed a sigh of relief. The prince was angry at Eleazar's race, not his parentage. "I'm ready to face your wrath, my prince." Eleazar chose the wooden sword with the longest blade to match the reach of the prince's thrusting ax. He took several swings and tossed the wooden sword from hand to hand, measuring its weight. He'd need to be quick and accurate to block Ram's fury.

The prince led him into the sparring arena where six other pairs had already begun midday bouts. Each pair fought within a circle of combat drawn in the dust, and Eleazar noted the prince walking toward the lone empty circle in the arena. Before Eleazar stepped inside it, Prince Ram turned and swung the ax. Eleazar ducked and diverted the shaft with his wooden sword, issuing a disapproving glare at his master. Ram never cheated. What was he thinking?

The prince returned his glare. "A soldier must be ready for unexpected battles, Eleazar." The fighting began in earnest. Swing, thrust, parry, jab—Prince Ram came at him relentlessly.

Eleazar defended every attack as Putiel had taught him. A royal guard must provide competition and training but never harm the prince's person or pride.

"Unexpected battles," Ram repeated. "Life is full of them." He swung low, and Eleazar jumped over the heavy ax blade. "Like the unexpected appearance of those two slaves this morning. And the unexpected way their serpent devoured the magicians' snakes." He swung the ax at an angle, nearly slicing Eleazar's shoulder.

Eleazar blocked with his sword, and the wooden blade split in half.

Prince Ram let his hands fall to his sides, stretched his neck, and smiled like a hyena circling his prey. "We must also prepare for the unexpected return of my putrid brother, Kopshef." As he spoke the name, fury launched Prince Ram's battle-ax at Eleazar's neck.

Eleazar ducked and, while Ram was unbalanced from his miss, he kicked the prince's legs from beneath him. Ram landed in the dust, and every sparring match ceased. All attention turned to the prince on the ground. Eleazar's first instinct was to offer assistance, to beg forgiveness, to show remorse. Any of which would have gotten him killed.

Instead, he offered his splintered sword and kept his voice at barely a whisper. "And if you attack Crown Prince Kopshef with uncontrolled rage, the unexpected will land you in the dust."

Prince Ram's lips curved into a slow smile before he barked orders at the others. "Get back to work!" He stood and shoved Eleazar from their sparring circle. "Follow me."

Eleazar retrieved the prince's battle-ax and handed it and his broken sword to the weapons keeper as they exited the armory gates. He walked silently beside his master toward the palace complex, waiting for Ram to share the inner turmoil that mirrored his own. Both of them hated Kopshef. Different reasons. Same intensity.

"Why do you think Father summoned my brother? Have I failed the great Pharaoh somehow?"

"May I speak plainly, my prince?"

"Be careful, Eleazar, but yes. You may speak." Though Ram shared Eleazar's disdain for Kopshef, there was still a bold line between master and slave, Egyptian and Hebrew.

"Your brother is not just high priest of Ptah but also the greatest magician in Egypt. When your father saw the Hebrews' serpent devour the magicians' snakes . . ." Eleazar paused, hesitant to say Ramesses was afraid. "Pharaoh seemed *affected* by the Hebrews' trick. It makes sense that your father would summon Prince Kopshef—a magician—to command Egypt's gods, but he trusts you to command Egypt's military."

Ram flashed a sideways grin. "My brother will certainly never command the military—no matter how many sword drills Putiel put him through as a child." Putiel, with Eleazar as his apprentice, had trained all four of Ramesses's oldest sons in military and life skills. Ram had learned well. Kopshef often balked at instruction.

Though Eleazar dreaded losing Taliah to a husband, he looked forward to seeing his old friend again. "Putiel always said a warrior's weapons were wisdom and strength, but a coward fought with deceit and trickery."

"Which is why my brother is a master magician and not a soldier." Ram's jaw muscle danced in rhythm with his steps. "Kopshef has tricked Pharaoh and others into believing he commands the gods, but Kopshef himself isn't a god until he sits on Egypt's throne." He looked at Eleazar, raising a single eyebrow. "*If* he ever sits on Egypt's throne."

Eleazar offered a simple nod, neither smiling nor frowning. His duty was to protect and serve Prince Ram—whatever that entailed. He'd worry about conspiracies and coups after Prince Kopshef arrived. For now, he was more worried about Kopshef's personal guard.

He'd ask Putiel face to face why he never responded to the message he'd sent, and then they'd sit down with their cups of beer and talk of Taliah's marriage. Eleazar would nod, smile, and give approval to whomever her abba chose. After all, what did it matter to Eleazar whom she married? She was no longer his concern. Doda would have one less mouth to feed, and Eleazar could return to life as normal.

So why did he feel dread each time he looked to the quay for Kopshef's royal barque?

21

The LORD said to Moses, "Tell Aaron,
'Take your staff and stretch out your
hand over the waters of Egypt—over the
streams and canals, over the ponds and
all the reservoirs—and they will turn
to blood.' Blood will be everywhere in
Egypt, even in vessels of wood and stone."

—EXODUS 7:19

The morning sun shone through the window, brightening Abba Amram's face as Miriam cooled him with a wet cloth. Taliah fed Ima Jochebed leftover rations from last night and regaled them with history lessons of Prince Mehy's battles.

She offered Ima a sip of cool water. "I still can't believe the same warrior in my stories now empties our waste pots each morning."

Moses had left no room for argument when he'd taken over the household's vilest chore. "The Hebrews would rather slit my throat than let me work beside them in the fields or mud pits. I must be of use," he'd told them.

Miriam understood the need to feel useful, so Moses emptied the pots. For the past two days, however, the chore had fallen to her. Yesterday, Moses and Aaron had left Goshen before dawn to confront Pharaoh. As expected, the staff-to-serpent miracle hadn't convinced Pharaoh to release the Israelites, but word spread quickly through Goshen that Aaron's serpent devoured the magicians' snakes.

Taliah's students asked her to tell them the story, and several Hebrews gathered around to listen. From there, whispers and gossip spread at the river as women gathered water for their families. Faith in Yahweh's power was growing, as was Moses's notoriety.

Yesterday afternoon he'd withdrawn, and Miriam knew he'd likely gone to their private palm tree. This time, she didn't follow. At dusk, she used the hand signals Moses had taught her to send Sattar to find him. Neither the dog nor her brother returned, but why worry? Surely, Yahweh would protect His appointed deliverer.

A few Judean elders came to the long house after dark. "Have you any dreams or visions for us, Miriam? Any word from Yahweh on what to expect next?"

She could hardly get the word past the lump in her throat. "No."

Was that pity in their gaze or condescension? Miriam let the curtain fall and left them standing at the doorway.

It was well after the moon's zenith when Sattar led her brother through the doorway, but Miriam pretended to sleep. Moses woke her before dawn, saying he'd heard from Yahweh again and must wake Aaron for another confrontation with Pharaoh at the river. He walked out that morning, leaning heavily on his staff, looking every bit of his eighty years old. Miriam tried to feel compassion for Moses, but found she could only yearn for his weariness. *Please, Shadd . . . Yahweh, use me for Your purpose among the Israelites. Take me to Yourself as a bride, as family, and let me feel Your love as I once did.*

Silence had shrouded her morning chores. She'd eaten little and spoken less as she tended to Abba and Ima's care. "Are you trying to wash off the dirt or my wrinkles?" Abba Amram grinned, but her distracted rubbing had left a red mark on his arm.

"Oh Abba. I'm sorry." Tears threatened. "I'll get some aloe to soothe it."

Before she could struggle to her feet, he caught her arm. "What's bothering you, my girl?" On the neighboring mat, Ima Jochebed pushed away the bread Taliah offered.

All eyes were on Miriam, and she felt her cheeks flush. If only an injured slave would walk through the door so she wouldn't have to confess the jealousy and self-pity that nearly drowned her. Why had Yahweh taken away her place of honor among the tribes? Had she displeased Him somehow? She closed her eyes, sending tears down her cheeks.

"Tell us what troubles you, daughter." Ima Jochebed reached across Abba to pat her arm.

"It's stupid and selfish and . . ." She took a deep breath. "I miss Shaddai's nearness." It was true but sounded too honorable. They deserved the whole truth, but she couldn't say it above a whisper. "I miss feeling important."

"Hmm." Abba quirked his mouth, completely noncommittal.

"I'm terrible, aren't I?" She covered her face.

"Awful," he said. "You're absolutely awful."

"Abba!" Horrified, Miriam looked up.

Abba's mischievous grin awaited her. "Yahweh is still near, Miriam. He's everywhere." He laughed and opened his arms. She fell across his chest, and he patted her back as he'd done since she was a girl. "When God is silent, He expects our patience and will reward our faith. Rest in the silence, and trust He's near." Ima turned on her side and stroked Miriam's hair. Even in her parents' weakness, they gave Miriam strength.

Eleazar's tortured voice came from the doorway, "What's wrong? Is Saba all right?" He knelt beside Abba Amram.

"I'm fine, my boy," Abba patted his hand.

Eleazar sat back and glanced at Miriam. "Then something is bothering you." It was an observation, not a question.

"I'm fine too, dear." She need not give her nephew another reason to be angry with Yahweh.

"Hmm." Eleazar looked dubiously at all four members of the household. Then with a single nod produced Abba Amram's favorite rations— cucumbers and nabk-berry bread. "This should make everyone feel better."

Taliah helped Abba and Ima divide their portions, while Miriam spoke quietly to Eleazar. "I was afraid you were late because Ramesses discovered your connection to Aaron and Moses."

He cast an uncomfortable glance at Taliah before answering. "I was late because . . ." He pushed to his feet and disappeared for only a moment behind the dividing curtain. He returned holding a blue byssus sheath, as sheer as a butterfly's wings, and shoved it in Taliah's direction—eyes focused on his sandals. "It's meant to be worn over a linen robe, but you'll make it look lovely even on rough-spun." Taliah's countenance brightened. Eleazar cleared his throat and continued, "Your abba Putiel is returning to Goshen and will undoubtedly make a marriage match for you very quickly. You'll need something special to wear for your wedding."

Taliah's whole countenance wilted, but she tried to mask it by slicing the bread. "I need no token gift to remind me of you, Eleazar. My leg aches every evening where you broke it." Her hand trembled as she offered some bread to Ima Jochebed.

Eleazar stepped toward her, extending the sheath. "Pharaoh summoned Prince Kopshef, so your abba could be here in a matter of days. You won't have time to make wedding preparations, Taliah." He shook the sheath, urging her to take it.

Taliah looked up, eyes pooled with tears, and then stood with the elegance of a queen. "Give the sheath to the next girl whose leg you break." She left the room, chin held high, but Miriam knew her heart was broken. Taliah hadn't spoken of her feelings for Eleazar, but they'd been clear since the morning they'd treated his whipping wounds.

"You're foolish, my boy." Abba Amram spoke the words on Miriam's mind, and Eleazar glared at her as if she'd said them.

Miriam shrugged. "Don't look at me like that. I—"

Ima Jochebed's shriek nearly split Miriam's head. Eleazar rushed toward her. "What is it?"

Her eyes wide with terror, she pointed to the bowl and rag Miriam had used to bathe Abba Amram earlier. "The water . . . it . . ."

Miriam glanced at the bowl. Startled, she quickly checked Abba's arm, his face, his chest. "No blood or injuries." Then she looked into the bowl. Smelled it. "The water has turned to blood."

Eleazar stood like a statue. "Where did the blood come from?"

Screams erupted suddenly all over the village, echoing beyond Goshen into the city of Rameses. Eleazar ran from the room, leaving unanswered questions in his wake.

Taliah returned holding the water jugs she'd filled at the river earlier. "Water to blood," she whispered and then looked at Miriam. "Didn't you pour water from a pitcher and it turned to blood at the elders' meeting on the plateau?"

Miriam covered a gasp, and then came understanding. "It's Yahweh, Taliah. Moses and Aaron went to Pharaoh this morning to display another miracle. Yahweh has turned Egypt's water to blood."

"All of it?" Taliah's voice squeaked in panic.

Miriam lifted one shoulder, excitement building. "It makes sense. Yahweh's miracle increased in grandeur from Aaron's first staff-to-serpent display on the plateau to the demonstration of power in Pharaoh's throne hall. And now the same increase with the water-to-blood miracles."

Miriam turned to Abba and found his face filled with wonder. "Perhaps we'll live to see Israel delivered from Egypt after all."

"What will we drink?" Ima's voice was small.

Miriam felt her first pang of fear. "Taliah and I made a two-day supply of beer." She eyed Taliah, coaxing her out of the room to check it.

The girl returned nodding. "The beer remains, but our bread dough mixed with honey and water to ferment for the next batch is ruined. That water turned to blood."

"Yahweh will show us how to survive." Abba patted Miriam's knee, smiling serenely.

But Taliah remained at the doorway, pale as fine linen. "This God of yours is real, isn't He?"

22

The fish in the Nile will die, and the river will stink; the Egyptians will not be able to drink its water.

—EXODUS 7:18

Eleazar stood at strict attention, holding the reins of Prince Ram's black stallion, waiting for Prince Kopshef's entourage to pass by. The crown prince traveled with as much pomp and ceremony as Pharaoh himself. Musicians, dancers, and priests led his processional from the quay, up the palatial hill, and through the royal gates as his train of servants followed carrying golden chests overflowing with robes, jewelry, and potions. Prince Kopshef himself rode a prancing white stallion, while Pharaoh waited on his throne atop three hundred steps of gleaming white marble. The aroma of lotus and acacia was nearly as overwhelming as the crowd's cheers.

As Prince Kopshef's stallion passed, Eleazar noted his personal guard was a massive Nubian, not Putiel. *Perhaps Putiel was demoted, sent back to the ranks of Kopshef's military detail.* Eleazar hoped it didn't have anything to do with the census request and veiled message he'd sent weeks ago. He scoured the throngs of military slaves that followed but didn't see Putiel. In fact, he saw no Hebrew slaves at all.

His heart began to pound an unsteady rhythm. Prince Ram, as commander of Egypt's army, had sent over a thousand Hebrews under Putiel's command to accompany the crown prince four years ago. They were to assist and defend the building of underground burial chambers where the future sacred Apis bulls of Ptah would be entombed after the entire country mourned their loss. As one of many ambitious building projects of

Ramesses, the Apis tombs of Saqqara had met with some resistance from local peasantry—which was quickly squelched by a small detail of Prince Ram's best warriors. The Hebrews were needed only to guard the workmen at the burial chambers, maintain the soldiers' weapons, and serve Kopshef's guards as the crown prince traveled to and from his palace in Memphis.

Prince Ram leaned over to stroke his stallion's neck and whispered to Eleazar. "My brother wouldn't last one round in a circle of combat with you."

Eleazar made no reply. None was expected. Prince Ram had spent his whole life competing with Kopshef—Nefertiry's firstborn. Prince Ram's mother, Isetneferet, had become Second Great Wife only after Nefertiry, the First Great Wife, died four years ago. Prince Ram had always been second. Second in succession. Second in temple ceremonies. Second in Egypt's heart. Ram was, however, first in his father's favor.

"Come, Eleazar." Ram urged his horse to a slow walk. "Let's hear what my parasitic brother says after sailing on a bloody Nile for four days. No doubt he's waiting for an audience with our father before changing it back to water."

Eleazar jogged alongside his prince, perhaps more anxious to hear the report than his master. When Eleazar had delivered his rations to Doda's household earlier, he'd found Saba Amram unconscious and Ima Jochebed delirious. Dehydration from rationed water had been hardest on the elderly and the infirm. Since Yahweh had turned the Nile to blood four days ago, all of Egypt had resorted to digging seep holes beside the river to filter out the blood through dirt, sand, and rocks.

Well, not all of Egypt had resorted to digging seep holes.

Pharaoh sat atop his tower of stairs, a table with a golden goblet at his right hand. He lifted the bejeweled cup to his lips, gulped lustily, and motioned for a servant to refill it. The maid poured from a large amphora, holding it a cubit above the cup, spilling wine on her white gown, the table, and even Pharaoh's hand. The Son of Horus laughed while the rest of Egypt licked dry, cracked lips.

Eleazar clenched his fists, straining to remain calm when he longed to burst through the crowd and snatch an amphora of wine for his family. How could Pharaoh waste the sweet nectar when Saba and Savta were dying? Doda Miriam's whole household had to dig and filter water from seep holes beside the river and then boil it before drinking. Even then, they barely gathered a cup per person each day.

Prince Ram dismounted his stallion with the grace of a falcon in flight. "Welcome home, Brother!" he said, affixing a smile as he approached Kopshef.

The crown prince slid from his mount and opened his arms wide, forcing the same feigned delight. "Little brother, I see the walls of Rameses are still standing." They locked wrists in a grip that would have felled weaker men.

Eleazar took his place at Ram's shoulder across from Kopshef's personal guard. The Nubian was a head taller than Eleazar and focused on a distant nothing. His ebony skin glistened in the midday sun, every muscle taut and bulging. Eleazar hoped he would never have to fight him.

Prince Kopshef's smile revealed perfectly straight teeth matching his pure white robe. The long byssus linen and simple gold straps were typical for priests, but the crown prince distinguished himself with two pieces of jewelry. He wore a golden uraeus band on each bicep—a rearing cobra and a perched vulture—signs of authority over both Lower and Upper Egypt.

The most impressive and costly piece of jewelry rested on Kopshef's chest, the Gold of Praise collar, bestowed on highly esteemed military men. Kopshef's was the most elaborate of all those belonging to Ramesses's firstborn sons. It was a mockery, of course. Only a few men had witnessed his cowardice at Kadesh during his rite of manhood, but hundreds had witnessed his blood lust on innocent Hebrew soldiers when he returned to the camp in shame. Kopshef had spent the rest of his life trying to prove his strength.

"You seem to have misplaced the thousand Hebrews I sent with you to Saqqara," Ram said, releasing his brother's wrist.

"I caught your Hebrews planning an insurrection and killed those involved."

Ram's eyes narrowed. "We never received your census report."

"Why would I send a report that said they're all dead?" Kopshef turned a wicked grin on Eleazar. "Putiel was the instigator."

Shock hit Eleazar like a blow, and horror sucked the wind from his lungs.

"You'll answer to Pharaoh." Ram said, turning shoulder to shoulder with his brother toward their father's throne. The princes began their three-hundred-step climb while Eleazar and the Nubian remained at the base of the stairway.

The last words Eleazar heard were from Ram. "Putiel saved your life. You know he would never . . ."

"I'm sorry." The Nubian focused forward, barely moved his lips, and kept his voice low. "Many of the Hebrews were good men."

Anger surged, but Eleazar gained control in light of the guard's compassion. "Putiel was like a father to me. What happened?"

"You don't want to know."

Eleazar shook with pent-up fury but remained silent, watching as Prince Ram and Kopshef bowed to Pharaoh at the top of the stairs. He had to know. "Putiel has been Kopshef's teacher and advisor since he was twelve. How could he kill him without—"

"That's why he killed him." The Nubian stole a quick glance at Eleazar and then quickly focused back on the princes, who waved to the adoring crowd and began their descent. "Kopshef summoned me to his chamber, while Putiel's body still lay dead on the tiles. Four advisors stood around the prince, who held a scroll in his hands. He said the message in it finally gave him reason to be free of the Hebrews that had plagued him his whole life. That's when he ordered the execution of all Hebrews in Saqqara."

Eleazar's stomach rolled. Was it his message? His scroll? Was Kopshef telling Ram right now about his secret message? "How long ago was this?"

"Weeks ago, at the end of the month of Thoth." The Nubian stepped back to clear the way for the princes who had almost reached the last step.

Eleazar could barely mask his emotion while both he and the Nubian readied their masters' stallions. The other guard worked as if they'd never exchanged a word. Prince Ram stepped to the sandstone tiles first, hurried over, and mounted his horse. If Ram discovered Eleazar had attached a veiled message, would he confront him immediately or wait until they were away from this crowd? He was so busy checking the bridle and reins, he hadn't noticed Prince Kopshef sidle up behind him.

The prince leaned close, whispering, "Pharaoh said I was right to squelch Putiel's rebellion and purge the holy tombs of the treacherous Hebrews." Eleazar whirled around to Kopshef's wry grin. "Perhaps I should find this she-camel mentioned in your message to Putiel and remove her as a threat as well."

Eleazar's mouth went dry. "I don't know what—"

"Get away from my guard, Kopshef." Prince Ram leaned down from his mount. "You stole Putiel, and look what happened."

"Yes, look what happened," he grinned, and then whispered to Eleazar, "Don't think you can deceive me the way you've deceived my dimwitted brother. I can't prove it was you who added that message, but I will find a way to make all Hebrews pay for the shame Putiel tried to hang on me."

He took two long strides and mounted his stallion. The beast pranced and reared, eliciting roaring approval from the crowd. Kopshef lifted his fist as if he were a conquering hero returned from battle—when his greatest accomplishment thus far had been remaining on his spirited horse. Still the crowd cheered, and Kopshef drank in the praise.

Ram reined his stallion in and bent to speak with Eleazar over the din. "What did Kopshef say to you?"

"I'll tell you everything," Eleazar shouted over the cheering, "when we can speak privately in your chambers." It was a lie. He could never tell Ram about his personal message added to the scroll or divulge Taliah's identity—especially now that Kopshef intended her harm.

Eleazar jogged alongside his master on their way to the stables, fear growing in his belly. It seemed Eleazar wasn't the only one still carrying scars from Kadesh. The Hebrew friends Eleazar lost had become the seedbed for Prince Kopshef's lifelong brutality.

How could Eleazar tell Taliah that her abba had been killed because

of the message he'd sent? The one man who could have found her a wor-
thy husband was dead. Eleazar's chest ached, not because he was running
from the palace to the stables, but because he wanted to care for her.
Taliah needed a husband, and despite all his protests, he wanted to marry
her—that lovely, spirited, intelligent daughter of Putiel.

But now more than ever, he couldn't.

While he was under Prince Kopshef's suspicion, she was in more
danger than ever.

Dust from the road felt gritty between his teeth, and there was no
water—only blood—to wash it away. Doda Miriam was right. Eleazar
couldn't protect any of them.

23

*The fish in the Nile died, and the river
smelled so bad that the Egyptians could not
drink its water. Blood was everywhere in
Egypt. But the Egyptian magicians did the
same things by their secret arts, and Pharaoh's
heart became hard; he would not listen to
Moses and Aaron, just as the LORD had said.*

—EXODUS 7:21–22

The river still flowed red, fish floating and decaying along the banks.
Every slave and peasant in Egypt was thirsty—boiling and ration-
ing fetid water. In the last rays of sunset, Eleazar knelt at the seep hole
he'd dug beside the Nile, dipping water from the rock-lined pit.

Prince Kopshef had taken this same posture at midday, bent over a
seep hole dug by some thirsty palace slave. Pharaoh had summoned all
the wise men, sorcerers, and magicians to observe his son, the great high
priest of Ptah, as the master of Egypt's dark arts demonstrated his skill.
Jannes and Jambres, the king's personal magicians, were there watching
as Kopshef scooped out a full bowl of clear water from the seep and
passed it among the spectators. After witnessing its relative purity, the
audience was held captive by the prince's gyrations, chanting, and shriek-
ing. Eleazar wondered if anyone else noticed the disparity between Kopshef's methods and Yahweh's quiet power.

With an exhausted sigh, Kopshef poured the water from the bowl,
and it hit the ground as blood. The gathered audience clapped politely,
but Ramesses lost all restraint. "Should I be impressed that you match the
skills of a madman? I have blood already. I want water!"

The crown prince threw down his magician's utensils and stormed back to the palace while Jannes and Jambres exchanged a satisfied grin and Prince Ram attempted to soothe his father's temper. "The blood has dissipated some, and our astrologers say it's not blood anyway. It's a red, slimy plant of some kind—the result of an exceptionally hot summer— that will disperse in a few days."

Pharaoh leaned close to his second firstborn, but Eleazar saw his fear and heard the whisper. "Whether blood or slime matters little, Ram. If the Hebrew god can strike the Nile, he's stronger than the Nile god, Hapi, and Kopshef can't command him." He then raised his voice to be heard by all. "Jannes and Jambres, find Prince Kopshef and do whatever chanting and sweating you must to make the Nile stop bleeding." Pharaoh placed his arm around Ram's shoulders and left the magicians by the river.

Eleazar sighed, dipping his cup into the seep hole. Out came a little water with a lot of dirt and sediment. He wasn't nearly as good at this as Taliah. She'd kept Doda, Moses, Saba, and Savta drinking a cup of water a day when the beer ran out. Eleazar threw the water and sludge back into the hole. Should he try again or hurry to Doda's long house? If he went to the long house, he'd have to tell Taliah about Putiel and face the truth about Saba and Savta's weakening condition. Dread pressed his hands back into the hole. He'd try harder to get water.

"I can't lose them," he whispered to no one. Others knelt nearby, mostly women, dipping water from the seeps they'd dug. They'd think he'd lost his mind if he kept whispering to himself. He closed his eyes. *Yahweh, if You hear me, be as merciful to my saba and savta as they have been faithful to You.*

The thought of seeing them once more pressed him to his feet. He was wasting precious time on a job Taliah could do better. He made his way toward the long house, nodding greetings to passersby, accepting sympathetic glances and words of concern. Everyone would mourn the loss of Amram and Jochebed. Their age had made them legends. But they weren't the only ones weakened by this plague. The elderly, infirm, and children struggled with only a single cup of water a day. Even Doda

Miriam stumbled with her first step this morning when Eleazar had delivered his rations. *Why Yahweh? Why kill the people You've promised to help?*

Dragging a hand through his hair, he removed the leather tie at the nape of his neck and saw teeth marks. *Taliah.* His thoughts were never far from her these days. She hadn't spoken to him since he'd tried to give her the blue sheath. Why did his first words have to report Putiel's death?

His chest constricted as he neared the long house. His private meeting with Prince Ram had uncovered disturbing news. When the princes met Pharaoh at the top of the stairway, Ramesses agreed to Kopshef's request that all Hebrew slaves be confined to two cities: Rameses and Pithom. Why move all Hebrews to two cities? Was Kopshef preparing a mass extermination? Would he systematically seek to harm anyone connected with Putiel, or would Ramesses keep him too busy with magician's tricks to bother with Hebrews? Perhaps Moses would have some wisdom on the matter. After all, he lived among the royals for the first forty years of his life. Eleazar arrived at the long house and shoved aside the curtain, finding Moses embracing Doda Miriam. Fear pierced him. "What's wrong?"

"She stumbled," Moses said. "She's becoming dehydrated."

Doda tried to push him away. "Stop fussing. I'm fine." Doda looked up, her face as pale as goat's milk. "Your saba and savta are feeling better this evening. They're both awake but weak." She tried to walk toward Eleazar but faltered.

He lunged forward, catching her. "You're not fine. You can't take care of everyone else and let yourself become weak." He leaned close for her alone to hear. "How can you help Taliah grieve for Putiel if you can't stand up?"

Doda covered a gasp and pushed away to meet his gaze. "What happened to him?"

Moses leaned close as Eleazar quietly recounted all he knew. "Kopshef killed Putiel and every Hebrew in Saqqara. He's always been fearful of rebellion and distrustful of his servants, but he used my veiled message about Taliah as grounds for conspiracy—and killed them all."

"If there hadn't been a message, he would have found another reason." Moses pinned Eleazar with a stare. "Believe me, hate like that finds a way to lash out. I don't know Prince Kopshef, but I grew up with men like him. My guess is that Putiel was too noble, too full of integrity. Men like Kopshef kill servants who are mirrors."

"Mirrors?" Eleazar asked.

"Servants who reflect a master's worst traits by treating the master exactly opposite of how he treats his servants."

Eleazar squeezed his eyes shut and nodded. "That describes Putiel perfectly."

"What describes him perfectly?" Taliah's bright voice shattered the hushed moment. "Did you bring Abba here, or am I to meet him at the palace?"

Near panic, Eleazar would rather have fought fifty men than face Taliah's hopeful look.

Doda Miriam laid her hand on Eleazar's forearm and stepped toward the girl. "Your abba didn't arrive with Prince Kopshef, dear. None of the Hebrews sent to Saqqara returned." She fell silent, allowing Taliah's quick mind to absorb the implications. It didn't take long.

Confusion flitted across her beautiful features, and then realization settled like a shroud. Taliah's chin trembled as she turned to Eleazar for answers. "Do you know what happened?"

He swallowed hard and thought of Putiel. *A warrior's weapons are wisdom and strength, but a coward fights with deceit and trickery.* He was tempted to lie. Tempted to run from responsibility. But it was time he use wisdom and strength to fulfill the vow he'd made to Putiel. "Everyone knew that Prince Kopshef was as ruthless and volatile as his father, but your abba Putiel had always been able to mollify him. No one realized that the prince had such deep-seated hatred for Hebrews and was waiting for an opportunity to revisit his vengeance that began twenty-five years ago."

He paused, preparing himself for the hatred he would soon see in her eyes. "When I sent Prince Ram's census request—and added a personal message—it gave Kopshef a viable reason to accuse Putiel of insurrection. He took out his hatred on every Hebrew soldier in Saqqara."

Doda and Moses bowed their heads, and Taliah covered a sob. "How many were killed?"

"Nearly a thousand."

She closed her eyes, sending a stream of tears down her cheeks, and shook her head. When she opened her eyes again, Eleazar saw pity, not anger, and it staggered him. "I'm sorry, Eleazar. You must know it wasn't your fault."

Emotion closed his throat, and he shook with the effort to stem his tears. Prepared for anger, her compassion was too much to bear.

He needed fresh air and started toward the door, but she stepped in front of him and cradled his cheeks between her hands. "It's not your fault," she said again.

Without thinking, he leaned down and kissed her full red lips, drinking in her scent of acacia and honey. When he lifted his head, she didn't look away, which gave him courage. "Will you marry me, Taliah?" Her pause and instant frown stole every drop of bravery.

"Why?" she asked. "Why would you marry me now? Is there suddenly less danger? Can you protect me?" She stepped back and crossed her arms. "Or do you feel so guilty about Abba's death that your sense of duty compels you to marry Putiel's poor . . . little . . . daughter?"

Her last words came out through tears on the verge of hysteria, and Eleazar felt panic rise again. An image of Ima Elisheba's tantrums and Abba Aaron cowed into doing as she wished flashed in his mind. But he also remembered the times Savta Jochebed had been upset and Saba Amram had calmly listened and replied. If he and Taliah were to live together for the rest of their lives, he refused to have a marriage like the one his parents had made.

Closing the gap between them, he circled her waist with his large hands. She wiggled but quieted as he looked deeply into her eyes. "Our lives will be no less dangerous, and though I'll try to protect you, I'm not sure I can." Her features softened, and she leaned in slightly as he continued. "I do feel guilty about your abba's death, but that's not the reason I proposed." He allowed himself a slight grin. "I must marry you so I can stop thinking about you so much."

She rewarded his humor with a swat and a smile, then poked her head around him to see Doda. "What's involved in a Hebrew wedding? I've lived in the harem since I was five, so I don't know."

Doda rubbed her chin, a mischievous sparkle in her eyes. "Normally, there's a betrothal and the two families negotiate a bride price—"

Taliah waved away the advice. "We don't need a betrothal, and I have no family to negotiate." She looked up at Eleazar, her eyes sparkling. "I come to you with no dowry."

"And you're a bargain—no bride price." He winked, causing her cheeks to bloom a rosy red.

"I'd say we can have the wedding tomorrow." Doda clapped her hands, delighted. "Abba Amram can say the wedding blessing since he's regained consciousness, and we'll invite Aaron, Elisheba, and your brothers." She grabbed Eleazar's arm. "Make sure you get word to Ithamar at the palace today."

Eleazar felt the joy drain from the moment like water from a cracked jar. "We can't invite anyone. This marriage must be a secret." He glanced at Taliah, noting her suspicious look returning. "We must be discreet. I've told Prince Ram I'm moving out of the barracks to care for my ailing grandparents, but no one can know I'm married."

Taliah shoved him away. "Because you're ashamed of me. Because everyone believes I was a harem concubine."

"No, because—"

"I almost believed you cared." She raised her chin, eyes narrowed. "Do you have other secret wives stashed around Goshen? Or maybe at the palace?"

"No, Taliah, I—"

"Don't worry, Commander, you won't have to hide me because we're not getting married." She stormed from the long house without letting him explain.

Somewhere between disbelief and fury, Eleazar turned to Doda and Moses, who stood silent. "I'm not ashamed of her. Kopshef knows Putiel left a woman in my care and threatened her." He looked down at his sandals and scuffed the packed-dirt floor. "Perhaps she'll be safer if I don't marry her."

The comment earned him another swat—this one from Doda. "You've finally done the right thing. Don't stop now just because she's running like a spooked desert hare."

"Taliah? Afraid?" Eleazar looked to Moses for input. "I don't think she's afraid of anything."

Moses stepped close and put a calming hand on his shoulder. "Son, all of us are afraid of one thing—being alone. Taliah has blustered about being independent since I met her, which means it may be the thing she fears most."

"I'll talk to her, dear." Doda patted his arm. "Send Hoshea with tomorrow morning's rations, and then you come tomorrow evening with rations fit for a wedding feast. I'll have your bride ready."

24

Miriam dabbed a damp cloth on Abba's lips and then offered Ima the same bit of moisture. Both were conscious but still severely dehydrated. They'd spent the day sequestered in the adjoining room, preparing a reluctant young bride. Taliah had consented to the marriage late last night, but only after Miriam assured her that Eleazar had explained his true motives after Taliah had stormed out. Her nephew was many things, but he wasn't a liar. Their marriage would be a secret not because he was ashamed but because he was cautious.

Taliah's nervous chatter helped distract Miriam from Abba and Ima's grave condition. "I haven't braided my hair or painted my feet with henna since my days in the harem. Without a mirror, it's hard to tell if my braids are even." She patted the top of her head, where she'd coiled the two long strands in a pile and fastened them with an acacia bloom. "How do I look?"

"Lovely, dear." Miriam set aside the cloth and cup of water. "I have something for you." She rolled to her knees and waited for the room to stop spinning before standing. She'd had no water yet since she awoke. "Ima Jochebed and I have some things tucked away in our linen basket.

We want you to wear them with the blue sheath Eleazar gave you." Miriam rummaged through the stack of baskets in the corner, digging beneath Abba and Ima's extra robe and tunic. "Here they are."

Taliah's gasp was exactly the reaction she'd hoped for. "I've never seen a Hebrew robe so fine, Miriam, and the head covering. Where did you get them?"

Ima Jochebed's voice crackled. "My wedding . . ."

Miriam winked and explained. "Ima wore the head covering when she wed Abba, and the robe was mine from when I was handmaid to the pharaoh's daughter, the woman who raised your Saba Jered."

Miriam dropped the garments into Taliah's waiting hands. "Step behind the stack of baskets and try them on."

Without any more coaxing, the girl hurried behind the baskets. She soon reappeared with the feather-light cloth gently hugging her curves and the head covering draped over her braids. "What do you think?" Radiant, Taliah twirled in a circle.

"Beautiful." Ima whispered the word through a smile and closed her eyes.

Taliah rushed to her side and kissed her cheek. "Thank you, Jochebed. I hope I get to wear them."

Abba Amram brushed her arm, stealing her attention. "Eleazar . . . will . . . come." The effort to speak cost him dearly, and Miriam returned to his side to dab his lips with the damp cloth again.

Taliah moved a few stray hairs off his forehead. "It doesn't matter. I have my students—three more since last week. I might be able to support myself by next year's inundation."

Miriam remembered what Moses said about Taliah's greatest fear. Could she really be afraid of the thing she's fighting so hard to achieve? "You have nothing to fear. Eleazar loves you, dear. He just doesn't know how to show it yet."

Taliah dropped her gaze, rubbing imaginary dirt from the palm of her hand. "It's I who know nothing of love." Before Miriam could ask what she meant, Taliah lifted her chin with the nobility she wore so well. "It's no secret soldiers are given women as rewards for their achievements.

I'm sure Eleazar has no misgivings about our wedding night." Her cheeks flushed instantly.

Miriam glanced at Abba and Ima for help, but both her parents rested with eyes closed. What did Miriam know of wedding nights and love between a husband and wife?

Yahweh, give me wisdom.

"You mentioned growing up in the harem, Taliah, observing the relationships of Ramesses with Queen Nefertiry and his other wives and concubines." The girl nodded, giving Miriam permission to forge ahead. "Don't assume that because Eleazar grew up in a Hebrew home he understands love and marriage. He's forty-seven years old and has lived with soldiers since he was twelve, when his abba and ima sent him to become a military slave. His ima Elisheba is an ox with sharp horns and a soft heart—though the soft heart has become harder to discern in recent years. My brother Aaron has never shown affection—not to his wife or sons. So Eleazar is . . . how should I say this?"

Taliah pulled the head covering off and revealed her consternation. "Just say it. I'm terrified I'll disappoint him or"—her voice broke, and she studied her hands again—"that he'll put me away after the wedding night."

There it was. Fear of being alone, abandoned again as she'd been as a child. She and Eleazar had that in common. Miriam reached for her hand and squeezed it, hoping to infuse the same confidence she had in Eleazar. "He will never put you away, Taliah. Eleazar knows how it feels to be abandoned. Though Eleazar could have lived at home during his first years of military training, Aaron and Elisheba refused him. Eleazar lived here with Abba, Ima, and me."

"Why? Why wouldn't they—"

"Elisheba felt Eleazar's temper could turn violent and harm her two older sons, sons she'd always pampered and preferred to Eleazar and Ithamar."

"Oh Miriam, that's awful." Her eyes misted and she reached for Miriam's hand. "But it explains why Eleazar loves you and Amram and Jochebed so much."

"We know him better than anyone, dear, and I'm telling you— Eleazar loves you. I see it in his eyes each time he looks at you. But he's like most men. He shows that love in practical ways. He's seen what love can do—good and bad—so love means action for him. He sees a need; he fills it. If something is broken, he tries to fix it."

Taliah kept her head bowed, her voice low. "If I were to someday believe your God created men and women, not that I do believe it, but if I did . . ."

"Of course, if you ever believed . . ." Miriam tried to hide her delight. The girl had asked several such questions in the past few days.

Taliah looked up, meeting Miriam's gaze. "Why would Yahweh create men and women so different? Eleazar is brave and honorable and compassionate. The way he takes care of you, Amram, and Jochebed, and the conviction with which he protects us is most admirable. He would make a wonderful abba if he'd simply learn to express his emotions." Frustration began seeping into her tone. "Why doesn't he talk more? He's very intelligent, but no one knows it because he seldom speaks."

Miriam chuckled. "Indeed, he is all those things and more, but you will not change him, dear." She brushed Taliah's cheek. What a gem Eleazar had found. "Love him as he is, and let Yahweh change him."

Moses poked his head around the curtain. "I saw Eleazar and Hoshea rounding the corner of the long house. They'll be here any moment."

Taliah pushed herself to her feet and smoothed Ima's lovely robe over her slender curves. "Do I look like a bride?"

Once again, Miriam stood slowly, allowing her body time to adjust to the change in position. She really must get that cup of water soon. The blue sheath Eleazar had given Taliah lay on the mats between Abba and Ima. Miriam snatched it up quickly and slipped it over Taliah's wedding robe and draped the head covering over her hair and lovely face. "Now you look like a bride."

Taliah's eyes fastened on the doorway behind Miriam. A short gasp escaped. "Are you all right?"

The girl's panicked expression turned Miriam around, and she found Eleazar standing in the doorway caked with blood and mud.

"It's been a long day," Eleazar said. "There were no clean robes at the armory, and I can't wash in a river of blood. So leave me alone, and let's get started."

Hoshea and Moses appeared beside him, looking like respectable Hebrews, hair and beards combed, robes clean. But Eleazar, clearly not injured but in a foul mood, looked as if he'd wrestled with pigs and then slaughtered them.

Miriam saw disappointment written on Taliah's face, and blind fury propelled her toward her nephew. "Is this how a bridegroom comes to receive his bride?" She took three steps before a loud roar inside her head and spotty vision nearly knocked her to the ground. When she came to herself, Eleazar's arm was around her waist, and his grimy hand was on her arm. She shoved him away. "You're filthy!"

"Doda, please." He clenched his teeth and nodded toward Taliah. "Do you think she's still willing to marry me?"

Miriam grabbed his arm and dragged her big, strong nephew out of the long house into the night air. The effort cost her. Another dizzy spell settled in, and she braced herself against the doorframe. When Eleazar reached for her, she wagged her finger. "Don't you touch me, young man. Since you can't wash in the bloody Nile, you will wipe dust in your hair, your beard, and on your body. You will comb it out and wipe it off until you are presentable to your young bride."

He started to protest, but Miriam silenced him with an uplifted hand. "Not a word! I spent most of last night convincing her that you'll make a fine husband, that you'll love her and will learn to please her. You will apologize to Taliah for appearing in anything less than your finest armor."

Eleazar's lips were pressed into a thin, straight line. He nodded but said nothing.

"I'll get you a comb and a towel. Get started." She left him throwing dust on himself and wondered if he'd ever learn what was important to a woman. *Yahweh, can You teach a stubborn old soldier to love a headstrong young wife and teach a fact-stunted wife to honor a life-wizened husband?*

25

That is why a man leaves his father and mother and is united to his wife, and they become one flesh.

—Genesis 2:24

Eleazar combed dusty mud from his tangled hair and cursed the gods, cursed Ramesses, and cursed the Libyans and Hittites. Why must Libya invade Egypt's western border? Why were Hittite prisoners of war expected to produce weapons for their captors? Eleazar knew the answers, of course. Libya needed food because of the worst drought in their history, and Egypt needed Hittite slaves because they alone knew the secret to forging iron weapons. But knowing the answers didn't simplify Eleazar's life.

Doda Miriam thought he'd arrived dirty and disheveled out of spite. Is that what Taliah thought too? "Women," he huffed.

A meaty hand landed on Eleazar's shoulder. "They're a mystery." Moses sat beside him. "Is the blood yours or someone else's?"

Eleazar choked out a laugh. It would have been nice if Doda or Taliah had asked. "Someone else's."

"Sparring?"

"Beating." This was Eleazar's kind of conversation. Simple.

"Did they deserve it?"

So much for simple. "Yes and no." Eleazar found Moses raising his eyebrows in question. The ex-general deserved an explanation. "Libyan rebels attacked our western border three days ago. Prince Ram needs more iron weapons. Hittite slaves show their defiance by making a few shoddy battle-axes, so we don't know which are battle-ready and which will break."

Moses nodded and stroked his long gray beard. "Prince Ram will hold you responsible for every battle-ax that breaks."

"He said if I can't manage this city's slave armory, I'll be punished or, worse, transferred away from my ailing grandparents." Eleazar stopped combing his tangled hair. "If he knew I was getting married—"

"Taliah wouldn't be safe. I know." Moses drew up his legs and rested his arms on his knees. "The Egyptians have always preyed on a slave's worst fear."

Eleazar resumed working the blood and mud out of his hair and beard. He'd gotten most of it off his armor, arms, and legs by the time his uncle spoke again.

"I never let myself love anyone while I was a soldier, and it was a mistake." Moses stood, brushing the dust from his clean linen robe. "You have a lovely bride waiting inside, and your saba and savta would like to celebrate with you. Don't make the same mistake I did." Moses disappeared inside the curtained doorway before Eleazar could respond.

Perhaps Moses understood better than he realized, but Eleazar was still determined to be discreet. It was the only way he knew to protect her. He picked up the dirty cloths and Doda's comb, hoping he'd cleaned up enough to pass inspection. When he stepped through the doorway, Moses was whispering something to Doda Miriam, and her expression softened.

She saw Eleazar and opened her arms. "All right. Come here and forgive your Doda."

He wrapped his fierce little doda in an equally ferocious hug. Oh, how he loved her. "I do forgive you, and you must help me with Taliah."

She wriggled from his arms and patted his cheek. "You needn't ask, dear. I'll always meddle." Moses laughed, and Doda grabbed Eleazar's wrist, leading him through the dividing curtain into Saba and Savta's room. Hoshea sat quietly in the corner, while Eleazar's bride, who had pushed the head covering around her shoulders, sat between his grandparents dabbing their lips with a wet rag. She wore a beautiful linen robe with the sheer blue sheath he'd given her draped over it. Lifting the head covering back over the braids piled atop her head, she looked like one of Pharaoh's queens—but more beautiful.

Taliah offered him a tentative smile. Perhaps she could forgive him for his shoddy appearance.

"Come here, boy." Saba Amram's voice was barely a whisper, but he had the strength to smile.

Eleazar hurried to kneel beside him and reached over to squeeze Savta Jochebed's hand. She lay on the other side of Taliah, tears leaking from her eyes—a sure sign of her approval. Moses and Doda stood over them like proud parents as Eleazar looked into his bride's eyes for the first time. Was it true joy he saw, or had his hope made him blind?

"God made woman . . . from man's rib . . ." Saba began the wedding blessing without warning. "He brought her to the man. . . . The man said . . . 'She is . . . bone of . . . my bones . . . flesh of my flesh' . . . "

Saba Amram paused, lifting his fingers as if grasping for Eleazar's hand. "Moses . . . finish."

"He's just weak, boy." Doda tried to sound reassuring. "Let Moses finish the ceremony."

Eleazar could only stare at the one man who had loved him without question, without conditions or judgment. *Please, Yahweh, if You hear me, please don't take my saba.* He sniffed back the emotion that threatened his manhood. "Fine. Let Moses finish."

He heard a sniff from his bride and cursed the head covering that hid her face from him. What was she thinking? Why didn't she speak her mind as she always did?

Moses knelt at Saba and Savta's heads. "Take Taliah's hand in yours, Eleazar." Awkwardly, Eleazar obeyed. Her hand looked so tiny in his. Moses began speaking as soon as their hands joined. "For this reason a man leaves his father and mother and is united to his wife, and they become one flesh. Now you may take your wife to the bridal chamber I've prepared for you."

Eleazar looked up at Doda in a panic. "I was going to bring a mat into Saba and Savta's room."

"You'll do no such thing." She waved away his comment.

Moses grinned like a child who'd eaten the last candied date. "I've prepared the roof as a private space for you and your bride, Eleazar. It's waiting with everything you need."

"But—"

Savta touched Eleazar's knee. "Love her . . . well." Her eyes remained closed, but her smile was unmistakable.

Taliah removed her hand from Eleazar's and bent over to kiss Savta and then Saba. She rose gracefully and stood at the doorway, face still covered, unreadable.

Eleazar felt helpless. Something inside told him this was the last time he'd see his grandparents. He didn't want to leave. "Help them, Doda." He stood, pleading. "Give them herbs or a potion. Something. Do something."

"There's nothing to do, boy." Doda's pallor suddenly went gray, and she steadied herself on Eleazar's arm while she regained her balance.

"Get her some water, Hoshea!" Eleazar shouted. "No, wait. Go to the palace and steal a bottle of Prince Ram's wine."

"No!" Miriam said.

At the same time, Moses rose to his feet and stepped in front of Hoshea, blocking his exit. "Hoshea will not risk his life to save those who would not survive our freedom. It is Yahweh's will that those who can't make the wilderness journey rest peacefully now with Abraham and Sarah in paradise."

"Yahweh's will?" Eleazar said, incredulous. "Your Yahweh wants to kill my saba and savta?" Eleazar glared at him. "Is this the God you serve?"

Doda stared at Moses, her face reflecting the same confusion Eleazar felt. "Surely, you don't believe Yahweh wants Abba and Ima to die now, when we're so close to freedom. They've served Him faithfully their whole lives."

"Which is better for Abba and Ima," he said, "to die in their beds, surrounded by the family who loves them? Or to die in the Sinai, sleeping on rocks and fighting scorpions?"

Doda Miriam stood silently for several heartbeats and then her whole body began to tremble. Her knees buckled, and Eleazar caught her before she fell.

Moses sent Hoshea to fetch a cup of water and then looked at Eleazar, sorrow deepening the weathered lines on his face. "Miriam is strong. She'll recover. But Yahweh has given you this precious time to say goodbye to your grandparents. Your saba looked on you with pride when he began your wedding blessing. Now, rejoice in the peace he'll soon feel, and take your bride up to the wedding chamber your grandparents instructed me to prepare for you."

Eleazar choked on a sob. "They told you to prepare the roof for us?"

Doda Miriam lifted her head from Eleazar's chest and wiped her eyes. "Abba thought of it this morning. Moses has been working on it all day." She wiped more tears and tried to smile. "I believe they held on to see you and Taliah married. You'll honor them best by loving your wife."

Eleazar felt as if a boulder had lodged in his chest. He stared down at Saba Amram and Savta Jochebed. How could this be the last time he would see them?

Yahweh, if You hear me, please take care of my saba and savta as they have cared for me. Uncontrolled sobs shook him. He had no idea how long he wept, but no one hurried his grief. When the emotion ebbed, he leaned over to kiss their foreheads and arranged their hands on their chests.

"Good-bye." He swiped both hands down his face and stood, eyes lowered. He halted at the door and offered his hand to his wife. She cradled his huge paw with both hands. Eleazar lifted his eyes to Moses. "Thank you," he said, and then led his bride through the adjoining curtain.

He noticed the interior ladder Moses had installed—overlooked when he'd passed through earlier. Pressing his thumbs against his eyes, Eleazar tried to stop the tears. What man went to his wedding bed a blubbering idiot? He jumped like a virgin when Taliah laid her hand on his back but regained some control with a deep breath.

"After you." Eleazar pointed to the ladder.

Taliah wiped her own tears and silently began the climb. He might have enjoyed the sway of her hips had his chest not ached so terribly. She pushed aside the ceiling cap that kept birds and animals from sneaking into the house. It also provided a place to knock for anyone who might wish to visit the newlyweds.

Eleazar climbed the last rung and stepped into their rooftop bridal chamber, amazed at the transformation. Moses had created a newlyweds' hideaway. A three-sided shelter with lamb's wool headpieces protected a new sleeping mat—no doubt woven by Doda—long and wide enough for both Eleazar and Taliah. The moonlight bathed Taliah's features, and Eleazar knew then he'd married the most beautiful creature on earth. He could never deserve her.

Taliah knelt at his feet and began unlacing his sandals.

Fire coursed through his veins. "Stop!" She jumped as if he'd shot her with an arrow. He softened his voice. "I'll do it."

She scooted onto the mat and hugged her knees to her chest. "Don't yell at me." She laid her cheek on her knees and faced the Nile.

With a frustrated sigh, he pulled at his laces and threw his sandals aside. He considered asking Doda to come up and tell Taliah that he hadn't *yelled*. It seemed everything he said to this woman was misconstrued. Instead, he replaced the cover on the rooftop entry, doomed to more misunderstanding.

He lumbered over and sat on the mat beside her. She scooted away. *Perfect*. "I didn't shout. I'm used to doing things myself."

"You did shout, and you're not by yourself anymore."

"Taliah, I . . ." What was there to say? His grandparents were dying. How could he enjoy a night of pleasure? "Good night." He stretched out on his back, crossed his ankles and rested his head on his hands. The stars were bright, the moon full, and he was losing two of the three people who had been his anchor in every storm.

Taliah didn't move. Then he heard it—the sniffing. The whimpers came next.

Feeling utterly despicable, Eleazar sat up and scooted closer, then reached for her shoulder. "Taliah, I'm sor—"

"I'll miss them too, you know." She shot to her knees and attempted to shove him. "I'm the one who's spent every day of the last two months with Amram and Jochebed, but do you notice my pain? Do you care how I feel? No, because all you think about is how their deaths affect you. How much you'll miss them. Well, here's something to think about, Eleazar. You have a wife now, someone else to consider." She lay down on her side of the mat, back toward him, curled into a ball. "Good night."

Stunned, Eleazar lay down again too—and began fuming. He stared at the moon and counted the stars, as well as the ways he'd tried to protect this ungrateful woman beside him.

He pushed himself to his feet and hoisted Taliah up to meet him toe to toe. "I'm sure you'll miss Saba and Savta, but don't you dare call me selfish. I consider everyone before myself. You eat my rations, you live in my doda's house, and I waited to marry you until every other possibility was spent."

"Oohh!" She stomped her foot. "And I'm supposed to thank you for marrying me because you had no other choice?"

He grabbed her face between his hands. "Anyone close to me is in danger, Taliah. I would have married you weeks ago if . . ." His inadvertent confession silenced him.

"You would have married me weeks ago?" Taliah's awe made her so vulnerable, so stunning, so irresistible.

Still cradling her cheeks, Eleazar touched her lips with his thumb. *So soft.* Their breathing grew ragged, expectant. He bent to swipe a gentle kiss across her cheek, her mouth, her neck. She tilted her head, parted her lips, and closed her eyes. This was his wife, and he barely knew her. He knew even less about being a husband.

Eleazar kissed her gently, timidly. Would she be afraid? But her hunger grew, and he knew then that his wife possessed all the passion and candor to teach him how to be her husband. He kissed her deeply and lowered her to the sleeping mat so carefully prepared by those they loved. They would grieve Saba and Savta in the morning, but tonight he would discover new depths of this woman he'd married.

26

Miriam gazed out her parents' small window at the half moon in the starry sky. Two oil lamps sputtered, their fumes mingling with air fetid with decaying fish and the bloody Nile. She sat between Abba and Ima, waiting, hoping—but neither had regained consciousness since Eleazar and Taliah's wedding this evening. Miriam had sent Hoshea to tell Aaron that their parents were failing quickly, but Hoshea returned with Aaron's regrets. He was too tired to visit tonight. Miriam thanked Hoshea and sent him home, refusing to show her disappointment in Aaron's continued indifference.

Moses sat on the other side of Abba, his head bowed, lips moving in silent prayer. How could he flaunt his communion with Yahweh when he knew Miriam yearned for such intimacy?

"I suppose Yahweh is telling you more of His plan for Israel." She heard the bitterness in her tone but didn't care.

His eyes opened, and he lifted his head slowly. "I don't understand Him any more than you do, Miriam. If Yahweh hadn't required me to return, Pharaoh wouldn't have ordered bricks with no straw. The overseers wouldn't have been beaten. And our parents wouldn't be dying."

Miriam felt a twinge of guilt. Moses need not carry the world's troubles on his shoulders. "Ramesses has imposed arbitrary decrees before. Slaves are beaten every day, and our parents are old." She reached for his hand, trying to ease the tension between them. "*We* are old, little brother."

"So why choose us, Miriam?" His eyes blazed. "And why has Yahweh brought only trouble when He promised rescue and deliverance for our people?"

Abba Amram's lips parted, his dry mouth crackling. "Must get worse . . . to show . . ."

Miriam dropped Moses's hand and reached for the damp cloth to dab on Abba's parched lips, while Moses leaned over him and tried to sooth his restlessness. "Save your strength, Abba. Don't speak."

"Let him speak," Miriam said. "These are our last moments to hear his voice, to learn from hi—" Emotion strangled her words.

Abba's chest rattled as he drew another breath to speak. "To see the true measure . . . of Yahweh's power . . . and authority . . . things must get . . . worse." The last words fell from his lips as if heaved off a precipice. His breathing grew more labored.

Moses leaned over, kissed his forehead, and let tears fall onto their abba's cheeks. He looked up at Miriam, his sorrow mirroring hers. "You've lived with this kind of wisdom all your life. I've only begun to glean from its depths. How can Yahweh take them from me now?"

"And so much more difficult when they're woven into the fiber of your being." Miriam lifted Ima's hand to her lips, closed her eyes, and rocked as waves of despair washed over her.

They wept together until Abba's voice rattled again. "Greater suffering means deeper revelation as you near God's promise." His words were barely above a whisper, but they were lucid and fervent. His eyes never opened. It felt as if Yahweh spoke directly through him.

Awed, Miriam glanced at Moses and then returned her attention to both parents. Ima lay silent, her chest still rising and falling, but haltingly. Abba exhaled a long breath—and then breathed no more. The panic she'd anticipated in this moment didn't come. Instead, she felt a strange sense of resolve.

She stroked Ima's feathery cheek. "Greater suffering means deeper revelation as you near God's promise." Repeating Abba Amram's words somehow extended his life—and would give Ima the peace she needed to join him in paradise.

Ima lingered as Miriam and Moses anointed Abba Amram's body

with bitter-almond oil and wrapped it for burial. Miriam shared count-less pearls of wisdom their parents had imparted during their long lives. Insights on life, and love, and Yahweh. They laughed a little, cried a lot.

Shortly before dawn, Ima Jochebed also breathed her last. Miriam was exhausted and could see the same weariness on Moses's deeply lined face. As they finished Ima's burial preparations, heavy footsteps sounded on the rooftop. Eleazar would soon come down. *Oh Yahweh, may his and Taliah's marriage bring comfort to this grieving house.*

Eleazar woke before dawn's glow brightened the eastern sky. Taliah slept snuggled against him. He carefully pulled his arm from beneath her head, trying not to disturb her deep, steady breaths. She stirred but didn't wake.

He donned his tunic and strapped on his armor, staring at the beau-tiful woman he now called wife. His chest ached at the responsibility. What if Prince Ram or Kopshef discovered her? What if Pharaoh had her beaten for Eleazar's mistakes? Taliah should stay close to the long house. Maybe she shouldn't fetch water from the river anymore. What if one of the slave drivers attacked her again? Eleazar would kill any man that touched her. Was this how every Hebrew husband felt?

He scrubbed his face and tried to wipe away his worry as he removed the rooftop cover and descended the ladder. A single oil lamp was lit in the main chamber, but he heard quiet whispers in Saba and Savta's room. He crossed Doda's chamber in five long strides and shoved aside the curtain.

Sattar was curled up in the corner, farther from Doda than normal. He perked his ears but didn't growl at Eleazar. The scent of bitter-almond oil filled the air, and the sight of Saba's wrapped body nearly felled him. "He's gone?"

Moses pushed to his feet, and Eleazar saw that he'd been wrapping Savta Jochebed's head with linen. The realization knocked him back a step, and he covered a sob. "They're both gone?"

Doda lifted her hand to Moses, requesting help to stand. Eleazar raced across the chamber to embrace her, and she hugged him fiercely. "They're together, boy. All is well."

He released deep, wrenching sobs. He'd known that last night would probably be the last time he'd see them, but the finality of death was too cruel. To face the rest of his life without Saba and Savta's love and encouragement—how would he survive? Eleazar held Doda Miriam tighter and tried to tamp down the overwhelming fear of someday losing her. He kissed the top of her gray head. "I'll help with the burial."

She gave him a final squeeze, released him, and nodded.

Hoshea peeked through the curtained doorway, concern etched on his brow. "I'm early with this morning's rations, but I wanted to see how . . ." His words trailed off as Eleazar gratefully accepted the rations. Hoshea offered a second bundle. "Take mine too."

Eleazar started to protest, but Hoshea interrupted. "I don't need them. And don't worry about your duties today. I'll tell Prince Ram your grandparents died, and that you're helping with the burial."

Eleazar grabbed Hoshea's breast piece, pinning him with a stare. "You'll tell him I'm ill from drinking unboiled water." He released Hoshea and addressed the others. "If Prince Ram learns my grandparents died, I won't have an excuse to live in Goshen. He can never discover I'm married. I will live with my wife." He felt his cheeks grow warm at the raised eyebrows around him.

Doda Miriam smiled, her eyes glistening. "Family first. Your saba Amram would be proud of you, Eleazar."

No one had ever said kinder words to him. He turned to Hoshea. "I whipped the Hittites last night. Make sure their wounds are cared for. Check every battle-ax before you send it with the troops to Libya. I return to duty tomorrow."

Hoshea pounded his fist over his heart, the warrior's salute. "You've taught me well. I'll take care of our men. You take care of your family. I'll return tonight with more rations."

27

*Seven days passed after the LORD struck
the Nile. Then the LORD said to Moses,
"Go to Pharaoh and say to him, 'This is
what the LORD says: Let my people go, so
that they may worship me. If you refuse
to let them go, I will send a plague of frogs
on your whole country.'"*

—EXODUS 7:25–8:2

Miriam woke to Sattar's nearness, his soft fur rising and falling beneath her hand as morning light invaded another dreamless sleep. The now-familiar ache assailed her—Abba and Ima were gone, buried two days ago. But what did time matter?

The Shaddai she'd once known had vanished. Eleazar had Taliah to care for him. And she'd proven Moses's observation on fear true. She was alone in a house full of people, and she was terrified.

The sound of clattering pots and bowls roused her. What was Taliah doing? Miriam turned her back to the noise. Hoshea must have delivered the rations and gone. She wasn't hungry.

Taliah should eat. She should keep up her strength in case she conceived quickly. But why should Miriam be concerned? Moses said the weak wouldn't survive the wilderness, and Miriam felt weak. She wouldn't survive freedom.

"Miriam." Taliah shook her shoulder. "Miriam, Moses is gone."

"What? Where—" Miriam sat up too quickly, sending the room into a spin.

Taliah helped her sit up and held a warm cup of water to her lips.

"Drink this. Hoshea brought more water this morning. The river is beginning to clear, and I've boiled enough to fill a jug." Miriam tried to push the cup away, but the girl held it steady. "All of it. You're not eating or drinking enough. Eleazar said it's my job to get you on your feet today. My only job."

Miriam was too tired to fight, so she relaxed into Taliah's arms, letting the girl lower her back onto the mat.

"Did you see Moses this morning?" Taliah's face looked like a cloud, blurred and wavy. Miriam blinked her eyes, trying to unmuddle her mind. Was the girl asking her or someone else? Concern shadowed Taliah's sweet face. "I left early this morning to get water from the seep hole, and Moses was already gone. He hasn't returned."

Miriam lay still, her mind clearing enough to let fear speed her heartbeat. She'd heard Hoshea's whispered rumors. A few disgruntled Hebrews had made plans to kill Moses. Her tears came unbidden. She couldn't lose Moses too. "You must go find him."

Taliah sat back on her heels and released a deep sigh. "I can't. Eleazar told me to stay near the long house." She drummed her fingers on her leg and fidgeted with a loose string on her sleeve. "Eleazar will just have to understand."

She grabbed Miriam's head covering from the peg on the wall and pulled it low over her forehead. She tied her long, black braid into a knot to hide it beneath the rough-spun cloth. "I'll be back as soon as I find him."

Miriam pulled Sattar close, digging her gnarled hands into his thick fur. "I'm of no use," she whispered into his perked ears. "I can't even look for my lost brother. What purpose do I have without Abba and Ima? Without Shaddai's dreams and visions?"

The only answer was Sattar's deep, steady breaths, wooing her to rest and sleep.

Miriam's next awareness was Eleazar's raised voice. Startled awake, she gasped and heard Sattar's warning growl as Eleazar entered holding Taliah's arm in a deadly grip.

"Was I unclear when I ordered you to stay in this long house?"

"No." Taliah's chin was raised in defiance despite Eleazar's anger.

Miriam struggled to sit up and felt surprisingly better after this morning's water. "Don't shout at your wife, Eleazar. I told her to find Moses."

He released his wife's arm and crouched beside Miriam, spewing his anger less than a handbreadth from her face. "And why would you risk my wife's life to save a man who's had more military training than I have and won more battles than the reigning king of Egypt?"

Miriam turned away. "Well, when you put it that way, it sounds ridiculous, but I was worried about my broth—"

"Ridiculous!" He stood and continued ranting. "Yes. Ridiculous."

Miriam felt her own anger rising. "Why are you in Goshen at midday anyway? You would never have known Taliah was searching for Moses if you hadn't come home—"

"Taliah came to the armory to enlist my help in finding my uncle."

Miriam looked to Taliah for an explanation, but her head was now bowed. Miriam lifted her hand to Eleazar. "Help me up, boy."

Once on her feet, Miriam grabbed Eleazar's hands to steady herself, but her destination was Taliah. She tilted the girl's chin. "Tell me you didn't name Moses as Eleazar's uncle."

"Of course not. I simply asked the guards to tell Eleazar that his elderly uncle had wandered away from home and his family needed help locating him." She turned to Eleazar. "With all the rumors of attempts on his life, I thought you'd want to know he was missing."

"Who's missing?" Moses stood in the doorway, staff in hand.

Aaron peeked over his shoulder. "Are you feeling better, Miriam? Elisheba is better today too."

"Aahh!" Eleazar roared his frustration. "Where have you been, Moses? These women have been clucking over you like hens, and every soldier in Ram's army has now seen my beautiful wife."

"Frogs." Miriam saw them in her mind's eye, piled higher than the palace gates. A sliver of light pierced her dark world. *Thank You, Yahweh.* She turned to Moses. "Thousands of frogs. Is that the next plague?"

Moses sighed. "Yes. That's where we've been. Yahweh spoke to Aaron and me this morning. We found Pharaoh on his way to inspect the new winery and"—the sound of croaking frogs grew louder as Moses told the story—"I told Aaron to say to Pharaoh, 'If you refuse to let our people go, I will send a plague of frogs on your land.'" Moses shrugged as a wave of frogs and toads slithered, hopped, and crawled into the long house through doorways and windows. It was a veritable sea of green creatures coming in waves. Taliah stared wide-eyed at the writhing packed-dirt floor.

Eleazar's fury was squelched by the more urgent issue now crawling over his feet. "I'd better get back to Prince Ram. I'm sure Ramesses has summoned all the princes by now." His first step squished at least five frogs. He grimaced but continued his destructive march out the door.

The frogs kept coming, while Miriam and the rest stood wide-eyed at the onslaught. Finally, Aaron lifted his voice to be heard over the croaking. "I suppose I should go check on Elisheba. Someone said the river is clear now, so perhaps she'll regain her strength with more water. I'd suggest we still boil it until the frog plague is over." He nodded his farewell before slipping this way and that on the layer of frogs beneath his sandals.

Taliah supported Miriam's elbow. "Perhaps you should sit down. I'm not sure you've regained enough strength to maneuver around these frogs."

"I feel much better after hearing from Yahweh." How could she explain that a simple picture of frogs in her mind had instilled more strength than a feast at Pharaoh's table? Perhaps Yahweh wasn't so different than Shaddai after all. Perhaps she wasn't alone.

Moses tried to clear a place for Miriam on her mat, but before she could kneel, more frogs filled the void. Moses and Taliah finally created a sort of fenced-in area for Miriam to sit.

Thankful, she looked up at her brother. "I pray Pharaoh lets us leave Egypt soon. I'm not sure how long I can live with frogs in my bed."

"Or in our food." Taliah scooped three frogs from the pot they used for cooking.

Moses reached for two large water jugs. "I'll go to the river," he shouted over the croaks. "We can prepare more water to drink. Surely, the frogs won't jump in the pot if the water's boiling."

Sattar caught a toad in his mouth but quickly released it, snorting his displeasure. Enthralled by their hopping, however, he stuck his nose into a pile of frogs, then leaped backward and whined at Miriam.

"Some protector you are," she chuckled. The others joined the laughter, releasing some of the tension. Perhaps Sattar's antics would keep them sane amid Yahweh's slithering, crawling, leaping show of power.

28

Moses said to Pharaoh, "I leave to you the
honor of setting the time for me to pray for
you and your officials and your people that
you and your houses may be rid of the frogs,
except for those that remain in the Nile."
"Tomorrow," Pharaoh said.

—EXODUS 8:9–10

Eleazar had spent most of the day watching Prince Kopshef prove his power by producing more frogs and listening to Pharaoh's unimpressed rant about the inadequacy of Egypt's gods to do more than add to the mess. Even Prince Ram, who usually yearned to see his older brother fail, had confided to Eleazar that he wished Kopshef could command the gods and end the plague. But it seemed no god could command Yahweh.

Eleazar sent Hoshea to Goshen with the evening rations while he remained at Prince Ram's side throughout the harrowing day. Eleazar arrived at the long house after Doda was asleep in the main room, and Moses was most likely tucked away in Saba and Savta's room behind the dividing curtain.

He climbed the ladder as quietly as he could. Taliah lay on her side, back turned toward him. Eleazar lay down beside her and watched the moon's progression across the night sky. Sleep had been a miser unwilling to share its peace since Saba and Savta died. When he finally nodded off, he dreamed of frogs crawling from Pharaoh's eyes, nose, and ears and then awakened with a frog on his head. The constant croaking threatened to drive him mad, but at least he and Taliah slept on the rooftop and only dealt with an occasional frog crawling up the ladder. How was that even possible? How was any of this possible?

He rolled to his side and found Taliah's eyes open, watching him. "I'm sorry I disobeyed you and left the long house," she said. "I was just trying to help."

Eleazar stared into her dark, round eyes, sparkling in the moonlight. Why talk about things they couldn't change? The damage was done. Afraid of saying the wrong thing, he said nothing and simply took her in his arms.

She molded her body to his, every curve perfectly matched, arms and legs artfully entwined. "I don't like it when you're angry with me. Have you forgiven me?"

Why did she need to hear the words? "I forgive you, Taliah."

The rooftop cover scraped to the side, and Eleazar was on his feet, cudgel in hand. Hoshea popped his head up, and only then did Eleazar lift his foot and see the frogs he'd stepped on to defend his fortress.

He threw down his cudgel. "What is it, Hoshea? You're early with the rations."

"All the princes have gathered in the throne hall. Pharaoh has summoned Moses and Aaron to get rid of the frogs." Even in the waning moonlight, Eleazar saw Hoshea's excitement. "I think this is it, Eleazar. I think Pharaoh's going to let Israel leave Egypt."

Eleazar quickly donned his tunic and armor, carrying his sandals down the ladder. He realized the error when he stepped from the last rung and frogs squished between his toes. His uncle was already emerging from the other room. Eleazar turned to Hoshea. "Go get my abba. We'll meet you on the way to the palace."

The women tried to feed them before they left, but Eleazar and Moses grabbed only a loaf of barley bread and a few dried figs to eat as they walked. Eleazar held the curtain aside for Moses, letting him lead the way through the sludge of live and dead frogs. How could there be more than there were last night? And yet they seemed to be multiplying no matter how many were stepped on.

"Is it over then?" Eleazar asked Moses. "If Pharaoh agrees to let the Hebrews worship in the wilderness, I mean."

Moses seemed deep in thought—or perhaps he was as tired as Eleazar. Surely, no one had slept a wink last night. "I don't think this is the end. When Yahweh speaks of our deliverance, He implies catastrophic displays of His power." Moses slipped on an especially large bullfrog. He wiped it off his sandal with his staff, disgusted. "Frogs are annoying, not catastrophic."

Abba Aaron and Hoshea joined them from the adjacent village. Hoshea sidled up to Moses, and Abba lagged behind, still wiping sleep from his eyes. He seemed utterly unaffected by possibilities and asked through a yawn, "If Ramesses summoned all the princes, does this mean he's giving in?"

"No," Eleazar said, annoyed. Why did everything about his abba irritate him?

Moses exchanged a glance with Eleazar before offering a kinder answer. "I don't think anyone but Yahweh knows what Ramesses will do."

As the first rays of dawn lit the path before them, the four of them hurried their pace toward the palace complex. Eleazar scanned the landscape of Egypt and saw toads and frogs like an undulating green blanket and wondered aloud, "Will Egypt ever be the same?"

Abba Aaron shot a scornful look at his third-born son. "Why would you care about Egypt when the Israelites could gain our freedom today? This is the day our forefathers have longed for. We could walk into that throne hall . . ."

Eleazar seethed silently, blocking out Abba's senseless drivel. Had abba heard nothing Moses said? No, he heard only what he wanted to hear.

"I have two sons." Moses blurted out the declaration, taking all of them off guard. He looked at Eleazar and then at Aaron. "I wanted to bring them with me to Egypt. In fact, they began the journey with my wife and me from Midian, but Yahweh nearly killed me before Aaron met me in the wilderness."

Eleazar stopped, sliding on a frog, and looked at his uncle, incredulous. "Why would Yahweh try to kill you? And why are we only now hearing this story?"

"You're hearing this story now because I wish someone had told me how important an abba and son relationship is. It's obvious you and Aaron don't like each other, and I'm telling you both." He pinned Abba Aaron with a stare. "Your son must be more important than your pride. He must be more important than your duty or your day's labor." He returned his attention to Eleazar. "And your abba will die someday—as my abba did—and then you can't make amends."

Moses resumed his march toward the palace, Abba and Hoshea falling in step beside him. Eleazar lagged behind, stinging from the rebuke. "You didn't answer my question. Why did Yahweh try to kill you?" He caught up with the others as Moses began speaking.

"After I fled Egypt and arrived in Midian, Jethro gave me his daughter Zipporah as a wife." He glanced over at Eleazar. "I was only a few years younger than you when our first son, Gershom, was born. Like you, however, I had little inclination toward the gods, and though Jethro was the high priest of Midian, he never pressured me to circumcise Gershom or our second-born son, Eliezer." He returned his focus to the frogs and his slippery footing. "Zipporah nagged me to spend more time with my sons, to teach them what I'd learned in Egypt, to make them honorable men. But I was always too busy tending Jethro's flocks and training my herding dogs."

Moses fell silent for a few steps, regret gathering with the tears on his bottom lashes. No one prodded him to continue, but each of them hung on his next words. "My sons are thirty and thirty-three. They chose to join Zipporah and me when Yahweh commanded me to return to Egypt. On the first night of our encampment, I heard Yahweh's voice like thunder: 'Say to Pharaoh, "Israel is My firstborn son. Let My son go, so he may worship Me." But Pharaoh will refuse to let him go; so I will kill his firstborn.'"

Eleazar grabbed his arm, panicked. "Which of Pharaoh's firstborns? Only Kopshef?"

"I don't know," Moses said, "but when Yahweh spoke, a flaming spear shot into the ground, barely missing me. Yahweh didn't speak again, but in that moment—I can't explain how—we all understood that I would die with the next fiery spear if *my firstborn* wasn't circumcised immediately." His chin quaked, and he shoved his thumb and finger against his eyes, struggling for control. Abba Aaron and Hoshea stood awkwardly, shoving frogs aside with their sandals.

Eleazar tried to imagine such a bizarre scene. "Did you do it? Did you circumcise Gershom?"

Moses shook his head. "I couldn't. I couldn't hurt my son to save my life. But Zipporah grabbed a flint knife and cut off Gershom's foreskin. She threw it at my feet and called me a 'bridegroom of blood,' leaving my firstborn writhing in pain and humiliation." He wiped his cheeks and set his jaw. "The complete failure I felt as an abba in that moment is what Ramesses will feel when his firstborn die. When I beg Pharaoh to let Israel go, it is with both rage and compassion—rage at his abuses against Israel, compassion that his pride will cost his sons' lives." He shrugged off Eleazar's hand and stepped toward Aaron, almost nose to nose. "And when I tell you, Aaron, to love your son Eleazar, it is with that same rage and compassion. Love your sons—*all* of your sons—before it is too late."

Moses turned on his heel and left the three men in awkward silence. Abba Aaron cast a sheepish glance at Eleazar before beginning his march again. Hoshea shrugged and began walking again in silence with Eleazar.

They entered the palace gates, and frogs dropped on their heads from the parapets above. None of them bothered to bathe or don a ceremonial robe to appear before Pharaoh. Any delay seemed unwise in light of the rising number of frogs beneath their feet.

Two Nubian guards opened the massive ebony doors as Eleazar and Hoshea escorted Abba and Moses into Pharaoh's presence. Would Ramesses notice Eleazar's family resemblance? Or would he be too focused on frogs to notice the Levite family traits in Prince Ram's guard?

Every chair in the gallery of Pharaoh's firstborns was occupied, though the princes and their guards looked as if they'd gotten little sleep.

Prince Kopshef stood at Pharaoh's right hand, Prince Ram at his left. Ramesses sat on his throne while slaves fought to keep frogs off the dais. They were losing the battle.

"The crown prince has matched your magic, Hebrew." Pharaoh's voice echoed in the empty throne hall. "Prince Kopshef also stretched his hand over the waters of Egypt and made frogs come onto dry land."

Eleazar and Hoshea halted when Ramesses began speaking, but Abba Aaron and Moses continued to the edge of the red carpet. Moses bowed slightly to the crown prince. "Congratulations. You've added more frogs."

Pharaoh leaned forward. "Pray to Yahweh to take away the frogs." He slammed his flail on the armrest at the precise moment a frog jumped onto it from the floor.

Eleazar winced as Pharaoh slid the lifeless creature off. *One less frog for Yahweh to take away.*

Pharaoh narrowed his eyes, seething. "If your god will take them away, I will let your people leave my city to offer sacrifices."

A deafening pause was Moses's response, and no one else dared breathe. Finally, he said, "I leave it up to you, Mighty Pharaoh, to determine the time when I will pray for you, your officials, and your people to be rid of the frogs—except for those that remain in the Nile, of course."

Pharaoh trembled with rage, and Eleazar braced himself for the execution order. No one spoke to Ramesses with such flippancy and lived.

"Tomorrow." The king spit out the word like a curse. Both Kopshef and Ram leaned down to whisper their protests, but Ramesses silenced them. "Tell your god the Son of Horus declares he should kill the frogs tomorrow."

Eleazar glimpsed the frustration in his master's features. Why hadn't Pharaoh chosen to have the frogs removed immediately? *Stubborn pride.*

"It will be as you say, Ramesses," Moses said. "Tomorrow the frogs will die, so that you will know that there is no god like Yahweh among your gods."

Abba Aaron bowed, but Moses simply turned his back and walked toward the yawning ebony doors, escorted by Hoshea. Eleazar again marveled at Moses's nerve and felt convicted. Pharaoh's stubborn pride prolonged a senseless plague just as Eleazar's pride continued to punish Abba for a past no one could change. Could he forgive and try to live at peace? The familiar anger burned in his chest, and he felt heat rising on his neck. He would try to forgive, but it would take more than one tomorrow.

Eleazar took his place behind Prince Ram's empty chair in the gallery of firstborns and glanced at the line of princes perched on their golden chairs. Would their father's pride cost them their lives? What might Eleazar's pride cost him?

29

Pharaoh summoned Moses and Aaron and said, "Pray to the LORD to take the frogs away from me and my people, and I will let your people go to offer sacrifices to the LORD."

—Exodus 8:8

Miriam sorted through her baskets of herbs and jars of ointments. Which ones should she take into the wilderness? She could never carry them all. Taliah had rescued the herbs from their frog-laden garden yesterday and carried in the last basketful as the croaking suddenly stopped. Every frog drew its last breath at the same moment, and every slave was given a shovel to start scooping dead frogs. By late last night, frogs were heaped as high as rooftops in Goshen, and Eleazar reported frogs in the city being shoveled from palace windows and piled along paths all the way to the river. But Miriam hadn't needed to see the frogs piled by the palace gates. Yahweh had already shown her in the vision.

Moses suddenly became a hero instead of a villain, and several elders had brought gifts as peace offerings—a goat, a camel, and three geese. Their household had enjoyed fresh camel's milk this morning for the first time since Abba Amram fashioned Nefertiry's wedding necklace thirty-seven years ago.

Miriam stuck her nose in a jar of mint aloe but could barely appreciate the aroma over the stench of decaying frogs. Leaving Egypt was more appealing now that it reeked of decaying fish and frogs, but the thought of leaving Goshen was still bittersweet. Freedom was a concept she could only imagine. What would she do all day without injured slaves to tend?

What would the Israelites do without masters to direct them? And who would organize their departure? Miriam hadn't had time to coordinate the elders as she'd promised Moses that day under the palm tree. How would everyone know where to go?

The enormity of change overwhelmed her as she rummaged through her basket of dishes and tossed out a broken clay cup. *"Nothing broken or worn out goes to the Promised Land."* Moses's command brought a fresh wave of grief. "Abba and Ima yearned their whole lives to see Your promise fulfilled. Why spare me and not them? Am I not as broken and worn out as they were?"

Miriam continued her cleaning, tossing the old, keeping the useful. *Keeping the useful.* Her stomach churned as she whispered. "I am no longer Your voice to the people of Israel. You have chosen my brothers as Your messengers. What use am I now, Yahweh?"

Miriam bowed her head, hands stilling on the basket of bandages. "What if I stayed in Egypt?" She peered over her shoulders, left then right, making sure no one heard—of course, no one was nearby. Taliah was teaching the village children. Moses had gone to meet with Aaron about naming more elders. "I could stay," she said a little louder, the possibility growing in her mind. "The Egyptian peasants accept me. They wouldn't mind—"

"I see you still talk to yourself." A male voice startled her from behind.

Sattar didn't growl or even move, but Miriam whirled to see an old man standing inside her doorway. His mischievous smile showed several missing teeth, but it was his eyes that took her breath. "Hur?" Surely, she was imagining her old friend.

"Shalom, Miriam. It's good to see you." He took two long strides and held her hand, warmth radiating from his light-brown eyes.

She stood speechless, mesmerized by a man she hadn't seen in over twenty years. A man once married to her friend Shiphrah. A man who had once captured Miriam's affections—although no one had known.

"Do I have frog entrails on my beard?" He chuckled and released her hand, swiping the long gray hair that reached from his chin to his waist.

"No. No! I'm sorry. I just . . . when Ramesses sent you to Pithom twenty years ago, after Nefertiry found a cobra in her bed, I thought I'd never see you again."

He waved away the memory. "That was an unfortunate event. I'm good at my job, but a snake-and-rat man can't guarantee he's cleared all vermin from a palace the size of Ramesses's." He shrugged. "But a Pharaoh doesn't listen to reason when his queen screams, 'Cobra!' in the middle of the night."

Miriam giggled like a maiden and thought how ridiculous she sounded. She cleared her throat and regained composure. "So what brings you back to Rameses?" She felt her cheeks warm. Why was she acting so silly?

"Pharaoh sent a cart for me in the middle of the night. It seems when the frogs died, rats and snakes emerged from every nook and cranny to find alternate food sources." Miriam shuddered involuntarily, and Hur chuckled again. "That's the reaction of most people to my job, but I've been teasing cobras and killing rats for as long as you've been alive. I'm fairly good at it by now."

His eyes sparkled with the same life and joy Miriam remembered. "I'm glad you're back. Have you seen your son Uri?"

The sparkle dimmed. "Not yet. Aaron said Uri and my grandson, Bezalel, work with Nadab and Abihu in the metal shop. These plagues have put them behind on a big project, so I'll try not to bother them . . ." His words trailed off as his eyes scanned the disarray in Miriam's main room. "Are you moving to another long house?"

"No. Haven't you heard? Ramesses released the Israelites to worship in the wilderness." She saw his expression falter but continued her explanation. "Moses returned from exile as Yahweh's prophet—Yahweh is El Shaddai's new name—and the recent plagues have convinced Ramesses to let Israel travel into the wilderness to worship . . ." Miriam stopped when Hur began shaking his head.

"It isn't happening, Miriam. I've been crawling around the palace halls since dawn. Pharaoh nearly bit off Prince Ram's head when he asked how to ensure the Hebrews would return from the wilderness."

"I don't understand. Why would the king be angry about ensuring our return?"

"Pharaoh called Prince Ram an imbecile for believing he'd ever let the Israelites leave Egypt." Hur's countenance softened. "I'm sorry, Miriam."

She didn't know what to say or even how to feel. Would Moses be devastated? Or had he expected Ramesses to default on his promise? That day by the palm tree, he'd told her Yahweh promised Pharaoh would *drive* them out of Egypt. Ramesses certainly hadn't come to that point.

"I should go," Hur said. "I've upset you."

"No!" Miriam reached for his arm as he turned to leave. "Please don't go." She felt her cheeks grow warm again. He must think her terribly forward. "Unless you need to get back to the palace."

"Actually, no. Snakes rest during the heat of the day. I'll return to work at the palace tonight."

Her heart fluttered erratically, and she reached for her walking stick to steady herself. "Would you eat the midday meal with us?"

Taliah ducked under the doorframe with a full water jar on her head. When she looked up, she was face to face with Hur and nearly dropped the jar.

"Taliah, this is my old friend Hur." He bowed slightly and helped her lower the jar, while Miriam's nervous chatter continued. "His wife, Shiphrah, was a dear friend who taught me midwifery and herbal skills many years ago. And Hur, this is Taliah." She pointed at her stiffly as if describing a bowl on a shelf. "She's Jered's granddaughter. You remember Jered—Mered's firstborn son?"

"Oh, you sweet girl." Hur grabbed Taliah's hands and kissed them. "Mered and Bithiah were special friends indeed, and your Saba Jered was like a big brother to my son Uri."

Taken off guard, Taliah chuckled and patted his blue-veined hands. "Well, it's very nice to meet you, Hur. I'm anxious to hear more about your friendship with Miriam." She turned to Miriam with wide eyes and a knowing grin.

"I hope to soon have more stories to tell about Miriam." Hur's eyes lingered too long on Miriam, causing heat to rise from the tips of her toes to the top of her head.

Taliah stood behind him, pointing furiously and mouthing, "He likes you."

Flustered, Miriam rattled off the first thing that entered her mind. "So you'll stay for the meal then?"

Moses walked through the door and heard the invitation. Brow furrowed, he inspected the stranger, but his countenance brightened the moment he recognized his long-ago servant. "Hur, you old snake charmer, it's good to see you."

Hur bowed at the waist. "Welcome home, Master Mehy. I heard you had returned."

Moses's delight dimmed but only slightly. "My name is Moses, my friend, and I'm a simple shepherd from Midian. I would be honored to take a meal with you and get to know more about the man who used to taunt cobras in my villa and kill rats in my granaries."

Hur smiled at Miriam over his shoulder as Moses led him through the dividing curtain into the other room. Sattar followed the men, leaving the women to prepare the meal. Hur was as kind as she remembered, and he'd retained the mischief that made him so endearing. The fact that he and Moses had fond memories of each other sent warmth coursing through her.

Taliah brought the large water jug closer and started teasing. "I've never seen you blush, Miriam. Hur must be very special indeed."

Miriam ignored the comment, busying herself instead with clearing a spot on the floor for their small dinner mat. She was thankful the girl hadn't made the connection between Hur and Miriam's confession of girlhood affection a few weeks ago. It would never do for Hur to discover she'd once loved him. The thought of it made her cheeks flame again. She reached for their wooden plates. They'd use Eleazar's plate for Hur.

Taliah began grinding grain with the hand mill. She looked up from her task, brows knit. "Where has Hur been all these years, and what brought him back to Goshen?"

"Ramesses sent Hur to Pithom as punishment after finding a cobra in Nefertiry's bed. Hur's wife, Shiphrah, died here in Goshen shortly after he left."

"How sad." Taliah was silent for several heartbeats, grinding the barley, then suddenly gasped, eyes as round as the wooden plates on the mat. "It's him, isn't it?"

"It's who, dear?" Miriam knew what she meant but needed time to form a vague reply.

"He's the one you told me about—the one you loved when you were a girl, but your friend married him, and they were happy, and then no one else could ever meet your needs like El Shaddai." She pointed at the dividing curtain. "It's Hur!"

"Shh!" Miriam was near panic. "Keep your voice down. Yes, but that was a long time ago."

"Well it's obvious he came back to Goshen to marry you."

"No, dear. Hur is the best ratter and snake killer in Egypt, and Ramesses brought him back from Pithom to clear the palace. That's why he's in Goshen."

Taliah stopped grinding grain, her expression void of silly teasing. "What if your God brought him back to you?"

Miriam waved away the comment. "Shaddai is not in the habit of matchmaking, dear. Hur and I are longtime friends. We have a shared past, and old people like to talk about old things. That's all."

Taliah shrugged and emptied the fresh-ground barley flour into a bowl. "Shaddai may not be a matchmaker, but Yahweh might just surprise you."

Miriam grabbed a cucumber to chop and chose to ignore the girl's comment, but she couldn't ignore the flutter in her belly.

She'd just heard that Pharaoh reneged on his promise to release Israel, and all she could think about was an old friend who had returned from Pithom. It was ridiculous . . . but true.

Yahweh, what's happening to me? Am I going mad? Surely, it was the grief of losing Abba and Ima. The tremendous strain of Moses's return and the plagues. The uncertainty of God's silence. Whatever was troubling her, she was tired of it. She needed to refocus her priorities.

"Taliah, I've heard on good authority that Pharaoh changed his mind and won't let us leave Egypt."

Disappointment shadowed the girl's face, but she didn't seem overly surprised. "Eleazar told me last night that I shouldn't bother packing our things." She added water to the barley flour, mixed it into a ball, and started kneading. "I think if your God delivers us, we'll know when it's time to pack."

30

*Then the LORD said to Moses, "Tell Aaron,
'Stretch out your staff and strike the dust
of the ground,' and throughout the land of
Egypt the dust will become gnats."*

—EXODUS 8:16

Eleazar stood under the penetrating stare of Egypt's king, using every shred of restraint not to scratch the burning, itching bites that covered his body. Pharaoh used no such restraint. He sat on his throne scratching his arms and legs and neck and abdomen as he questioned Eleazar. "Do you know these Hebrews, Moses and Aaron?"

"Yes, my king." Eleazar's voice echoed loud in the empty throne hall. He prayed they wouldn't press him further.

"Are they responsible for this infestation of biting midges?" Prince Kopshef shouted the question in Eleazar's right ear.

Eleazar paused, forming his answer carefully. "I saw Aaron strike the dust of the ground with Moses's staff, and the dust became biting gnats."

"There, that's how you do it." Pharaoh extended his flail toward Kopshef. "Take one of your magic rods and strike the dust."

"I've tried that, Father." Kopshef looked to the other magicians for support, but they merely bowed their heads, defeated.

Pharaoh's fury turned to quiet rage—a condition far more lethal. "Are you telling me that none of Egypt's gods can overpower this Yahweh?"

Kopshef's typical arrogance was suddenly replaced with trembling lips and hands extended like a beggar's. "Jannes and Jambres have tried every spell and chant. I, too, have called on every god and dark spirit, but our magic can't duplicate this plague." He left Eleazar's side, ascended the steps of the dais, and bowed at his father's feet. "This plague is the finger of the Hebrew god. Please, mighty Pharaoh, Keeper of Harmony and Balance, what harm would come of letting the Hebrews go worship this Yahweh of theirs?"

"No!" Pharaoh shouted, slamming his flail on the armrest again. "Am I the only one strong enough to stand against a god of slaves? Must my sons and officials whine like old women every time they endure hardship? Get out of my sight, all of you!"

Eleazar joined Prince Ram as they exited the throne hall. The prince leaned close and whispered, "If you know these Hebrews, then go back to Goshen and beg them to lift this plague. My wife and children are suffering, Eleazar." The ebony doors closed behind them, and Ram grabbed Eleazar's breast piece, jerking him to a halt, eyes pleading. "Make this stop, please."

"I will try, my prince."

Ram hurried away, rattled. He'd never spoken to Eleazar about his wife and children before. They talked only of weapons and battles and war. And when had Pharaoh's second firstborn ever begged help from a Hebrew slave? He hadn't even gloated over Kopshef's failure to duplicate the miracle.

Eleazar felt a peculiar peace amid the turmoil. Not because he or his family had been spared the suffering. No. Doda, Taliah, and the others were as miserable as the Egyptians, but the fact that the Hebrew God had proven His power superior to other gods had given Eleazar a sense of inevitability. Not today, and perhaps not tomorrow, but someday and somehow Pharaoh would indeed let Israel leave Egypt. Though Yahweh had done nothing for Eleazar personally—He might even punish Eleazar for years of rebellion—this Hebrew God was powerful enough to make Prince Ram beg. And that fact alone lightened Eleazar's step.

His journey to Goshen seemed shorter today. Perhaps it was because the mud pits and fields were deserted. It was the last month of Akhet, and the waters had reached their height. Whatever canals needed digging had been dug. The fields were too wet to plant. It was the perfect time for a plague.

Eleazar chuckled and let himself scratch his arms, moaning aloud at the fiery pleasure. He passed piles of frogs along the way and marveled at the amount of decay in only a week's time. They'd shrunk to half their original height, and the stench had become so familiar he now ceased to notice it. As he approached Doda's village, Eleazar saw a discarded robe in the tall grass. The robe groaned, and he hurried over to see an elderly man shivering and curled into a ball. Eleazar lifted him into his arms and carried him to Doda Miriam's.

"I need help!" he shouted as he shoved aside the curtain. Doda was applying some sort of balm to Moses's arms. "Hurry. I found him on the roadside."

Sattar greeted him with the familiar growl, and Doda grabbed her walking stick to push herself to her feet. When she saw the man, she gasped. "Oh no, it's Hur."

Eleazar looked at the man again and remembered the friend of their family who'd been unjustly exiled to Pithom when Eleazar was a young soldier. Every exposed surface of Hur's skin was covered in tiny red dots. The man's delirium was a blessing in disguise. Were he conscious, with so many bites he'd be more miserable than the rest. Eleazar laid Hur on Doda's sleeping mat with extra care. She appeared with a wet cloth, a bowl of water, and aloe. Moses followed with a basket of rolled bandages.

Taliah stood an arm's length from Eleazar. He felt her cold stare. "He's a friend of Miriam's from long ago. He's been visiting nearly every day. We were worried because we didn't see him yesterday or this morning." She stepped closer and dug her fingers into his arm. "You'd know all this if you were here more often."

Eleazar pulled his arm from her grasp but remained silent. She wouldn't understand a soldier's duty to his master. They'd been married less than two weeks, and already she was nagging. Granted, he had slept at the barracks a few nights, but he'd been home more nights than not. Didn't she see he was trying?

"Where did you find him, Eleazar?" Doda Miriam glanced over her shoulder, eyes glistening.

"He was lying in the grass between the city and Goshen."

"Miriam?" Hur whispered the name, and every eye turned to Doda.

She knelt beside him and dabbed his forehead with the wet cloth. "I'm here," she said. "What are you doing taking a nap in the tall grass, my friend?"

"I don't want . . . be a burden . . . Uri and Bezalel." Hur turned toward the soothing cloth, his face covered with the fiery red midge bites.

"Do you suppose he's been sleeping outside all this time?" Doda spoke, it seemed, to no one in particular. "He's over ninety inundations old. He can't sleep outside in the night air—" Her voice broke, and she covered her face with the cloth she'd used to tend Hur.

Eleazar couldn't bear to see Doda upset, not after she'd just lost Saba and Savta. "Why can't Hur sleep here, with Moses in Saba and Savta's chamber?"

"Of course," Moses said.

"No, he shouldn't. What will people say?" Her cheeks flushed instantly pink.

Since when had Doda Miriam cared what gossips said? Eleazar noted the grin exchanged between Taliah and Moses and realized he'd missed more than a few of Hur's visits while tending Prince Ram at the palace.

Hur lifted his hand to Miriam, and she cradled it in her own. "I don't want . . . to be a . . . burden." He closed his eyes.

Doda swiped at her cheeks and took a deep breath. "Eleazar, get a cup of water. Taliah, start some barley porridge. He needs hydration and nourishment." She glanced over her shoulder. "Moses, get your room tidied up. You've got a new roommate."

Each one snapped to the assigned duty, while Miriam tended her patient with extra care. Eleazar delivered the water, bent to kiss the top of her head, then proceeded to find Moses in the adjoining chamber.

He was unrolling Saba's old sleeping mat for Hur and pointed to a basket of linen. "You'll find a wool blanket in that basket. Hur might need it as the nights get cooler."

Eleazar followed instruction without comment, considering how he might present Ram's request to his uncle. He found the blanket and began unfolding it on the mat as he unveiled the prince's request.

"Ram sent me here to ask mercy for his wife and children."

Moses stopped tidying and gave Eleazar his attention. "Has Prince Ram convinced Pharaoh to let our people go?"

Eleazar saw something of the war-hardened general in his uncle and didn't appreciate it. They were just having a friendly conversation. "No."

"Then Yahweh will extend no mercy." Moses resumed his preparations for Hur, cutting a new lamb's wool headpiece, rearranging the sleeping mats.

"But the women and children are suffering terribly. There's no need—"

"No need?" Moses stood suddenly, issuing the challenge in Eleazar's face. "Hebrew women and children have been needlessly suffering for four hundred years. I don't think a few midge bites on Egyptian royals are so ghastly. Do you?"

Fire raced into Eleazar's veins. He would have struck any other man. Through clenched teeth, he spit barely controlled venom. "It's always ghastly when it's your family."

The reply seemed to dowse the fire in his uncle. Moses rubbed both hands down the length of his face and groaned. "And there's the heart of the matter, Eleazar, the very reason I want to rail at the God who has promised to deliver us." The surprise on Eleazar's face must have provoked Moses to continue. "Why does Yahweh attack His own family?" Moses held out his arm and pointed to the fiery red dots that no doubt burned and itched as much as those on an Egyptian. "Why must God's people suffer along with those He's punishing? I don't understand it."

Stunned at his uncle's confession, Eleazar grasped at his own reasoning. "I don't understand why either, but these biting gnats must be from the hand of Yahweh because Pharaoh's magicians couldn't duplicate it. And if the gnats are from Yahweh, they must be a part of His ultimate pla—"

"They can't duplicate the biting gnats?" Moses's eyes lit with surprise.

"Kopshef called this plague the 'finger of the Hebrew god' because it surpassed the power of all Egyptian gods." Eleazar chuckled. "Pharaoh was furious."

Moses covered a laugh. "They are seeing His undeniable power. Surely, you see it too."

Eleazar shifted awkwardly. Of course, he saw the Hebrew God's power, but there were too many unanswered questions for Eleazar to trust Him. "I see His power, Moses, but I refuse to place my life—and the lives of those I love—in the hands of another capricious god."

"Excuse me." Taliah poked her head around the curtain. "Miriam needs your help to move Hur. She'd like to get him settled in before she tries to feed him."

Moses patted Eleazar's shoulder on his way toward the doorway. "Thank you for speaking honestly about Yahweh. Remember, He told us we'd know His nature by His actions, and those actions have begun, Eleazar. Watch what He does next."

Taliah folded her arms across her chest, her eyes hard as flint stones. "It seems you open your heart to everyone but your wife."

Eleazar reached for her, hoping to show the love his words had been so worthless to convey, but she bolted from the adjoining room alone.

Doda poked her head through the doorway a moment later. "I need your help too, Eleazar. Hur is too heavy for Moses to move himself."

Eleazar stepped into Doda's main room, looking for Taliah. She must have fled to the roof. With as much authority and precision as Egypt's generals, Doda directed her friend's transfer to the adjoining room, then kept him and Moses busy with Hur's care until dusk.

Taliah hadn't come back down, and Eleazar saw no reason to follow her to the roof. What would he say? She'd made her feelings clear. She wanted nothing to do with him.

While Doda and Moses ate servings of barley porridge with Hur and reminisced about the old days, Eleazar said his good-byes. He'd return in the morning with rations, but he'd stay in the barracks with Hoshea again tonight. At least there he didn't have to explain himself.

31

*If you do not let my people go, I will send
swarms of flies on you and your officials,
on your people and into your houses.*

—EXODUS 8:21

Miriam rose before dawn again, stealing glances at the dividing curtain for any sign of wakefulness on the other side. Since Hur had moved in three weeks ago, Miriam liked to have her hair braided and head covering in place when the men emerged from their room. Moses usually woke first, but Hur followed close behind.

Taliah must have heard her stirring and groaned a sleepy, "Good morning." She'd begun sleeping in the main room with Miriam since Eleazar had moved back to the barracks. Rolling up her sleeping mat, Taliah moved like those wooden shabti dolls in Pharaoh's nightmare—stiff, listless, and pale. Taliah seldom had a smile even during her classes—now filled with Egyptian and Hebrew students.

"Do you want to get water this morning, or should I?" Miriam reached for a jug, but Taliah beat her to it.

"I'll do it. I need the fresh air." She coiled her single braid into a knot at the nape of her neck and snatched her head covering from the peg. "We should probably make a new supply of beer this morning as well."

Their mornings were dedicated to daily chores, but after their midday meal, when Taliah gathered the village children for lessons, Hur and Miriam enjoyed their quiet afternoons reminiscing about dear ones they'd loved and lost.

"Good morning." Hoshea peeked around the curtain carrying two partial bundles of rations. Taliah stepped back, her eyes downcast.

"Good morning, boy. Where's Eleazar?" Miriam asked the same question every morning and evening since her nephew had begun sending his apprentice to deliver rations. Didn't Eleazar realize they needed to see him far more than they needed his food?

But every morning and evening, poor Hoshea mumbled some sorry excuse he'd invented on the way to Goshen. "Eleazar sends his apologies, but he's coming tonight for the evening meal."

Taliah choked out a laugh. "Why?"

Hoshea looked from Taliah to Miriam and back. "He uh . . . well, he . . . he misses his family." He'd obviously hoped for a more favorable reaction.

"If he truly missed us, he'd wake up with me each morning and kiss his doda every night." Taliah stared at him as if poor Hoshea had an answer to Eleazar's truancy.

"I must get back." Hoshea offered her the bundle with an apologetic shrug. "Perhaps if you welcome him with a smile and . . ."

Taliah's fiery glare silenced the young apprentice. He slipped through the curtain before she ate him for breakfast. Poor boy. Eleazar had put Hoshea in an impossible position.

"Perhaps if you'd tell Eleazar how much you miss him, dear. You can draw more flies with honey than—"

"I know you're trying to help, Miriam, but I won't pretend I'm happy when I'm not."

"Good morning, beautiful ladies." Hur's cheerful voice intruded.

Taliah turned from Miriam. "Good morning, Hur. Sleep well?"

"I always sleep well because I'm well loved." He alternated glances at the two women, his head cocked in question. "I'm sure you find the same to be true—"

"Don't. Don't speak of love to me—ever." Taliah's eyes flashed dangerously, but Hur was undaunted.

Crossing the small room, he clasped her hand. "No matter who else disappoints you, Yahweh's love endures. We need never doubt His love—ever." He winked and kissed her hand.

Miriam held her breath. Would Taliah berate him or accept his encouragement? She let out her breath when Taliah responded.

"Thank you, Hur. You're very kind." Eyes misty, she removed her hand from his grasp, grabbed the water jar, and fairly fled out the doorway.

Miriam's heart broke for her. "Eleazar is coming for the evening meal."

"Ah, so that's why she's especially sensitive this morning."

Miriam nodded and glanced over his shoulder toward the dividing curtain. "We should warn Moses. He's usually awake by now. Is he ill?"

"No. He was gone when I woke up. I assumed you'd seen him."

A gnawing dread rumbled in Miriam's stomach. She hoped it was merely hunger, but that was unlikely. Their household had eaten like kings since the biting midges had subsided. Not only had the Hebrews realized Moses was Yahweh's true messenger, but even some of the Egyptian peasants left offerings at their doorway. Their household now enjoyed boiled goose eggs for breakfast, goat cheese to share with neighbors, and fresh camel's milk to flavor their porridge. Yahweh had supplied what they needed and more.

But Moses's early-morning departure signaled trouble. Miriam sensed it.

"Bring the rations please." Miriam grabbed the hand mill and took out her fears on the barley they'd been given by the family of one of Taliah's students. Her teaching responsibilities had increased since her pupils showed higher aptitude in bartering, writing, and geography—all of which improved a parent's worth in a given craft or market booth. The poor girl would no doubt have traded every accomplishment for a kind word from her husband. The most heartrending part of it all was that Miriam knew she and Eleazar loved each other. They just didn't know how to show it.

Hur stood behind her and leaned close. "What's bothering you?"

She stilled but couldn't speak past the lump in her throat. He knelt before her and removed the hand mill from her lap. The eyes looking back were the ones that had captured her heart as a girl. Even when he'd married Shiphrah, Miriam had respected this lighthearted, steadfast man. "I want Eleazar to love Taliah the way you loved Shiphrah." The words were out before she realized how much of her heart they revealed.

Hur raised an eyebrow and grinned. "And how exactly did I love Shiphrah?"

Her face and neck were on fire. She wanted to hide but refused to run out the door like a skittish mare.

He tilted her chin up, capturing her once again with those eyes. "Shiphrah and I were married a long time. It may take years before Eleazar can share the depths of his emotion with his wife. A man's heart is more fragile than a woman's."

How could anyone's heart be more fragile than the one in her chest, skipping like a stone on the Nile? Miriam forced words from her dry throat. "But a woman's heart withers over time." She pushed his hand away and left the house, unable to staunch her tears. So many things to strike at her emotions in such a short period of time. Shaddai's absence and the deaths of Abba and Ima. *Why—oh Yahweh, why must I struggle now with loving a man when I'm old and my life is over?*

32

But on that day I will deal differently with the land of Goshen, where my people live; no swarms of flies will be there, so that you will know that I, the LORD, am in this land. I will make a distinction between my people and your people. This sign will occur tomorrow.

—EXODUS 8:22–23

Eleazar left the palace complex as the sun began its descent behind the western hills. He should have stayed. Prince Ram had become even more dependent on him since the plagues began, finding solace in a Hebrew guard amid the Hebrew god's judgment. Eleazar chuckled as he jogged. Poor Ram had no idea Eleazar and Yahweh weren't exactly friendly.

The industrial section of Rameses behind him, Eleazar slowed his pace. He was in no hurry to reach Goshen. Would Taliah be pleased he'd honored his promise and come home this evening? Or would she stare at him with those deeply wounded eyes and make more cutting remarks? Why couldn't she understand that these were unusual times, special circumstances? The frogs came days after Saba and Savta died, then the biting midges. Eleazar was a military soldier, personal guard to Prince Ram. If she wanted a brick maker who would be home every night, she should have considered that before—

Eleazar couldn't even complete the thought. He knew he was making excuses. He could have been home more. Ram had even told him to go home to his ailing grandparents, but he'd stayed at the barracks because Taliah wanted words. She wanted Eleazar to talk, to share his feelings, to recount his day, when all he wanted to do when he arrived in Goshen was forget.

The long house was in sight. He slowed his pace to a walk, sighed, and kicked a rock, sending it skittering into the crusty remains of a shrinking frog pile. Instinctively, he scratched his hand and then looked down where the midge bites had been.

"Will you really plague only the city?" he whispered to the God he refused to acknowledge.

Moses and Abba Aaron had interrupted Pharaoh's morning bath at the river to proclaim tomorrow's plague—flies, biting flies. Ramesses had cancelled all court activity to meet with his officials and magicians. Maybe Taliah expected him to talk about these things as well. She loved to debate, but Eleazar wasn't a teacher or philosopher. He was a soldier, a man of few words, and he wasn't about to betray Prince Ram to entertain his wife.

Besides, Moses sat at their evening table. How could he discuss the details of Egyptian argument at court? Once Moses had announced that the plague would begin *tomorrow,* he left and the debates began. Kopshef suggested *tomorrow* was an omen. A punishment from the Hebrew god because Pharaoh had been too proud to plead for relief from the frogs immediately. Ramesses's fury had equaled the desert sandstorms, so Jannes and Jambres proposed an alternative for the fourth plague's delay. Perhaps the Hebrew god was taunting Egypt's gods, giving the magicians a chance to match power against power. This glimmer of hope soothed Pharaoh and gave Kopshef and his conjurers a full day to fend off the swarm of flies Moses had promised.

Eleazar was a Hebrew. He loved Doda and Taliah—and Moses. But to reveal the inner workings of the palace still felt like a betrayal.

He rounded the corner of the long house and approached Doda's doorway. Light glowed around the curtain, but the family banter was displaced by an eerie quiet. He peered through the curtain and found four people seated around the reed mat, eating in complete silence. Something was very wrong.

Taliah leapt from her spot and hurried over to greet him. She stretched up on her toes and whispered, "Miriam and Hur had some sort of quarrel, but no one knows what it was about." She cleared her throat, resumed a normal voice, and led him to the mat. "One of the elders killed a goose and shared it with us, so we're eating like kings tonight."

"I see, and it looks like we have enough to feed the neighbors." Eleazar dropped his small bundle of rations and sat directly across from Moses who nodded toward Miriam and shrugged an *I-don't-know-what-happened* look. Miriam and Hur kept their heads bowed. Eleazar clapped his hands loudly, startling everyone. "I'm starving. That goose looks delicious." Taliah piled up his plate with the juicy, dark meat covered in leeks and onions and then ladled on a honeyed-yogurt sauce that rivaled palace cuisine.

Finding himself the leading conversationalist, Eleazar stepped out into uncharted waters. "So, Moses, I wasn't there for your announcement. Tell us about tomorrow's plague."

"There's another plague?" Miriam looked up for the first time, betrayal written on her features. "Why didn't you tell me?"

Moses tilted his head and answered softly. "I didn't want to add more tension to the evening."

"Perhaps I should go." Hur rolled to his knees, struggling to stand.

Moses stopped him and shot a glare at Miriam. She closed her eyes and let out a huff. "You're not leaving, Hur. I'm sorry. I'm acting like a child. Moses, tell us about the plague." She kept her head down and began shoveling goose into her mouth as if it were the first meal she'd had in years.

Hur sat down and smiled sheepishly. Eleazar felt sorry for him. Hur wasn't even married to Doda and he was in trouble.

"Yahweh is sending a swarm of flies tomorrow," Moses began, "but this time He's making a distinction between Egypt and Israel. The flies will swarm only the city of Rameses but will leave Goshen untouched."

Doda Miriam shoved her plate away. "Yahweh will make a distinction." Her eyes sparked, her voice crackling with anger. "He's good at choosing favorites." She struggled to her feet, and when Hur tried to help, she cried, "Stop! I can do it," and left the house with Sattar trailing behind her.

All eyes turned to Hur for an explanation. "She'll be all right. Every great love goes through the fire. She and Yahweh will work this out." He used his walking stick to help him stand. "Thank you, Taliah, for a wonderful meal. This household has shown me such warm hospitality, but if Miriam wants me to leave, I should go. I'll speak with her about it as soon as possible." He excused himself and disappeared into the room he and Moses shared.

Eleazar and Taliah sat with Moses in uncomfortable silence. Both Moses and Taliah had eaten most of their meal, and Eleazar felt a rush of guilt. He was late for the meal. He'd come, but he was late—again. Dragging both hands down his weary face, Eleazar felt Hur's words like a cudgel to the gut. *I'll speak with her about it as soon as possible.* If Hur was willing to talk to Doda—a woman who was merely his friend—perhaps Eleazar should make more effort to talk to his wife.

He brushed Taliah's arm. "May I speak with you on the roof?"

Startled, she flinched, and then her cheeks instantly pinked. "I should clean up—"

"No, no. I can do it." Moses began gathering dishes and waving the couple toward the ladder. He stole Taliah's plate from her hand. "You cleaned while you cooked. There's hardly anything to do. Go on. Go on." He forced a yawn—badly. "It's well past dark. Time for bed, you two."

Eleazar climbed the ladder to escape the awkwardness. He shoved aside the rooftop cover, stepped off the ladder, and assessed their deserted hideaway. The palm branches needed straightening on their three-sided shelter, and the sleeping mat had been skewed by the wind. He grieved what was lost between them and what had never been built.

Taliah stepped close behind him, laid her head against his back, and circled her arms around his middle. "Will you stay with me tonight?" Her voice was barely a whisper.

He squeezed his eyes shut. Ram would need him when the swarm of flies came tomorrow. Eleazar turned toward his wife and tilted her chin to see her deep, dark eyes. "I want to stay. Do you believe me? I want to stay every night."

Tears pooled on her lashes. "Will you stay with me tonight?"

No shouting. No accusations.

His wife needed him too. Bending to kiss her, Eleazar stopped just before their lips met. "I will stay, Taliah, because I love you."

The moon and stars witnessed the purest love Eleazar had ever known. Surely, this was the meaning of the ancient wedding blessing, *one flesh*. Long into the night, he and Taliah shared the intimacies known only to husband and wife. Love. Desire. Passion. And finally, the complete rest of a satisfied soul.

Eleazar's next conscious thought was an annoying buzz that wouldn't be stilled, a vibration that stirred the breeze. Taliah must have woken at the same time. She grabbed his hand but didn't move. A whirling black cloud moved over Goshen, blocking the fading stars and moonlight. Eleazar dared not sit up for fear he'd disturb the thick swarm of flies above them. He turned onto his stomach and crawled to the edge of the roof, Taliah by his side, and they stared in disbelief as the swarm descended on the city of Rameses. Beginning in the industrial section and peeling off into the armory, the palace complex, and the noblemen's homes. Every part of the city grew black and pulsated with a thick layer of the buzzing insects—and the sky over Goshen became clear.

"I must go." He jumped up, grabbed his armor, and hurried to the ladder.

"Eleazar." Her voice stopped him. "I love you too."

A ferocious yearning swept over him. She loved him. "I'll be home again as soon as I can." He cursed each step that took him away from his beautiful wife.

33

*Then Pharaoh summoned Moses and Aaron and
said, "Go, sacrifice to your God here in the land."*

—Exodus 8:25

Moses and Doda waited at the bottom of the ladder with four
empty grain sacks. Before Eleazar could question their purpose,
Moses began wrapping the sacks around Eleazar's arms and legs. "If these
are the stable flies I remember from my days here at Avaris, they're blood
feeders and you'll need this protection."

Eleazar didn't argue though he looked like a fool with sackcloth
wrapped like wings around his limbs. "I'll send Hoshea with word if
Pharaoh relents and decides to release us."

Moses finished tying the last sack to his leg and rose to meet his gaze.
"I'll see you in a little while."

The certainty on his uncle's expression told Eleazar he'd already
heard from Yahweh. The soberness told him this would not be the last
battle with Ramesses. Eleazar kissed Doda's cheek and began his brisk jog
toward the city. He reached the edge of the industrial section and waved
off the first fly. He'd jogged ten camel lengths, and his face was on fire. A
few more strides and the pests started biting through the sackcloth.

He ran to the throne hall first, but it was empty—not even a guard
at the ebony doors. The sounds of shrieks and cries of pain grew louder as
he checked one empty audience chamber after another. Eleazar decided
to find Hoshea in their underground military barracks. Perhaps he'd
know where Prince Ram and Pharaoh were meeting.

The swarms of flies lessened as Eleazar descended the ramp to the
Hebrew barracks. He stepped over Hoshea's morning rations and pounded

at the door of the chamber they shared. Hoshea turned the iron latch and swung open the door, looking at Eleazar as if he had two heads. "What's wrong?" He appraised Eleazar's winged arms and legs and then slapped at a fly on his neck.

Eleazar rushed inside and closed the door behind them, astonished that not a single fly entered the chamber with him.

"I was just ready to open my door and collect my rations when I heard your knock." Hoshea helped Eleazar remove the sackcloth. They found welts the size of grapes on his arms and legs.

Eleazar could only imagine what his face looked like. He collapsed on Hoshea's sleeping mat. "We have to find Ram. No one is in the throne hall."

Hoshea swallowed hard, staring at Eleazar's wounds. "Are you sure that's a good idea? It appears the distinction Moses prophesied is all about location, not the person. As long as we're in the Hebrew section of the palace or in Goshen, we're safe."

"We're soldiers, Hoshea. We serve our commanders. I serve Prince Ram, and you serve me, live or die." Eleazar saw a shadow of doubt cross his young apprentice's face, and it startled him. Hoshea had never shown fear. His honor and courage had been faultless.

The boy extended his arm to help Eleazar stand, but he held Eleazar's gaze. "If I ever have to choose between obeying you or Yahweh, I will choose Yahweh, Commander."

Eleazar released his arm and felt a sting of betrayal. "At least we know where your loyalty lies. Will Yahweh allow you to look for Prince Ram?" He could see his sarcasm wounded Hoshea, and he regretted it immediately.

The boy offered kindness in return. "Of course, I'll help you find the prince." He reached for the sackcloth to retie them, but Eleazar stopped him.

"It doesn't help." He squeezed the boy's shoulder. "My comment was uncalled for. I'm sorry."

"Not as sorry as I'm going to be in a few moments." Hoshea grinned and cringed as he reached for the door.

Eleazar chuckled with him and wondered why he couldn't talk with Taliah so easily.

They began their search in the residential wing, swatting flies and crying out in pain as they tried to ignore the overwhelming wails of women and children. But Eleazar and Hoshea found Prince Ram by following the sounds of quarreling. He, Prince Kopshef, and Pharaoh were sealed in an alcove three doors down from Prince Ram's private chamber. They'd stuffed cloth beneath the door, presumably keeping flies out, but it did nothing to muffle their sharp disagreement on how to stop Egypt's decline.

Eleazar recognized Prince Ram's voice first. "Kill Moses and Aaron! If they can't announce the plagues, the plagues won't happen." Should Eleazar knock on the door or run back to Goshen and warn Abba and Moses?

"You imbecile!" Kopshef screamed. "It's not Moses and Aaron that overpower Egypt's gods. It's their Yahweh. Who's going to kill him when we can't even match his tricks?"

Eleazar pounded on the door and heard Pharaoh bark, "What?"

"It's Eleazar, my king. How may I serve you?"

"I've already sent my chariot to Goshen to collect Moses and Aaron. Make sure they find us."

Hoshea slapped a fly from his neck and shrugged, glancing around the deserted palace hallway. "We might as well get comfortable," he said, sliding down the wall and landing in a heap.

Eleazar stood, arms crossed over his chest, assessing the eerie sight. The morning sun streamed in the long, narrow windows showing dust dancing on marble tiles, intricately carved pillars, and luxurious tapestries. That same dust had become biting gnats weeks ago, bringing pain and destruction to the three most powerful men in the world—men now huddled in a locked room hiding from . . . flies. Couldn't a God who turned the Nile to blood, turned dust to gnats, and caused flies to swarm on a single city free the Israelites in a single day? Eleazar grinned. Yahweh was indeed teaching both the Egyptians and the Israelites many things about Himself in these days of plagues and patience.

With the thoughts still rumbling in his head, Eleazar noted four silhouettes at the far end of the hallway. Flies swarmed all around the two Egyptian guards, but none landed on Abba or Moses. Eleazar pointed to the sight. "So much for our theory of God's distinction being geographical, not personal."

Hoshea's face lit with wonder. "We're discovering Yahweh can do most anything." They waited impatiently for the two elders to arrive. When Hoshea could wait no longer, he shouted, "Has a single fly landed on you?"

But Moses was sober, his countenance more melancholy than triumphant. "No, but we've seen much suffering on our way here." He pointed to the closed door. "Is Ramesses in there?" Without waiting for an answer, he opened the door. No knock. No warning. He simply barged through the door Pharaoh had barricaded shut and closed it behind him. The Egyptian guards were as stunned as Eleazar and shoved him aside to press their ears against the door.

There was no need. Everyone in the city could hear Pharaoh shout. "Go, Moses! You may sacrifice to your god in our land."

"Not good enough." Moses's reply was calm but commanding, also easily heard. "Our sacrifices are detestable in the eyes of Egyptians. We might be stoned while we worship if we remain here. No. We must be allowed a three-day journey into the wilderness to sacrifice as Yahweh commands."

"Aahh!" Pharaoh growled, and Eleazar heard increased swatting and more groaning. "All right! You may sacrifice in the wilderness, but don't go far. Now pray for me!"

The Egyptian guards exchanged a stunned glance, as did Hoshea and Eleazar. Pharaoh, deified Son of Horus, asked for a blessing from a slave's god.

"As soon as I leave the city, I will pray to Yahweh, and *tomorrow,*" Moses emphasized, "the flies will leave Pharaoh, his officials, and his people. But be sure you don't deal deceitfully again with Yahweh's people, Ramesses."

The door swung open, and the leaning Egyptian guards nearly fell into the room. Moses stepped back, allowing them to regain their balance—and their composure.

"Wait!" Pharaoh pointed his flail at Moses. "I will not wait for tomorrow. Tell your god the flies must leave today."

Moses grinned. "Yahweh gave you one chance to choose the time of your deliverance—with the frogs—and you were too proud to ask urgently. The flies leave tomorrow." He slammed the door closed behind him.

Eleazar glimpsed Prince Ram before the door closed, his welted face mottled with rage. Was he angry with Moses? Or maybe Kopshef or Ramesses? Or had he summoned Eleazar this morning and found him absent?

Moses stepped within a handbreadth of Eleazar's face. "Now that Yahweh has made a distinction between Goshen and Egypt, you would do well to do the same, son." He motioned to Abba Aaron. "Come, let's return home. We've done all Yahweh requires of us here."

As they lumbered down the long hallway in silence, Eleazar felt torn. Should he escort them back to Goshen or remain outside this door in case Prince Ram emerged? Hoshea squashed a few flies under his sandal, glancing up at his mentor for direction.

"Escort Abba and Moses back to Goshen. Tell Doda and Taliah I'm staying at the palace until the flies are resolved."

Hoshea drew a breath to comment, but thought better of it. "As you wish, sir." He hurried to catch up with the elder Hebrews, and Eleazar watched them go, fearing he'd made the wrong choice.

34

Pharaoh said, "I will let you go to offer
sacrifices to the LORD your God in the
wilderness, but you must not go very far.
Now pray for me."
    Moses answered, "As soon as I leave you,
I will pray to the LORD, and tomorrow the
flies will leave Pharaoh and his officials and
his people." . . .
    But this time also Pharaoh hardened his
heart and would not let the people go.

—EXODUS 8:28–29, 32

Miriam sat beneath her palm tree, Sattar by her side, listening to the shrieks and moans of suffering Egyptians. The flies had been relentless, coming in waves and swarms all day long. Yet not a single bloodsucker had landed in Goshen. Her people were safe. They were witnessing the mighty hand of Yahweh judging their oppressors and shielding His beloved Israel.

So why was Miriam crying? *I'm a ridiculous old fool.* It was the only explanation. She ached for life as it was before. Abba and Ima in the next room, sharing their daily wisdom. El Shaddai's intimate whisper throughout her day and in her dreams—yes, *El Shaddai,* not Yahweh. It didn't matter anymore whether she was important among the tribes. She simply yearned for the constant presence of those who knew her intimately. This loneliness was too much to bear. *Please, Shaddai, I don't want to live another moment without feeling You near.*

Sobbing into her hands, she knew she must confess to Him the greatest foolishness of all. She couldn't whisper it. She could barely even think it. *Forgive me for falling in love with Hur.* Mortified, Miriam shook her head in shame. She was too old to fall in love, and she'd never needed anyone but El Shaddai. Why now was she suddenly acting like a besotted maiden? Throwing tantrums. Worrying about her appearance. Guarding her words. *I want You, El Shaddai, only You.* She felt as if she had betrayed her first love, her true Husband.

Only silence answered.

Who has betrayed whom? The bitter accusation rose up in her before she could stop it. Her God, now called Yahweh, seemed busy elsewhere, but she couldn't give in to resentment. If she believed her God loved her—and she did—why would He choose to harm her?

Sattar stirred beside her. Miriam glanced over and saw his tail thumping the ground wildly. She needn't look behind her. Only Moses roused that kind of welcome.

"May I sit with you?" But it wasn't Moses. It was Hur.

Miriam's heart jumped to her throat. "Of course." She wiped her face with her mantle.

He sat on the other side of Sattar and dug his fingers into the thick black-and-white fur. Sattar laid his head on Hur's leg, and Miriam rolled her eyes. *Traitor.*

"It appears you've made a friend," she said coolly.

"It appears I've lost one."

Tears stung her eyes again, and she struggled for control. "That's how I feel about El Shaddai—an old Friend who changed His name and chose other people to spend time with."

"Why do you suppose He did that?" Hur asked the question as if pondering how much garlic to add to a stew.

Annoyed, she swiped at tears and glared at him. "If I knew I wouldn't be sitting here crying."

He nodded slowly and turned his focus toward the Nile. "Why are you angry with me, Miriam?"

There it was. The question she'd dreaded. She shook her head and pressed her lips into a thin line, refusing to release the words that burned within.

"You've never been shy about speaking your mind." He grinned and turned to her then, searching her eyes. "Do you feel you're betraying Yahweh if you love me?"

Stunned at his audacity, she opened her mouth, but no words came.

He leaned over and kissed her cheek and then went about the lengthy process of standing up. "That's the wonderful thing about Yahweh, Miriam. We don't have to choose between Him and those we love. His love flows through us." He reached down and brushed her cheek. "Consider yourself kissed by Yahweh today."

He walked away as she covered a sob. *Kissed by Yahweh.* Her heart ached at the tenderness she felt in that moment. Months since she'd had a dream, weeks since her last vision—who could have guessed she'd feel Yahweh's presence through the persistent kindness of a longtime friend.

She pulled up her legs, rested her forehead on her knees, and wept. Cleansing, grieving, refreshing tears. The sun had begun its western descent when she raised her head and untangled her creaky body. She was too old for these depths of emotion. *Yahweh, keep me bobbing in the shallows.* She chuckled, feeling as if her God grinned with her. Yes, right there with her.

The cries of suffering from the city had dissipated. Miriam wondered if the biting flies had gone, if they'd had their fill of human blood, or if people had resigned themselves to the pain. She should get back to the long house and see if they needed her. She paused at the thought. No, they didn't need her, but they would certainly miss her if she was gone.

35

Then the LORD said to Moses, "Go to
Pharaoh and say to him, . . . 'Let my people
go. . . . If you refuse to let them go . . . , the
hand of the LORD will bring a terrible plague
on your livestock in the field. . . . But the
LORD will make a distinction between the
livestock of Israel and that of Egypt, so that no
animal belonging to the Israelites will die.'"

—EXODUS 9:1–4

It had been three weeks since the flies began, but they'd known within moments of the swarm's departure that Pharaoh would not let Israel leave Egypt. Slave drivers were dispatched in droves to Goshen, most of them still welted and bleeding from fly bites. The season of *Peret*—the months Egypt sowed barley, flax, wheat, and spelt—was a few weeks away, so the field-working Hebrews were reassigned to brick making. Slower and less skilled, the displaced brick makers drew the brunt of the pained Egyptians' wrath, and Miriam's herb supply dwindled again.

In spite of the increased workload and beatings, Yahweh's distinction during the fourth plague caused more Hebrews to return to the faith of their forefathers. While Hur helped Miriam tend the wounded, others gathered at the door hoping for a peek at Israel's deliverer. Notoriety had become both a blessing and curse for Moses. As a result, he began spending long hours away from the long house. He'd lost any shred of anonymity, and gifts continued piling up: grain, livestock, robes, even jewelry. They traded most at the market for food supplies to give back to Goshen neighbors who barely had enough to survive. Not so long ago, it had been those in Miriam's household whose bellies had rumbled through the night.

Taliah had taken leftover rounds of bread from today's midday meal to her students gathered outside the long house. Hur and Miriam listened to the children's questions and Taliah's knowledgeable replies.

"She's so good with them." Hur's observation broke their companionable silence.

Miriam crushed more dried thyme, letting it fall into the bowl. "Mm-hmm."

"Where are your thoughts right now?" Hur touched her cheek, startling Miriam from her task.

Miriam's face flushed as she ducked her chin. Since that day beneath the palm tree, Hur seemed to understand she wasn't ready to voice her feelings, but she'd at least stopped fighting them. "I was thinking how blessed we are," she said. "In spite of Pharaoh's second refusal to let us leave Egypt, I feel like Yahweh is in control and will deliver us at the proper time."

"It helps that we've seen Him confound orders from pharaohs in the past, doesn't it?" The impish grin on Hur's face reminded her of younger days.

"Do you remember pompous King Tut?" She shook her head and rolled her eyes. "He was such a little boy, yet he thought himself a god who could order your wife and Puah to throw our male infants into the Nile. Our midwives were very brave to defy him."

Hur gazed at a spot far beyond their small window. "I remember the day the Medjay guards arrested Shiphrah and dragged her and Puah before the king. It was a miracle Tut didn't order their executions."

Miriam nodded. Their afternoons of memories nourished her soul. "Moses's whole life is a miracle. Do you remember how Ima Jochebed hid him for three months? Then one night, he cried all night—"

"I remember!" Hur's eyes were full of excitement. "And Jochebed and Amram coated a basket with pitch and—"

"And put Moses in it, then floated him on the Nile. I followed him into the bulrushes where Pharaoh's daughter was bathing. I couldn't believe it when Anippe rescued him."

Hur patted her hand, looking deeply into her eyes. "Yahweh never looked away from your little brother. He provided Moses with an education and military training that would someday lead our people out of Egypt."

As Hur recounted God's handiwork, envy constricted Miriam's chest—and she hated herself for it. *Yahweh, forgive me for being so petty.*

Hur squeezed Miriam's hand. "Plagues and destruction aren't Yahweh's only miracles, are they? Sometimes we're slow to notice the miracles right in front of us."

His gaze held her and made her heart flutter. Her mouth went dry, her mind utterly blank. What does one say when she's too old for passion yet too smitten to turn back?

Aaron chose that moment to enter the curtained doorway. "Where's Moses?" No greeting. No formalities. Typical.

Miriam jerked her hand from Hur's grasp, hoping Aaron hadn't seen their intimate touch. "He took Sattar and said they were going to pester Pharaoh's flocks."

Aaron lowered himself to the mat beside Miriam. "Well, I'm tired of being ignored."

"Am I ignoring you, Aaron?" She hoped he would say yes so she could gut him like a fish for the years he'd ignored Abba and Ima.

"Of course not, Sister. It's Moses who ignores me."

Miriam felt a little guilty for her thoughts, but was more interested in Aaron's sudden readiness to confide in her. "I thought you were busy with metal shop projects that Nadab and Abihu brought home for you. Why do you care if Moses ignores—"

"Moses was supposed to let me speak to Pharaoh and the elders. When I met him in the wilderness, he told me he didn't speak well in front of others, so Yahweh chose me to be the spokesman. God was supposed to speak to Moses, and then Moses should tell me what to say. But Moses has been progressively doing more of the talking."

Miriam thought Aaron sounded like the spoiled little brother she remembered growing up. What did he have to complain about? At least he was chosen by Yahweh. "Have you talked to Moses about your concerns?" She tried not to sound cranky.

"I was planning to wait until we prepared for the next plague, but Moses informed me earlier that he approached Pharaoh this morning in the royal stables and proclaimed the fifth plague would kill the livestock of Egypt." Aaron's eyes bulged. "He did it alone! Without me!"

Miriam felt the news like a spear to her belly. Why had Moses not mentioned it to her? He had been in and out of the long house several times today. Annoyance began to boil. "What else did he say about the plague?"

Aaron raised one brow and leaned close. "He told me all livestock belonging to Egyptians will die, but God will again make a distinction and spare all Hebrew livestock. He refused to tell me how the animals will die, but Yahweh has set tomorrow again as the day of reckoning."

Miriam's mind whirred with concern for the Egyptian peasants of Goshen. Many households of Taliah's students depended on livestock for their livelihood. "All Egyptian livestock or just the king's? Every animal or just certain types?"

"Moses said the plague would kill . . ." Aaron lifted his hand to count off the species, "Horses, donkeys, camels, cattle, sheep, and goats."

Miriam thought of the camel and goats and geese they'd received, some of which came from Egyptian neighbors. Should they help their neighbors prepare for the plague? If they slaughtered the animals and began drying the meat now, they'd at least have something to eat later. But no one would believe her. Why hadn't Moses announced the plague to everyone so they could prepare? Her seething turned rancid. "I know how you feel, Aaron. When my services were no longer needed, I was given no fond farewell. I'm no more than a discarded midwife these days."

She turned to Hur for support, but his expression was passive, unreadable.

"And he's arrogant." Aaron jabbed the air with an accusing finger.

"Moses lets the elders bow to him as if he were king. Some of the Egyptians even bow when he passes by."

Miriam hadn't seen the bowing, but she was weary of the constant intrusion of visitors with gifts. "My patients must shove their way inside to get treatment. And did you see the goats in our pen outside? Moses won't let me sell them. Why do we need so many goats?"

Hur finally joined in. Leaning toward Aaron, he asked, "Why do you suppose Moses went to Pharaoh without you?"

"He's hungry for power, I suppose." Aaron looked first at Miriam and then at Hur. "He wants all the glory now that Yahweh's plagues no longer harm the Israelites."

Hur grasped Miriam's shoulder, gentle but firm. "Do you believe that?"

She swallowed hard. Did she really believe Moses was seizing glory for himself through Yahweh's miracles? No, even as an Egyptian prince, he hadn't sought fame and recognition. But he'd definitely hurt her by disregarding her position among the Israelites. "I think Moses should realize he's not the only one to whom Yahweh has spoken." Miriam raised her chin, straightened her spine, and silently dared him to ask another question.

The sparkle in Hur's light-brown eyes faded, and he released a weary sigh. "I'm sure if you asked Moses why he went to Pharaoh alone, he would explain his decision. My guess is he was following Yahweh's orders, as I've watched him do since I arrived from Pithom." He shook his head. "I'm sorry you two see Yahweh as a bauble to be traded and hoarded. I believe God is infinite, and we experience Him more fully when we share Him with others."

He got to his knees, the silence magnifying every creak and pop of his joints. When he pushed to his feet, he looked down at Miriam. "I once knew a girl who heard El Shaddai whisper in her dreams. She delighted in God and her delight was contagious. But your delight is gone, Miriam." Miriam drew a breath to defend herself, but Hur leaned down and kissed the top of her head, silencing her. "Yahweh's presence is con-

stant. He never abandons us, but I think He grows tired of our flailing."
He disappeared through the curtained doorway before she could spew
her protest.

Miriam sat fuming, and Aaron shuffled quickly to his feet. "I must
get back to Elisheba. She'll wonder where I've been."

"Can't you stand up to her once, Aaron? Can't you tell Elisheba that
your sister needed you? You didn't get to say good-bye to Abba and Ima,
and your two youngest sons won't step foot in your home. Haven't you
sacrificed enough for your overbearing wife?" The words rushed out,
heavy with years of bitterness.

Aaron stood, head bowed, silent under their weight. Miriam thought
she'd feel relief at releasing the emotions she'd restrained for so many
years. Instead she felt like Elisheba, battering Aaron with a stronger will.

"Go." It was all Miriam could muster. And he obeyed.

Miriam sat alone in the home she'd known all her life, but she felt
like a stranger in it. The baskets of grain sat in the same place, the jars of
balm were arranged exactly right, and bundles of herbs hung from the
proper rafters. Village children sat outside her window in the afternoon
sun with a skilled teacher. *Your delight is gone,* Hur had said. Yes, her
delight left when El Shaddai stopped whispering in her dreams—or had
it gone before that? Hur said Yahweh's presence was constant, that she
was fighting Him. Was it true?

A warm breeze wafted through the window, lifting a few stray hairs
off her forehead. *Yahweh, is that You?* It was how she used to sense His
presence.

But she neither heard nor sensed His reply. Instead, she remembered
the conversation with Abba and Ima when she'd determined to experience Yahweh anew. Had she ever really tried?

Perhaps she hadn't tried, but Yahweh had revealed Himself anew in
spite of Miriam's lack. He'd replaced the nighttime dreams and detailed,
candid visions of her youth with shorter glimpses of an event that required discernment and were immediately fulfilled. Like when Aaron
and Moses had been in danger and the warning Yahweh had given her of

the frog plague. Hur's kiss was definitely a new experience of Yahweh's tenderness. Even Sattar's constant presence and protection felt like a provision of Yahweh's care.

She dropped her head into her hands, voice trembling. "Thank You, Yahweh, for Your sweet wooing. Forgive me for being so blind to Your presence."

But something else nibbled at her heart, ate at her spirit. Why not speak the words to the One who already knew her thoughts? With a deep sigh, she spoke into the stillness. "Why are the delightful moments with You so fleeting? Why am I so easily drawn into bitterness and pettiness?"

Because you're angry with Me.

The words came as a knowing within her, not audibly, but as real as if Yahweh stood before her and spoke as a man. She hadn't dared admit the truth, but she was indeed angry with her Shaddai. Yahweh, who turned the Nile to blood; Yahweh, who sent frogs to Pharaoh's bed; Yahweh, who set boundaries on swarming flies. How dare she, a flawed human, a simple Hebrew slave, have the audacity to be angry with Him? But she was.

Still, He had the patience to woo her as she made these discoveries at her own pace. Her heart broke at the reality.

36

Then the LORD said to Moses and Aaron,
"Take handfuls of soot from a furnace and
have Moses toss it into the air in the presence
of Pharaoh. It will become fine dust over the
whole land of Egypt, and festering boils will
break out on people and animals throughout
the land."

—EXODUS 9:8–9

The cloying smell of smoking hooves, flesh, and offal hung in the air over the city of Rameses after the total annihilation of Egyptian livestock four days ago. Eleazar much preferred the smolder of the armory forges and the distraction of the skilled Hittites pounding and shaping new battle-axes. He'd worked hard to restore his relationship with the Hittites after disciplining them and would work harder still.

"Thank you for your work," he said to the chief iron worker, meeting his hard stare. "It's not easy to aid the nation that enslaves you."

The Hittite paused his hammering. "I don't forge weapons for Egypt. I do it to save my back from the whip." He plunged the hot iron into a tub of water, sending a rush of steam into the air and ending their exchange.

And Taliah wonders why I struggle with conversations. Eleazar moved to the next Hittite, their burly red-haired leader. Surely he would understand that Eleazar couldn't allow the sabotage of ax heads to go unpunished. As slave commander, Eleazar walked a fine line between his fellow slaves and his Egyptian master. Prince Ram must trust him implicitly, but the slaves must also know Eleazar was their brother, subject to the same ruthless masters.

As he approached the central furnace, he noted one Hittite elbow another and point behind Eleazar. Curious, Eleazar looked over his shoulder, and his knees nearly buckled. Moses and Abba Aaron had gained entry through the armory gates and were headed toward Eleazar.

The metal worker leaned close and chuckled. "Aren't they the Hebrew magicians? Maybe they'll set the Hittites free too."

Eleazar rushed to meet them, hoping to send them on their way before Prince Ram arrived for their sparring session. "What are you doing here?"

Moses kept walking. "Yahweh told us to collect ashes from a furnace." Abba Aaron glanced nervously right and left. Sparring soldiers in the circles of combat ceased their training, and several Hebrew soldiers bowed as Moses passed by.

Eleazar stepped in front of his uncle, halting his progress. "You can't just walk into the armory and take what you want."

"I won't take it, Eleazar." He paused, eyeing the forge. "You're going to give it to me." He stepped around him and walked directly to the central Hittite furnace and greeted the chief iron worker. "I'll need some soot to take to the throne hall."

The Hittite turned to Eleazar for approval but suddenly looked from Moses to Aaron to Eleazar and back. "Commander, you resemble these old Hebrews. Are you related to the magicians?" He goaded his Hittite buddies. "Maybe the commander will turn his cudgel into a serpent."

"Enough!" Eleazar took a single step toward the furnace, when a hand abruptly whirled him around.

Prince Ram stood inches from Eleazar, betrayal written on his features. He stared at his personal guard as if seeing him for the first time, then examined the enemy Hebrews. "You're related, aren't you?" The muscle in his jaw danced as he waited for an answer.

Eleazar's thoughts whirred, trying to condone his deception, but a soldier made no excuses. "Moses is my uncle. Aaron, my abba."

Ram's nostrils flared, and Eleazar prepared himself for the blow that was sure to come. He deserved death, perhaps torture. Instead, the prince stepped back and addressed Moses. "Conduct your business, and I'll escort you to the throne hall myself."

Moses pointed to the furnace's lower compartment where the ashes fell, and the chief Hittite slipped on his glove, turned the latch, and opened the grate. He scooped several handfuls of soot onto a tray to cool, stirring the ashes. No one spoke.

"Cool enough?" Moses asked. The Hittite nodded, giving Moses the go-ahead to scoop the ashes into a pouch on his belt. He paused near Eleazar for an excruciatingly long moment. "Your family misses you."

In that moment, Eleazar wanted to spar with Moses—using real swords. How dare he and Abba march into the armory without warning, without Eleazar's permission? Despite his anger, he was relieved they hadn't revealed Taliah's identity or the fact he was married. The reminder that Eleazar hadn't been home in weeks heaped burning coals on his already guilty conscience. He hadn't visited Goshen since the plague of flies, but it wasn't because he'd forgotten his wife or his responsibilities.

Prince Kopshef had offered to send Egyptian physicians to check on the condition of Eleazar's failing grandparents—a threat veiled in kindness. As far as those in the palace knew, Saba and Savta had died the next day, and Eleazar's excuse to live in Goshen died with them.

"Very convenient that your grandparents should die the day I plan to send my physicians to check on them." Kopshef's smirk had hinted at victory.

Eleazar made no reply, but he'd noted Prince Ram's suspicious glare. As the only Hebrew among the royal guards, Eleazar had always been singled out for scrutiny, but Ram had defended him as unimpeachable. The plagues—especially after Yahweh made the distinction between Hebrew and Egyptian—had driven a deeper wedge between all Hebrew slaves and their masters. Eleazar had been trying to regain Prince Ram's trust by proving himself loyal and available, day or night.

Today's revelation of family ties had demolished any trust he'd rebuilt.

Eleazar's silence communicated his anger, and Moses returned his attention to Prince Ram. "I'm ready to see Pharaoh."

Ram extended his hand in the direction of the palace. "Well, if you're ready, lord Moses . . ." His sarcasm preceded a seething glare at Eleazar. "You will follow us to the throne hall."

"Yes, my prince." Eleazar noticed Hoshea watching from one of the weapons compartments, and he prayed the boy stayed away. If Ram meted out his fury on Eleazar, Hoshea was fully capable of assuming the role of commander.

Prince Ram led Abba and Moses out of the armory toward the palace complex, and Eleazar provided rear guard. No one spoke as they passed through narrow pathways between charred remains of animal carcasses. The cleanup had almost finished, and Egyptian shepherds were now choosing which Hebrew animals would be taken as Egyptian flocks and herds. By the time they entered the palace gates, the sun was directly overhead in a cloudless sky.

Prince Ram led Moses and the others into the palace through the back entrance, again forgoing the public baths and formal linen robes. "I'm sure Pharaoh's public forums are over for the day, but he may still linger in the throne hall. I'll show you to the princes' quarters."

They climbed a marble staircase and walked through a large court-yard where Ram's wife played with their children. The youngest daughter ran to her father and hugged his legs. Ram leaned down and hoisted the little princess into the air, inspiring giggles and more hugs. As the prince set her down and patted her behind, she ran back to join her brothers.

Ram turned to the men, narrowed his eyes, and clenched his teeth. "These are the ones who suffer from your plagues, Moses." Without wait-ing for a response, he turned and led them up the second marble staircase and then down a narrow hallway with intricately carved doorways lining both sides. Eleazar knew this route to the courtroom as well as he knew his own name, and he'd grown immune to the luxury until he saw won-der fill Abba's expression. Persian pottery sat atop marble half pillars. Luxurious tapestries bearing the purple shades of Phoenician dyes graced every wall. Floor tiles the size of grapes fit together in a splendid sea of designs. Prince Ram opened the gold-plated door at the end of the hall, and they emerged directly onto Pharaoh's dais.

The throne hall was nearly empty. A few stragglers from the day's petitioners remained to settle accounts with the scribes. Eleazar saw his brother Ithamar rolling up his scrolls and neatly arranging his pigment and reeds. Six firstborn princes were gathered around the king, as well as a few of his advisors and magicians.

Ramesses glanced over his right shoulder at the same time some of his officials spotted Ram and his motley band emerging from the prince's entry. Pharaoh failed to hide his disgust. "What are you doing, Ram? Why did you parade Hebrews through the palace?"

"I wanted them to see where my children play and where your sons sleep." He led Abba and Moses off the dais, down the steps, and pointed to the spot on the red tapestry where they were to stand. Eleazar followed, taking his place behind Ram, keeping his head bowed as the prince addressed Moses. "I want you to realize who is being harmed by these plagues of yours. When your god killed Egypt's horses last week, it was my sons' army he weakened. When your god killed our goats, he took milk from my children, and dead cattle means less meat for our tables."

Moses kept his tone even. "What about the Hebrew children who have never tasted goat's milk or eaten red meat? What about Hebrew households who now have no livestock because you seized their animals when your own died in the plague?"

"We take only enough to survive," Ram said. "We'll purchase more from the traders when they arrive."

Moses raised an eyebrow. "Am I to believe you'll return the Hebrews' livestock when you buy more?"

"Enough!" Ramesses slammed his flail. "Every animal in Egypt belongs to Pharaoh because every slave belongs to Pharaoh. I will not quibble over hooves and snouts." He glared at Moses. "Why are you here?"

Without a word, Moses reached into his pouch and threw a handful of soot in the air. He repeated the action until the soot was gone and every Egyptian in the room groaned in stunned agony. Festering boils appeared on every scar left from the biting flies. The wounds that had healed weeks ago now bulged with angry sores.

Eleazar examined his hands and arms. The remnants of his fly bites remained a light brown on his olive skin. No sign of the plague that caused the Egyptians in the room to writhe in pain. He met Ram's gaze and saw more silent accusation. Did he think his suffering brought Eleazar pleasure? They heard screams from the residential wing through which they'd come.

"Out!" Pharaoh screamed. "Get out!"

Abba Aaron turned in a hurry to flee, but Moses bowed slowly, holding the king's gaze as he backed all the way to the exit. A retired soldier knew better than to turn his back on a wounded enemy.

Prince Ram drew near Eleazar and whispered through gritted teeth. "Make your choice now, slave. Are you a son, or are you a soldier?" His whole body trembled, and Eleazar wasn't sure if it was rage or the painful sores that caused it.

"I am Hebrew by birth, but I am loyal to you by an act of will, my prince." Eleazar bowed his head in submission. "And my will is stronger than Hittite iron."

"Then escort your father and uncle to the palace gates and return with a report on when these cursed sores will leave us." Eleazar turned to go, but Ram grabbed his arm. "And find a way to stop their god, or I will find a way to make you suffer with us."

The fine hairs on Eleazar's arms stood at attention. He rushed from the great hall and found Moses and Abba descending the ramp at the northeast corner of the palace.

Moses saw him first, and a smile graced his weathered face. "You've decided to come home! Miriam and Taliah will be delighted."

"I've decided to rebuild my master's trust, which you destroyed when you marched into that armory."

Moses's expression turned to granite. "When Yahweh commands, I obey. He said to get soot from a furnace. That's what we did." He began his march without awaiting a reply.

Eleazar stepped in front of him. "I understand that you're a soldier under authority, but I'm a *slave* soldier whose only armor is his honor. It's all that protects me from Ram's wrath. You stripped away my protection today, and I must regain it, or none of us will be safe." He grabbed a handful of Moses's robe and pulled him to within a handbreadth, grinding out the words. "Make sure you don't ever reveal Taliah's connection to me. That would be the last foolish thing you do."

Moses's expression was full of pity. "Do you really think you can protect Taliah when you can't even protect yourself? Taliah is under Yahweh's care—as are we all."

Eleazar released Moses with a humorless laugh. "You'll forgive me if I'm not comforted that my wife is guarded by a God who is destroying the strongest nation on earth. All I've seen is Yahweh's wrath. I see no compassion."

Abba Aaron's head was bowed, silent as usual in the face of conflict. But Moses met the challenge with fire in his eyes. "You want compassion? You, who refuse to be a husband? You, who ignored Miriam's grieving? Are you really standing in judgment of our God, who has come down to rescue His people after four hundred years of ruthless bondage?"

"Yes!" Eleazar growled. "I judge a God who kills the righteous with the unrighteous."

"Do you condemn a God who blesses you with a child though you deny Him and abandon your wife?"

Eleazar staggered backward, the words hitting him like a blow. "What did you say?"

Moses's features softened. "Taliah is pregnant, Eleazar. She was hoping to tell you when you came home, but since you refuse to return . . ."

Eleazar felt the blood drain from his face. Words failed him. *A child.*

"Miriam says Taliah should deliver during next year's inundation— if we're still in Egypt." Moses stiffened. "But you need not worry. Both Taliah and the child will be cared for."

Eleazar looked at Abba Aaron, and shame crawled up his neck and cheeks. At least Abba and Ima had raised him for the first twelve years of his life. "Perhaps it's best I not return to Goshen at all. I'll have Ithamar draw up an Egyptian document of divorce, and I'll provide a healthy sum for her and the baby. Taliah will have what every woman wants—a child—and she need not keep suffering my failures."

"You may be the most cowardly soldier I've ever known." Revulsion twisted Moses's features.

But Eleazar wouldn't be baited. "I will continue sending my rations. Please make sure Ram and Kopshef never discover Taliah is my wife." He turned before his humiliation found new depths and immediately realized he'd failed to get the information Prince Ram had asked for. Eleazar had no idea when the plague of boils would end, but he wasn't about to beg answers from Moses. He'd heard enough self-righteous tirades to last a lifetime.

A child. The thought burned and twisted in his belly. Taliah would make a fine ima. She loved children and had the knowledge to teach them well. What did Eleazar have to offer a child? Nothing. Moses was right. Eleazar knew nothing of compassion or love or grieving. He'd provide the practical items for the child to live and grow but no more.

Eleazar's sandals echoed in the empty hallway outside the throne hall. He pressed his forehead against the tall ebony doors, listening to the painful groaning within. Closing his eyes, he inhaled slowly and repeated his words, "A soldier's honor is his armor." The life he'd chosen seemed hollow now, but he must convince Prince Ram—and himself—his life was worth living.

37

The magicians could not stand before Moses because of the boils that were on them and on all the Egyptians. But the LORD hardened Pharaoh's heart and he would not listen to Moses and Aaron, just as the LORD had said to Moses.

—EXODUS 9:11–12

The midday meal was quick and light, a few cucumbers, sliced melon, and bread with cheese. Miriam helped Taliah clear the dishes and roll up the reed mat. Hur and Moses sipped warm water and leaned against the wall, stroking Sattar who sat between them.

Hur had been kind but distant since he'd challenged her last week about losing her delight for Yahweh. He usually found an excuse to leave the long house after the midday meal, leaving Miriam alone to ponder her commitment to delight in Yahweh and dig out the root of anger from which her jealousy had sprouted. Hur's words had penetrated Miriam's soul and planted a small seed that felt as if it might be growing—even starting to blossom. At least now when she woke after a dreamless sleep, she looked forward to searching for Yahweh throughout her day and hadn't been disappointed. He'd shown her small glimpses of His presence each day—a sweet birdsong, a child's laughter, a distant memory that came to mind.

"Why are you smiling?" Taliah asked. "I could use some good news."

Miriam set aside the plate she was scraping into the garbage pot and cradled Taliah's cheeks between her hands. "I'm smiling because Yahweh is revealing His presence in many ways." Miriam kissed the tip of her nose. "And that precious life growing inside you is another proof of His touch. Eleazar's stubbornness won't rob us of that joy."

Taliah nodded as fresh tears wet her lashes. Pregnancy brought all sorts of wild emotions, and if anyone deserved a few tears, it was this girl. Resuming her chores, Taliah banged spoons and pots with the fervor of a woman scorned. She'd alternated between anger and despair since Moses returned with Eleazar's plan for a divorce this morning.

"How can he abandon a pregnant wife?" she fumed. "Has he no heart at all?" She lost a short spoon in a large bowl of beer mash and growled her frustration.

Miriam cast a glance over her shoulder at Moses and Hur. They'd nodded off despite the noise, both of them softly snoring. "Why don't you go weed the herb garden, dear?" Miriam's suggestion was partly self-ish. The girl had broken two cups and ruined one recipe of bread dough with too much salt. "A little fresh air will be good for the baby."

Taliah had cancelled her afternoon classes because she didn't feel up to teaching today, but Miriam was running out of things to keep her busy. The girl had already ground herbs, spun wool, and made more bread.

Sattar perked his ears and growled, and Taliah shot a panicked look at Miriam. "He only growls like that when—"

Eleazar's heavy footsteps pounded the dirt outside their window, and suddenly his large form filled the doorway. He looked tired, haggard. Miriam wanted to give him a fierce hug and then offer him warm bread with goat cheese. It had been weeks since she'd seen him.

"Why are you here?" Taliah's tone sparked like flint rocks.

Hur snorted loudly, waking at the disruption. "Eleazar, good to see you, boy."

Moses woke but offered no greeting.

Eleazar's gaze was fixed on Miriam, his expression pained. "Pharaoh has summoned Doda to treat his boils." He turned to Moses. "I think it's a trap. She can't go."

Miriam crossed her room and grabbed his hand. He was trembling. "Come over here and sit down, boy. What are you talking—"

"No!" He pulled his hand away and pinned Moses with a stare.

"Months ago, I mentioned Doda to Ram. I know it's my fault she's in danger now, but you can stop this, Moses. Pharaoh and Kopshef are afraid of you. Neither will admit it, of course, but the king and all his officials are afraid of Yahweh and you as His prophet. If I tell Ramesses you won't allow Doda to come to the palace, Doda can stay here. She'll be safe."

Moses stood, his features softening. "Why do you think it's a trap? Perhaps Pharaoh simply wants Miriam to treat his boils."

"After you threw the soot this morning, I was ordered to follow you and find out when the plague would end and how to overcome Yahweh's power—or Ram would make me suffer as he was suffering." Miriam gasped, but Eleazar didn't acknowledge it. "When I returned having done neither, Ramesses ordered me to fetch my doda, the midwife who was Isis in the flesh."

"You see, dear." Miriam patted his hands, trying to calm him. "That's why he's summoned me. Pharaoh called me *Isis in the flesh* when I interpreted his nightmares."

"He has an army of physicians, Doda. He has no need for a Hebrew midwife."

Miriam waved away his nonsense. "I'm going." She began collecting herbs and balms into a shoulder bag.

"No, you can't." Eleazar turned his pleading to Moses. "Please, stop her. I can't lose her too."

"Yahweh will protect her." Moses stood firm.

"Like he protected Saba and Savta?"

The venom in his tone stilled Doda's hands. He was right. Yahweh could choose not to protect her. What if Yahweh let her die today? Fear weakened her knees, and black spots blurred her vision. A deep breath cleared her vision, and with it came a calming peace as she turned to face her nephew. "I don't want to die, but if Ramesses kills me today, it will be after I tell him of Yahweh's power and faithfulness. There is a purpose in everything Yahweh allows, boy."

Hur winked at her, his smile sending a lovely jolt of courage through her.

Desperate, Eleazar looked to his only remaining ally. "Taliah, please.

You, of all people, know the gods can't be trusted. Yahweh let Kopshef kill your abba and a thousand Hebrews. Why should we trust him to protect Doda—to protect anyone we love?"

"I don't know if Yahweh will protect Miriam," she said, "but Yahweh has done everything He promised, Eleazar. He keeps His word." She stepped forward, moving the soldier back. "Which is more than you've done."

Finished with her packing, Miriam shoved the bag into Eleazar's arms and grabbed her walking stick. Sattar was immediately at her side. She reached down to scratch behind his ears and motioned for him to stay. He whined and laid his ears back as she left—his version of arguing—but the journey to the palace complex was meant for Miriam and Eleazar alone. Her nephew needed to be reminded of a few things he seemed to have forgotten. Or perhaps told things he never knew.

Miriam nudged Eleazar out the door without a word.

He lagged behind at first, but she soon heard his footsteps shuffling behind her. "You must wait for me to escort you."

"I knew you'd catch up. Do you still have the bag?" She glanced over to be sure he carried it properly. The last thing they needed was to arrive with aloe gumming up the turmeric. "Let's address this nonsense about Yahweh's part in killing Putiel, Abba, and Ima."

"It's not nonsense. If your God is powerful enough to save them but chose not to, then isn't He responsible for their deaths?"

"It's not that simple, and you know it."

Eleazar's voice rose. "Why isn't it that simple? Yahweh caused the Nile to turn to blood, so Saba and Savta died of dehydration. Yahweh killed my grandparents. That's simple."

Miriam shook her head but didn't reply. Nothing she said would penetrate his heart right now. He was angry, scared, frustrated, and exhausted. He wasn't ready to listen. "I don't have all the answers, Eleazar. I don't even know all the questions. But I do know"—she remembered Hur's words that penetrated her angry heart—"God's presence is constant. When you stop fighting and flailing, you might just find Him waiting with some answers."

"I've had to fight my whole life." His gaze was fixed on the palace.

"And that's Yahweh's fault too? Couldn't your pain have something to do with human choice—you having to reap the consequences of others' poor decisions? Or perhaps some of your own poor choices?"

He lifted an eyebrow but didn't say a word. He didn't have to. She ached for the harsh life her boy had led.

"You have a wife now who loves you deeply, and you'll soon have a child, Eleazar. Will you cause your child to believe Yahweh is harsh because his abba chose to abandon him?"

Her words hit their mark. His nostrils flared, eyes misted. "I'm leaving them to save them. Kopshef hated Putiel with a singular passion. If he discovers Taliah is his daughter, he'll kill her. Prince Ram has caught me in one deception, and if he discovers I've hidden Taliah from him, he'll execute us both. Who will feed our child then?"

Miriam's heart flopped over in her chest. So Eleazar's aversion to Goshen was more than loyalty to Ram. He truly believed both his life and Taliah's would be forfeit if the royals discovered their marriage. "It seems you're more of a slave than the rest of us."

His brow furrowed, his patience growing thin. "I'm Prince Ram's personal guard. I have more freedom and power than many Egyptians."

"And yet Yahweh offers you *true* freedom. You said yourself the Egyptians were afraid of Him and of Moses. What makes you think Ram would dare touch you or Taliah if you were truly committed to Yahweh?"

Eleazar halted and grabbed her shoulders, eyes ablaze. "What makes you think I would ever be committed to a God who destroys a nation and sends boils to torture women and children?"

Startled, Miriam could only breathe her reply. "You mean the God who has seen our people tortured, raped, and murdered for four hundred years? The same God who has promised your freedom?"

"I never asked to be free." He released her and stared into the distance.

"And your ancestors never asked to be slaves." She nudged him, trying to ease his tension, but he wouldn't soften. So she snuggled against his side and wrapped her arms around his waist. "I love you with all my heart, Eleazar, but it saddens me that you insist on blaming God for the bad and taking credit for the good."

With a begrudging rumble, he squeezed her closer. "And it angers me that you attribute to Yahweh only the good and ignore His responsibility for the bad."

She looked up, still holding him tight. "I don't deny Yahweh lets bad things happen. We simply disagree on *why*."

He peered down, uncertainty knitting his brow. His hesitation spoke louder than all his questions. Finally, he gave in. "All right, Doda. Why does Yahweh let bad things happen to the ones we love?"

There it was—that tiny spark of searching. He was finally listening. *Yahweh, please give me something wise to say.* "I don't know the reasons bad things happen, but I know—because of all the good things that happen in between—that Yahweh has good reasons."

Eleazar shook his head and grinned, still unconvinced, but no longer contentious. They resumed their walk to the palace, lost in their own thoughts. Everything in creation needed a guiding force. Egypt had the Nile. Sailors had the stars. Miriam and her brothers had Yahweh. Eleazar must determine his. As long as he viewed Yahweh as the enemy or another capricious deity among Egypt's many gods, his course would never be steady.

They arrived at the palace complex under a shroud of silence. Eleazar brooding; Miriam praying.

The palace had changed dramatically since Miriam had visited four months ago. Eleazar escorted her directly to Pharaoh's private chamber, where two Nubian guards stopped him but invited Miriam in.

"I'm Prince Ram's guard," he said, panicked. "This is my doda. I must accompany her at all times."

The largest guard shoved Eleazar back. "Only the midwife." He grabbed Miriam's arm and roughly dragged her inside.

"My bag!" she said, reaching for the supplies Eleazar carried. The Nubian grabbed the bag and unceremoniously shut the door on Eleazar's protest.

Ramesses lay moaning on a large linen pad stuffed with wool. A dozen men—presumably his physicians—knelt around him, hands clasped, barely able to lift their heads. They too were in severe pain with their own festering wounds. This would never do.

"Out!" she said. "I'll treat the physicians after I treat Pharaoh."

Ramesses lifted a hand to wave them out, and she couldn't tell if they were relieved or resentful at her intrusion.

As Miriam reached for her supplies, she noticed the Nubian's face and chest were covered with boils. "I can soothe those wounds with the contents of my bag."

He dropped his eyes and kept his voice low. "Thank you. I'm sorry I couldn't let your nephew join you. You'll be safe with me."

She patted his arm in a spot where there were no boils. "I'm not afraid. Yahweh protects me, and He's bigger than you."

A slight grin creased the guard's lips before Ramesses's voice rumbled through the room. "There she is. Lady Isis in the flesh. Come to heal me."

Miriam rolled her eyes and coaxed the Nubian to follow her with the bag of supplies. "Don't be ridiculous, Ramesses. You know I'm not a goddess, and only Yahweh makes a seed grow into herbs." She arrived at his bedside and looked down on the boy who'd become a man—who then proclaimed himself a god. How entirely human he looked now. "Let's tend these nasty boils, dear."

38

*Then the LORD said to Moses, "Get up early
in the morning, confront Pharaoh and say
to him, 'This is what the LORD, the God of
the Hebrews, says: Let my people go, so that
they may worship me, or this time I will send
the full force of my plagues against you. . . .
At this time tomorrow I will send the worst
hailstorm that has ever fallen on Egypt, from
the day it was founded till now.' "*

—EXODUS 9:13–14, 18

Eleazar sat in the dust, legs splayed, leaning against the palace wall.
He'd watched the eastern sky transform from amethyst to deep
pink to the clear brilliance of another cloudless day. He'd sharpened
seven daggers, four spearheads, and Prince Ram's favorite sword. All of
them Hoshea's responsibilities. During the two months since Eleazar had
promised Taliah a divorce certificate, he'd undertaken Hoshea's morning
and evening duties while sending his apprentice to deliver Doda's rations.
He refused to be tortured by a wife he still loved, who carried a child he
could never raise. And why listen to Doda's heartfelt lectures about a God
no one understood?

Eleazar threw the last sharpened dagger across the wide alley, sinking
the blade into the doorpost of a stable. He wished it was Kopshef's head.
If it weren't for the crown prince, he might have a chance at being a husband. Kopshef's hatred for Hebrews increased with every plague, and
now that two months had passed since the boils, the crown prince had

time to plan his assault. "If we kill the Hebrews," he had said to Pharaoh last week, "their god will have no people to save."

"And who will build my cities and temples?" It was obvious Ramesses's patience had grown thin with the firstborn of his flesh, the best of his magicians—yet the most impotent and cowardly. "You, Kopshef? Will you bend your back from dawn until dusk, all day, every day? Will your wives and your children?"

Kopshef abandoned direct anti-Hebrew tactics and began more subtle methods, like driving a wedge between Prince Ram and his Hebrew bodyguard. In a week's time, Kopshef had paired Eleazar against a dozen Nubians in the circles of combat, taunting him, tempting him to lose control, which would shame his master and other Hebrews.

Approaching footsteps roused Eleazar from his brooding. Hoshea was late returning from Goshen this morning.

"Your doda Miriam wanted me to tell you that she's trained Sattar to steal a piece of dried fish from between her teeth." Hoshea chuckled. "She demonstrated. It's impressive."

Eleazar pushed himself to his feet, heart aching, but he couldn't let on. "That dog would chew off my face if I tried such a trick."

"He'd eat anyone's face but Miriam and Moses—and maybe Hur. Sattar likes Hur almost as much as Miriam does." Hoshea bounced his eyebrows.

"That's foolishness." Eleazar snorted. "Doda Miriam has never needed a man, and I refuse to get involved in her personal life." He poked Hoshea's chest. "Perhaps you should let Hur know that my only involvement would be killing him if he hurts her."

Hoshea chuckled again, no doubt thinking Eleazar was teasing. He wasn't.

"Come, Hoshea, we must get to the throne hall before the princes arrive."

They began their morning trek through the wide barracks hallway and up the ramp. Hoshea kept sucking air through his front teeth, an annoying tic only prevalent when he was nervous.

"What is it, Hoshea? Do you need to confess something?"

"Confess? Me? No, I don't need to conf—well, there is something . . ."

Eleazar waited, but Hoshea's hesitation began to unnerve him. "Just say it."

"Taliah wants to know why you haven't sent her the certificate of divorce, and she felt the baby kick for the first time."

The words tumbled out like boulders down a cliff, burying Eleazar under a mound of guilt. He stopped, grasping the side of the ramp to steady himself. Which was worse, the fact that she wanted the divorce or that he wasn't there to experience his child's new life?

"I'm sorry." Hoshea stood at a distance, head bowed.

"Never speak to me of Taliah's condition again. Do you hear me?"

"Yes, Commander."

"And you can tell her . . ." Eleazar took a breath. He hadn't asked Ithamar to write the divorce papers for fear that Kopshef or Ram would find out about Taliah. But how could he explain his caution without alarming her unnecessarily? "Tell her I'll send the papers when I'm ready."

Hoshea nodded but didn't look up. Why was he so timid? A new fear nearly stole Eleazar's breath. "Why is she in such a hurry for divorce papers?" Proof of Eleazar's abandonment would mean she'd be free to remarry. "Is there another man waiting to take my place?" He would kill any man who touched her.

Hoshea's head shot up, anger blazing like fiery arrows from his eyes. "Taliah won't even look at another man. She hardly smiles. Miriam makes her eat for the child's sake. She's broken, Eleazar. Is that what you want to hear?" He stormed toward the palace entry before Eleazar could answer.

They reached the throne hall in silence. Hoshea opened the ebony door, allowing his commander to enter first, but both men came to a breathless halt.

Moses stood alone before Pharaoh's throne; Kopshef and Ram standing on either side.

Shock gave way to fear, and fear gave way to curiosity. Eleazar and Hoshea hurried down the crimson carpet, and Eleazar leaned over to whisper, "Where's Abba Aaron?"

"I don't know. I didn't see him or Moses in Goshen when I delivered this morning's rations to Miriam."

The morning sun shone through the tall, narrow windows but hadn't yet reached the far edge of the room. No princes filled the gallery. No supplicants were present to offer petitions. There weren't even any scribes to record Moses's words.

As Eleazar and Hoshea approached, they heard Moses speaking, but it didn't sound like him. He spoke as the very voice of Yahweh. "By now I could have stretched out My hand and struck you and your people with a plague that would have wiped you off the earth. But I have raised you up, Pharaoh Ramesses, for this very purpose, that I might show you My power and that My name might be proclaimed in all the earth. You still set yourself against My people and will not let them go. Therefore, at this time *tomorrow* I will send the worst hailstorm that has ever fallen on Egypt, from the day it was founded till now."

At the pronouncement of another plague, Prince Ram shot a burning glare at Eleazar. For two months, Eleazar had forestalled disaster for the Hebrews by rebuilding his master's trust. He would not allow Moses—or Yahweh—to jeopardize it in a single morning. "Is there something we can do to avoid the plague?" Eleazar's voice echoed in the empty throne hall.

Startled, Moses turned to see Eleazar and Hoshea behind him. "Ramesses could let Israel leave Egypt."

"Never." Pharaoh's single word brought Moses's attention back to the throne.

"Then give an order now to bring your remaining livestock and slaves to a place of shelter. The hail will fall on every person and animal that is still out in the field, and they will die." Moses turned on his heel and brushed Eleazar's shoulder on his march out of the throne hall.

When Moses cleared the ebony doors, Eleazar pointed Hoshea in his direction and said loud enough for Pharaoh to hear, "Follow him. I want to know his every move. Report at midday, sunset, and at the moon's zenith." Hoshea bowed and hurried to obey.

"Well, Ram," Pharaoh said, rubbing his chin, "it appears your Hebrew has chosen sides wisely." He leaned forward, motioning Eleazar closer to the throne. "What do you suggest we do about Moses's latest prediction, Hebrew?"

Did he truly believe, or was he testing Eleazar? Kneeling on the first step of the dais, Eleazar bowed his head. "My king, I suggest we shelter every animal and servant before the hail comes tomorrow."

Silence drew out long and painful, but Eleazar kept his head bowed. If death was coming, let it come swiftly.

"And you, Kopshef, my crown prince," Pharaoh purred. "How do you suggest we handle Moses's threat?"

"Kill him. Kill every Hebrew that hides their animals under a shelter. It's the first plague in over two months. Their god is weakening, and Moses is grasping at the last dregs of his power."

The king's flail was suddenly hooked under Eleazar's chin, drawing his eyes upward. "What do you think, Hebrew? Is your god weakening in power, or will he strike back if I harm his messenger and his people?"

"I can't pretend to know the mind of a god, my king." Eleazar swallowed hard, and chose his next words carefully. "Of the stories I remember from childhood, the Hebrew God does not react kindly to those who challenge Him directly."

Ramesses's eyes narrowed to slits, his thoughts unreadable. He sighed and removed the flail from Eleazar's throat. "I will not bow to this god's threats by ordering animals and people to cower from a hailstorm that may not come. If his god's power is waning as Kopshef believes, the hail will not come, and we'll kill Moses—*tomorrow.*" He chuckled at his wit, but Eleazar saw no humor in the recurring theme of delayed retribution and rescue.

"Leave me." Pharaoh waved them away like the gnats of months ago. "Kopshef, tell the chief scribe to cancel court today." He rose from the throne and skulked toward his private exit.

Kopshef glared at Eleazar. "I'd rather kill all of you and be done with it."

Ram stepped in front of his guard. "I believe you have a message to deliver to the chief scribe." The brothers stood in silent challenge before Kopshef stalked off.

Eleazar released the breath he was holding and waited for orders from his master. Prince Ram said nothing, but turned and walked toward the exit. Eleazar followed him into the prince's wing, remaining silent until they reached his private chamber. When Eleazar stopped beside the door to stand guard, Ram spoke quietly, keeping his eyes on the floor. "Do you believe in this god, Eleazar? Is the hail coming?"

Such simple questions, but they sent Eleazar's heart into a race with his thoughts. Did he believe? If he did, why was he living in this palace instead of with his wife and doda? If he didn't believe, why did he feel so certain they should bring in the livestock and servants? Many lives counted on his answer.

"Yes, my prince. Yahweh is real, and we should shelter every animal and servant you own."

"Make it happen," Ram said.

Eleazar nodded as Ram closed the door, and then he hurried to the stables to begin warning the herdsmen and servants to shelter Prince Ram's property before dawn tomorrow.

39

Throughout Egypt hail struck everything in the fields—both people and animals; it beat down everything growing in the fields and stripped every tree. The only place it did not hail was the land of Goshen, where the Israelites were.

—EXODUS 9:25–26

Miriam awoke when the earth beneath her shuddered. Sattar snuggled closer, whining. A long and violent roll of thunder shook the long house, and flashes of lightning shone brighter than the midday sun.

"It's happening just as Yahweh said." Taliah's voice was full of wonder, and not a trace of sleep lingered. During the past two months, she had soaked up every ancient story of Yahweh like dry ground drinks the inundation. "Is it safe to watch from the rooftop?"

"It's safe. Not a pebble of hail or a drop of rain will fall in Goshen." Moses spoke from the curtained doorway, staff in hand. "But this is only the beginning of Yahweh's full fury of plagues that will break Pharaoh's will. When I stretched out my staff toward the sky as Yahweh commanded, the hailstones began battering the city, the fields, and the river. It's awesome—and terrible." His face was ashen.

Hur shoved aside the adjoining curtain, eyes wide. "I've never felt the ground shake like this."

Miriam pushed to her feet, knees and back creaking, and offered the men her mat. "Come, you two. Sit down." She poured cups full of watered wine, while Taliah spread generous portions of soft goat cheese on last night's bread.

More thunder shook the long house, while lightning provided an almost continuous glow through the window. Taliah crouched beside Moses. "Am I awful to be curious? I want to see God's newest wonder for myself."

"It's not awful to desire to witness Yahweh's power, but none of us will take delight in the wrath that is to come." Moses rested his head against the wall, staring at the ceiling. "Eleazar will come soon to summon me to Pharaoh."

Taliah shot a panicked glance at Miriam and then back to Moses. "Eleazar? What about the hail? Is it safe for him to come?"

Moses looked at them then, a slight grin replacing his despair. "We'll know soon enough." His answer did little to stem the fear growing in Miriam's belly.

Taliah hesitated, the stormy emotions on her face rivaling the weather in the city. "I don't want to see him, but I can't stay away if he's braving this storm." She rushed out, Miriam, Hur, and Moses close behind. They joined the crowd already gathering on the path leading to Rameses.

Heaps of ashes from burned livestock carcasses glowed eerie lavender in the unearthly light of the storm. All brick making had ceased after the plague on Egypt's livestock. The slaves were needed to process the hides of the dead cattle, spin the wool of the sheep and goats, and burn the remaining carcasses. Now deadman's land overlooked the charred remains of Egypt's prized stables, and Goshen was stripped of its animal supply to put milk and meat on noblemen's tables.

"Will the hail kill the rest of Egypt's livestock?" Miriam breathed the question to no one.

Several observers peered over their shoulders, but none answered. There were no answers, only God's terrible majesty on Israel's behalf. If it hadn't been so devastating, it would have been beautiful. Lightning flashed. Thunder rolled, as hailstones the size of onions and small melons crashed to the earth. And like an invisible shield, God cupped His hands around the villages of Goshen. Not a pebble of hail or a flash of lightning touched the ground.

"Astounding," whispered a Hebrew man.

"How can it be?" an Egyptian peasant asked Miriam. "Why would your God include us in His mercy?"

Miriam paused, wishing she knew the whole answer but praying her partial understanding would suffice. "We have seen the distinction He made today, and together we've learned about His nature. Yahweh sometimes extends mercy to those who haven't asked, but it is His way alone that leads to deliverance."

Taliah's student, Masud, ran to the man who spoke and wiggled into his embrace. Miriam realized it must have been the boy's father, and her heart squeezed in her chest. *Oh Yahweh, please work in Masud's family to believe. These children have become so precious to Taliah.*

"Someone's coming from the palace!" One of those staring at the hail pointed to a large metal object moving toward them in the distance.

Miriam felt Hur's presence behind her. He placed his hand at the small of her back and leaned over her shoulder. "Is it Eleazar as Moses predicted?"

Was her heart pounding because of Hur's touch or the knowledge that it was almost certainly Eleazar beneath those storm-beaten Egyptian shields? "I'm sure it's him."

"Oh Miriam, look at the dents in those shields." The concern in Hur's voice matched her own. He immediately bowed his head, and his lips began moving in silent prayer. This good and godly man captured her heart a bit tighter.

Taliah rested a hand on her slightly rounded belly and watched the metal cocoon draw nearer. A reverent hum spread over the crowd as some whispered prayers and others wondered if the shields would last until they reached Goshen's clear skies.

Two sets of sandals peeked from beneath shields held above and around the visitors. When they reached the edge of Rameses's industrial section, they crossed into the calm of Goshen, unscathed. They let the battered shields fall from their hands and unstrapped others from their backs. Eleazar and Hoshea stood in silent awe, gawking at the raging storm only steps behind them.

A mighty cheer rose from the gathered crowd, and without thinking, Miriam turned and hugged Hur. He lifted her off her feet, laughing as they rejoiced together.

When he set her back down, his light-brown eyes sparkled. "I'd like to kiss you, but this time it wouldn't be from Yahweh."

Miriam stepped back, the declaration seeming utterly inappropriate, but before she could scold, he laughed and announced, "But I'll wait for my kiss until Yahweh frees us from Egypt." He clapped his hands and joined the cheering crowd, while Miriam tried to refocus on Yahweh's miracle.

Eleazar and Hoshea met the crowd and were greeted like conquering heroes. Slaves and peasants alike chattered and patted their backs, lauding their bravery in making the harrowing journey. Men inspected the shields that had been battered and torn by the large hailstones and the wind that had hurled them. By the time Eleazar spotted Miriam, he was near panic. "Pharaoh summons Moses and Abba to the palace. Now!"

Taliah was among the throng trying to reach Eleazar and Hoshea. Too late, Miriam saw her stumble and fall. He must have noticed her at the same time because he shoved three men and two women out of the way to get to his wife.

Eleazar scooped her into his arms, his face ashen, and Miriam could only read his lips over the noise. "Are you all right?" Taliah buried her head against his chest in reply.

Hoshea ran toward Aaron's village, undoubtedly in a hurry to collect him for their return to the palace. Moses, Miriam, and Hur trailed behind Eleazar as he carried Taliah to the long house. Sattar cleared a path for them through the crowd.

As soon as Eleazar entered Miriam's doorway, Taliah wriggled out of his arms. "I'm fine." She stumbled, and he tried to steady her, but she jerked away. "Don't," she said, eyes blazing.

An awkward silence settled over the room. Miriam saw crimson creeping up Eleazar's neck. "I thought you were hurt. I'm sorry."

Taliah set her jaw. "Are you injured from the hail?"

"No." Eleazar's voice was barely a whisper. He stared at her rounded belly. "I thought you were hurt."

"You said that already." Taliah swiped at her tears and raised her chin. "If Pharaoh summoned Moses and your abba, you should go."

Eleazar cast a pleading glance at Miriam, and she saw the war raging in his soul. What was she supposed to do? He was a grown man. "You always have a choice, Eleazar, but it's not just you who lives with the consequences anymore."

"What am I to do, Doda? Tell Ram and Kopshef I've been married to Putiel's daughter for nearly five months and let them kill her?"

Taliah gasped, covering her mouth with a trembling hand.

Eleazar cursed, squeezed his eyes shut. "I didn't want you to know." He opened his eyes and reached for Taliah, but she drew back. Clenching his teeth, Eleazar's jaw muscle danced. "Yahweh has left me no choice. If I show the slightest disloyalty to Ram now, if the royals discover I've deceived them by marrying Putiel's daughter, we'll all be executed." He turned to Miriam. "I'm more of a slave than anyone. Remember, Doda?" In three strides he'd nearly cleared the doorway. "Come, Moses. Pharaoh is waiting."

Moses brushed Taliah's cheek on his way past, and she fell into Miriam's arms.

"Eleazar loves you, dear." Miriam patted her back. "If Yahweh can deliver Israel from the most powerful nation on earth, He can certainly deliver Eleazar from Pharaoh's vindictive sons."

Hoshea arrived with Abba Aaron as Eleazar exited the long house. "What's wrong?" A single look at Eleazar's sullen expression seemed answer enough for his young friend. "I'll keep three of the battered shields to protect your abba and me. You take four to cover you and Moses,"

It was then that Moses emerged from the long house, issuing a glare at Eleazar. "Let's go." He didn't pause to receive his shields or instructions on protecting himself. The eighty-year-old marched toward the city like a foot soldier on his first mission.

Eleazar grabbed his shoulder. "Wait. You can't walk into the hailstorm unprotected."

Whirling on his nephew, Moses's eyes flashed. "I'm never unprotected, boy. If you would put your shields down, perhaps you'd witness Yahweh's spectacular power on your behalf." He was referring to more than a hailstorm, and Eleazar knew it. Without waiting for a response, Moses resumed his march.

Eleazar threw down his shields and jogged to catch up. "Fine, but we'll both be dead before we reach the winery."

"If you believed that, you wouldn't have dropped your shields." Moses kept his eyes on the palace, his arms and legs pumping.

Abba Aaron kept one shield but finally dropped it when he couldn't keep stride while carrying it. Hoshea also dropped his shields and let out a howl about three steps from the storm. The Egyptians were silent in battle. Hoshea evidently refused to die like an Egyptian.

The four men met the storm in perfect stride, each crossing into the city with their right feet. Eleazar expected the immediate impact of the first icy boulder—but it didn't come. Nor did it come with the second step or the tenth. He realized he'd closed his eyes, so he opened them and saw a handbreadth of space around them was repelling hailstones. Hoshea and Abba marched on Moses's left and Eleazar on his right. The four men stayed in tight formation and walked gingerly through the palace gates to the astonished stares of the guards inside the parapets.

The farther they walked, the faster Eleazar's heart beat. "Pharaoh planned to kill you if the hailstorm didn't come," he said to Moses as they climbed the palace ramp.

"Pharaoh tried to kill me before." Moses's lips curved into a mischievous grin. "It didn't work forty years ago, and it won't work now." He looked at his companions. "God has other plans for me—and for all of you."

They reached the grand ebony doors, and for the first time, Eleazar didn't want to go in. He would have preferred to return to Goshen with

Moses and beg Taliah's forgiveness, to forget Prince Ram, to wait in the relative quiet of Doda Miriam's long house for Israel's deliverance. Yahweh was real. Would He really protect Eleazar? Would He protect Taliah? Eleazar needed time to think, time to consider all the possibilities. But here they stood at the throne hall, and Pharaoh waited.

Eleazar opened the heavy door. The princes were seated in their gallery and all Pharaoh's officials lined both sides of the crimson carpet. Prince Kopshef stood at Pharaoh's right hand, Prince Ram at his left.

As the Hebrews began their first steps onto the carpet, Pharaoh raised his voice. "This time I have sinned, Moses." He paused until the four men reached the edge of the tapestry and stood directly before the throne. Then Pharaoh held out his hands in contrition. "The Lord is in the right, and I and my people are in the wrong. Pray to the Lord, for we have had enough thunder and hail."

Moses's expression remained placid. "What about Yahweh's command to let His people leave Egypt?"

"I will let you go," Ramesses said too quickly. "You don't have to stay any longer."

Prince Kopshef descended the dais and met Moses face to face. "My father asks you to pray. He has agreed to your demand." He rested his hand on his short sword. "Pray, Hebrew."

Eleazar glimpsed a slight grin on Prince Ram's face and felt dread twist in his belly. He reached behind Moses and squeezed his waist, hoping he'd realize something was desperately wrong.

Moses politely but confidently stepped around Prince Kopshef and addressed Pharaoh. "When I have gone out of the city, I will pray to Yahweh. He will stop the thunder and hail so you may know the whole earth obeys our Hebrew God." He stepped back and met Kopshef's sneer. "I know that you and your officials still don't fear my God, but you should. This plague only destroyed Egypt's flax and barley. Since wheat and spelt ripen later, there's still time for you to release my people before Egypt is completely ruined."

"Get out." Kopshef ground out the words between clenched teeth and then shouted, "Guards!" Abba Aaron jumped as if he'd been bitten by a viper, but Moses stood like granite as the crown prince announced their fate. "Escort Eleazar to the king's prison. His apprentice will escort Moses and his brother to the edge of the city to pray." He turned to Hoshea. "Make sure the hail stops before you release them, or you'll share a cell with your trainer."

40

Miriam, Hur, and Taliah stood among the crowd at the eastern edge of Goshen, watching the hail continue to pummel the city as dawn turned into day. Clouds shrouded the sun, making it impossible to judge how long since Eleazar and Hoshea had taken Moses and Aaron to the palace, and the storm raged on, building rather than declining in strength. Tortured cries competed with sounds of thunder, while field slaves, forced by their Egyptian masters, ran into the pelting hail to herd cattle, goats, and sheep into shelters. But it was too late. Miriam wondered why the Egyptians hadn't sheltered them yesterday when Moses warned them. Why must more Hebrew slaves die because they lived in the city with their masters? *Why, Yahweh?*

Miriam tried not to question as the devastation mounted. She should be thankful, standing in the safety of Goshen's protective boundaries, but what about the bodies of dead slaves and animals strewn over the fields, battered and covered by the giant balls of ice? Sheets of rain swept across fields of barley and flax in bloom. Would the dikes hold, or would the Nile overflow its banks? How completely would Yahweh protect them? Just to the border of Goshen? Or would His protection travel with them when they were set free?

Hur's arm slipped around her waist as he pointed toward the city with his other arm. "They're coming. See?" Each flash of lightning illuminated an unnatural bubble of calm moving through the swirling rain and hail.

"Moses!" someone yelled. "Here come Moses and Aaron!"

Miriam nudged her way to the front of the crowd and saw Hoshea leading her two brothers home.

"Eleazar." Taliah stood at her right shoulder. "Why isn't he with them?"

Miriam reached for her hand and waited in silence until the three men reached Goshen. Elisheba was there to greet Aaron. Even Nadab and Abihu embraced their abba when he stepped over the threshold of Goshen's safe haven.

Moses's countenance was more troubled on his return than when he'd left, and Miriam's heart sank. "What is it? What's wrong?"

"Prince Kopshef ordered Eleazar to Pharaoh's prison."

"No!" Taliah stifled a cry.

Moses immediately closed his eyes and lifted his hands to Yahweh. No words spoken, only Moses's silent tears petitioned Yahweh for reprieve. In the blink of an eye, the thunder and hail stopped, and the rain no longer poured down on the land. A collective gasp brought Moses's hands down.

With tears still wet on his cheeks, Moses turned to Hoshea. "I don't know what Kopshef will do to you if you return to the palace. You could stay here in Goshen . . ."

The young apprentice stood tall and lifted his chin. "How could I tell Eleazar to trust Yahweh and return to Goshen if I can't trust Yahweh and return to the palace?" Hoshea met each one's eyes—Moses, Hur, Miriam, and finally, Taliah. "I'll find out what's happened to Eleazar and bring back word." He turned and ran toward the ruins of what was once the world's richest kingdom.

Without barley, how could Egyptians make beer and bread to feed themselves? Without flax, how could they make linen to clothe the nations? Food and commerce destroyed in one short morning—and all of this, Yahweh said, was only the beginning of the full force of His plagues.

Miriam squeezed Taliah's hand and smiled, trying to instill courage she didn't feel. *Please, Yahweh, use some of Your power to protect our Eleazar.*

✿✿✿✿✿

Eleazar waited for the next sting of the whip. *Snap!* He sucked in a breath but refused to cry out. How many lashes had there been? He'd lost count at twenty-four.

"You told Moses we planned to kill him, didn't you?" Ram leaned in close, his breath smelling of leeks and garlic.

"Yes." How many times must Eleazar confess?

"You told him we'd kill him in the throne hall as soon as he prayed for the hail to stop, didn't you?"

"No." They'd been over this. Before the beating started.

Eleazar had told Moses they planned to kill him if the hail didn't come, but he hadn't known they planned to kill him in the throne hall if he prayed immediately and stopped the hail. What idiot decided on that strategy?

Another lash. Had he spoken his thoughts aloud?

"You're lying, Hebrew." Kopshef shouted from behind him and brought the whip down again. "Why did Moses insist on waiting to pray in Goshen unless you warned him of our plans?"

Eleazar's tongue felt swollen, his lips cut and bleeding. "He thinks strategies . . . like a soldier . . ."

"You belligerent . . ." Kopshef's voice drew near. "I know how a soldier thinks." Ram stepped between them, warding off further abuse.

He could hear the brothers struggling, fighting, but Eleazar couldn't see them. His arms were bound above his head, forcing his eyes forward. He'd seen only the dirty, torchlit walls of this cell for most of the day, perhaps into the night. Time was irrelevant in Pharaoh's prison. Would he ever leave, or had he seen Taliah for the last time?

Eleazar heard a *crack!* and then a hard thud. Someone had landed on the floor. "Sit there until you can think like the soldier you claim to be

rather than the worthless high priest of Ptah!" Ram said, standing behind Eleazar, his heavy, uneven breaths testimony to Kopshef's improved
fighting skills. "I don't know why Father listened to you and changed his
mind anyway. It's ridiculous to kill Moses when it's the Hebrew god that's
destroying us. We should be working toward a solution instead of angering this god further."

The other guards stood like statues; none offered comment or aid to
the quarrelsome princes. A scraping sound on the dust signaled Kopshef's
rise to his feet. "All right, Brother, what do you suggest? Invite Moses to
banquet at Pharaoh's table?"

Ram suddenly appeared with a cup of water and held it to Eleazar's
lips. Drinking deeply, Eleazar let the cool liquid bathe his aching body,
inside and out.

"Don't drink too quickly." Ram set aside the cup and motioned for
two guards' assistance as he untied Eleazar's hands and helped him sit on
the packed-dirt floor. He grabbed Kopshef's whip, coiled the thinly
braided papyrus in his hand, and tilted Eleazar's chin with the handle. "I
believe you, Eleazar. I don't think you knew we planned to kill your uncle
in the throne hall, but I'm offended that you warned him about our plan
if the hail didn't come. That's a breach in loyalty, my Hebrew friend."

"Does it help that I didn't tell him until after the hail came?"

Kopshef kicked his left side, and Eleazar felt a rib snap. Spots danced
before his eyes as he clung to consciousness.

Ram shoved his brother away. "What matters is finding the Hebrew
god's weakness." He glared at Kopshef. "You said every god has limita-
tions, so Eleazar must help us find Yahweh's."

Consistency certainly seemed a weakness. Why had Yahweh protected him from the killing hail to let him be beaten to death in prison?
What was the point?

"So you'll be our eyes and ears in the villages," Ram was saying. He
looked at Eleazar with raised brows, waiting for an answer.

Mind cloudy from blood loss, dehydration, and pain, Eleazar could
only stare.

Kopshef came at him again, but Ram held him back and nodded at one of the guards. The man signaled someone behind Eleazar. The sounds of doors opening and closing preceded scuffling feet—and then Hoshea stood before him, bound and looking terrified.

Eleazar, suddenly alert, focused on Ram. "What do you want?"

"You will continue your duties as my personal guard during the day, but you will return to Goshen each night, living with your uncle and gleaning information about his god. Your apprentice will serve me while you're in Goshen. Each morning, you'll report on your findings. If your reports displease me, your apprentice will suffer for your incompetence."

Hoshea met Eleazar's gaze, courage replacing his fear. The boy had made it clear through both word and action that he would die for Yahweh—but he need not suffer for Eleazar.

Struggling to his feet, Eleazar stepped toward Ram and drew the restraint of two guards. "I will learn about the Hebrew God, but you need not harm the boy."

Ram leaned forward, spitting the words at his guard. "I've given you this assignment before with no results." He looked over his shoulder, signaling Kopshef, who buried his fist in Hoshea's belly. "This time, you *will* find Yahweh's weakness and report back to me."

41

Surely I spoke of things I did not understand,
things too wonderful for me to know.

—Job 42:3

Miriam, Moses, and Hur sat around their small mat for the evening meal and shoved morsels of food around their wooden plates. No one was hungry. Earlier in the day, when the slave drivers raided their village for Hebrews to replace the house slaves killed in the storm, they'd hidden Taliah on the roof. Women had been taken from their children, screaming, to live and serve in Egyptian households—never to return to Goshen. Men, too, were taken, but most husbands were allowed to return home in the evenings. Masters used only women to warm their beds.

"When did Taliah eat last?" Hur broke the long silence.

Miriam tried to recall. "I think we ate a little something after Eleazar and Hoshea left with Moses."

"Should I go get her?" Moses asked. "Or maybe take up some cucumber and melon? They may sweep for more replacements tomorrow. Taliah should stay on the roof for a few days."

The sound of heavy footsteps outside their doorway silenced them all. A burly Egyptian guard slapped the curtain aside and entered, inspecting the interior. His eyes landed on Moses. "Do you live here?"

The few dates Miriam had eaten felt as though they might reappear. She swallowed hard, exchanging a terrified glance with Hur.

Moses stood, meeting the guard eye to eye. "I live here."

"Your nephew will live with you from now on."

A second guard, a large Nubian who matched Eleazar's size and wore the royal guards' dress armor, helped Eleazar through the doorway. Lowering Eleazar gently to his knees, the Nubian turned his attention to Miriam. "His ribs are broken on the left side. Wrap his chest tightly, and then don't try to move him tonight."

Eleazar lay facedown, struggling to breathe, his fingers digging into the dirt. Miriam met the Nubian's gaze, surprised to see caring eyes and a compassionate nod. "Thank you," she whispered, not wanting to draw attention to the man's kindness.

The first guard threw Eleazar's breast piece and arm bands at him, all of which landed on his wounded back. Eleazar cried out, and the guard smirked. "He'll need to be in full-dress armor when he reports to the throne hall for duty in the morning." Both guards disappeared through the doorway into the night without a backward glance.

Moses pulled the curtain closed after making sure they were gone, while Hur and Miriam hurried to collect the needed supplies. Whipping wounds covered Eleazar's back from his neck to his ankles, but it was his wheezing and labored breathing that was most concerning.

"We must get you on your knees, my boy," she said through tears. "Can you—"

Without further coaxing, her brave soldier began the arduous process of pressing his bulk up to his hands and knees. Hur helped, but if Moses was nearby, she didn't see him.

Miriam looked behind her and found him standing over them, trembling with rage. "Which one did this, Ram or Kopshef?"

Eleazar drew a wheezing breath. "I've been ordered to live with you as a spy"—he drew another breath—"to find Yahweh's weakness and report it to Ram." He coughed and cried out, holding his left side. "Or they'll do this, or worse, to Hoshea."

"Adonai, help us." Hur prayed quietly as he slopped honey on the bandages for Eleazar's wounds.

Moses knelt beside his nephew, teeth clenched in barely controlled rage. "Yahweh has no weaknesses, but He most certainly will not let them kill Hoshea."

Eleazar shook his head doubtfully, as if words were too costly.

"Are you sure, Moses? Don't say it if you're not certain." Miriam's hands shook on the bandages she began winding around Eleazar's torso. Hur took the bandages from her as Moses pulled her into a tight embrace. Helpless to withstand the men's tenderness, Miriam released the sobs she'd held captive all day. "How can we know when Yahweh will protect us and when He'll welcome tragedy into our house? Why did He protect Eleazar from the hail and then allow this?"

Hur finished wrapping Eleazar's ribs while Moses held Miriam. How foolish she felt. The prophetess of Israel, weeping like a spoiled child in her brother's arms.

Moses laid his cheek atop her head and waited to speak until her emotions calmed. "Our trust in Yahweh grows like trust in any other. The better we know Him, the more we can trust Him. But because He is a Being beyond our knowing, His ways will always be beyond our understanding. That's where trust and faith divide." He kissed her head and tilted her chin to capture her gaze. "Even when I can't trust Him, I can have faith in the fathomless God of Abraham, Isaac, and Jacob, whose power and promise work for the *eternal* good of His people."

Eleazar lifted an eyebrow in challenge. "This beating did not feel like Yahweh was working for my good."

"You're home, aren't you?" Moses grinned. "And I said 'eternal good,' Eleazar. Yahweh is more interested in you knowing Him than pleasing yourself—or even pleasing others." He released Miriam and scooted close to his nephew. "Have you even considered what Yahweh has done for you, boy?"

"He let Kopshef nearly kill me!" Eleazar grabbed his side, the shout punishing.

"What if Yahweh used this beating to send you back to Goshen so you could be a husband and father again?"

Moses's words gained Eleazar's attention. His eyes narrowed as he pondered the possibility.

"Perhaps Ram's command to discover Yahweh's weakness will be the key that unlocks Yahweh's power for you."

The roof cap scraped before Eleazar could respond, and Taliah peered through the opening, gasping when she saw him. She began a hurried climb down the ladder. "What happened?" she asked, nudging Moses aside to kneel in front of her husband.

Eleazar, still on hands and knees, spoke just above a whisper. "I've come home, wife. I won't ever leave you again."

Hur reached for Eleazar's right arm. "Let's get you settled on your stomach so we can treat the rest of your wounds." Moses hurried to support his left side as the gentle giant lay facedown on Miriam's sleeping mat.

Taliah stood aside, waiting, watching, seemingly hesitant to draw near to her husband.

Eleazar noticed too. "Aren't you pleased I've come home?" His voice was small, like a child's.

"Why did you really come home, Eleazar?"

Miriam exchanged a glance with Hur. The truth would sound worse than a lie, but he couldn't deceive her.

Eleazar released a shuddering sigh while Miriam and Hur began treating the open wounds on his legs. "Prince Ram sent me back to Goshen to live with Moses so I could discover how to stop the plagues. I'm to report my findings every morning, and if what I've discovered doesn't please Ram, they'll do this to Hoshea."

Taliah stood behind Miriam, so she couldn't see the girl's face. The silence was almost as excruciating as Eleazar's pain. He gripped the sleeping mat and sucked in air as they poured turmeric powder and honey directly into the wounds. Still Taliah remained quiet, unmoving. What was she thinking?

"All done with the herbs, boy." Miriam pressed a calming hand to his head, the only place without a whipping wound. "Now the bandages."

He propped his chin on his fist and turned toward his wife. "Why were you on the roof when the guards brought me home?"

She sniffed. "Miriam hid me because the slave drivers came looking for young Hebrew women today."

Eleazar's chin trembled as he turned to Moses. "I suppose you'd attribute that to Yahweh's protection."

Moses grinned. "I no longer believe in coincidence."

"It's good to know I'm not the only one struggling to believe in Yahweh's protection." Eleazar looked up at Miriam. "Taliah should remain on the roof for a while, day and night—"

"But I've got classes to tea—"

Moses lifted his hand to silence her. "Eleazar is right. We don't know how long they'll be looking for replacement slaves for the city."

Eleazar buried his face in his hands. "When my wounds are healed, I'll sleep in the adjoining room with Moses and Hur."

Everyone waited in silence for Taliah to object. She didn't. Instead, she walked to the ladder, climbed it, and closed the roof cap without a word.

42

*If you refuse to let them go, I will bring
locusts into your country tomorrow. They
will cover the face of the ground so that it
cannot be seen. They will devour what little
you have left after the hail, including every
tree that is growing in your fields.*

—EXODUS 10:4–5

Miriam pulled the last rounds of bread from their small clay oven and tossed them in the basket to share. Hur poured camel's milk in five clay cups, Eleazar dispensed the boiled goose eggs, and Taliah passed the basket of dried figs to Moses. Their household was among the few with enough for two meals a day.

It had been a month since the hail had destroyed more livestock, the barley, and the flax. Once again Pharaoh had taken from Goshen to provide for his palace and noblemen's tables. Rather than blaming Moses for their plight, neighbors continued to bring gifts to Yahweh's messenger. Moses, knowing the givers' poverty and hunger, always offered a gift in return which was often accepted with humble thanks. Israel's deliverer was gaining favor with his fellow Hebrews and the Egyptians, who were realizing just how crazed Ramesses had become.

"What will you tell Ram of Yahweh this morning?" Moses popped a fig into his mouth and passed the basket to Eleazar. It had become a morning ritual, this quizzing of Yahweh knowledge.

"Well, I can't tell him the story you told me last night. Abraham's willingness to offer up Sarah's firstborn, Isaac, would not bode well with Ram."

Taliah shifted in her seat, anxious to interject as always. "But isn't that exactly what Ram wants? He'll perceive Yahweh as illogical and therefore weak." She hadn't skipped a single chance to debate about Israel's God. It was as if she thrived on it.

"Ram might think Yahweh weak at the moment, but when Moses announces the final plague . . ." Eleazar shot an accusing glance at his uncle but let the air crackle with his unfinished thought.

"What final plague?" Taliah asked the question burning in Miriam.

Moses, looking distinctly uncomfortable, heaved a deep sigh. "When I left Midian, while I was on my way to Egypt, Yahweh said Israel was like His firstborn, and because Pharaoh had so mistreated His firstborn and refused to let us go . . ." He dropped his gaze and then spoke quietly. "He will kill Pharaoh's firstborn."

Miriam heard her heartbeat pounding in her ears. *Kill Pharaoh's firstborn?* "Which one?"

Moses lifted his hand, forestalling more questions. "I don't know any more than that. You know how the plagues have been. Yahweh tells me some details but seldom a full description. He told Aaron and me to use the staff for the first three plagues but didn't bother to inform us that the Egyptian magicians would duplicate the plagues with their dark arts." He kicked his plate, sending wine and food flying.

The room grew silent in the wake of Moses's uncharacteristic outburst. Miriam laid a hand on his arm. "What is this about, Brother?"

He wiped both hands down his face and then looked up at those he loved. "I'm the abba of a firstborn son, Miriam. I know what losing him would do to me." He pointed to Taliah's belly and pinned Eleazar with a stare. "Your firstborn may be a boy. What if he was killed because of *your* stubborn pride and disbelief?" He pulled his hands through his hair and expelled a deep breath, regaining a measure of calm. "Ramesses will not let us go for a simple three-day journey into the wilderness, and because of his prideful resistance, he will lose his wealth, his power, and his sons."

Eleazar's features clouded. "Don't tell me you feel sorry for him." He looked to Hur and Miriam for answers, but they remained silent. His anger returned to Moses. "How can you feel pity for a madman?"

Moses raised his head slowly, his features drawn and weary. "It's more than pity, Eleazar. I'm angry at his obstinance. Confused by his stupidity. And I'm ashamed that he calls himself the son of my friend Sety."

Moses began tidying the mess he'd made, blowing dust off bread and dates. Miriam stilled his hands. "Go. Take Sattar to the palm tree and talk to Yahweh."

He paused, deep sadness in his eyes. "Yahweh has already spoken, Miriam. Aaron and I will pronounce the eighth plague to Pharaoh today. Locusts will cover the land tomorrow and destroy what's left of the crops and vegetation. The Egypt my friend Sety left to his son will be unrecognizable."

Moses's words summoned the images of Ramesses's nightmare, and she turned to Eleazar. "Yahweh is the invisible force that cut off the ten toes of Sety's statue until it toppled over and shattered into a million pieces."

Moses looked perplexed, but Eleazar nodded. "Doda was summoned to interpret Ramesses's nightmare shortly before Abba and Hoshea left to meet you in the wilderness. We're seeing the dreams fulfilled."

"What can we do to prepare?" Miriam sat back on her knees and took Moses's hand.

His shoulders visibly lifted as if her words shared the burden. "You and Hur organize the elders. Taliah, talk to the Hebrew children. Harvest everything from our Hebrew gardens today—even if it's not quite ready. Onions, cucumbers, garlic, leeks, herbs, melons, figs, wheat—everything. Nothing green will survive the army of locusts coming tomorrow."

"We can't harvest all of it." Miriam glanced at Taliah who would help her organize the women. She was strong but nearly six months pregnant. "And what will we do with everything? We don't have room to store it all."

"Dry it," Moses said. "Wrap it. Prepare it for our journey to God's Promised Land. Pharaoh still thinks I'm asking for a three-day journey, but when he finally drives us out, it will be forever." He pushed to his feet and offered a hand to Eleazar. "You can escort me to your abba Aaron's long house and then to the palace. We'll concoct a convincing weakness to report to Ram before I declare to Pharaoh God's coming power."

Hoshea pressed his forehead against his sleeping mat as Eleazar tended fresh wounds. "Aahh! Are you scrubbing my back with hyssop branches?"

"I'm sorry. We have only wool bandages since the palace confiscated all linen for trade."

Ram had beaten Hoshea every day for the past two weeks since the plague of locusts began. The army of insects had come with the east wind in a single night, and by morning the ground had undulated with them. They weren't just creeping, crawling creatures, but messengers of destruction that devoured every green sprig and growing fruit in Egypt. When Pharaoh summoned Moses to plead for Yahweh's deliverance, a mighty west wind caught up the locusts and swept away all hope with them.

Egypt was ruined, and Ram meted out his frustration on poor Hoshea.

The boy's back looked like the braided reeds Ram used to whip him, fresh wounds crisscrossing the partially healed ones. Though the prince usually alternated Hoshea's beatings in method and location—some days a cudgel to the belly, other days a whip to the back—today, the prince had discovered from Hebrew spies that Goshen was hoarding dried vegetables, fruits, and grains that they'd harvested before the locust attack. Ram had decided to make a spectacle of Hoshea's beating, tying him to a whipping post in the armory so every military slave under Eleazar's command could watch.

And he'd told them it was Eleazar's fault. Perhaps he should have told Ram about the dried food, but would it have spared Hoshea a beating? No. Clearly, nothing Eleazar said now made a difference.

"All the men hate Ram, you know." Hoshea sniffed, and Eleazar knew he was crying. "Even the Hittites respect your strength, Eleazar. They know your loyalty is to your people and our God. Every slave soldier under your command would turn on Ram after the way he's treated us."

Eleazar clenched his teeth against the ache in his chest. "My actions aren't about strength or loyalty. They're about protecting my wife and child."

Eleazar spread more honey and dried henna on a bandage before placing it on another long stripe on Hoshea's back. They no longer had the luxury of pouring out honey or using full henna leaves. The healing supplies had dwindled from the plagues.

"I suppose something good has come from all this." Hoshea spoke quietly, laying his cheek on his hands.

Eleazar tried to chuckle, but the effort sounded brittle, forced. "What possible good has come from poverty and starvation?"

"Other than Pharaoh and his officials, most Egyptians have become far kinder to Hebrews." He let loose a real belly laugh. "A slave master apologized for accidentally hitting me with the butt of his spear yesterday. Can you believe it? He apologized."

The sounds of sudden screams cut off Hoshea's levity and brought Eleazar to his feet. Light from their doorway disappeared as soldiers giving orders drew both Eleazar and Hoshea into the underground hallway—and into total darkness.

"How can it be dark?" Hoshea whispered. "It's midday."

Eleazar looked in the direction of the arched entries at both sides of the tunneled hall and saw nothing. He reached for the doorframe to secure his bearings, and Hoshea stood shoulder to shoulder with him.

"What do we do?" The boy's voice sounded small in the whirling roar of a violent wind.

"It's a khamsin, Hoshea, nothing more." Eleazar heard the tremor in his voice and knew he hadn't convinced his apprentice or himself. The typical spring windstorms blew in sand from the desert and could cause temperatures to climb from unbearable to dangerous. This was different. Though sand was collecting at the edges of the entries and sweat was already stinging his pores, Eleazar had never known a khamsin to render the sun completely dark. He held his hand in front of his face but couldn't see it.

"Hoshea, I'm going to stay here while you go back into our chamber and find the flint stones. Feel your way along the wall, and you'll find the stones lying with my sandals and dagger at the head of my sleeping mat." Eleazar followed the outer wall to his left and lifted a torch from its strap. "I've got the torch. We'll light it and make our way to the throne hall. Pharaoh will want to see Moses again, and we need to be ready to fetch him."

"In this?" Hoshea's voice squeaked like a maiden's.

Eleazar chuckled. "Yes, my friend. We'll see if Yahweh's protection works for sand as it did for hail."

43

Then Pharaoh summoned Moses and said,
"Go, worship the LORD. Even your women
and children may go with you; only leave
your flocks and herds behind."

—EXODUS 10:24

Eleazar and Hoshea lay in their dark chamber on their sleeping mats. Bored. When the khamsin began, they'd donned full-length robes to protect them from the blowing sand and ventured to Pharaoh's throne hall. It had been deserted. They went next to Prince Ram's chamber, where the guard refused them entry. The prince did not wish to see Eleazar, the betrayer of Egypt.

"I'm sorry," Hoshea said as they walked in the small circle of torchlight. "You've given your life to serve Ram, and he calls you a betrayer."

Eleazar pondered the strange peace he felt and wondered why Ram's words hadn't bothered him more. "I haven't given him my life, and I stopped serving Ram when I returned to Goshen and committed never to leave Taliah again." Though he was caught in this sandstorm in the barracks, he fully intended to keep his promise, even though his wife had limited their relationship to the debates on Yahweh. At least Eleazar had been able to watch her belly grow with the promise of their firstborn son. Yes, he was sure their first child would be a son.

"I'm hungry." Hoshea sighed. Eleazar heard the telltale *swish-thump* of Hoshea's new talent, throwing a small ball of twine into the darkness and catching it. His friend had mastered the skill.

They'd been holed up in their chamber since the first day of the storm and hadn't ventured far from the barracks since. They'd occasionally snuck out to find a morsel of food in the kitchens or leftovers in a vacant chamber.

"Are you hungry enough to get the robes and clean sand out of your teeth when we return?" Eleazar would rather wait until he was starving. The high winds and burning temperatures made torchlight tricky, and sand snuck into every crevice. He had no idea how long the khamsin had raged. With no sun or moon to measure time, the darkness pressed in on them like a grinding stone.

A loud pounding on their door startled Eleazar. He heard Hoshea try to shuffle toward the door, but his whipping wounds had crusted with scabs, so he moved rather slowly. "I'll get it. Lie down so I don't plow you over." Waiting until the sound of shuffling ceased, Eleazar moved toward the door and turned the iron latch. A sudden stream of torchlight flooded their room and made him squint.

Kopshef's Nubian guard stood holding the insufferable light. "Mighty Pharaoh commands you to bring the Hebrew Moses to the throne hall immediately." He hurried away before Eleazar had a chance to thank him. Though the Nubian hadn't done anything to mitigate Eleazar's beating, he'd transported Eleazar gently to Goshen and treated him with respect. It was an unusual kindness.

"We'd better get out the flint stones and robes." Hoshea's voice came from the yawning darkness of their small chamber. "Are your flint stones still at the head of your sleeping mat?"

Eleazar's heartbeat quickened. "What if we don't take a torch?" Would Yahweh provide light as He'd provided protection from the hail?

Hoshea answered with silence. What was he thinking? Had he even heard Eleazar's question over the roar of the wind in the hallway?

A hand on Eleazar's shoulder startled him. Both men chuckled, but Hoshea spoke first. "I think Yahweh will honor our faith."

Eleazar took a deep breath and blew it out slowly. Was he really ready to try this—without Moses? Yahweh *liked* Moses. Eleazar wasn't sure how Yahweh felt about him. "Let's go."

Hoshea had already gathered their full-length robes. He shoved one at Eleazar and presumably donned his own to protect the crusted wounds

on his back. Completely covered, Eleazar led the way along the dark walls
of the barracks hallway. When they reached the arched entryway leading
to the open avenue of the palace complex, Eleazar shouted over the wind's
roar, "Ready?"

"Absolutely!" Hoshea let out a horrendous yowl and charged into the
swirling darkness.

Eleazar followed closely, and both men were swept into an ethereal
bubble of light and peace. They stared at each other, astounded, and then
reached a hand beyond the light to feel the harsh sand and heat. They
pulled their hands back into the bubble and felt the wonder of their
protection.

Without a doubt, Yahweh surrounded them, enfolded them, shielded
them.

With each step toward Goshen, the light and peace moved with
them. The dust beneath their feet was bright and undisturbed, the terrain
familiar, marking the way toward Doda's long house.

Finally, they stepped into another world. Goshen. No wind. No
darkness. No swirling sand. A few Hebrew children halted their play to
examine Eleazar and Hoshea. One ran away, crying, "Ima, soldiers came
out of the darkness!"

Eleazar knelt and held out his callused hand to the little boy who
remained. Someday his son might be frightened. "We won't hurt you."

Instead of taking Eleazar's hand, the little boy ran into his arms and
hugged his neck, nearly toppling the big man. Startled, Eleazar realized
he'd never been hugged by a child before. *What a wonderful feeling.* He
squeezed the boy gently, careful not to break him, as tears stung his
eyes.

"Hoshea?" Moses came around the corner of the long house and
then spotted Eleazar with the child. "Eleazar? What's happened?"

Suddenly conscious of how strange he must appear, Eleazar released
the boy and struggled to his feet. "Kopshef's guard sent us to retrieve you.
Pharaoh wants to end the darkness."

Moses raised an eyebrow and rubbed his beard-covered chin. "Three
days. It took his hard heart three days to relent."

"It's been three days?" Hoshea asked. "We couldn't tell because of the darkness. I don't suppose Goshen has seen any wind or sand."

"Not a grain." Moses's smile faded when he turned to Eleazar. "Before we return to the palace, I need to tell you . . ."

His pause made Eleazar's heart skip a beat. "Is it Taliah?"

"No. It's another plague—the final plague."

"Yahweh is planning another plague before this one is over?"

Hoshea was shocked, but Eleazar remembered Moses's words on the morning before the locusts. *Ramesses will lose his wealth, his power, and his sons.*

"Remember, Hoshea, I told you about the final plague during the plague of frogs." The boy's blank stare goaded Moses. "Yahweh warned me of the last plague on my way from Midian to Egypt. He said—"

"Israel is My firstborn." Hoshea's face paled. "Has He revealed which firstborns will die?"

Eleazar squeezed his eyes shut, afraid to hear the answer.

"Every firstborn male in Egypt, Eleazar." Moses spoke softly. "Men and animals. From the lowest slave's house to Pharaoh's palace."

The three of them stood in silence. What was there to say? Yahweh had given Ramesses every chance to let Israel leave peacefully, yet Ramesses had broken every promise and chosen deception over truth every time.

Eleazar forced a single word from his dry lips. "When?"

"Yahweh has set our deliverance in motion. The plague of darkness began on the first day of the first month of the Hebrew New Year. Nothing Pharaoh says today matters. The tenth plague is coming." Without another word, he began walking toward the storm.

Hoshea and Eleazar rushed to flank each side, and again the strange bubble of protection carried them through the darkness of Rameses. This time, however, Yahweh ushered them through the palace courtyards and into Pharaoh's presence. Ramesses, Prince Ram, and Kopshef sat huddled in the dark throne hall around a single torch. Wind and sand blew through the tall, narrow windows, threatening their sputtering source of light.

Eleazar noted their awe as the Hebrews approached in the glow of Yahweh's protection. Prince Ram met his gaze and held it. Pharaoh's second firstborn had become hard as Hittite iron. What degradation would he plan for Eleazar and Hoshea after this confrontation? Hoshea must return to Goshen with Moses. He wouldn't survive another beating. For reasons Eleazar couldn't define, he knew in his gut *he* must remain at the palace. Leaning over, he whispered to Moses, "Hoshea goes home with you. I'm staying. Tell Taliah I love her, and I'll be at her side when Israel leaves Egypt."

To his credit, Moses never broke stride. The three Hebrews continued their march to the edge of the crimson carpet, halting before the throne.

Pharaoh stood, inspecting the light and calm surrounding the three men. His awe abruptly gave way to fury. "Go, worship your god. Your women and children may go with you, but leave your flocks and herds behind."

"No." Moses spoke firmly. "Our livestock goes with us for the sacrifices and burnt offerings we present to our God. Not a hoof is to be left behind. We won't know the number of sacrifices required for our worship until we arrive at our destination."

Ramesses began to tremble with rage, and both princes stood. "Get out," he seethed, descending two steps. "Get out of my sight, and don't appear before me again! The next time I see your face, you will die."

Eleazar stepped nearer to Moses, ready to take the blow if Prince Ram or Kopshef advanced with a sword, but Moses nudged him aside and offered a respectful bow. "As you say, I will never appear in this throne hall again."

44

*Tell the people that men and women alike
are to ask their neighbors for articles of
silver and gold.*

—Exodus 11:2

Miriam sat beneath her favorite palm tree, Sattar snoring softly by her side. She buried her hands in his fur and let the new sounds of Egypt waft over her. Though the season of *Shemu* had come, no harvesters picked ripe fruit. No slaves swung sickles in the fields. Only the slosh and slurp of the Nile interrupted the silence of devastation. There was no barley for beer, no flax for linen, no normalcy in the wake of Pharaoh's stubborn resistance.

The day Moses had been summoned to end the darkness, the khamsin's wind faded. As shadows lifted from the city of Rameses, the safety and peace of Goshen's three-day light-cocoon had drawn Hebrew slave and Egyptian peasant together. Both had tasted freedom from Ramesses's malevolence and formed stronger bonds than Pharaoh's edicts imposed.

Taliah's village school had been a powerful melding force. She invited any child who wished to learn, and her classes had grown to three sessions a day of thirty children each. Little heads bent to watch as she scribbled maps and letters and pictures in the dust. Dirty faces lifted in rapt wonder as she recounted Egypt's history—and that of Abraham, Isaac, and Jacob. Moses appeared each day to authenticate the military tales and thrill the young boys who ran off after lessons to play with wooden swords.

But Taliah's cheerful expression was replaced with distant stares each evening when she left the long house to stand at Goshen's edge and wait for Eleazar.

Miriam wiped tears from her cheeks. "He isn't coming home this time, is he, Yahweh?" Did Taliah sense her husband's death? Is that why she ignored the message Moses brought home from Eleazar, promising they'd be reunited when Israel left Egypt? Miriam pressed her fists against her eyes, forcing the tears to stop. *I'm trying to trust You, but must You take everyone I love?*

"I thought I'd find you here." Moses's voice intruded, and she looked up to find not only one brother but Aaron, Hoshea, and Hur as well.

Sattar never stirred. She tousled his fur. "Some watchdog you are." Miriam shaded her eyes against the midday sun, levity fled, fear of the worst nearly choking her. "Have you heard something about Eleazar?"

"No, no!" Moses knelt beside her, holding her gaze. "We're here to make preparations for the journey into the wilderness."

She searched his eyes for anything held back but saw nothing. Then she measured the others' expressions. The men sat down in a half circle around her with the stoic calmness of their gender. Relief swept over her like a wave, and she swatted Moses. "Don't scare me like that again."

"I'm sorry, but I needed to speak privately with those I trust." He drew her close and whispered, "Eleazar will be all right. Yahweh has plans for our nephew." Miriam's throat tightened with emotion as Moses began his impromptu meeting. "Each of you has a vital role during our last days in Egypt."

Our last days in Egypt. The words cut Miriam like a sword. "This is really happening, isn't it? We're really leaving Egypt." She blurted out the thought, interrupting whatever Moses was saying.

His face lit with that lazy grin. "Yes, Miriam. In a matter of days, you will no longer be a slave in Egypt." He wrapped his arm around her shoulder and pulled her close. "How does that feel?"

As a matter of fact, it was terrifying. Everything that had happened in the past eight months had been beyond astonishing, but far more upheaval than an eighty-six-year-old woman expects to encounter at the end of life.

But Moses hadn't waited for her reply. "Hur, you and Aaron will work together to reconfigure our tribal leadership. Yahweh requires seventy elders—six from each tribe with the exception of the Levites, from which Aaron and I will serve as two of the six."

Miriam laughed, wide eyed. "You want to give the Reubenites the same number of elders as Judah?" She looked at Hur and then Aaron. "Tell him. The righteous tribes—Naphtali, Levi, Judah—will never allow Reuben and Ephraim and—"

"Yahweh commanded it, Miriam." Moses's voice was soft but firm. "We must learn now to obey or remain in Egypt."

The finality of his words settled into her spirit. *Learn now to obey or remain in Egypt.* "All right, Moses. What can I do to help?"

"Aaron will call the whole assembly of Israel together for a meeting in three days at dusk. At that meeting we'll announce the final plague and describe Yahweh's precautions for His people in order that no one in Goshen will die. I need you to work with the women after that meeting to make sure their meal preparations are precisely as Yahweh has instructed. The women know you and trust you. You've either been midwife for the births of their children or brought them into the world."

Miriam sat a little taller. Finally, something she felt equipped to do. "I'll ask Taliah to accompany me. That way she'll get to know more women, and they'll see her devotion to Yahweh."

"Good, good." Moses paused, looking nervously at each member of the group. "The next task will likely sound as strange to you as it did to me when Yahweh spoke." He tore at some sprigs of grass and tossed them in the air with a sigh. "Yahweh wants every Hebrew—men and women alike—to ask our Egyptian neighbors for articles of gold and silver."

Miriam stared, incredulous. Hur rubbed his chin, Hoshea's eyebrows rose like the eastern hills, and Aaron studied his sandal laces. Was she the only one willing to ask the hard questions? "Our neighbors have barely enough grain to put bread on their tables. How can we ask them to give us their treasured possessions when we've only recently gained their trust?"

Moses rubbed his temples, eyes closed. He wasn't convinced this was a good idea either. "Some Hebrews work for Egyptians in the palace, others for noblemen, so they have more to give. Yahweh said every slave is to ask his or her neighbor for gold and silver—and for clothing. This is how we will plunder Egypt's wealth without lifting a single weapon." With another deep breath, he lifted his eyes, weariness heavy on his brow. "Again, Miriam, I need you to speak to the women about this. Hur will talk to the men in the villages." He turned his attention to Hoshea. "We're to gain weapons in much the same way. I need you to go to the armory and find Eleazar. He must ask Ram to give us weapons—"

"No!" Miriam would hear no more. "It's too much, Moses! Yahweh asks too much. We don't even know if Eleazar is alive, but if he is, must he tempt the executioner further by asking Ram for weapons? No!"

She grabbed her walking stick and tried to push to her feet, but Moses stopped her. "Does Yahweh ask more of you than He's asked of me? Haven't I given up my wife, my sons, my parents? I'm asking you to do no more than I've done myself. Obey, Miriam. We must all obey in order to reap the promises of the God who loves us." His words stung, but worse was his quick shift of attention to Hoshea. "Will you go to the armory?"

"I will."

The boy's two simple words smothered Miriam in shame—inescapable, binding shame.

Hoshea stood immediately, and Moses lifted his hand for help to stand. "I'll go with you. I want to see if Eleazar is there." He looked back at Miriam. "At least then I can assure my sister he's alive."

Did Hoshea's courage spring from the exuberance of youth or from stronger faith? Did it matter? Looking up at him and Moses, Miriam shielded her eyes from the sun. "When are we to begin asking our neighbors for gold and silver?" She didn't even try to hide the defeat in her tone.

"As soon as Yahweh provides the opportunity." He patted Hur's shoulder. "When you tell the people, let them know God will make a way."

"We will," Hur said. "Be careful at the armory."

Moses and Hoshea walked away, and Hur scooted into the shade with Miriam, Sattar between them. "I'm not sure which will be more difficult. Getting gold from our Egyptian neighbors or prying Judah's hands from the scepter they think they inherited from Jacob's ancient blessing. Those elders will not give up their authority willingly."

His friendly banter was endearing but not helpful. "So you're not oblivious to the obstacles, just silent when it matters." Why didn't he speak his mind instead of watching quietly while others made decisions for him?

"I believe Yahweh speaks to Moses clearly. I trust Yahweh. I trust Moses. What more is there to say?"

"But it's not that simple!" Hadn't she said those same words to Eleazar when he was criticizing Yahweh?

"Of course it's simple, Miriam. It's simply not easy."

She glared at him, this man with his integrity and wisdom and faith. Why couldn't he do something hideous so she could have a reason to be angry with him?

"Marry me, Miriam." His penetrating stare stole her breath—those light-brown eyes so full of love—for her.

Surely, she hadn't heard him correctly. Better not to say anything than to make a fool of herself and—

"Did you hear me? I asked you to marry me." He gave her a lopsided grin.

"I . . . I . . . heard."

"My son Uri and grandson Bezalel have given their blessing. They thought it foolishness at first—because we're old—but when I pointed out that you and I will need help traveling through the wilderness, they agreed we could be very useful to each other."

"You want to marry me because I'm useful?"

"No, no, no." Hur reached for her hand, brow furrowed. "That didn't come out at all the way I'd planned. I want to marry you because I have loved you for as long as I can remember—first as a friend, then as Israel's prophetess, and now as a woman. Please, Miriam, honor me by becoming my wife."

Yahweh, what are You doing? Where are You? She'd had no warning this was coming, no time to adjust. How could she become a wife after a lifetime of serving only One? She loved Hur, yes, and she'd come to grips with that, but to betray her calling as Israel's prophetess by marrying another?

"No, Hur. I can't marry you."

She pulled her hand from his grasp and reached for her walking stick, but he rested his hand on her arm to stop her. "Why? I know you love me. Tell me why."

Tears threatened. Her first thought, her commitment as Yahweh's prophetess, was far more noble, but was it the truth? Or did the reason come from a much deeper, darker place in her soul?

Miriam pushed herself to her feet. "I will not marry you because I can't lose you too."

"Lose me? What do you mean?"

Miriam kept walking, Sattar at her heels, leaving Hur to his questions and herself drowning in her fears. She had served El Shaddai her whole life. He'd been enough—her love, her life, her all. But in the past eight months, He'd revealed Himself as Yahweh and had revealed His nature by His actions. She had always known Shaddai's love. Now, she was seeing Yahweh's power, and it terrified her. He'd taken Abba, Ima, and Eleazar from her—everyone she held dearest in the world. If Yahweh meant her to be alone, she dare not let Hur get too close. With a will of iron, she would pursue an obedience like she'd seen in Hoshea—even if her heart felt like a boulder in her chest.

45

On that same night I will pass through Egypt
and strike down every firstborn of both people
and animals, and I will bring judgment on
all the gods of Egypt. I am the LORD.

—EXODUS 12:12

Eleazar held a bronze shield in one hand and a *khopesh*—sickle sword—in the other. The curved sword with its hooked end could snag the Nubian's shield away, but if Eleazar got too close, Kopshef's guard would bring down his battle-ax and split Eleazar's head.

It was the third day Ram and Kopshef had pitted their personal guards against each other in the sparring ring. All other matches ceased, and a chorus of Egyptian soldiers chanted, "Kill the Hebrew. Kill the Hebrew." Evidently, Eleazar's blood would suffice as partial retribution for Yahweh's plagues.

"The Egyptians will not kill you themselves." Mosi leaned heavily on distracting his opponent while fighting.

"Why would any Egyptian hesitate to kill me?"

Eleazar lunged with his khopesh, but Mosi was quick. He swung the ax in the opposite direction, barely missing Eleazar's right shoulder. "Kopshef is sure the Hebrew god protects you as it protects Moses." He smiled, revealing white teeth filed to points. "We'll see if you are protected."

Another swing and miss, and this time Eleazar smiled. "Don't blame Yahweh for your poor skills, my friend." Circling the ring, he watched for an opening, any sign of weakness in the Nubian. He didn't want to harm him, only disarm him.

Mosi lunged to his right but swung the ax to his left, inflicting a minor cut on Eleazar's thigh. "It would appear your god lets you blee—"

Tipping Mosi's ax with his shield, Eleazar then hooked his opponent's shield with his sword and flicked it aside, slicing the battle-ax's shaft with an upward swing of the khopesh.

Mosi stood defenseless with a wooden stick in one hand; his smile turned to resolve. "Finish it."

Eleazar stepped to within a handbreadth. "I wouldn't give them the satisfaction." He threw his weapons in the dust and stalked over to the Hittites' forge to check on the progress of the new iron spearheads.

"It's the third day in a row Kopshef's Nubian has lost." The chief metal worker pointed to the center sparring ring, where Mosi stood like a statue while Prince Kopshef lashed him with his whip.

"Perhaps if Kopshef would stop beating his best fighter, the Nubian would be able to kill me." The whole row of Hittites laughed as if they'd been drinking and brawling all night. Barbarians, all of them, but somehow Eleazar had won their loyalty, and for that he was grateful.

Prince Ram glanced in their direction and shoved his brother away from Mosi, perhaps offering the same advice Eleazar had mentioned to the Hittites. The two princes stormed from the armory, leaving Eleazar under the watchful eye of the man who tried to kill him each day.

Eleazar hurried over to the Nubian, who drew his dagger and turned when he heard the quick approach. Eleazar lifted his hands in surrender. "It's just me."

Mosi relaxed and sheathed his weapon. "We serve fools."

On that much, they agreed. "Are you to be my watchman again today?"

"I'm to report to Kopshef if you have any contact with your uncle or father."

"I have too much work in the armory today. The Libyan revolt has resolved since Egypt no longer has food supplies to raid, but we need to replace all the spearheads for Ram's division." He started back toward the iron forges and raised his fist in the air, shouting, "Looks like another day of banter with the Hittites!" The barbarians jeered and cursed, already starting their good-natured goading.

Mosi groaned behind him. The Nubian hated the Hittites.

"Eleazar! Eleazar, wait!"

The deep male voice struck dread into his soul. *Moses.* Eleazar whirled on his uncle and found Hoshea escorting him. "What are you doing here?"

Mosi joined them, exchanging a concerned glance with Eleazar. He'd have to report their presence to Kopshef. Too many Egyptian soldiers stood staring at Moses to keep this visit a secret.

Hoshea's pitiful expression apologized before he opened his mouth. "Listen to the whole message from Yahweh before you say it's impossible, and remember all the impossible things we've already seen Him do, and—"

"Can we trust him?" Moses nodded toward Mosi, and then recognition swept over his features. "Aren't you the guard who brought Eleazar to the long house after his beating?" He grabbed Mosi's arm and turned him to see the fresh whipping wounds. Shaking his head, he didn't wait for Eleazar's answer. "You'll want to hear what we have to say."

More curious than ever, Eleazar glanced right and left at the gathering crowd of onlookers. "Let's at least move to a private corner in the slave quarters." He led them to the eastern wall of the armory, and noticed Moses's lazy grin appear. "Why are you smiling?"

He pointed to the weapons cabinets. "We've come to talk to you about those." Shaking his head, Moses chuckled and placed his hands on his hips. "Just when you think Yahweh isn't paying attention, He intervenes on a small detail like that. Israel needs those weapons when we leave Egypt, Eleazar, and Ram will give them to you."

"Hah. Oh really?" Now, it was Eleazar's turn to laugh, and Mosi joined him.

"I know this Hebrew god commands nature," said the Nubian, "but he does not command royalty, or your people would have worshiped in the wilderness by now."

Moses's humor dissolved, and he shot a questioning glance at Eleazar. Could they divulge Yahweh's plan to free Israel, not merely give them a festival reprieve? Eleazar nodded his approval to Moses.

"In three days' time, Aaron will call a meeting at the base of the plateau at dusk for the whole assembly of Israel. At that time, we'll announce the last plague." Moses looked at Mosi. "The final plague will kill every firstborn in Egypt, both man and animal, unless the inhabitants are within the walls of a house with lamb's blood on the doorframe. Yahweh has issued strict rules for the meal that night while the death angel passes over. Pharaoh will drive Israel out—along with all foreigners who align themselves with the Hebrews and are obedient to His instructions." Moses pointed to the weapons cabinet with one hand and placed the other on Eleazar's shoulder. "When we leave, we must have that sparring gear and extra weaponry. It's up to you and Hoshea to get these cabinets unlocked and arm every man in Israel."

Panicked, Eleazar looked at his apprentice. As usual, Hoshea's expression fairly glowed with faith. "Yahweh will make a way."

While Eleazar still processed the magnitude of the task, Mosi leaned into their circle, keeping his voice low. "May I attend this meeting with Eleazar and eat the strict meal in the house with the lamb's blood?"

Moses's expression reflected Eleazar's surprise, but something more caused his uncle to hesitate. "I must tell you, my Nubian friend, that there is one other requirement that must be met for a foreign man to be saved from this plague and be counted among the people of Yahweh."

Abraham's covenant. Eleazar knew the moment Moses spoke of being counted among Yahweh's people.

"Anything," Mosi said. "I'll do it."

"You must be circumcised."

If a Nubian's skin could grow pale, Mosi's most certainly would have. He stepped back as if Moses might seize him to do the cutting then and there. Eleazar waited silently, watching perhaps the fiercest fighter he'd known make a decision about a man's most delicate part.

Finally, he took a deep breath and exhaled slowly. "I'll be at the meeting with Eleazar, and you'll have your weapons."

Moses and Hoshea nodded their approval and walked away, leaving Eleazar with the man he'd known for only a short time, but had truly come to know only within the last few moments.

"What made you decide to follow Yahweh?" He spoke barely over a whisper.

Mosi watched the retreating figures of Moses and Hoshea. They stood in silence for so long that Eleazar assumed his new friend chose not to answer. But when he moved away, Mosi grabbed his arm and met his gaze. "My name is Mosi—meaning firstborn. I was first among twelve brothers in my tribe."

PART 3

*Now the LORD had said to Moses, "I will bring
one more plague on Pharaoh and on Egypt.
After that, he will let you go from here, and
when he does, he will drive you out completely."*

—EXODUS 11:1

46

*Now Moses was tending the flock of Jethro his
father-in-law, the priest of Midian, and he led
the flock to the far side of the wilderness and
came to Horeb, the mountain of God.*

—Exodus 3:1

Miriam's weary body woke to the sound of shuffling feet. Sattar's tail thumped on the dirt floor beside her. Moses was awake. Opening one eye, she saw the azure glow of predawn through their single window. Today was the day. The meeting.

Hoshea stumbled out of the adjoining room, fastening his armor as he hurried past Moses. "I'll give Aaron the message. 'Meet at the palm tree when the sun clears the eastern hills to determine the final list of elders.'" Moses nodded, and Hoshea rushed out the door without a bite to eat.

Breathing deeply, Miriam sat up, yawned, and stretched. "Elisheba will shake that boy like a dusty mat if he wakes her now."

Moses chuckled. "Why do you think I sent Hoshea instead of going myself?"

Taliah stretched and rubbed her rounding middle. "Good morning, Miriam." Without waiting for a reply, the dear girl folded her linen sheet, rolled up her mat, and immediately started meal preparations. While the rest of them slept with wool blankets during these cold winter nights, Taliah's extra blood flow meant rosy cheeks, a bigger appetite, and a constant sheen of sweat on her brow.

Thankfully, it also meant more energy. She and Miriam had spent most of the past three days visiting every village in Goshen, introducing themselves and encouraging the women to attend the upcoming meeting with their children and husbands. News of Eleazar's safety had stirred Miriam's faith in Yahweh's power to work in men's—and women's— hearts. They would build strong trust by talking with Hebrew women about the meal instructions and let Yahweh guide them into the right moment to ask for Egyptian treasure.

Moses nudged Miriam out of the way to retrieve the kitchen garbage and went about his usual tasks. Israel's deliverer had become quite proficient at emptying waste pots. Miriam grabbed a water jug and started for the river. It was quiet this morning with only four women at the shadoof gathering water. She'd already talked with them about tonight's meeting, so she wished them *shalom* and hurried home, balancing the full jar on her head.

Bowing under the doorway, she lowered the full jug to the floor and looked up to find both Moses and Taliah staring at her. "What?" She scanned the room. Nothing seemed amiss. What could have happened in the short time she'd gone to the river?

Her chest constricted. *Hur.*

"Where's Hur?"

Moses stepped forward, hands extended to calm her. "He must have left in the night. I'm surprised Sattar didn't wake you."

Relief warred with anger. Thankful he wasn't dead, Miriam might kill him for scaring her. "Why would he leave?"

She knew the answer, as did Moses and Taliah. Hur had told Moses about Miriam's marriage refusal, and Miriam had told Taliah. But they'd all been so busy preparing for the meeting, it hadn't been unbearably awkward—except at mealtimes. When they finally settled around the mat to eat a meal, the silence was deafening.

Taliah returned to the hand mill and resumed grinding their morning grain. "He commented to me yesterday that he wasn't 'comfortable' here anymore and planned to speak to his son about moving in with him."

"And you didn't think to mention it to me?" Miriam's voice squeaked with barely controlled emotion. She squeezed her eyes shut and took a deep breath. "I'm sorry, Taliah. Of course, Hur should live with his family."

"Hur was living with his family." Moses's jaw muscle flexed. "You're too stubborn to accept it."

"Stubborn? I've been extremely flexible considering all the changes I've endured." She ground her teeth, fighting the words that clawed to get out. "Especially with a God who has changed beyond my recognition."

Moses's features softened, and he exchanged a glance with Taliah. Both left their chores, and Moses guided her to her mat. "Sit down, Miriam. We must talk."

"You won't convince me to marry Hur. I—"

"Whether you marry Hur or not is your decision." Moses sat across from her, quieting her with a stern look from beneath furrowed brows. "We must talk about Yahweh. He does not change, Miriam."

She looked at Taliah, afraid her continuing questions might rattle the girl's burgeoning faith. Taliah held up her hands. "I won't debate. I'll sit quietly and listen. I promise." That wasn't Miriam's concern, but Taliah's silence might be helpful.

Moses reached for Miriam's hand and brought it to his lips. "Sister, you're the one who taught me as a child that God is constant, and it's still true. The changes you sense are merely changes in your knowledge of Him, not changes in Yahweh Himself."

"That may be true," she said, "but it's not just my knowledge that's changed. My relationship with Him has changed because I don't know how to *feel* about this new knowledge or how to incorporate the new knowledge into my daily living."

Moses fell silent, staring into the distance. Miriam knew he was listening to the Voice as she'd never heard it—clear, succinct, indisputable words, not vague impressions or images to decipher.

When he turned to her again, his eyes were full of compassion. "The day I saw the burning bush, I'd led my flock to the far side of the desert and climbed up the only path I knew on Mount Horeb. I had to leave that path to see the bush burning, to speak with Yahweh, and learn His name. I was on uncharted ground." He chuckled and added, "I've been on uncharted ground ever since. Yahweh said we would come to know Him through His actions, and so we have. We are still learning who He is, if we watch carefully and open our hearts to each revelation He gives."

"The El Shaddai I knew was powerful. He revealed the future in dreams and visions, and His presence was like fresh-baked dark bread— warm and inviting, never threatening or strange. But Yahweh reveals His power through extraordinary and frightening plagues. What am I to believe about His nature now?"

Moses's expression softened. "He is still warm bread, Miriam, but He has added red meat and calls us to His banqueting table to eat and grow." He let his hand fall back to his lap. "After Yahweh spoke to me from the burning bush, He led me down the other side of the mountain. I cut a new path through the briars and rocky crags. Did Mount Horeb change because God revealed a new path?"

Miriam rolled her eyes. Of course, a mountain couldn't change, but Miriam hated briars, and she didn't like this new path.

Moses chuckled. "Yahweh is bigger than a mountain, Sister, and we'll never come to the end of His newness."

"Can I say something?" Taliah was nearly bursting.

Miriam couldn't keep from grinning. "Go ahead."

"The strange and frightening things that make you question Yahweh are the very things that help me believe." She reached for Miriam's hand and squeezed. "I don't want a warm-bread god that I can understand. I need a God who hears my hopeless cries at the edge of Goshen when I think my husband is dead. I need a God I can't explain to do the things I know are impossible."

Tears came unbidden at the untainted wonder in Taliah's countenance. She was utterly enamored with Yahweh. He had revealed Himself at the core of Taliah's identity—her intellect—and she was entirely captivated by this God who was both powerful and personal.

Miriam drew the girl's forehead down for a kiss. "Thank you, my precious Taliah, for reminding me of His wonder." She released her and used Moses's shoulder to push herself to her feet. "And thank you too. Now, let's get on with our day."

The abrupt end to their conversation drew raised eyebrows, but Miriam wasn't ready to talk more about Yahweh or Hur with them. All these words and explanations did little to nourish her soul. She needed time alone at her palm tree, quiet moments with her Creator.

But that couldn't happen until after tonight's meeting.

47

*Tell the whole community of Israel that on the tenth day
of this month each man is to take a lamb for his family,
one for each household. . . . Take care of them until the
fourteenth day of the month, when all the members of
the community of Israel must slaughter them at twilight.
Then they are to take some of the blood and put it on
the sides and tops of the doorframes of the houses where
they eat the lambs. That same night they are to eat the
meat roasted over the fire, along with bitter herbs, and
bread made without yeast.*

—Exodus 12:3, 6–8

After nearly a week of sparring, both Mosi and Eleazar were cut,
bruised, and scabbed—but still alive. Ram and Kopshef finally
tired of the sport, perhaps realizing their two guards had no desire to kill
each other. The princes left their personal guardians to work in the armory all day since Pharaoh had abandoned all audiences in his court after
the locusts ended Egypt's trade.

No one knew what occupied Prince Kopshef's time, but Prince Ram
had brokered a deal with Canaanite traders to replenish Pharaoh's stables
with Arabian stallions, his fields with Amorite oxen, and his sheepfolds
with the finest Canaanite flocks. The royal granaries would once again
teem with barley for beer and emmer wheat for bread—staples of life and
health for every Egyptian. Rumors swirled that even melons, grapes, rad-
ishes, onions, and cucumbers would once again grace Pharaoh's table at a
banquet to celebrate his business-savvy son. Ramesses had given the pal-

ace slaves four days to make preparations for a celebration that even the gods would envy.

"The barley and wheat arrive tomorrow." Mosi twirled his dagger on a wooden plank, deep in thought. "So the bakery and brewery slaves will begin working nonstop again." He stopped the dagger and looked up at Eleazar. "Do you think it coincidence that the Hebrew meeting is tonight and their workload resumes tomorrow?"

Eleazar chuckled, remembering Moses's words from a few weeks ago. *"I no longer believe in coincidence."* He pointed at the sinking sun. "It's almost dusk. We should go."

They walked together across the armory compound, assessing the two sparring matches in progress. Since the Libyan crisis had resolved and Pharaoh was more interested in eating than war, fewer Egyptians trained for battle, which meant less work for the slaves. This allowed the Hebrew slaves to slip away for the meeting, leaving only the Libyans, Nubians, and Syrians trying to look busy.

Eleazar and Mosi arrived at the central forge as the chief iron worker doused a new sword in the cooling bath and steam shot into the air. He pulled the blade from the bath and smiled. "Good timing, Commander." Then, pointing to a new sword resting on a bench with twenty others, he said, "Try one."

Mosi grabbed a hilt, tossed it hand to hand, and then brought the new sword down hard on top of a wooden whipping post. The sword cut the wood like a warm knife through fat.

The Hittite sneered. "Oh, how I wish it was an Egyptian head."

Ignoring the comment, Eleazar pointed to the other swords on the bench. "Can I trust them all, or will some crack like an eggshell—as did your battle-axes?"

The Hittite metal workers exchanged uneasy gazes, and their spokesman cleared his throat. "Every sword is true, Commander. You have our promise and our loyalty." He pounded his fist against his breast piece— over his heart—prompting the Hittites near him to signal the same allegiance.

Eleazar returned the gesture and eyed Mosi, coaxing him to do the same. The Hittites knew their commander was up to something when the Nubian showed them respect.

Eleazar leaned in close to the chief Hittite. "Can I trust you to cover for the Nubian and me? We'll be gone for the length of the evening meal. If our princes should return unexpectedly, tell them we've gone to the stables to prepare their new Arabian stallions that arrived this morning."

The Hittite smiled, revealing missing and rotted teeth. "What do we get in return for our help?"

Mosi patted his shoulder. "The opportunity to be circumcised, my friend."

The remark won a ribald laugh from the Hittite, assuring Eleazar and Mosi of his cooperation. They hurried through the gate, talking loudly about the new Arabian stallions Prince Ram had secured from traders to replace the horses killed in the plagues. Jogging at a steady pace, they cleared the first rise. Once out of the armory's clear view, they abandoned their course, backtracking toward Goshen. Staying low, they crossed ruined fields and hid behind mounds of burned carcasses until they reached the cover of long houses and peasant huts.

Weaving through a sea of people, Eleazar hurried through Abba Aaron's village first since they'd come in from the north. Hebrews and Egyptians lined up in the alleyways between long houses, shoulder to shoulder, on their way toward dead-man's land. Most of them moved aside when they saw Eleazar and Mosi in full-dress armor.

"There they are." Eleazar pointed to the edge of the plateau where Moses and Abba Aaron stood above them. When they reached the main road that connected the villages to the city, he noticed many of the Hebrew leaders standing in the waste piles directly below the plateau.

"Why are the people standing in the refuse, my friend?" Mosi curled his nose.

Eleazar had no answer. Then he saw Doda, Hur, Taliah, and Hoshea among them and was determined to find out. "I don't know, but that's where we're going."

Shouldering his way through the crowd, Eleazar had no time for pleasantries. Abba Aaron had raised his hands for silence, and the rumble of the people stilled.

Eleazar and Mosi began climbing the slippery, smelly waste pile at the base of dead-man's land. The stench was overpowering. Finally reaching Doda, Eleazar tapped her shoulder. She turned and slipped in the sludge. He steadied his doda, but his eyes caressed Taliah, who looked back at him with joy welling on her lashes.

Doda released him. "Go, go hug your wife." She waved him away and noticed Mosi. "Well, here you are. Moses said you'd be joining us, boy. Welcome." She reached for Mosi's hand, pulling him toward her and startling the Nubian with her waste-pile hospitality.

Taliah was trembling as she threw her arms around Eleazar's neck, clinging like she'd never let go. Hoshea slapped his shoulder. "Welcome, Commander," he said, beaming.

Several around them began shushing. "We're trying to hear Moses." Hur, ankle-deep at the pinnacle of the sludge three rows ahead of them, turned to greet Eleazar.

Still holding his wife, Eleazar whispered in her ear, "Why isn't Hur standing with Doda?"

She released him, then cautioned him with a finger pressed to her lips and a sheepish glance at Doda. Leaning close, she whispered, "The immediate reason is because Hur is a newly appointed elder. The other reason is your doda refused his marriage proposal."

"His what?" Eleazar said too loud, earning more growls from neighboring Hebrews. He pulled Taliah close and spoke against her head covering. "Of course, she refused. They're too old to marry." His wife elbowed him and issued the first stern look since their reunion. He hugged her to his side. Oh, how he loved her!

Abba Aaron bounced his hands on the night air, and a throbbing silence fell over the crowd. Moses lifted his voice over the whole community of Israel. "Yahweh has declared seventy elders to serve you. They stand in the waste piles today, symbolic of their calling. We will serve Yahweh as elders above you, but we're mired in life with you, so we will never lord over you."

Eleazar looked over his shoulder at the vast sea of Israelites behind them. From this vantage on the waste pile, God's people stretched out into Goshen like branches of the Nile. The reality struck him. Israel's deliverance was at hand.

"Yahweh will bring one final plague against Egypt," Moses continued. "Because Israel is Yahweh's firstborn and Pharaoh has refused to release us from his cruel bondage, Yahweh will strike down every firstborn son in Egypt, both man and beast."

A nervous flutter spread through the crowd.

"When, Moses?" a man in the crowd shouted. "When will the plague begin?" Others in the crowd began shouting questions, and panic started to ripple through the masses.

"Will the plague strike Egyptians in Goshen?"

Taliah looked over her shoulder and then turned to Miriam in a panic. "That was Masud's father. He believes in Yahweh, Miriam, but as only one god among all Egypt's deities."

Eleazar knew Masud and his siblings held a special place in Taliah's heart because they were her first three students, and their parents had been the first to trust her with their children. How many others believed Yahweh was one of many gods? He looked at Mosi, standing under Doda's protective wing. What did he believe about Yahweh?

Moses tried to shout, but the crowd only grew more agitated.

Abba Aaron stepped closer to the edge of the plateau. "People of Goshen," he shouted, lifting his hands again. "Hear me! Hear me!" The crowd settled, and fell silent as he began, "My brother, Moses, will tell you all we know about the details of our deliverance, but you must be ready to leave Egypt at a moment's notice, for when the plague of firstborns sweeps through Egypt, Pharaoh will not simply release us. He will *drive* us out of Egypt, and there will be no time for planning."

Moses stepped forward again. "Today is the tenth day of Israel's first calendar month. When you return to your homes, those of you who have been able to replenish your flocks from the market, choose a male yearling lamb or kid without defect. Care for it in your homes until the fourteenth day, when at twilight you will slaughter the beloved creature and smear its blood on the sides and tops of the doorframes with hyssop branches. That same night, you will eat its meat roasted over the fire—all of it. If your family numbers less than fourteen, invite another family, who may not own a yearling, to eat the sacred meal with you. None of the meat is to be left until morning. If any meat is left until morning, you must burn it.

"Eat the meat with bitter herbs and bread without yeast. You will eat it standing, with your cloak tucked into your belt, your sandals on your feet, and your staff in your hand. We must eat in haste. It is the night when Yahweh goes through the land to strike down the Egyptians. He will see the blood on the top and sides of the doorframe and will pass over that doorway. He will not permit the destroyer to enter your houses and strike you down but will pass over Israel's firstborn. But in Egypt every firstborn male will die."

Not a sound could be heard. Eleazar held his breath as questions whirred in his mind. Where would he spend this *Passover* night? A quick count of people in Doda's household assured him there would be enough meat for Mosi to join them if he chose to. But what about the foreigners? Moses had promised to give instruction for the foreigners to be sav—

"Because the meal preparations fall to our women, the prophetess Miriam and our niece will visit your villages to give instruction to the women on the various ingredients and cooking instructions. For those foreigners who live among us and wish to be grafted into Yahweh's people, any male eight days old or older must be circumcised."

Murmurs rippled through the gathering at the severe condition. Moses lifted his hands for silence, and the people stilled. "It is a sign of the covenant Yahweh made with Abraham generations ago, a covenant that we—this generation—will see fulfilled as we receive Abraham's promise and take possession of the Promised Land. We learn to obey Yahweh's commands now so we can enjoy His promise forever."

Silence again, and Moses let it speak to those who would listen. After several heartbeats, he raised his voice again. "When Pharaoh releases us, your newly appointed elders will spread the word through your tribes. Until then, Yahweh commands all men and women who count themselves among His people to ask your Egyptian neighbors and masters for articles of silver, gold, and clothing to aid us on our journey."

The Egyptians in the crowd erupted.

"Haven't we already been plundered?" Masud's father shouted. Several others shouted and shook their fists at Moses, but he raised his voice over the few dissenters.

"Yes. Egypt has been plundered. But those within the sound of my voice have a chance at new life." Without another word, Moses and Abba Aaron turned and began their descent down the rocky plateau.

Eleazar stood silently, listening, observing, as the people of Israel began to worship the Lord—quietly, reverently, bowing down where they stood.

Mosi knelt beside him but simply watched the others, seeming intrigued but unsure how to participate. Eleazar knelt too, bowing his head in silence, listening as those around him raised their voices to the God he was only beginning to know. *Yahweh, if You hear me, know that I will serve You, but I still fear Your vast silence, Your great unknown.* Was it enough to serve and obey though uncertainties still lingered? He almost laughed, realizing he'd served Egyptian masters who never gave explanations. Why not serve an all-knowing, all-powerful God?

As the crowd began to disperse, Mosi and Eleazar rose from their knees, and Mosi leaned over to whisper, "Does your uncle really expect Ram to open the weapons cabinets for a nation of slaves?"

Eleazar closed his eyes, silent for a moment. "My uncle expects Yahweh to do another miracle."

"And there is only one God who could do it." Mosi held up one finger.

Doda patted his arm. "That's right, dear. One God alone." She grabbed his strong arm and started following him down the mountain of sludge. "Why don't you escort me home?"

"I would be honored."

Hoshea fell in step behind them.

Eleazar had planned to return to the palace without going to Doda's. Extending their visit would only make the good-bye harder. "We'll wait at the long house only until Moses returns."

"You're going back tonight?" Taliah's voice was barely a whisper, her eyes swimming in tears. Eleazar's heart seized.

"We'll go ahead," Doda called over her shoulder. "You two catch up."

Eleazar placed his hands on his wife's rounding belly, but she nudged them away, not violently, but intentionally. "I thought you'd come home to stay, like Hoshea."

He tilted her chin up to look into her eyes, those deep, dark pools that sparked with life and passion. "Someday soon I will come home, but it won't be to a slave's long house in Egypt. We will have a home where our son is free."

"Our son?" She lifted a brow in challenge.

He brushed her ear with his lips. "An abba knows these things."

"Don't leave." Her arms circled his waist, squeezing as if he were a lifeline. "Stay with me."

He laid his cheek atop her head and held her. People dispersing from the meeting walked around them, but it didn't matter. Eleazar and Taliah stood in the waste pile until they were alone in the darkness and rats began their evening feast. The first furry brush across Taliah's ankle released her grip. "Oh! Let's go!"

Eleazar swept her into his arms and carried her down the slippery mess. Resting her head against his shoulder, Taliah held on tighter when they reached the path. "I take it you're comfortable?" he asked.

She giggled and nodded.

Fine with him. She felt good in his arms. When they reached Doda's long house, he didn't want to go in. "I wish we could have our own home now." He bent to kiss her, tasting the sweetness of love that had endured pain and survived.

He set her feet on the ground, and she kissed him again. Leaving tonight wouldn't be easy. "Taliah, I'll be here for the Passover meal. I don't know what lies between here and there, but I promise—I'll see you on the night of our deliverance."

48

Ram's business deal with the Canaanite traders had changed the palace from a tomb to a temple. After three days of nonstop preparations, the throne hall had been transformed into a grand feasting room. Pharaoh, the crown prince, and Prince Ram sat on the elevated dais, while Pharaoh's guards, Eleazar, and Mosi stood behind their respective royals, overlooking the festivities.

Scented wax cones perched on every noble head, dripping a heady aroma into the elaborate wigs of the noblemen and their ladies. A cacophony of sound filled the air as musicians beat drums for scantily clad dancers and jugglers sang ribald songs to entertain Pharaoh's honored guests. Huge platters of roast goose, wild boar, and tender antelope were served with a steady stream of imported wine. The new grain stores were lavishly served in the forms of bread and beer—the customary double portions doled out to the firstborn of every household. Liberal helpings of imported fruits and vegetables were added to Egypt's only remaining food supplies: cheeses, dried fruits, and nuts.

The atmosphere was bright and cheerful, but Prince Kopshef sat brooding over his third pitcher of the strongest dark beer in Egypt. He'd been moping all night at Pharaoh's blatant praise of Ram. Pharaoh's first and second firstborns seemed doomed to a life of rivalry. Eleazar felt the gnawing betrayal of knowing their rivalry would be short lived.

Tomorrow night at twilight, households in Goshen would sacrifice a yearling from their flocks and save their firstborns—and every Egyptian household would mourn and wail. Eleazar shivered, scanning the table to his right where all the firstborn sons of Pharaoh sat, their guards positioned behind them. How many guards were firstborns like Mosi, and would die with their masters? Eleazar shifted his attention to the nobles. How many of them would join their firstborn sons in death? And the male slaves serving the heavy meat platters—two Libyans and three Assyrians—would they die because they hadn't been at the meeting and didn't know of Yahweh's deliverance? Surely, Yahweh would find a way to offer deliverance to those He knew would choose to follow.

"I'd like to propose a contest." Prince Kopshef raised his voice and stood on unsteady legs, swaying such that Mosi had to steady him. "Tomorrow at dawn. A hunt. My brother Ram leads a team of noblemen, and I lead a second team. Whoever kills the most antelopes, wins."

"Wins what?" Pharaoh asked, noticeably perturbed.

Kopshef bowed, spilling his beer on his father's shenti. The guests' unified gasp sobered the crown prince. "Wins your favor, mighty Pharaoh, Giver of Life, Keeper of Harmony and Balance."

Every sound stilled, waiting for the king's reaction. "Very well," Ramesses said, eyes narrowed. "The city is overrun with antelope since our crops were destroyed. A hunt is in order."

A cheer rose from the noblemen, but Eleazar caught Mosi's slight sneer. A hunt meant a long night of preparation for the royal guards. The Arabian stallions needed care—hooves trimmed, manes clipped, and tails wrapped. The princes would expect their mounts to be fully garbed in feathered headgear, jeweled reins, and metal-worked blankets. Exhaustion swept over Eleazar just thinking about the night ahead.

Prince Ram motioned Eleazar near and whispered, "I'll make sure I get the best noblemen for the hunt. You make sure you secure the best horses for their chariots. We'll win this. Do you understand?"

"Yes, my prince." Eleazar resumed his statuesque posture and watched his master fume. How could he ask Ram to give weapons, gold, and silver to the Hebrew slaves now? Moses had been adamant that Eleazar and Mosi were a crucial part of Yahweh's plan to plunder Egyptian weaponry. Eleazar had suggested they wait until their masters were in high spirits at tonight's celebration before asking for such a gift—but now this.

He stole a glance at Mosi. The Nubian stood like a granite pillar behind his drunken prince. Kopshef might give half the kingdom, but he wouldn't remember his promise tomorrow.

Yahweh, guide me to ask for Egypt's weapons at exactly the right moment.

Eleazar inspected every plank and strap of Prince Ram's chariot and the two prancing stallions harnessed to it, his vision blurred from exhaustion. Ram wouldn't care that he'd worked all night if a stallion broke free in the middle of the hunt. After the feast, Eleazar had escorted Prince Ram to his chamber, and the prince had made it painfully clear that winning today's hunt would determine his life's journey. Eleazar ached to tell the firstborn prince that his life's journey would be considerably shorter than he realized.

Prince Ram interpreted his hesitation as rebellion and used his whip on Eleazar for the first time in weeks. Eleazar was banished to the stables to prepare the chariot and horses.

Wincing as he reached up, Eleazar straightened one black stallion's feathered headpiece. Without Hoshea in the barracks to tend his wounds, he'd quickly slathered honey on a piece of cloth and trapped it under the back straps of his breast piece. It wasn't nearly as effective as Doda Miriam's bandages.

"Let me help." Mosi grabbed the horse's headpiece and nudged him out of the way, keeping a keen eye on the noblemen and princes, making sure he wasn't seen. "Did you ask Ram for weapons? Is that why he beat you?"

"The beating came when I kept my mouth shut." Eleazar shoved Mosi aside. "Get back to Kopshef's chariot before you get us both killed." Mosi stepped away, but Eleazar grabbed his shoulder, keeping his voice low. "Did you ask Kopshef for weapons?"

The Nubian gave him a dark look. "I'm still standing here, aren't I?"

The knot in Eleazar's belly tightened. Moses was counting on them to get the weapons before tonight's plague.

"Let's go." Prince Ram strode past him to address the team of nobles he'd carefully chosen. Over fifty royal officials had arrived before dawn, feigning neutrality. To choose a prince's team publicly was political suicide, but bribing a firstborn privately curried favor. Ram raised his voice above the chaos in the stable. "Brothers, my team has been given red flags to tie onto your chariots—the color of blood, the color of victory!" A resounding cheer made Eleazar's sleep-deprived head pound harder.

He led the twin stallions out of the stables, through the palace gates, and toward the linen shop, where servants had worked through the night to erect a massive papyrus-woven arch as the starting point for the hunt. Prince Kopshef waited in his chariot, with Mosi holding the reins. Pharaoh, too, waited impatiently with a falcon on his shoulder and a charioteer to guide his own stallions. Every man had a bow strapped to his back and a quiver full of arrows. Many antelopes would die today, providing the main course for another feast this evening.

Eleazar took his place in the chariot beside Ram and snapped the reins to hurry the twin blacks to the left side of Pharaoh's chariot. The red-flagged team followed, dimming the predawn light with a rising cloud of dust. Kopshef and his team lined Pharaoh's right flank and choked on Ram's dust.

The king raised his voice above the clanging harnesses and squeaking chariots. "The Son of Horus greets you as Ra emerges on his golden barque from another victory in the underworld. May this day hold victory for us all!" With his blessing, he lifted the falcon into flight, and the stallions' taut muscles lurched into action.

Eleazar guided their chariot safely between two of Kopshef's noblemen, but a third cut him off, nearly tangling the chariot wheels. Prince

Ram grabbed the reins and shoved him into the chariot wall, driving his stallions as if being chased by the dread goddess Ammut, devourer of the dead. Careening around the linen shops, he led his red-flagged team to the Nile's southern shoreline.

"Take the reins," he shouted, shoving the leather straps into Eleazar's hands and bracing himself against the chariot rail. He reached for the bow on his back and nocked an arrow from his quiver. A herd of antelope lifted their heads and bounded away along the grassy banks of the river.

"Keep us steady." Ram drew the string back, letting his first shot fly. A bull eland, the largest and slowest male of a Delta herd, dropped to the ground. The first kill belonged to Ramesses's second son. "Ha-ha!" Ram raised his arms, victorious. Arrows flew past them. Wounded antelopes ran frantically in every direction, barking, whistling.

"Well done, my prince." Eleazar slowed the stallions to field dress his kill.

"What are you doing?" Prince Ram grabbed the reins and slapped them to speed the horses onward. "Keep going. We'll dress the kills later." He shoved them back at Eleazar and brought an arrow to his bow for another shot.

Eleazar weaved between wounded and dead animals, arrows whizzing past them. Men shouted. Ram could be struck by a stray arrow or speared by an injured antelope. The prince would die by plague tonight, but he wouldn't die under Eleazar's watch this morning. "My prince, this is insanity. I can't protect you here."

Ram laughed like a madman. Had he heard the concern? Eleazar had seen battle fury, the blood lust that steals a man's reason and conscience, but never in a hunt for wild game.

Ram pointed ahead, where it seemed several chariots had circled around a lone palm tree. "Kopshef and father are slowing down. Go! Go!"

"It's chaos, my prince. I can't get you in there."

Just then, the feathered fletching of an arrow grazed Eleazar's shoulder, and Prince Ram cried out in pain. Eleazar's gaze met Kopshef's sinister grin as the crown prince lowered his weapon and nodded as Prince

Ram slumped over the rail of their chariot. Reining the stallions to a walk, Eleazar noted the arrow protruding from Ram's back above his left shoulder blade. Painful, but not a mortal wound.

Ram pushed himself up to stand and offered a wry smile. "Get us to the front of the crowd. I'll win father's favor with this injury."

Eleazar felt pity for the young man, and rage at Kopshef who was too much like Ramesses. "There is Another whose favor is more important." Courage swelled inside him. Now was the time to speak plainly to his master.

But before he could speak, a shout rose above the clang and rumble of chaos around them. "This is what Yahweh, the God of the Hebrews says." Eleazar reined his horses and searched for the source of the voice among the throng of chariots.

Moses stood sheltered at the base of Doda's private palm tree, the place she'd always met with her God. Chariots had slowed and then halted at his appearance. Ramesses stepped out of his chariot and marched toward the Hebrew, bow still in hand, but he stopped when Moses raised his arms and shouted so every nobleman could hear.

"Yahweh says to all of you, 'About midnight I will go throughout Egypt, and every firstborn son in Egypt will die—from the firstborn son of Pharaoh who sits on the throne to the firstborn son of the female slave who works at her hand mill. The firstborn of your newly purchased cattle will die as well." Moses let his words settle in the silence. "There will be loud wailing throughout Egypt—worse than there has ever been or ever will be again—but among the Israelites not a dog will bark at any person or animal.'"

Not a single Egyptian flinched. Moses lowered his arms and surveyed the dead antelopes strewn along the banks of the Nile. He began shaking his head, and his face and neck turned crimson. Eleazar remembered Moses saying he would mourn the moment he was forced to proclaim death to Ramesses's sons.

But death was a toy to Pharaoh. Perhaps his uncle had just realized that.

Moses turned a hard stare on Ramesses, this time shouting at him directly. "After tonight, you will know that Yahweh makes a distinction between Egypt and Israel." He opened his arms wide, pointing to the gathered chariots. "All these officials of yours will come to me, bowing down before me and saying, 'Go, you and all the people who follow you!' And finally, Israel will leave Egypt."

Without waiting for Ramesses's response, Moses stormed away. No one tried to stop him. No one spoke a word. Pharaoh, chin held high, returned to his chariot and signaled his charioteer back to the palace. Kopshef followed, leaving Mosi behind to help field dress the antelopes. Other noblemen joined the retreat, also leaving their drivers to process the kills. Would they serve these antelope at tonight's scheduled feast or cower in their homes, waiting for the plague to come?

Eleazar kept his head respectfully bowed, unsure how Ram would respond to Moses's declaration. "Would you like me to stay or return to the palace to dress your wound?"

When the prince remained silent, Eleazar looked up to find him staring into the distance. "So I'm to die tonight at midnight?" He turned then to face Eleazar, eyes glistening. "How long have you known?"

49

A foreigner residing among you who wants to celebrate the LORD's Passover must have all the males in his household circumcised; then he may take part like one born in the land. No uncircumcised male may eat it.

—Exodus 12:48

Miriam stepped into the sunshine and stretched her back, lifting her face to the warmth of the morning sun. *Thank You, Yahweh, for the obedience of one more Egyptian family.* She wiped and rewrapped her bloody flint knife and tucked it beside the extra bandages and herbs. Miriam had performed twenty circumcisions in ten households during the past three days—not many considering she and Taliah had visited nearly every village in Goshen—but they were twenty foreign males who would live through tonight's plague.

Stepping into the alleyway between long houses, she glanced left and right. Around every corner in every village, she looked for Hur. It was silly, she knew, but he'd practically ignored her at the meeting, and she hadn't seen him since. She'd lived with a constant roiling in her belly, and no juniper tea or caraway seeds helped. *Yahweh, I've never needed a man before. Why now?* She hadn't had time for that private chat at her palm tree. Just quick, frantic prayers every time she ached to see Hur.

Sattar snuggled close and pressed his head under her hand, seeming to sense Miriam's mood. He'd become her shadow, waiting outside the door of every home they visited.

Taliah emerged from the two-room mud-brick hut looking as weary as Miriam felt. "I've instructed Bahiti on cooking the yearling, and she's agreed to host the meal here and share it with Khepri's family who will supply the herbs and bread." This girl could teach a bee to buzz and organize the hive.

"Thank you, dear." Miriam looped her arm through Taliah's and began walking. "We have only our village to visit before we go home to make preparations." They'd begun their teaching quest at the farthest northern village—with the tribes of Asher, Dan, and Zebulun—on the day after Moses announced the plague.

Miriam poked her head into every doorway, greeting the women inside. If it was a Hebrew household, she and Taliah made sure they understood Yahweh's instructions. If the residents were Egyptian or other foreigners who refused Yahweh's commands, they offered a blessing and then asked for gold, silver, or clothing. As the day of Yahweh's judgment drew nearer, the foreigners' generosity grew larger. No doubt, they hoped to win Yahweh's favor with gifts as they believed other gods could be swayed. Sattar had become their beast of burden, and the baskets of treasure strapped across his back grew heavier each day.

Miriam and Taliah turned into the alley of their own village and saw a few women working outside, shaking out mats and emptying waste pots into the central channel. Most had been sent home from their work on the plateau or in the city as word of Moses's dawn announcement spread through Rameses.

"Leah!" Miriam called to a young Hebrew ima. "Are you prepared for the Passover meal?"

The young soldier's wife seemed hesitant, eyes darting this way and that. "I hope so." She ducked her head and disappeared behind her curtained doorway.

Miriam exchanged a puzzled glance with Taliah. "I hope so? That won't do." They marched across the narrow path between long houses and signaled Sattar to wait outside. Poking her head inside the curtain, Miriam offered another greeting, "Shalom, Leah."

The woman looked startled, but who wouldn't with four young children running around like wild boars in the marsh. "What troubles you, dear?" Miriam studied the children and noted the oldest was a boy with curly black hair and lively dark eyes.

The woman's eyes filled with tears. "We have no yearling. Hur said I'm supposed to share my neighbor's lamb, but we have no grain to offer in return—"

Miriam waved off her concern. "I'm sure Sarah and Eli will welcome you. I've known them all my life. Come."

A little girl reached up and poked Taliah's rounded belly. "Is there a baby in there?"

"Yes, there is. Do you think it's a boy or a girl?"

The little darling eyed her three brothers, her rosebud lips twisting into a frown. "You'd better hope it's a girl. Boys are mean."

Miriam giggled and grabbed the oldest boy's hand. "Why don't you walk with me. I'm not as steady as I used to be." He nodded and squared his shoulders—such a darling, this one. *Yahweh, pass over him.*

Escorting the little family to the neighboring doorway, Miriam moved the curtain aside with a gentle "Shalom to this house."

"Shalom to you, Miriam," Sarah said. She was an old woman now, but Miriam was the midwife who had brought her into the world. Sarah furrowed her brow as Leah, the four children, and Taliah trailed in behind Miriam. "I hope they brought bread to share."

Sarah's husband Eli snored in the corner, and her daughter Gittel offered a sad smile—a silent apology for her ima's harsh welcome. Gittel's six children played quietly in the corner. No doubt their savta Sarah had made sure of that.

Miriam nudged the young ima farther into the main room. "Leah will share much more than bread. Her little ones will play with Gittel's children, and you'll enjoy each other's company while we await Yahweh's deliverance."

"More mouths to feed," Sarah grunted and reached for the hand mill. "We'll make more bread."

"I can help." Leah stepped forward.

Gittel set aside her spindle. "Leah and I will take care of the meal, Ima. You and Abba rest."

"You can help," the old woman said, wagging her finger at the new-comer, "but don't think you'll take over my grinder."

Leah glanced over her shoulder at Miriam and Taliah with a timid smile. The children had already begun a game when they slipped out the doorway.

They'd walked only a few steps when Taliah's pace slowed, her gaze focused on the small mud-brick hut of her three favorite students. "I don't think I can ask Masud's father again. He's already refused us twice."

Miriam pressed her hand to the girl's arm, halting their steps. "What if we hadn't encouraged Leah to join her neighbors? Would shyness or uncertainty have cost her firstborn his life?" Remembering this girl's earlier passion for children's welfare, Miriam knew what would move Taliah's heart. "You loved those children enough to fight for their education. Love them enough now to fight for their faith."

Sattar remained close as they approached the small hut. Miriam quickly checked her bag for circumcision supplies. She had just enough bandages and herbs if Beb, Masud's father, agreed to believe and obey Yahweh's commands.

Taliah cleared her throat and rustled the curtain. "Shalom to this house."

They heard shuffling inside and then Masud, Haji, and Tuya appeared at the curtain, eyes bright. "Peace to you, Taliah."

"Good morning." She ruffled the curly black hair of each child.

Haji stared down at the baskets strapped across Sattar's back. "You have a lot of gold!" He reached out to touch, but his big brother slapped his hand.

Taliah tipped each little chin to see their bright, black eyes. "I've come to say good-bye. I'm leaving Egypt, and I won't see you again."

"Father said we couldn't go with you." Masud stood straight and tall, but his round black eyes welled with tears. "I asked why, and he said he's afraid of your god."

"Masud!" Beb appeared and pulled the children inside. His eyes never left his sandals. "Thank you for teaching our children. We owe you a great debt."

"You owe me nothing." Taliah's voice wavered, but she cleared her throat again and lowered her voice. "Please, Beb, Yahweh asks for your obedience, but He promises you new life and freedom. You need only take it."

Miriam stepped close, whispering, "I have herbs and bandages for your wounds. Your family can join us for the meal. Please, Beb. Please."

"Thank you for your kindness," he said with a polite nod. "Safe journey." The curtain fell closed, hiding the man and his family in their dimly lit hut.

Taliah covered a sob, and Miriam squeezed her eyes shut against the truth that left her breathless. Masud would die tonight—that bright, beautiful, happy boy. Because of Ramesses's hard heart. Because of Beb's fear. Because four hundred years of evil men had brought two nations to this impasse. And because Yahweh's gift of human choice comes wrapped in irreversible consequences.

"Come, dear. We have a few more visits before we go home to begin our own preparations." Miriam guided Taliah toward the next doorway, hoping they could save the firstborn inside.

50

*The LORD made the Egyptians favorably
disposed toward the people, and Moses
himself was highly regarded in Egypt by
Pharaoh's officials and by the people.*

—EXODUS 11:3

Eleazar didn't know which of Ram's wounds to tend first—the arrow
in his shoulder or the betrayal of keeping the plague from him.

"How long have you known?" Ram shouted the question this time.

Insides twisting, Eleazar held his master's gaze. "Several days."

Ram choked on a laugh. "I suppose I deserve your hatred."

"I don't hate you, my prince." Eleazar paused, and decided a dying
man deserved the truth. "But I couldn't trust you. I have a wife to
protect."

The look of betrayal deepened. "A wife? You said you'd never marry."
He sounded like a child—a lonely little boy.

"I married to keep a vow, but I will leave Egypt with a wife I love."
Taking a deep breath, Eleazar revealed more. "I hid her to keep her safe."

"From me," Ram said—a statement, not a question.

Eleazar nodded once. "And from Kopshef. She's Putiel's daughter."

Ram looked away, turning his back. They watched in silence as the
servants dressed the antelopes. Eleazar noted blood pooling on the floor
of their chariot. "My prince, your wound must be tended. Please, let me
take you back to the palace."

"Why bother if I'm going to die at midnight?"

Eleazar placed the prince's hand on the chariot rail and snapped the reins, turning the horses toward the palace. "There's a way for you and your son to survive this plague if you're willing."

Ram glanced at Eleazar suspiciously, wincing as the chariot jostled his wounded shoulder. "Why would you help me after the way I've treated you?"

Eleazar felt this might be his only chance to obey Yahweh's command. This might be the softest his master's heart would ever be. "I hold no grudge against you, my prince. I'll tell you how to save yourself and your firstborn when we've reached privacy, but for now I'd like you to consider a request."

Ram's brow shot up. He paused, considering, and then nodded permission to continue.

Eleazar focused on the stallions ahead of him. "Our God commands Israel to leave Egypt peacefully, but every Hebrew is to ask his master for items of gold, silver, and clothing—only that which our Egyptian masters are willing to give. I'm asking you to offer items from Egypt's armory." He didn't dare look at Ram but simply waited for the refusal.

"I'll give you the key hanging around my neck when we get back to my chamber. It unlocks every weaponry cabinet in the armory. Take only what you think the slaves can manage." Ram's voice grew husky. "A man who remains loyal after what I've put you through deserves my trust."

They finished the ride in silence, arriving at the stables to concerned glances and scurrying slaves. "Should I call the palace physicians, my lord?"

"No!" Ram marched past every offer of help and entered the palace through the servants' hall, avoiding the royal residence. He grasped Eleazar's arm, and kept his voice low. "If word reaches my wife that I've been injured, don't let her or my children see me until you've bandaged the wound. I don't want them frightened."

"Yes, my prince."

Ram stumbled as he resumed his walk, blood still oozing. Eleazar steadied him and then followed without a word as Ram led them through the palace and into the empty throne hall. Several scribes lingered near the doorway leading to their quarters, and Eleazar noticed Ithamar among them.

His youngest brother saw him too; their eyes met. Had Ithamar heard about the plague? Had he attended the meeting and made plans to eat the prescribed meal within the home of a blood-stained doorway? Ithamar wasn't a firstborn, so surely he'd be safe even if he spent the night in the palace, but how would he find their family when it came time to flee Egypt? Torn between love for his brother and compassion for Ram, Eleazar remembered the weapons key and knew he must find Ithamar later. *Please, Yahweh, find a way to care for my brother through someone else.*

Ram mounted the dais and slipped through the prince's entry leading to the residential wing. Eleazar knew the guard at his door. "Go to the palace physicians and get all the supplies they use to treat an arrow wound."

"But don't bring the physicians!" Ram snarled, opening his door. "I'm sure I'll see them at midnight." Weak now from blood loss, he stumbled toward his bed.

Eleazar ducked under Ram's healthy arm, helping him walk a few more steps. "I'm telling you, I know how you can save yourself and your son."

"Oh, now you're going to stop Yahweh? When I'm dying from a chest wound?" Ram sat on the edge of his wool-stuffed mattress while Eleazar removed his sandals, leather breast piece, and wristbands.

"You're not dying." Eleazar threw the last wristband on the floor. "The occurrence of the other plagues depended on one man's choice—your father's—but with this final plague, Yahweh gives every man a choice. Everyone who chooses to obey is extended mercy."

"Quite noble of your god, Eleazar. What must I do?" Ram's head drooped, and he was struggling for consciousness. The arrow still protruded through front and back, but Eleazar dare not remove it until he had bandages to pack the wound—his battlefield training had taught him that much.

A knock came just in time. "Come!" Eleazar looked over his shoulder at the guard, weighed down with four baskets of every bandage, herb, and potion the Canaanite traders had offered. Ram's business deal had benefited him in more ways than he imagined. "Leave it and go," Eleazar barked.

"May I get you anything else?" The Egyptian guard bowed humbly—to Eleazar.

Ram chuckled. "You must be a firstborn." He lifted his head and narrowed his eyes. "Get out. You'll die with the rest of us." The man hurried from the chamber, closing the door quietly behind him.

Eleazar's blood ran cold at Ram's cruelty. He grabbed two wads of bandages and pressed them into Ram's hand. "Hold these. I have to break off the tip of the arrow and pull it through. It won't be pleasant."

Crack! Swish! Eleazar did it quickly, something he'd done dozens of times on the battlefield—but never for a prince.

Ram screamed and then panted when it was over, wide awake now.

Eleazar grabbed a wad of bandages and held it against the wound in his back and pressed Ram's handful of bandages against the wound in the front. "Are you ready to listen to me now? Are you ready to save your son's life?"

Ram glared at him. "You enjoyed that, didn't you?"

"A little." Eleazar grinned.

"I'm listening."

"You and your son are already circumcised, so you've already met one of Yahweh's requirements. You need only believe He is the One God, bring your family into this chamber, and smear a yearling lamb's blood on the top and sides of your doorframe. Do these things, and the death angel will pass over you tonight."

Ram's expression remained unchanged. Had he heard, or was he fading again?

"Do you understand me?"

"Do you understand that my father would kill me and all my children if I even mention the name of Yahweh in this palace?" Ram wiped sweat from his face. "Besides, if I live through the night, I think I may win the throne. I'm not about to trade Pharaoh's favor for a slave's god—even if that god threatens my life."

Eleazar wanted to shake him. "Even if you and Kopshef survive this plague—which you won't—the crown prince would never let you sit on Ramesses's throne. You'd be dead now if he'd been a better archer."

Ram's face grew paler. "Kopshef shot me?"

Eleazar's single nod hardened Ram's features to stone.

The bandages were soaked with blood, so Eleazar reached for fresh ones. "Press this against your chest wound and lie on your stomach while I pack the back wound." Ram did as instructed, and Eleazar worked quickly. The use of ground and crushed herbs he'd learned from Doda Miriam as a child had made him invaluable as a soldier's medic on the battlefield. How had he not seen Yahweh's hand on his life all these years?

"Turn over, and I'll pack your chest wound."

Without comment, Ram did as he was told, staring at the ceiling, deep in thought. Eleazar wanted to say more, to try to convince him to save himself and his son, but what good would it do? If a man refused to believe, refused to value his own life and others, no words in the world could save him.

"Sit up now, while I secure the wrappings." Again, the prince of Egypt obeyed his slave without hesitation. After tying the last bandage in place, Eleazar lowered his master's head onto a down-stuffed pillow, lifted his legs onto the bed, and covered him with a light linen sheet. "Will there be anything else, my prince?"

Ram reached for the key around his neck and snapped the chain. Finally, he met Eleazar's gaze once more. "Take it. Give your Hebrews the weapons they need." Eleazar reached for the key, and Ram held his hand as he received it. "Take whatever gold and silver you can carry when you leave my chamber. I don't want to see your face again, Hebrew—whether I live or die."

A cold shiver worked up Eleazar's spine as he took the key. "As you wish, my prince."

Ram closed his eyes, and Eleazar began collecting gold rings, belts, and chains into a shoulder bag. He stared for a long moment at Ram's

Gold of Praise collar. Should he? Could he? Yes, after four hundred years of his ancestors' slavery, he most certainly could take it. Fitting the heavy piece of jewelry around his neck, he slipped out the door and came face to face with the Egyptian guard who had retrieved the medical supplies. He looked at the golden collar on Eleazar's neck and lifted a single brow.

Eleazar placed a hand on the man's shoulder. "If you are willing to trust Yahweh as the One God, you can save yourself, my friend."

A moment of hope dawned before weary sadness washed it away. "A soldier serves his master unto death." Shoulders back, eyes forward, he let Eleazar pass.

51

*Take care of [the lambs] until the fourteenth
day of the month, when all the members
of the community of Israel must slaughter
them at twilight.*

—EXODUS 12:6

Miriam and Taliah finished their last visit with a family of Libyan
slaves. The father and his sons chose to be circumcised, and the
family would join their neighbors for the sacred meal, saving them from
tonight's grief and securing their freedom tomorrow. Now, past midday,
they should still have enough time to make preparations for their own
meal and pack the few things they would need for their journey.

Hoshea stood waiting for them outside their doorway, holding the
halter of their bleating lamb. "It's your turn to care for our friend here
while I do something important."

Despite her weariness, the sight of the brawny young soldier imprisoned by their tame yearling lamb made Miriam smile. "Caring for our
lamb is very important, Hoshea. Did you crush the bitter herbs as I
asked?"

He looked left and right, refusing to shout his answer across the alleyway. He'd been appalled when Miriam asked him to help with "wom-
en's" work. "Yes, I finished crushing the blue succory, *marrob* root, and
coriander," he said as Miriam and Taliah walked past him into the house.
"But I . . ."

Miriam saw that only half the chores she'd asked him to do were
finished. "But what?"

"But I've been thinking about what Moses and I discussed late last night—shelter for everyone in the wilderness, food, water, transportation for the elderly, sick, and new imas."

"You couldn't work while you were thinking?"

Taliah giggled as she unpacked her basket. "It's all right, Miriam. One woman can accomplish twice as much as a man in half the time. Let him go find Moses."

Miriam held Hoshea with her sternest look while he waited with raised brows. "Go then."

"Where is he going?" Moses shoved aside the curtain. "I had hoped to get some bread and cheese. I'm starving."

"There's bread, hard cheese, and dates in the basket." Miriam shoved it toward the men with her foot. "Taliah and I have work to do."

"It's past midday, Miriam. Sit down and eat with us." Moses slipped the bag off her shoulder, removed the basket from her arm, and then guided her to the mat Taliah had spread for them. "We'll eat quickly and share our news."

Frustrated but a little relieved to sit down, Miriam sliced the bread and broke off pieces of cheese while Taliah passed the dates. "Taliah and I visited all the villages and were able to delegate some teaching to other women so that every household was reached."

"Good, good." Moses bit off a piece of bread and chewed as he talked. "After announcing the plague to Ramesses and his nobles at dawn, I went to the armory and told the Egyptian soldiers. Most of them went home to be with their families—as I'd hoped—leaving me there with the slaves to work out shelter and transportation plans for our departure." He looked at Hoshea. "Why didn't you tell me there are hundreds of tents and at least fifty wagons at this armory and just as many at Pithom?"

Hoshea's mouth gaped. "I didn't know the exact numbers. Eleazar is in charge of the battle equipment."

"Where is Eleazar?" Taliah asked Moses. "Was he with Prince Ram this morning when you announced the plague?"

Moses shot a withering glance at Miriam and took another bite of bread. "Yes, he was with Ram."

"Out with it," Miriam said. They had no time for hedging.

"Eleazar and Mosi were driving chariots for their princes this morning when I announced the plague. Prince Ram looked like he'd been shot with an arrow—"

"Shot?" Taliah said. "Was Eleazar hurt?"

"No," Moses said. "It must have been some sort of hunting accident. I left right after the pronouncement, so I assume Eleazar returned to the palace with Ram. I'm not sure where Mosi is. Neither of them came to the armory this morning."

"When will they come for tonight's meal?" Miriam asked the question she knew Taliah was aching to ask.

Moses issued her a chastising grunt. "They know we slaughter the lamb at twilight. They'll be here."

An awkward silence followed. Of course, they knew when the lamb would be slaughtered, but Miriam wanted answers. And she wanted to talk to Hur. When she and Taliah had visited his son's village to teach the women, Hur had been at an elders' meeting. When Moses had met with him, it had always been elsewhere, never here in her long house.

Was she really keeping him safe by keeping him at a distance? Suddenly, her finely shaped arguments felt more like thinly veiled excuses. *Yahweh, please speak to me clearly—as You used to. Show me Your will in a way I can't deny.*

"We asked Masud's father to reconsider the circumcisions." Taliah changed the subject. "He refused again." No tears this time, simply a report of the tragic reality.

Miriam felt a twinge of guilt, pining over Hur when people's lives were at stake.

Moses leaned over and covered Taliah's hands with his own. "I'm so sorry. I know how much you love Masud."

She nodded. "If you love someone, you don't give up. You don't rest until you're sure they're all right." She looked up at Miriam. "Right?"

Miriam's throat tightened with emotion. Was Hur all right? She forced the word out. "Right."

"Absolutely," Moses said, patting her hands. "We won't give up until our loved ones are safe. I'll find Aaron and send him to the palace to get

Ithamar. Though the boy isn't a firstborn, he'll be safer in Goshen with his family." He turned to Hoshea. "You go to the palace and find Eleazar. He'll know where to find Mosi. You bring them both to the armory, and we'll organize the wagons. I'll go now and ask Hur to have the elders get a count of how many sick, elderly, and imas with newborns need a place on those wagons." He lifted his eyebrows to the group. "Everyone know their job?"

Miriam wanted to volunteer to speak with Hur personally—but not about wagons. There was simply no time. "Yes, General." She forced a grin and winked. "Go, while Taliah and I prepare for tonight's meal." She pushed to her feet, bones creaking and muscles screaming their protest. She hoped Hur saved a place for her on one of those wagons.

Perhaps she could find him when they left Egypt, seek him out among the tribe of Judah. What would she say? At least she could apologize. But for what? Maybe he'd find a nice widow to help him travel. Miriam had cheated herself out of the happiest days of her life.

Shaking her head to clear her thoughts, Miriam refocused on the tasks at hand. They'd need more water for their meal tonight. "Taliah, would you . . ."

She looked around the room and found herself alone. Well, not completely. Sattar sat at the doorway, making sure the yearling lamb didn't escape. "Where did that girl go?" Miriam asked her furry protector.

He didn't answer, but it was all right. Miriam was almost certain the girl went to plead once more with Masud's father.

52

*For the generations to come every male
among you who is eight days old must be
circumcised, including those born in your
household or bought with money from a
foreigner—those who are not your offspring.*

—GENESIS 17:12

Eleazar hurried away from Prince Ram's chamber and out the palace gates under the weight of a shoulder bag filled with gold—and the iron key to Egypt's weapons. Unbelievable.

No one tried to stop him; in fact, he saw dozens of other Hebrews with similar parcels full of treasure headed for Goshen. The guards on the walls seemed blind to the evacuation, or more likely they'd caught wind of the coming plague and feared angering Yahweh further.

Eleazar broke into a run just outside the palace gates and sprinted toward the armory. The sun was well past midday, but Yahweh's faithfulness gave his feet wings. He should still have time to unlock the weapons cabinets, disperse the weapons, and return to the palace for Ithamar.

Cresting the rise, he saw the armory ahead. No guards manned the towers, and when he passed through the gates, a chill skittered up his spine. The sparring arena was empty, the forge and furnace areas deserted. He walked directly to the weaponry cabinets and found slaves but no masters. A group of men huddled in the corner in a heated dispute, while the larger gathering idled the day away with wooden swords, wrestling, and games of chance.

"Where are the Egyptians?" he asked the Hittite captain. "And why aren't you making swords?"

The barbarian stood and grinned. "The Egyptians scurried home like rats to their holes when your uncle came this morning and announced tonight's plague. We've been waiting for you."

"Waiting for me?"

"Moses said you'd get the weapons key from Ram. I told him you'd have to pry the key out of Ram's dead hand." He pointed to the men arguing a stone's throw away. "We've got wagers on whether you would bring the key or not."

Eleazar took a second look at the loitering slaves—Hebrews and foreigners alike. They'd started walking toward him, interested in the conversation. "So Moses told you about the plague and that foreigners willing to covenant with Yahweh and obey His commands will be free when Pharaoh releases the Hebrews."

The Hittite laughed. "Covenant with Yahweh you say? If you mean any man willing to be cut—yes, we heard that part."

"What exactly did the men wager?"

"Some of the men think if this Yahweh of yours could make Ram give you the weapons key, He would be a god worth—obeying." He suddenly noticed the Gold of Praise around Eleazar's neck, and his mouth gaped. "Did you get the key?"

Eleazar reached into his shoulder bag, the Hittite watching every move. Eleazar pulled out a gold ring and grinned. The Hittite narrowed his eyes, not amused. Several in the gathering grumbled. Eleazar reached into the bag again and felt the long shaft of the iron key.

Slowly, Eleazar pulled the key from the bag and lifted it above his head for all to see. "Yahweh is the only God." He turned to face the men. "And He is worth obeying."

A murmur rippled through the soldiers, first slight and then building. Men hardened by years of battle and bondage stood on the cusp of freedom but must make a hard choice.

Eleazar returned his focus to the chief Hittite. "Are you with us?"

Only a moment's pause preceded the barbarian's battle cry, and he pounded his fist on his chest in pledge. "I will submit to the knife for a God who can bend the will of Prince Ram."

Eleazar began to chuckle and then laughed. "I never imagined Yahweh would provide Israel with the best iron workers in the world." He clamped the man's shoulder. "I don't even know your name."

"I am Taruna. My men call me Ru."

"Well, Ru," Eleazar said, offering him the key. "We must get a weapon into the hand of every fighting man who leaves Egypt with us. I'll find Hoshea to help us."

"Hoshea is at the palace looking for you." Taliah's voice squawked like a hen among lions, and Eleazar whirled to find his pregnant wife standing in the lions' den. The men jeered and taunted, and he felt crimson creeping up his neck.

"Touch my wife, and you'll have no need for circumcision." Eleazar glared at his men, halting their teasing. "Taliah, you will wait by the gate until I'm finished here." What was she thinking, coming to the armory unescorted? Shouting at him as if he was a child. "Go now! To the gate." Her cheeks grew crimson, and he regretted his tone, but her fiery spirit needed a bridle.

"Relax, Commander." Ru nudged his shoulder, drawing attention from his retreating wife. "I'll get the men to help me sort the weapons while you find your apprentice and escort your lovely wife home." He pointed to the stacks of equipment on the south side of the weaponry cabinets. "Are we taking armor as well or weapons only? What about sandals and helmets—"

"So this is Putiel's she-camel left in your care." Prince Kopshef shouted across the sparring yard, and Eleazar felt as if the ground tilted.

There by the gate stood his obedient wife with Kopshef's arm around her belly, a dagger to her throat. The prince pulled her head covering off and smelled her hair, her neck. Taliah turned away, whimpering.

Releasing a war cry, Eleazar hurtled across the yard, but Kopshef pointed the dagger at Taliah's belly. "Are you prepared to lose a wife *and* a child today, Hebrew?"

Eleazar skidded to a halt in the dust. "What do you want?"

"I want everything," Kopshef said. "I want your god to relent. I want the throne. I want my pandering brother Ram to die." He nodded toward the Hittite. "But for now, I'll take that key to the weapons cabinet."

Mosi stood three paces behind Kopshef and slowly drew his cudgel from his belt.

Eleazar forced calm into his voice, hoping to give his friend a chance to overpower the maniacal prince. He turned slightly, calling over his shoulder to the Hittite. "Ru, bring me the key." When he sensed no movement behind him, he kept his eyes on his wife but shouted. "I said, bring me the key—"

Mosi drove the cudgel into Kopshef's side and grabbed for the dagger. Taliah shrieked, and blood stained her robe.

"Taliah!" Eleazar lunged for his wife while Mosi and Kopshef struggled.

The slave soldiers rushed the prince, enraged, with wooden swords and cudgels in hand. Eleazar knelt amid the chaos with Taliah in his arms.

She was shaking and clutching under her belly as blood seeped through her fingers. "The baby, the baby!"

Panic surged through him. Blood. So much blood. He lifted his face to the sky and screamed, "Yahweh, don't take them!"

"I'm well," she said. "I'm well." Her eyes rolled back, and she was gone.

"Taliah, no!" He listened for breath and heard it. She'd only fainted, but he must find a way out.

He looked up, heard more shouting—then silence. Moses and Hoshea had joined the fray, shoving the soldiers away from Kopshef, lying in the dust. The prince struggled to his knees and then to his feet.

He ran.

Eleazar scooped Taliah into his arms and started toward the gate. Soldiers gathered around another body.

Mosi.

Eleazar stopped, bending over his friend with Taliah in his arms. "Nooooo!"

Moses saw the blood on Taliah and shoved Eleazar toward Goshen. "Go! We'll bury Mosi. Take her to Miriam. Go!"

Eleazar stumbled through the gate, gained his footing, and ran, heart pounding in his ears. *Yahweh, please, please. Yahweh, please.* He had no words.

53

Abram believed the LORD, and he credited
it to him as righteousness.

—GENESIS 15:6

Miriam mashed a few more dates in the bowl, then added a little honey to make the paste spreadable. It was a treat that would taste especially good with the bitter herbs Yahweh had required for their meal tonight.

Sattar slept peacefully near their lamb. Both had finally settled in the corner on the fresh straw Hoshea had gathered for bedding—one of the chores he'd completed this morning. Miriam stretched her hands, working the muscles out after grinding and mashing all afternoon.

She let her mind wander to Hoshea's early years. He was a good boy. A shame his abba had been killed at Kadesh. Eleazar and Putiel never spoke of how Nun died, only that he was one of many Hebrews needlessly killed on that dreadful campaign. Two things had changed when Eleazar returned from Kadesh. He'd taken Nun's son, Hoshea, under his wing to train and protect, and he'd turned his back on Yahweh—but that seemed to be changing. To think of him here tonight, celebrating Yahweh's deliverance with his wife . . .

Her heart was full. *Thank You, Yahweh.*

But tonight would be a somber celebration. She swished the wild lettuce, milk-thistle, and endive in water; these would be part of their bitter herbs for this evening's meal. They'd grown wild since the locusts ate everything else. Bitterness grew naturally in Egypt. It was the grain and livestock that took time to replenish.

Because of Yahweh's early warning, the Hebrews would have enough grain for tonight's unleavened bread and the seven-day supply Moses had instructed them to grind, but what then? Would they arrive in the Promised Land before the grain ran out?

"Enough worrying!" Miriam waved her hand as if shooing away flies. "If Yahweh can send frogs and flies and locusts, surely He can lead us to a city to buy a little bread." Sattar perked his ears and cocked his head as if she'd gone mad. "I haven't lost my mind yet, but I might if these young people don't help me when I ask."

Where was Taliah? If Masud's father had agreed to the circumcision, she would have returned for Miriam's help. If he refused, why wasn't she—

"Doda!" Eleazar's voice cut through the village noise. "Doda, help her." He nearly tore down the curtain, running through the doorway with Taliah in his arms.

Miriam dropped the bowl in her hands and splayed her sleeping mat on the floor. "Lay her here." She grabbed the basket of bandages and herbs she'd carried from village to village, while Eleazar placed his wife gently on the mat.

Blood stained Eleazar's arms and Taliah's abdomen. "Where is she hurt?"

"Dagger to the belly."

"Yahweh, help us." Nudging him out of the way, she knelt down and ripped Taliah's robe away. "Are you hurt, Eleazar?" she asked as she pressed wadded linen to a cut as long as a blade that sliced Taliah's bulging belly just above the bend in her leg.

"Just tend to her."

"I asked, are you hurt, boy?" Miriam barked, trying to remain calm.

"No." His chin quivered, and he pushed his thumb and fingers against his eyes, pressing back tears. "But Mosi is dead. He saved her."

"Where was she? I thought—"

"She came looking for me at the armory."

Miriam lifted the bandages and pulled the wound apart to determine its depth. Taliah groaned, drawing her legs up in pain. "Hold her legs down." Eleazar did as she asked, pressing his face against his arm, unable to watch.

Replacing the bandages with clean linen, Miriam wiped the sweat from Taliah's brow. "I don't think the blade sliced through the muscle. The baby's sack is still intact." She grabbed Eleazar's hand and pressed it against the wound. "Your hands are larger. Keep even pressure all the way across the cut."

Taliah moaned again, regaining consciousness though still groggy. "Eleazar? Oh, it hurts." She started to roll, curling her body into the pain, but Miriam pressed down on her shoulders while Eleazar kept pressure on the wound.

"You must be brave, my girl." Miriam spoke quickly, firmly. "Poppy seeds would dull the pain but they would also induce labor. Your baby could not survive yet, so you must be brave while I stitch up the wound." She kissed Taliah's forehead and eyed Eleazar. "Talk to her. Keep her calm. This will not be easy."

Miriam pushed to her feet, reached back into her basket for the flint knife, and removed Eleazar's hair tie. Without asking permission, she cut a few strands of his long, curly mane and retrieved the small bone needle she used for stitching deep cuts.

Taliah began to whimper and turned away, covering her eyes with her arm.

"You're going to be all right," Eleazar said. "Our son is alive, and you are going to live."

Having threaded the needle with three strands of Eleazar's hair, Miriam nudged his hand aside to begin. Taliah whimpered again, panicked.

"Wait!" Eleazar grabbed his hair tie and placed it between her teeth. "Remember? Bite down on this." He smiled through his tears and grabbed her hand, letting her squeeze as Miriam made the first stitch.

Taliah growled against the pain, and Eleazar stroked her forehead. "Our son will be born a free babe. He'll grow up in Yahweh's promise, own his land, marry a wife, and give us fat grandbabies we can bounce on our knees."

Miriam sewed as fast as caution allowed. "Keep talking. Keep talking."

"And I'll build you a home with four walls, a real door, and more than one window. We'll have a cow and goats—I hate sheep. They're stupid animals. Goats are much smarter."

Taliah chuckled through the groaning and tears, clenching her teeth on the same hair tie that bore her teeth marks from almost a year ago. Miriam worked and listened as the two of the people she loved most celebrated life and freedom amid their pain. *Yahweh, how far You've brought us and what a journey lies ahead.*

Taliah rested quietly, exhausted from blood loss and pain, Eleazar at her side. Doda tossed the soiled bandages in a basket to be washed in the Nile before they left Egypt. They must conserve since there would be no linen shop a short walk away after tomorrow's deliverance.

Eleazar rubbed his face, weary at the thought of the military march to come with a whole nation of women and children. It was insanity. Marching an army across the Philistine Highway had been dangerous, but marching the Israelites to Canaan would require power from Yahweh beyond anything He'd displayed yet. Of course, if He could change the wind to direct the locusts' flight and make the mighty Nile bleed, Yahweh could somehow protect a traveling nation—but how?

He cradled his wife's delicate hand between his large, callused palms. Taliah wasn't the only person in Israel who would need special care for the journey. Gently resting his hand on her belly, he wondered about women in labor or those who delivered a child tonight. What about the elderly or infirm? Israel would be free of Ramesses's cruelty, the slave masters' whips, and the endless days of hard labor, but what of food, water, provisions? Had Yahweh's people considered the costs as well as the benefits of leaving Egypt? Had he?

Footsteps outside their window intruded on his thoughts. Moses hurried in, covered in dirt. "How's Taliah? And the baby?"

"Both will be fine." Doda wiped her hands, beaming. Her confidence lifted Eleazar's spirits. "You're filthy. What have you been doing?"

Moses offered Eleazar a sympathetic look. "I took a few slaves from the armory to the Levite burial cave. We didn't have cloth or herbs for Mosi's body, but we placed him beside Abba and Ima. Hoshea is still at the armory to organize weapons distribution."

Eleazar nodded, swallowing the thick emotion. "Thank you for honoring my friend and burying him with Saba and Savta." He wanted to believe his friend's soul dwelt in paradise with Abraham, but he didn't know the deeper things of faith. For all those years, he had refused to listen when Doda or Saba spoke of such things. Now, he must know. "Will I see Mosi again in paradise?"

Moses glanced first at Doda then back at Eleazar. "I wish I could give you the answer you want, Eleazar, but the truth is, I don't know. Yahweh hasn't revealed to us as much about the afterlife as we'd like to know, and our fathers have refused to invent stories like the Egyptians."

Eleazar felt like a rock landed in his gut. "Is there a paradise where Abraham waits?"

"Yes," Doda chimed in. "Those who believe in Yahweh's promise by faith are welcomed into Abraham's bosom upon their death to await the eternal fulfillment."

Eleazar reached for Taliah's hand, wishing she'd wake. She was the one who loved words and debates and all this intellectual nonsense. But she was still sleeping, and he had to know. "Mosi never had a chance to be circumcised. Does that mean he . . ."

Again Moses hesitated, allowing Doda to answer. "Circumcision is a necessary element of our faith, it's true, but God considered Abraham as righteous before circumcision, because of his faith. Do you think Mosi had faith in Yahweh?"

Relief washed over Eleazar as he remembered his friend's words the night of the meeting at the plateau. "Absolutely. He said only Yahweh could get Ram to give the weapons key to a slave nation. He believed, Doda. I know he believed, and he intended to be circumcised and eat the Passover meal with us this evening."

"That's why I buried him in the Levites' cave." Moses eyes shimmered with unshed tears. "I think you'll see your friend again someday, Eleazar."

Lifting Taliah's hand to his lips, Eleazar pressed a kiss there and wept. *Thank You, Yahweh, for Mosi, for Taliah's life, for our deliverance.*

"You must come at once!" Abba Aaron stood in the doorway with Ithamar, breathless and panicked. "Kopshef rallied the army, and they've sealed off the armory—with the slaves inside."

Eleazar was too stunned at Ithamar's presence to fully appreciate the urgency. "Ithamar, you're here."

Abba shot an accusing stare at Eleazar. "I went to retrieve him for tonight's meal just as Kopshef returned to the palace, bloody and beaten! We heard him say it was you who—"

"Yes, he was beaten! Do you even care what Kopshef did to my wife?"

Moses stood, pressing a hand against Abba Aaron's chest. "What do you mean the Hebrew slaves are trapped?"

"When Kopshef returned to the palace, he went straight to Pharaoh and told him Ram had given Eleazar access to the weapons cabinets. He said the slaves mutinied when he tried to retrieve the key. Furious, Ramesses sent guards to Ram's chamber and placed him under house arrest, stripping him of his title. He immediately made Kopshef military commander of Egypt, and Kopshef's first order was to surround the armory and lock the gate—with the slave soldiers and all the extra weapons inside."

Moses turned to Eleazar. "We have a bigger problem than weapons. Every firstborn in that armory will die tonight unless we get them out of there by twilight."

Fear coiled around Eleazar's throat, nearly choking off his words. "Hoshea was Nun's only son." He watched the realization settle on Moses's features. "Hoshea is a firstborn."

Eleazar scrubbed his face, frustration and dread warring inside. "Ram had the only key to the weapons cabinet, and only Pharaoh and his commander hold keys to the armory gates. No one is escaping that armory unless the Egyptian army helps us tear down the walls or the king or Kopshef opens the gate."

He stared at Moses, waiting for a brilliant idea, but his uncle walked to the corner where their Passover lamb stood nervously bleating. He knelt down beside it and stroked its muzzle. Eleazar hoped his silent chat with the lamb inspired a miracle. Eleazar looked down at his sleeping wife, thankful she didn't know Hoshea's life hung in the balance.

A gentle hand rested on his shoulder. "I'm sorry, son. Tell me what happened to Taliah." Abba stood over him, genuine concern etched on his brow.

Eleazar searched for lingering accusation, perhaps some hidden blame, but saw none. Since he and Ima had sent Eleazar to become a military slave, they'd treated him like a barbarian—like a Hittite—thinking his only talent was violence. Any injuries or tragedies of war were Eleazar's own fault. Even Kadesh. "Kopshef sliced her abdomen, trying to kill her and our child, but Mosi saved them both. That's why the slaves beat Kopshef, Abba."

He squeezed Eleazar's shoulder, and gave a gentle nod. "None of us are safe from Egyptian hatred, son. You did all you could to protect your family, and Yahweh preserved their lives."

"Houses!" Moses released the lamb and marched toward the others. "Yahweh told us to paint lamb's blood on the tops and sides of the doorways of our *houses,* and eat the meal inside."

Everyone stared at him, perplexed. Doda was the first to speak. "And? How does that help Hoshea and the other firstborns in the armory? They can't get to their houses."

"Guardhouses, Miriam. There are buildings at the four corners of the armory where the overnight sentries take turns sleeping. The soldiers could shelter in the guardhouses and paint the doorframes with the lamb's blood."

Eleazar stood, meeting his uncle eye to eye. "You've obviously taken note of the armory and its contents, so you realize there are no sheep or goats in there, right? And it's surrounded by Egyptian soldiers. How do we get the meal provisions inside?"

"Aaron will go get Nadab and Abihu." Moses ran to the window and checked the position of the sun. "Time is running out, but if we spread the word among the elders, we can get their provisions to them and be home by twilight. We need all the elements for the meal taken to the armory—sheep, goats, herbs, and bread. Yahweh will make a way."

Eleazar pulled both hands through his hair. "What about the Egyptian guards? Blood sacrifice is detestable to them. They never see the offerings inside their temples. Do you think they'll just watch while we sacrifice lambs and toss them over the walls?"

Moses grinned. "Actually, I'm hoping they'll help."

54

*Each man is to take a lamb for his family, one
for each household. If any household is too
small for a whole lamb, they must share one
with their nearest neighbor, having taken into
account the number of people there are. You
are to determine the amount of lamb needed
in accordance with what each person will eat.*

—Exodus 12:3–4

A gentle evening breeze lifted a few gray curls off Miriam's fore-head. She leaned against their long house, waiting for the men to return, watching the sun descend behind the western hills. They'd been gone so long.

When the Levite elder had come seeking donations for the armory soldiers, Miriam shared some of their bitter herbs. He'd told her that a few women had set up ovens by the armory walls and were baking bread, tossing over the warm rounds to the soldiers waiting on the other side.

O Yahweh, what a sight! She wished she could help, but Taliah had needed a tender hand this afternoon after waking in pain. Poor dear. The girl would be sore for a few days, but what a miracle that both she and the babe were safe.

Miriam walked to the end of the alley and searched the path toward the city. No Eleazar or Moses. Would they make it home by twilight? Would Yahweh have mercy if they disobeyed a command while helping others obey Him?

A sudden flash stole her consciousness and placed her in a white linen robe at the edge of a vast sea. An overpowering wave—taller than Ramesses statues—piled up on both sides but didn't sweep her away. Hur was beside her, holding her hand. He leaned over and kissed her cheek. *A kiss from Yahweh.* He kissed her lips. *A kiss from me.*

The vision left her, and she was back on the dusty path in Goshen, trembling. She pressed a hand to her throat and drew a shaky breath. Yearning nearly felled her, and she covered a sob. *Yahweh, I love him. I don't want to, but I love him.*

But to realize her need for him now did no good. Hur was in his son's home—so close and yet twilight was almost upon them. She couldn't leave Taliah unattended, and if the men didn't arrive soon, she must sacrifice the lamb herself at twilight. Turning toward home, she was so deep in thought she didn't hear anyone approach until the voice startled her.

"Shalom, Miriam." Hur stood a step away with Elisheba at his side.

The pairing was so unlikely, Miriam could only stare. The two had barely spoken in all the years she'd known them. Why were they together now, here?

"Miriam?" Hur's brow furrowed. "Are you all right?"

"Yes, yes. Oh, I'm sorry. Shalom." She noticed the laden baskets on Elisheba's arms and the wineskin Hur carried. "Are you on your way to share tonight's meal with someone?"

Hur chuckled, but Elisheba turned to go. "I told you I wouldn't be welcome."

He grabbed her arm, soothing. "Miriam didn't say we weren't welcome, and you haven't told her why you wanted to join her household for the meal." He raised his eyebrows, grinned at Miriam, and waited.

Though considerably flustered, Miriam's curiosity overruled. "Elisheba wanted to join us?"

"Is it so hard to believe I could care about my grandchild?" Elisheba's chin quivered as she stared into the distance.

Confused, Miriam looked to Hur for answers, but he lifted a hand, advising her patience.

The silence forced Elisheba to explain. "When Aaron came home to get Nadab and Abihu to help at the armory, he mentioned Taliah's injury and that she'd nearly lost our grandchild." She swiped at tears and turned on Miriam. "Only Aaron, the two boys, and I were going to eat the meal together tonight since we hadn't found anyone to share our lamb with, so I gave our lamb to the armory."

Compassion chipped away at Miriam's defenses. Elisheba and her two sons had alienated nearly everyone in their village. Of course, no one wanted to share a meal. Whether she was truly concerned about Taliah was yet to be proven, but at least she acknowledged the babe as her grandchild. "We would be happy to have your household join ours for the meal, Elisheba."

"You see?" Hur patted Elisheba's back as a rare grin almost erased her frown lines. "Didn't I say we'd be welcome?"

"We?" Miriam, eyes wide, couldn't find more words.

Elisheba shuffled through her baskets. "I brought plenty of bread to feed Nadab and Abihu. They like my recipe. I add a little honey—"

"The elders and I have allotted the wagons for the elderly, sick, and new imas," Hur interrupted, his light-brown eyes never leaving Miriam. "Taliah will, of course, have a place in one of the lead wagons—either with Aaron and Elisheba or my new wife and I."

Miriam felt the blood drain from her face. If she spoke, she'd cry, so she nodded and tried to smile. Elisheba filled the silence. "I hadn't realized you married again. Who's the lucky bride? Do I know her?"

"I hope she's standing in front of me, Elisheba, and if you'll go check on your daughter-in-law, I'm going to ask Miriam to marry me properly."

"Well, I—"

"Please, Elisheba. Go now."

Miriam covered her mouth, not sure whether to laugh or cry. Hur took a step toward her, closing the distance between them. His eyes penetrated the depths of her soul.

Tears came without permission as Miriam thought of the torturous last few days. "Why didn't you talk to me at the meeting or come see me after?"

He reached beneath her head covering to tuck a stray hair behind her ear. "You'd heard enough from me. You needed time to hear from Yahweh."

His simple words and gentle touch sent her heart into a gallop. How could she explain the changes she'd felt during his absence? "So much has happened in the last few days, and with every experience, I wanted to share it with you. Yahweh already knew my thoughts and feelings, so when you were gone, I didn't have anyone to help sort it out." She shook her head and sighed, frustrated at her inability to express in words what their relationship meant.

He tipped up her chin. "You will be bone of my bone and flesh of my flesh. When the others return, one of them can pronounce the wedding blessing, and we'll have the rest of our lives to share our thoughts and feelings." Hur leaned down for a kiss, and Miriam tilted her head back, receiving it willingly. For the first time in her life, she belonged to another. A man who loved her. A man Yahweh had chosen as her special gift.

Hur brushed her cheek. "We need to prepare the lamb. It's almost twilight."

She nodded, and they leaned on each other as they walked back to the long house. When Hur pushed aside the curtain, Miriam entered and was pleased to see Elisheba helping Taliah drink a cup of herb tea.

Taliah perked up when she saw Hur. "Welcome home." Miriam glanced over her shoulder and thought she saw a faint blush on his cheeks. Taliah strained to see around them, her countenance falling when the curtain closed behind them.

Miriam knelt beside her. "Eleazar will be home soon, dear." She glanced up at Hur. "Did you see them at the armory?"

"I didn't go to the armory. Moses asked me to remain in Goshen and reassign families to share meals since we sent so many lambs to the armory. I'm sure they'll be back any time." Hur glanced out the window again. "It's twilight . . ." He looked at the lamb now lying beside Taliah. "We must paint the doorframe."

Taliah dug her fingers into the lamb's thick wool and bowed her head. Miriam knew she was crying. Elisheba wasn't as subtle. "Why did Moses say to care for the lambs in the house for four days? They grow tame and become so dear to us."

"I believe that's the point, Elisheba." Miriam picked up the lead rope. "A sacrifice is only a sacrifice if it costs us something."

Miriam reached for a bowl, and Hur retrieved Moses's dagger from the private chamber. Miriam called over her shoulder as she led the lamb outside. "Elisheba, light the lamps. Get the cook fire and spit ready. We'll bring in the lamb after we paint the doorframe."

When she and Hur stepped outside, she handed him the lead rope. "This is my household. I must sacrifice the lamb."

Hur kissed her forehead. "For a few more hours that's true." He gave her the dagger.

Their single row of long houses was lined with others performing the same grizzly task. Men crouched over bleating lambs—and then the bleating stopped. Hur bent on one knee and held their yearling securely against him. He looked at her with so much compassion.

Miriam swiped at stubborn tears and exhaled a deep breath. "I've delivered half the babies in Goshen and seen too much death, but I've never deliberately taken a life."

Hur positioned the bowl under the lamb's neck and then placed his hand over Miriam's on the dagger. "Make the cut all the way across. Swift and deep. It's the most merciful way."

Without further thought, she slashed the knife and turned her eyes away, letting her tears fall. Only a few moments passed, and she felt Hur's hand on her shoulder. "It's over."

Timidly, Miriam turned her head. The bowl was full of sticky red blood, and the lamb lay lifeless on the ground. *How gracious, Yahweh, that the death of one should save the lives of many.* Still, her tears fell for the little creature. She leaned down to kiss its soft black muzzle, and whispered through a tight throat, "Thank you."

55

*Take a bunch of hyssop, dip it into the blood
in the basin and put some of the blood on the
top and on both sides of the doorframe. None
of you shall go out of the door of your house
until morning.*

—Exodus 12:22

Covered in lamb's blood, Eleazar walked between Nadab and Abihu toward Goshen. Ithamar walked in front of them, flanked by Abba and Moses. They would reach Doda's by twilight but barely.

"How many lambs do you think we slaughtered?" Abihu trudged along the path, exaggerating his fatigue.

"Three hundred twenty-one." Ithamar beamed, just waiting to be asked. "That should be enough to feed the thousands of soldiers—"

"Of course, the scribe would know." Eleazar taunted his favorite brother, nudging him in the back.

Nadab tried to lift his arm but halted his trembling limb midway. "I think my arms are too tired to lift food to my mouth."

"Here, Nadab dearest," Abihu squeaked in a feminine voice, "I'll chew your meat for you if you're too tired."

Nadab growled, laughing, and reached over Eleazar to shove the second born. "Ima can't help herself. I'm too handsome to resist."

All three brothers groaned, but the banter soothed years of pain. Working beside his abba and brothers had filled Eleazar with joy though the occasion was anything but happy. The purpose and selflessness with which they came together had filled an emptiness he had clung to so long.

Doda's long house came into view too soon, and the group of men grew quiet. Though they were closest kin, Abba Aaron and his brothers would walk on to another village when Moses and Eleazar turned down the alleyway to rejoin Doda and Taliah. Perhaps things could be different when they left Egypt.

Rounding the corner, Eleazar saw Doda and Hur bent over the lamb, and he felt a twinge of guilt that Doda had to take a life. It would affect her deeply. Pressed by the time, he reached for Abba's shoulder to begin the good-byes. "I'm sure we'll see each other as soon as Pharaoh summons—"

"Wait!" Doda shouted. "Elisheba is here. You're all invited to eat with us."

She waved them toward her, and Abba slapped Eleazar on the back. "We need not say good-bye after all." The sparkle in his eyes assured Eleazar he'd felt the same dread at parting.

Covered in blood from head to toe, they must have been a horrendous sight, but the six of them strode toward Doda like victors.

Ima Elisheba shot through the curtain, wagging her finger. "I thought you'd never get here. Can't you see the sunset from the armory? I don't know why you insist on trying my patien—"

Abba Aaron pulled her into a hug. "I'm sorry we worried you, but we're home now. We'll hear no more about it." She grumbled about his blood-stained robe, but he silenced her with a single finger pressed against her lips.

"How's my Taliah?" Eleazar ached to go inside, but he knew there was work to be done.

"Go check on your wife." Moses nudged him toward the door and gave Nadab the blood-soaked hyssop branch he'd brought from the armory. "Your brothers and I will take care of skinning the lamb and painting the doorframe."

Anxious to see his wife, Eleazar needed no coaxing. He hurried through the curtain and saw Taliah propped against some baskets and blankets. She'd regained a little color.

Her countenance lit when she saw him. "You made it."

Before he took a step, he realized he was still covered in blood, but there was no time to bathe in the river. Eyeing a large jar of water, he grabbed it, careful not to slosh any, and kissed Taliah's forehead on his way to the adjoining room. "I'll be back when I can hold you in my arms."

Within a few moments, everyone was safely inside, and the lamb was roasting on the spit. Abba, Moses, and Eleazar's brothers washed their hands and arms in the adjoining room—the best they could do without a bath. Perhaps there'd be time tomorrow before leaving Egypt to enjoy one more bath in the Nile.

Eleazar nestled down behind his wife, propping her against him instead of the lumpy baskets. She settled into him, her warmth the essence of home. The small room was crowded and filled with noise—family noise. Ima Elisheba and Doda Miriam argued over who would mix the bread dough, while Abba and Eleazar's brothers began a game of chance with rocks and sticks. Moses and Hur leaned against the wall with Sattar huddled between them. Ten family members would share a lamb that could feed up to fourteen, but because seven hungry men hadn't eaten much all day, they probably wouldn't have leftovers to burn in the morning.

Eleazar's stomach growled, and Taliah reached up to brush his cheek. "Miriam said the lamb wouldn't be fully cooked until midnight —about the time the deaths begin. Were you able to talk with Hoshea at all, explain that he needed to get at least all the firstborns inside the guardhouses?"

"We didn't need to explain much. His passion for Yahweh has made him quite a leader among the captive soldiers. Even Ru, the chief Hittite, shows him respect and has committed to circumcision before this evening's meal."

"You're proud of him, aren't you?"

Eleazar's throat tightened. How could he describe his awe at Yahweh's far-reaching plans? Since Kopshef had killed Hoshea's abba at Kadesh, Eleazar and Putiel had taken responsibility for the boy's training—Eleazar for his military skills and Putiel for his faith. "It's you who should be proud, Taliah. Your abba taught Hoshea of Yahweh. It's Putiel's legacy that will save many lives tonight."

A smile mingled with Taliah's tears. Eleazar brushed her hair from her forehead and gazed at the beautiful daughter of Putiel, his wife, his love. *Thank You, Yahweh.*

She reached for his hand and kissed his palm. "Miriam told me about Mosi, Eleazar. I'm sorry."

"I'm sorry too, but Yahweh honored his sacrifice by saving your life and our son's."

A sparkle returned to her eyes. "I still don't know why you think it's a boy."

"I'm telling you. An abba knows these things."

She laughed out loud and let a genial silence fall between them. "Mosi's name meant firstborn, didn't it?"

Eleazar's hope soared. It was a Hebrew ima's right to name her children, and he would be so pleased if she'd give their son Mosi's name.

"*Firstborn* would be meaningful for our son, but it's not a Hebrew name."

Eleazar tried to hide his disappointment. "What name then?"

"I wondered about the Hebrew word for Nubian, *Phinehas.* It would still honor Mosi—"

Eleazar kissed her to show his approval. He'd never been good with words.

Whistles and jeers erupted from his brothers. Eleazar took off his wristband and threw it at them, and Taliah's cheeks pinked. The elders in the room laughed and applauded.

Hur exchanged a furtive glance with Doda, lifting his brows in silent question. She shook her head, expression clouding, and turned away. Whatever Hur's silent question had been, Doda had said no. What were they up to?

Hur turned to Abba Aaron. "How does it feel to have your whole family under one roof for tonight's meal?"

A loaded question, considering their history. Eleazar held his breath.

"You should have seen my boys working together, Hur." Abba's eyes glistened. "As children they couldn't work together without bickering, but today was another miracle in Egypt."

More laughter, and Eleazar relaxed. "Speaking of more miracles, you should have seen the guards helping us. Yahweh had completely turned their hearts. They helped slaughter more than three hundred lambs and lift them over the gates."

"Were any of the guards firstborns?" Hur's wiry eyebrows shot up with hope. "Did you tell them how to be saved?"

"A few were firstborns, and many had firstborn sons." Eleazar placed a possessive hand on Taliah's rounded belly. "Unfortunately, we heard the same reply from them that I heard from Prince Ram. If Pharaoh saw the blood on their doors, they'd be killed."

Ima Elisheba looked at Nadab with that date-syrup sweetness she reserved for only her two eldest. "I don't know how any parent could forfeit a firstborn." An uncomfortable silence settled over the room. Would tonight's meal be spoiled by the same hurtful patterns?

Hur spoke into the void. "When people care more about their lifestyle than the people they love, they are as imprisoned by their desires as we are enslaved by Pharaoh."

Ima's hands stilled on the spit. "We can love people and still enjoy the comfortable lifestyle they provide for us."

There it was. Ima's driving motivation for relationships. She had forced Abba to ignore his parents so she could have finer robes and meat on the table. And she'd kept Nadab and Abihu from marrying to provide for her in old age.

Eleazar stared at the most selfish woman he knew. "When we leave Egypt, we'll all give up our comfort and prove how well we love people."

Gasping, Ima turned to Abba. "Are you going to let him speak to me that way?"

"He included us all, Elisheba, and he spoke wisdom. You should consider his words—in silence." Even Nadab and Abihu covered grins.

Hur clapped his hands, startling everyone. "Miriam and I have an announcement to make." Pushing himself to his feet, he held out his hand to Miriam. "We plan to be married—tonight."

Moses and Abba Aaron rose to offer their congratulations, but Eleazar looked down at Taliah. "Did you know about this?"

She fairly glowed with excitement. "No, but isn't it wonderful?" When he didn't respond, he got a poke in the stomach. "What's wrong with you? Go over and congratulate them."

"Why can't they stay friends? They're too old to be married." His voice carried in the small space, and silence replaced the jubilant atmosphere. The hurt on Doda Miriam's face made him ache. "I'm sorry. I just don't see—"

"You don't have to see, boy." His feisty little doda spoke softly. "Hur can tell you all the practical reasons we need each other to travel through the wilderness, but the truth is, Hur is a part of Yahweh's new revelation to me. Since that morning I interpreted Pharaoh's nightmares, I've begged the One God to speak to me clearly." She turned and scanned the room. "All these months, He's been speaking through Moses, Hur, Taliah— even Sattar—but I've still been pounding my fists and begging Him to speak clearly, unable to perceive Him over my own rantings."

She looked intently into Eleazar's eyes. "We'd like you to pronounce our wedding blessing because you above all people know that sometimes people are stronger together than apart."

Panic shot through him like a hot iron. "I don't know the blessing. I only remember parts of it from Saba Amram—"

Hur rested a wrinkled hand on Eleazar's shoulder. "You'll have the words Yahweh gives you."

Doda and Hur looked at him with such hope. How could he refuse? Taliah poked him again. "I'd be honored." The words escaped him before he could stop them.

"Gather around the couple." Moses rallied the troops in the center of the room, forming a snug knot of family support. Eleazar replaced the baskets behind Taliah and left a space in the circle so she could watch.

Suddenly as nervous as he'd been for his own wedding, Eleazar swallowed hard. "Doda, Hur, take each other's hand and face me." He took a deep breath and looked into their rheumy eyes, overwhelmed at all they'd seen during their lifetimes.

"In the twilight of your lives, Yahweh has melded you into one sword, like Hittite iron—strong and true. Two are better than one for the journey that lies ahead, and you will be a gift to each other." Hur reached for Doda's hand and squeezed. Why had Eleazar placed an age limit on love?

He glanced at Taliah, trying to remember the words Amram and Moses had pronounced on their wedding night. Happy tears streamed down her cheeks, and the words came rushing back. "When Yahweh made woman, the man said of her, 'You are now bone of my bone and flesh of my flesh. You are called woman, for you were taken from me.' Hur, Miriam is now your wife."

Hur kissed her cheek. "That is from Yahweh." He kissed her lips gently, and then held her head and kissed her thoroughly. As the family applauded, Hur looked into his bride's eyes and said, "That was from me."

56

During the night Pharaoh summoned Moses
and Aaron and said, "Up! Leave my people,
you and the Israelites! Go, worship the LORD
as you have requested. Take your flocks and
herds, as you have said, and go. And also
bless me."

—EXODUS 12:31–32

Miriam's wedding had truly been a celebration. Her whole family surrounded her, laughing and chatting as the night grew dark and the stars grew bright. Everyone took a turn spinning the lamb on the spit, the large cook fire nearly baking them all. The pungent aromas of herbs, bread, and lamb ripened their hunger to sweet expectancy.

Moses went to the window and searched the sky. "The moon is too high to see from the window, which means the plague should be—" A neighbor's scream pierced the night air, and Moses bowed his head. "Yahweh, pass over us."

Every eye turned to Nadab, whose face went pale. Elisheba squeezed his hand and pushed herself to her feet, weeping and moving her lips without a sound. It was the first time Miriam had seen her sister-in-law pray.

Miriam used Hur's shoulder to push herself to stand. The others rose to their feet as well, following Yahweh's commands. More shrieks echoed outside as those in Miriam's home donned their sandals and tucked their robes into their belts. The men grabbed their walking sticks, while Miriam and Elisheba hurried to set out the food they'd been waiting to serve.

Elisheba's forehead was beaded with sweat. "I don't know if the lamb is cooked through."

An Egyptian mother's wail tore at Miriam's heart. She closed her eyes and placed a calming hand on her sister-in-law's shoulder. "Yahweh said we would eat in haste. He knew how much time we'd have to cook the lamb." Elisheba nodded and began carving the meat onto a platter to cool while Miriam distributed clay cups and plates to everyone. Baskets of bread and bitter herbs filled every space of Miriam's sleeping mat, used tonight for the family's meal.

Miriam pulled out the wineskin Hur contributed. "A gift from my son for our wedding," Hur announced, emotion clipping his words. "Yahweh, pass over my boy Uri." Tears blurred Miriam's vision as she filled everyone's cup. She squeezed the last drops of wine into Hur's cup, leaving her own cup empty.

"Here, beloved, take mine." Hur reached for her empty cup, but she stilled his hand.

"Please, no. I'll drink water." She took her place between him and Taliah. "I drank my cup of joy when I became your wife."

Elisheba hurried from where she stood between Nadab and Abihu and retrieved a water pitcher to fill Miriam's cup. Surprised, but grateful, Miriam nodded her thanks.

Moses lifted his cup and the others followed. "Yahweh has said, 'I will bring My people out.'"

They echoed his words, "I will bring My people out."

As the men tipped their cups, Miriam noted the dried lamb's blood still caked around their nails. "Wait, I'll get a bowl of water to wash our hands." She hurried to the task and draped a towel over her shoulder, waiting before each person as they dipped their hands in the water and dried them.

Miriam washed her hands last. Plunging her hands into the water, she thought of the many bloody bowls she'd dipped her hands into—the thousands of wounded slaves she'd tended. *Freedom, Yahweh. What will it be like?*

Moses leaned over to retrieve three small loaves of bread from a bas-

ket and lifted the middle loaf. "These three signify Abraham, Isaac, and
Jacob. The middle of anything signifies the heart." He broke the middle
loaf into two pieces. "When Abraham was willing to sacrifice Isaac, it
broke Isaac's heart—but both father and son were willing and obedient to
follow Yahweh." Moses let silence massage his message into their souls.
"Obedience to Yahweh is seldom an easy path, but it is ultimately the
only path to freedom." He passed the bread around the circle, and each
one took a piece, devouring both the bread and its significance.

Moses lifted his wine cup again. "Yahweh said to Abraham, 'Your
descendants will be strangers in a foreign land for four hundred years,
enslaved and mistreated, but I, Yahweh, will free My people.'"

His words sent a shiver down Miriam's spine, and the cool drink of
water chilled her insides. She tasted salty tears as they ran down her
cheeks and tried to imagine what tomorrow might be like.

Moses reached for the bitter herbs from the basket and stuffed several
leaves into his mouth. He chewed, grimaced, and everyone chuckled.
Miriam and the others followed his lead. The pungent greens typically
accompanied a meal, made palatable by sweet fruits or roasted nuts. But
when eaten alone, their bitterness couldn't be diminished, ignored, or
masked. The tongue must endure the assault as Israel had borne slavery
all these years.

A father's cry joined the wailing, and Miriam squeezed her eyes shut.
Indeed, the bitterness of slavery had set Israel's teeth on edge for four
hundred years. *Yahweh, pass over us.* She opened her eyes as Elisheba
offered the platter of lamb in one hand and the basket of her honeyed
bread in the other. Miriam thanked her for serving and Yahweh for His
provision.

They stood ready to flee, as Yahweh commanded, eating solemnly,
listening to the cries outside their door. Earlier this night, they'd celebrated each other, marriage, and freedom, but there would be no laughter
or teasing now. Their deliverance was at hand—but at a great price.

Hur's arm circled Miriam's waist and he kissed the top of her head.
"Freedom means a new life for us all—wherever Yahweh leads."

The reminder of their uncertain path turned every eye to Moses. Did he know where Yahweh would lead? Miriam saw his discomfort but asked the question on everyone's mind. "Has Yahweh revealed the next step, Brother?"

Another Egyptian father joined the wailing, and Moses's eyes slid shut. He sighed before opening his eyes to speak. "Yahweh said Pharaoh would drive us out of Egypt, but how and when still hasn't been made clear." The answer did little to reassure them. The wailing seemed louder. More shrieks filled the air. Moses's countenance remained calm. "Yahweh will protect us through this night." He raised his wine once more. "Yahweh said, 'I will redeem My people.'"

Cries of mourning surrounded them. How could they endure it all night? Just then, Miriam remembered a special treasure one of the Egyptian families had given her. She quietly slipped from Hur's embrace and dug through a basket for the timbrels and found three. She gave one to Elisheba and one to Taliah and kept the last for herself.

With a single clap, Miriam began the familiar chorus she'd sung since childhood. "El Shaddai, You—" Realizing she'd used the name for God she'd used all her life, she hesitated.

Moses grinned and lifted his wine cup to her. "*Yahweh* will make us His treasured possession. He said, 'I will take you as My very own people.'" Moses drank and lifted his deep, baritone voice, beginning the chorus again with God's most intimate name. "Yahweh, You have been our dwelling place throughout all generations."

Everyone joined in, the women clapping their timbrels and singing in the presence of Yahweh while He moved through the land judging the Egyptians and their gods. Occasionally, they'd stop, eat more bread, herbs, and meat until the wailing overcame them. Then they'd lift their voices and timbrels in song again, losing all sense of time. Miriam closed her eyes as she sang, allowing the music to lift her into Yahweh's presence. Her Yahweh. Israel's Yahweh.

Suddenly, Taliah shushed the group. "I think I hear horses coming." Wide eyed, everyone stilled, waiting.

Moments later, the clanging of a chariot harness drew near, and a loud voice shouted over the mourning, "Pharaoh Ramesses summons

Moses and Aaron. Show yourselves!" Repeatedly, the crier shouted the message as the chariot rolled down the first alley of Goshen's long houses.

Moses hurried through the curtained doorway. "I am Moses." He ducked back inside the long house, baiting them.

Miriam snuggled close to Hur, while Eleazar laid Taliah against the wall behind him and covered her with a blanket.

An Egyptian prince sliced the curtain with his sword. "My father summons you to—" He nearly stumbled over his tongue when he saw Eleazar. "What are you . . ." Rattled, he paused, trying to gather his wits. The poor boy's eyes were swollen and bloodshot, and his bald head was exposed. He hadn't even taken time to don his wig. He wasn't much older than Hoshea. Settling his gaze on Miriam's brothers, he barked, "Are you Moses and Aaron?"

Moses nodded. "And which son are you?"

The question seemed to unsettle him further. "I am Prince Khaem-waset, second born of Isetneferet." His cheeks quaked, and he pointed an accusing finger at Eleazar. "My brother Ram is dead because you let his wound fester."

Eleazar stepped toward him. "Is that what Pharaoh told you, Khaem?"

"Yes, and it's true." The prince stepped back and lifted his sword.

Moses lifted both hands, trying to settle the boy. "Did your father lie about all the firstborn deaths in Egypt? Surely, you realize Ram's death wasn't a result of Eleazar's negligence—but Yahweh's wrath."

Like a caged beast, Khaem glanced from one Hebrew to another. "Pharaoh says the double portions of Canaanite grain given to firstborns must have been tainted."

Miriam could stand it no longer. "Psshh, that's nonsense!" She waved her hand and stepped around Eleazar. "You are a grown man and can think for yourself, young Khaem. Check your slaves, your livestock. I'm sure the firstborns are dead, and they ate no Canaanite grain."

Grinding his teeth, he spoke with barely controlled rage. "I need only check my newborn son's crib, woman. He ate no grain either." He lifted his hand to strike her but hesitated, growled, and stormed out.

Moses spoke quickly. "Eleazar will escort Aaron and me to the palace. Nadab must stay inside the house to be safe, but Hur, Abihu, and Ithamar must get word to the elders. Our deliverance is at hand. Israel should be ready to depart by sunrise. We mustn't give Pharaoh a chance to change his mind again."

57

Moses gave Hoshea son of Nun the name Joshua.

—NUMBERS 13:16

The journey to Pharaoh's palace was torture. Prince Khaem drove his chariot in front of the three Hebrews, kicking up dirt and sand in their faces, while his three guards followed behind them, pressing their pace beyond what Abba Aaron could manage.

Finally, they arrived at the palace, Eleazar nearly carrying Abba Aaron, who was panting from the harried journey. Prince Khaem led them directly to the throne hall, his sandals clapping on the marble tiles. The moment the grand ebony doors opened, Pharaoh's fury erupted.

"Dead! How could you take every firstborn from me?" He slammed his flail on the armrest and stood to await their arrival at the dais. "You've taken my strength, my life, my legacy!" Pharaoh may have publicly blamed firstborn deaths on tainted grain, but he knew the true source of Egypt's mourning.

Prince Khaem mounted the dais and took his new place at Ramesses's right shoulder. Two new Nubians guarded Pharaoh—evidently his previous guards had been firstborns. Standing utterly still, their eyes darted from the Hebrews to the sky as if expecting an attack from above.

Abba Aaron removed his arm from Eleazar's shoulder and stood at Moses's side. Eleazar stood behind and between them. The Hebrews offered no answer to Pharaoh's accusation.

No matter. Ramesses didn't expect one. "Leave my people, Moses. You and the Israelites, go worship Yahweh as you've requested. Take your flocks and herds, your wives and children." He leaned forward and gritted his teeth. "But pray your god's blessing on me before you leave."

Pharaoh's echo faded into the empty throne hall before Moses replied. "Every Israelite must leave Egypt—even the slaves in the armory." He nodded to the key hanging around Prince Khaem's neck.

The prince stiffened as Pharaoh sat down on his throne, rubbing his chin violently while considering the request. Sweat formed on Eleazar's upper lip. Had Moses pushed too far? Would Pharaoh refuse again?

"Take everyone, and get out." Ramesses waved his hand at Khaem. "Give him the key."

Moses held out his hand, and Khaem, shaking with rage, unlatched his necklace and dropped the key into Moses's hand. "My brothers' blood is on your head."

Moses stared at him unflinching. "Four hundred years of slavery cancelled that debt." The Hebrews turned their backs on Egypt's king and left the throne hall in quiet victory.

No one dared speak until they reached the palace gates. Eyes followed them everywhere. Guards were posted at every door and atop the complex wall. When they reached the palace gate, Abba Aaron stumbled and nearly fell. Eleazar caught him and then checked the guards' reaction. No bows were drawn, only empty stares from a beaten people.

Abba braced his hands on his knees, breathing hard. "Please, I must rest a moment. My old legs can't run back to Goshen."

Eleazar exchanged a grin with Moses. "We aren't going to Goshen. The armory is much closer."

Abba Aaron's lips curved into a wry smile. "My legs are suddenly stronger."

"That's because you're a free man." Moses patted Abba's back. "Let's go."

Moses began jogging to the armory.

"Wait for me!" Eleazar chuckled, surprised at his uncle's stamina.

"I'll catch up." Abba Aaron hurried at his own pace.

Eleazar arrived at Moses's side, and his uncle teased, "I'm a shepherd, son. You Hebrew soldiers are soft." His smile dimmed, and he checked the waning moon. "Everyone will be pushed beyond their strength to leave by sunrise, and that's only the beginning. Sinai will test us all."

"Sinai." Eleazar shook his head, thinking of Taliah. She could never climb Sinai's bluffs and plateaus in her condition. "The Hebrews have no idea what kind of terrain we're facing. Most of the slave soldiers that marched with Pharaoh's army are dead at Kopshef's hand."

"That's why we're borrowing the wagons and tents. The elders have already assigned the tribal order of march and know where to meet at daybreak." He cocked his head and winked. "What do you think we've been doing while you've been getting those weapons?"

Eleazar shook his head, newly amazed at the man Yahweh had chosen to deliver Israel. When Moses had mentioned the need for weapons, Eleazar's only concern had been the immediate hurdle of wrestling the key from Ram, but Moses had already been planning to defend against the desert tribes in the wilderness. That was the difference between wavering doubt and steadfast faith.

As they neared the armory, they passed a dead Egyptian guard on the path—then another. Eleazar recognized some of them as those who'd helped sacrifice lambs yesterday. He halted Moses before they reached the gate, assessing the Egyptians still guarding it. "Will they attack us in retaliation?"

One of the guards spotted them while he spoke and fell to his knees. "Take your people and go," he shouted. "Leave us, or all of Egypt will die." Other guards rushed toward Eleazar and Moses, begging them to leave.

Moses showed them the gate key, and they eagerly escorted them. Hands shaking, Moses nearly dropped the key in the dust.

Impatient, Eleazar shouted through the gates. "Hoshea? Are you there? Hoshea?"

No answer. They heard only wailing from inside.

Moses finally unlatched the heavy iron lock, and the Egyptians helped swing open the gates. The sparring arena was strewn with dead slaves and others who mourned them, but torchlight glowed in all four guardhouses.

"Hoshea!" Moses shouted, hurrying toward the nearest shelter. The curtain rustled, and Hoshea appeared in the doorway.

"Are we free?" Hoshea hesitated.

Tears burned Eleazar's eyes. "We're free."

Hoshea ran from the guardhouse into Eleazar's embrace. Others poured from the shelters in numbers far exceeding his expectations. Hebrews first, and then foreign slaves walking gingerly. Eleazar held him at arm's length. "How many agreed to be circumcised?"

"Not many at first, but I told the Hebrews in each house to recite the ancient stories—Creation, Noah, and Abraham's journey—and the foreign soldiers listened from outside. Before midnight, many believed and filled the guardhouses." Hoshea's wide-eyed wonder was infectious.

Moses shook Hoshea, eyes glistening. "You're no longer *Hoshea,* my boy, because you weren't merely *saved* as the name implies." Wrapping his arm around the boy, he declared to the gathering crowd, "This man is now called *Yehoshua*—*Joshua*—because *Yahweh saved* all of you through his faithfulness." A great roar rose among the soldiers, shaking the ground beneath their feet. Eleazar joined the victory cry, energy pumping through his weary body.

Moses shouted at Eleazar over the noise. "It's up to you to get weapons to every household in Goshen by the time we leave at dawn."

"Not me," Eleazar said, gripping Hoshea's shoulder. "The men have a new commander—Joshua."

Joshua's eyes looked as big as the moon. "But you're the slave commander."

"True, but I see no slaves here." Eleazar spread his hands over the sea of rejoicing soldiers. "You rallied the men, and Yahweh saved their lives. It's you who will assign their defensive positions as Israel marches out of Egypt."

Abba Aaron arrived then, covering his ears against the ruckus. "What did I miss?"

Eleazar patted Joshua's chest. "Abba, meet Israel's new military commander, Joshua."

Abba's eyes sparkled, and he opened his arms, welcoming the young man who'd escorted him safely across the Sinai. "I can think of no one

better to lead us—except perhaps my son." He released Joshua and studied Eleazar. "What will you do now?"

"I'll return to Goshen with you. Those who have been too afraid to
ask their Egyptian neighbors for gold, silver, and clothing should have no
problem doing so now."

58

The Israelites journeyed from Rameses to
Sukkoth. . . . Many other people went up
with them, and also large droves of livestock,
both flocks and herds. With the dough the
Israelites had brought from Egypt, they baked
loaves of unleavened bread. The dough was
without yeast because they had been driven
out of Egypt and did not have time to prepare
food for themselves.

—Exodus 12:37–39

Waiting for official word of their deliverance was excruciating, but the required patience grew less painful when families found musical instruments among their treasures and began singing to Yahweh. As sounds of praise echoed in Goshen's villages, Egypt's wailing ebbed. The night wore on. The praise endured.

When Eleazar and Aaron finally returned home, the household celebrated loudly enough to alert their whole village that Yahweh had kept His promise. By the time Moses returned to Goshen near daybreak, he found Hebrew men wearing spears and bows across their backs as they tethered baskets and bedrolls to donkeys and oxen. Children draped in gold and silver jewelry chased sheep and goats down the alleyways between long houses. Tired imas dressed in Egypt's finest linen kneaded bread dough without yeast—timbrels and drums strapped to their backs.

"Why are you making bread?" Moses shouted at Miriam when he found her kneading like the others.

"It's what women do when we're nervous." She pushed to her feet, clapping excess flour from her hands. "You'll be happy about it when your stomach growls at midday. It's not like Yahweh will drop bread from the sky."

The call to march had come, and kneading troughs—with bread dough still inside—were wrapped in fine linen and tossed on strong Hebrew shoulders.

Miriam sat beside Hur on the wooden bench of an ox-drawn cart as the sun peeked over the eastern hills. Taliah lay snuggled in the cart on a cloud of blankets with eight elderly caretakers to tend to her. Aaron and Elisheba's cart pulled up beside them, carrying the precious cargo of their ancestor Joseph's bones. Miriam had feared there might be bloodshed when the Hebrews broke into Joseph's elegant mastaba on palace grounds to retrieve his mummified remains, but Eleazar assured her, "The Egyptians will give us anything as long as we leave quickly."

Hur reached for her hand. "Look to the east, Miriam. It's the last time we'll see a sunrise in Goshen."

She scooted closer and laid her head on his shoulder. Married. She was *married*.

A warm breeze lifted her sheer linen head covering. She didn't consider whether it was Yahweh's breath or simply the wind. She knew now that Yahweh could speak in any way He liked. She need only lean into the people He placed in her life to hear Him clearly.

"Prophetess, prophetess!" A little voice called up from beside her cart. She thrilled at the sight of Haji, younger brother of Masud and Tuya. "You're wearing a lot of gold!"

Touching the heavy jewelry on her neck and wrists, she unlatched an ankle bracelet and tossed it to the boy. "Give this to your mother." All three children walked past the cart with their parents. The boys and their father were in pain but joyful. They'd searched out Taliah at the front of Israel's procession to deliver the happy news that they'd obeyed Yahweh's commands and now believed in the One God.

Miriam scanned the sea of faces behind them. So many—some familiar, some foreign—stretched through the streets of Rameses, ready to embark on uncharted freedom.

Moses used Miriam's cart as a ladder to climb the pedestal of Ramesses's statue. He raised his staff above his head and shouted on the morning breeze, "Remember this moment—this day—and tell your children and their children that Yahweh, the God of Abraham, Isaac, and Jacob, brought you out of Egypt with a mighty hand." Thousands cheered, sending a rumble through the foundations of Egypt itself. Eleazar and Joshua helped Moses climb down—the man who was once Egypt's prince had become Israel's deliverer.

Miriam raised her voice with the others. What a joyous day. Glancing at Aaron and Elisheba in the cart beside them, she saw even Elisheba laughing. Was the old ox losing her sharp horns? Never. Miriam laughed all the more.

Joshua mounted the black stallion he'd been given by a happy-to-be-alive, second-born Egyptian soldier. Eleazar led the two oxen pulling Miriam's cart, and Nadab led his parents' oxen and cart.

Miriam watched as they passed the Egyptians lining the streets. Most were silent. Some wept. One soldier cried out, "Canaan is northeast. You're already lost." A few joined the mocking.

Troubled, Miriam shouted to Eleazar, "Does Moses know where he's going?"

Eleazar cast a wry grin at her, and Hur patted her leg. "Yahweh is leading us, not Moses. We will do well to remember that in the coming days."

When they stopped for a midday respite, her questioning became a bit more subtle as she asked her husband questions quietly. "Eleazar spoke of the Way of Horus when he marched to Canaan. Why aren't we taking that well-traveled highway?"

Hur brushed a stray hair from her eyes and offered her the last bites of his bread. "Moses said the Way of Horus was a shorter route to Canaan, but it's traveled by many merchants and patrolled by foreign armies."

"But we have weapons," Miriam said. "Yahweh is with us."

"Our men may be armed for battle, but they'll run back to Egypt like whimpering children if we face war now. Most of our men aren't trained, and until now Yahweh has fought and won our battles for us. We're learning to know Him, but we have no idea who we are as a nation."

The second part of their day was longer and harsher. The sun cooked both men and beasts, and their meager supplies ran low before they reached the first encampment.

"Sukkoth is over that rise," Moses said. "There's water for the animals, and we're out of Egypt's grasp." Joshua sent his messengers down the flanks of the procession, spreading the message to the nation. A cheer rose from behind them, giving hope to finish strong.

When they crested the rise, Miriam saw what looked like paradise after the dry plain they'd traveled that day. A wadi flowed through softly rolling hills with a few patches of grass and clustered palm trees. Dozens of shoddy tents were already set up there, but she resolved to keep her questions to herself.

Miriam squeezed Hur's arm, letting the reality of the moment settle in. "Our first night of freedom."

He bounced his eyebrows. "Our first night as husband and wife."

Miriam swatted his arm, her cheeks warming. They were too old for such nonsense. Surely, he didn't think . . .

He pulled her into a tender kiss. Her body responded, deepening her blush and speeding her heartbeat. When he looked into her eyes, she saw the man she'd loved since she was a girl.

"You'll always belong to Yahweh," he said, "but He shared you with me, and we'll honor Him every day we're together."

Those already camped at Sukkoth came out of their tents to see the mass of people descending on their quiet camp. Moses approached a few, embracing them like long-lost friends. Perhaps his years as son-in-law to a Midianite chieftain had prepared him in more ways than Miriam realized. Yahweh wasted no experience, no matter how seemingly insignificant.

The weary Hebrews made camp, the women baking more of the bread dough they'd kneaded before dawn. Small cook fires littered the countryside as far as the eye could see. Aaron and his family joined Miriam's household while Sattar nestled beside her, exhausted from his busy day of herding sheep, playing with children, and keeping watch over an entire nation. Taliah lay in Eleazar's arms, sore from the jostling, but refusing to complain. No one spoke, weariness claiming them all. Freedom, they were all discovering, was hard work.

The night was utterly still when Moses left their fire, climbed a nearby rock, and let his voice carry on the wind. "Commemorate this day, the day you came out of Egypt, because the Lord brought you out of it with a mighty hand. When the Lord brings you into the land of the Canaanites, Hittites, Amorites, Hivites, and Jebusites, you are to observe a special ceremony in this month, on this day each year: For seven days, we will eat bread made without yeast and on the seventh day we'll hold a festival to the Lord. On that day tell your children, 'We do this because of what the Lord did for us when He delivered us from Egypt.'"

One man shouted, "We will!" Others took up the chorus, and the nation rose to their feet and shouted as one, "We will! We will! We will!"

Moses returned to their family circle amid the chorus of commitment, looking as weary as Miriam felt. "I'm not sure we have enough grain for seven days of bread, brother."

He grinned at her. "We'll have enough."

Of course, they would. Why must she always question? Exhaustion swept over Miriam in a wave, and she leaned against Hur. "I'm tired."

Eleazar was on his feet immediately, helping both Miriam and Hur to stand. "I've prepared your wedding tent," he said with a wink.

She swatted him. "Stop that!" Her cheeks flamed as Hur placed his hand at the small of her back, gently guiding her to the tent made of sticks, linen sheets, and palm branches.

Sattar followed, but Hur stopped him at the tent flap. "You sleep outside tonight." The dog sat at the entrance and watched Miriam crawl into the small space. She rolled onto their sleeping mat and felt the warmth of Hur's body beside her.

"Come," he said. "Lie in my arms so we can stay warm."

She obeyed without a word, trembling like a maiden. Who had ever heard of an eighty-six-year-old virgin?

Hur kissed her hair and whispered softly, "Yahweh created man and woman to delight in one another. On the night you rest in my arms without trembling, we'll explore those delights."

59

Pharaoh will think, "The Israelites are
wandering around the land in confusion,
hemmed in by the desert." And I will harden
Pharaoh's heart, and he will pursue them.
But I will gain glory for myself through
Pharaoh and all his army, and the Egyp-
tians will know that I am the LORD.

—EXODUS 14:3–4

On the seventh morning of Israel's freedom, Miriam sat beneath the canopy, watching children playing in the sand. Yahweh had sent a pillar of cloud by day and fire by night to lead them off the well-traveled paths into uncharted wasteland, through a valley until they reached the sea at Pi Hahiroth.

Miriam hummed a wordless tune and tapped gently on the timbrel that had become a comforting friend. She, Elisheba, and Taliah had prepared their food earlier in the day—fish over the coals, nuts, dates, figs, and plenty of flat rounds of the unleavened bread they'd eaten since leaving Egypt. Tonight, Miriam would mix a little flour with warm water and honey to begin a new start of leavening for their family. Yes, a new start.

"Why are you smiling, Miriam?" Taliah reclined against a rock, hands beneath her belly as though to lift some of the weight of it.

"I'm thinking of all the new things we'll see on our way to Canaan." She pointed at the families splashing in the water. "They're swimming with dolphins and sea cows, animals I never knew existed until a few days ago."

Taliah perked up. "The children said the dolphins are friendly. Masud grabbed one of their thick fins and rode it through the water."

"They would also make a tasty meal." Nadab ducked his head, anticipating his sister-in-law's ire. Taliah threw Eleazar's cudgel at him.

Usually quiet Ithamar had joined their camp and jumped into the fray. "Sea-cow hides make the best tent covers." A pregnant pause emphasized his mischievous grin. "They're water repellant."

"Oohh!" The women groused at the thought of the fascinating creatures used for such common purposes.

The ruckus roused Hur, who'd been napping beside Miriam. He let out a horrendous snort, smacked his lips, and nestled his head in her lap. She brushed his hair off his forehead, listening to the soft snoring that had become as soothing as the splashing of waves. The tenderness he'd shown in their private moments was beyond a young girl's dreams and an old woman's hopes.

ﮔﮔﮔﮔﮔ

"Pharaoh's fury will ignite again when he realizes we left Egypt for more than a few days' worship," Moses said, eyes scanning the horizon.

Eleazar's heart squeezed in his chest. "Do you really think he'll pursue us after all the devastation?"

"He'll pursue us." Moses sighed and combed his fingers through his silver hair.

Behind the camp, their soldiers trained with Ru and the other captains Joshua had appointed. Good men, all of them, but not skilled enough to defend against Egypt's army. The whole camp would be wiped out if Yahweh didn't protect them. "It makes no sense to wait for an army that would annihilate us."

"It may seem that we're trapped," Moses said with a raised brow. "But Yahweh told me last night that we're to camp here, near Pi Hahiroth. If Yahweh says stay, we stay. We obey Him in everything, or we wander as a people alone. It doesn't seem like much of a choice to me."

Eleazar turned his back while he searched the seaside camp for his wife, a way to calm himself. Taliah's wound had healed well without festering, and she was even walking a bit now. Another reason to trust Yahweh, right?

A hand on his shoulder stopped his musing and turned him around. "There." Moses said.

Eleazar shielded his eyes from the blazing sun and followed the direction of Moses's pointing finger. Chariots. Hundreds of chariots. With Ramesses's chariot leading.

Without waiting for directives from Moses, he ran to the shoreline, calling for Joshua, Aaron, and Hur. By the time they returned, a cloud of dust rose in the distance.

Their flurry roused the attention of others, throwing the camp into chaos.

"Why did you bring us into the desert to die?" A man shouted at Moses. Women wailed and children cried. Fear crawled through the tribes like a living thing, devouring the already slippery hope to which they clung.

"We shouldn't have left Egypt," one woman cried.

They saw the first glint of iron weapons as a seemingly endless line of chariots snaked through the mountain foothills. Horsemen followed the chariots.

Screams grew louder. Panic rose. People ran. But where could they go? They were hemmed in by mountains all around, the sea at their backs. Some collapsed where they stood, weeping.

Eleazar scanned the terrified faces. Where was Doda? Finally, he spotted her among the crowd. Standing—just standing—terror etched on her features. He'd seen her discouraged and even grief-stricken but never terrified.

He ran toward her, and she shouted as he approached, "What did Yahweh say to Moses? What must we do?"

Without answering, he hurried Doda back to their family's campsite amid the people's hysteria. "Was it because there were no graves in Egypt," one man shouted, "that Moses brought us to the desert to die? Didn't we say to him in Egypt, 'Leave us alone; let us serve the Egyptians'?"

Eleazar peered over his shoulder and saw Moses drop to his knees and fall face down in the sand as he reached the shore. Doda must have seen it too. She covered a sob and fell into Hur's arms as they reached the tent, hiding her face against his chest. Taliah rushed into Eleazar's arms, trembling—or was it Eleazar's fear that shook them both?

ممممم

Miriam heard Joshua shouting orders to his men. Hittites, Nubians, Libyans, and Hebrews—right flank, archers, and other military talk. She couldn't grasp the commands, but any defense was futile. Did he think slaves could resist the most powerful army in the world?

Moses leapt to his feet—sand still clinging to his forehead and beard—and ran back toward the panicked Israelites. His countenance had completely changed. "Hur, look." Miriam pointed at her brother. "He's heard from Yahweh."

Running into the middle of the chaos, Moses waved his staff and shouted, "Don't be afraid. Stand firm. Stand firm!" Jumping and bellowing, he gained their attention by the absolute certainty of his manner and the absurdity of his gestures. "Stand firm and you will see the deliverance Yahweh will bring you today. The Egyptians you see today you will never see again."

The crowd's hysteria became quiet weeping.

"Yahweh will fight for us," Moses cried. "We need only be still."

With a magnificent *Whoosh!* the pillar of cloud—in which some swore they'd seen the angel of God—suddenly swirled overhead, transforming into the fiery pillar that warmed their desert nights. The fiery pillar surged and expanded, creating an impenetrable barrier at the mountain pass, protecting the entrance to their camp from the advancing Egyptians.

The light and heat drove many Hebrews to their knees, their weeping turned to wonder, their wonder to praise. The enormity of God's majesty roared in fiery glory, and His firstborn Israel responded with a roar of worship, shaking the ground. As one, the nation lifted hands and voices, basking in the protective shelter of the One True God.

Yahweh blew a warm east wind, like a sigh of pleasure. Miriam lifted her face to the breeze and felt it intensify, the breath of God growing stronger.

Within moments, the gusting wind nearly toppled her.

Miriam searched for Moses. He stood at the edge of the Sea of Reeds with his staff extended over the water. The mighty wind whipped the water into the air, forming a strange sort of tunnel at her brother's feet. The tunnel exposed a patch of earth, and the wind kept blowing.

Israel scattered, rushing back to their campsites to batten down their tents and belongings. Miriam, too, scurried to grab rounds of unleavened bread as their meal skittered across the beach.

"Leave it!" Hur shouted, laughing. "We'll bake more on the other side."

Miriam hurried back to their campsite. "What do you mean, on the other side?"

He directed her to look back to the shoreline. Moses stood with his hands raised to heaven, worshiping. The wind had now formed a narrow alley, almost two camel-lengths long and one camel-length wide, driving the water into walls on each side.

"Unbelievable," Miriam said, pinching her husband's arm.

"Ouch! Why did you do that?" He rubbed the tender spot.

"It's not a dream if we experience it together." She grinned.

Others began to point and gawk in silent wonder as the alley between walls of water began to widen. The wind blew violently, remarkably, precisely. Miriam closed her eyes, letting herself feel the wind, Yahweh's touch—like an impassioned Lover, determined to rescue His people. She reached for her timbrel, shook it in lifted hands, and raised her voice in song—her highest praise.

"Yahweh, You have been our dwelling place throughout all generations. Before the mountains were born or You brought forth the whole world, from everlasting to everlasting You are God."

60

*The Egyptians pursued them, and all
Pharaoh's horses and chariots and
horsemen followed them into the sea.*

—EXODUS 14:23

When the moon reached its zenith, Moses sent Aaron and Hur to call the elders to a meeting at the family's campsite. "Yahweh is giving us until dawn to prepare our hearts. He will continue to divide the water so we can cross on dry ground."

Taliah squeezed Eleazar's hand and snuggled close, the assurance offering welcome relief.

Moses's smile ebbed, and his countenance grew somber. "We will be safe, but Yahweh will harden the hearts of all the Egyptians, and . . ." Eleazar watched his uncle struggle for words. "Pharaoh's army will pursue us."

The elders erupted into panicked questions, but Moses steadied the doubters with his unshakeable certainty. "Yahweh has promised that He will gain glory through Pharaoh and his army. He will prove to the Egyptians by this final act that He is the One God, and there is no other."

Moses turned to Joshua. "There are two changes to our order of march. Rather than having the army surround Israel on all sides, we'll assign all our soldiers as rear guard."

"My men are ready." Joshua seemed eager for a fight. "We'll hold the line when Pharaoh's army approaches."

"There'll be no battle." Moses sighed again, hesitating as he addressed the elders. "Joshua's men will gently prod any panicked Israelites who try to turn back. In fear, our people may become disoriented in the midst of the walls of water. They'll need firm direction and compassionate leadership to steer them to the opposite shore."

He looked over the elders' heads at Eleazar and Hur. "That's why I want Eleazar to wait with Hur and Miriam's cart to cross last, with our army. Our nation must see me leading Aaron's cart at the front and Hur and Miriam's cart at the rear while they are flanked by Yahweh's mighty protection. Stability and security. It's what our people will need when they see Pharaoh's army charging toward them."

Without comment or question, the elders dispersed to inform their tribes. Ru sounded the ram's horn, the signal for the army to gather, and he and Joshua left to assign the army's new positions.

Eleazar drew Taliah near. "I want you in Abba and Ima's wagon at the front."

She snuggled into his embrace and whispered, "I'm staying in your cart. Besides, it will take a miracle of Yahweh to get your Ima Elisheba to go first across that divide."

As if on cue, Ima's voice shattered the quiet. "Aaron and I need to be in the middle of the people, not in front. They depend on his strength and calm among them. Choose another cart to rush in first."

Moses took two steps, placing himself directly in front of her. "Elisheba, my wife Zipporah is much like you. She loves loud and requires a quiet assault to breach the walls of her heart." He leaned forward and spoke within a handbreadth of her face. "But yours and Aaron's cart *will* lead the nation across the sea at dawn."

Remarkably, Ima grew still, but the flutter of fear spread through the camp as elders imparted news of the coming confrontation.

Dawn. Yahweh had given them until dawn to prepare their hearts.

The clang of a timbrel startled Eleazar, but Doda's low hum soothed. Soon, the whole camp pulsed with the rhythm and sway of quiet praise. Eleazar even dozed a little.

As Moses approached the mighty standing waves, Miriam watched Aaron sit like a stone on the driver's bench while Elisheba's grousing could be heard over the rushing water. Her eldest nephew Nadab stood on the ground beside his ima, trying to soothe her, while Abihu held the frightened oxen steady. Miriam wasn't sure which of her nephews had the more difficult task. Ithamar offered encouragement to six elderly people in a nearby cart. Such a good boy.

"Yahweh, protect them," Miriam whispered as Moses took the oxen's reins from Nadab and began his march toward a long patch of fallen reeds marking the entrance of God's escape.

Miriam felt as if Pharaoh's horses raced inside her chest. The prospect of being trapped on all sides by people and deep water didn't appeal to her, but she refused to show fear.

The tribes fell into order, pouring onto the dry land between the divided waters. A handful of families hesitated slightly, but others gathered around them to encourage and help them across. The sight was staggering. Thousands of people—mostly Hebrew, but also a sprinkling of Egyptians, Libyans, Nubians, and Hittites—hurried into God's alleyway of escape. Women led donkeys that carried household goods, and children helped drive flocks of sheep and goats, while men managed herds of cattle and oxen.

"Are you ready?" Eleazar called back to them. "The tribes of Ephraim and Manasseh have crossed the reeds. We should line up behind Benjamin."

Hur drew Miriam close and raised his bristly brows. Hands trembling, she clutched the timbrel in her lap. "I'm ready," she said. "Let Yahweh be praised."

Eleazar clicked his tongue, and their oxen began plodding through the sand, giant hooves digging deep and dragging the cart across the beach. Joshua's ram's horn sounded, signaling Israel's army to fall into position as rear guard.

As the final band of Hebrews drew nearer the towering walls, Miriam experienced their sheer magnitude. The water rose higher than any of Ramesses's statues with a roar that was deafening. Light from Yahweh's fire shone into the mist from the towering walls, creating an iridescent glow through which the nation walked. A reverent awe settled over God's people as they walked the dry ground of His provision.

Fear was gone. Yahweh reigned.

Hur reached out to brush droplets from her cheek, his eyes shining with tears. "Remember this moment, Miriam. We must recount it to every generation."

She bent to rest her forehead against his. *Thank You, Yahweh, for this man who is Your voice to me, Your love to me, Your presence in my last days.*

The sound of a trumpet rent the air, stealing Miriam's attention. Looking over her shoulder at Yahweh's fiery blockade, terror shot through her. "The fire is changing!"

When the lower portion of God's pillar became a cloud—a veil that couldn't stop chariots—a second trumpet launched Pharaoh's chariots into action.

"Go! Go! Go!" Joshua shouted behind them. Some of his men rushed to prod their cart's oxen while others ran past them to hurry the tribes ahead.

Hur gathered Miriam into his arms, and she looked back again at Yahweh's fading protection. The last Hebrew soldier had just passed over the threshold of broken reeds. "Pharaoh's army will overtake us." The words came out in a whisper. She closed her eyes and buried her face on Hur's shoulder. Yahweh had warned them of Pharaoh's pursuit, but not this. *Not this, Yahweh!*

Lost in a fog of pandemonium, she could do nothing but wait. Trapped in the rear of this procession with these vexatious oxen. Anger welled up with fear as panic spread ahead of them. Thousands screamed. Donkeys brayed. Children cried. Terrorized by Pharaoh, King of Two Lands, Ruler of Egypt.

Why? Why were they terrified when Yahweh had warned them of His plan? Yahweh had even told them the precise moment at dawn to begin their march.

Miriam sat up as straight as a measuring rod and looked over her shoulder again. The fire of God still shimmered, but its brilliance had almost completely faded into a cloud with morning's light. The chariots reached the beach, Ramesses leading them. His double crown and regal bearing were unmistakable.

Memories of Ramesses as a child flashed in her mind. With angry tears and willful tantrums, he'd always gotten his way. Sety had never denied his son. No one had—until Yahweh.

"Look at the walls of water, everyone!" Miriam shouted, pointing to the right and left. "Focus on God's glory!"

Eleazar repeated the command to those ahead. "Look at the walls. Focus on God's glory!" Soon, the words echoed through the nation, forming a rhythmic marching mantra. "Look at the walls. Focus on God's glory. Look at the walls. Focus on God's glory. . . ."

Hur and Miriam grabbed each other's hands and shouted the refrain, staring at the magnificence of Yahweh's escape route. Then curiosity caused Miriam to look behind them again.

Pharaoh's horses strained forward across the beach where God's people had camped, flinging sand and spinning chariot wheels until they were mired to their axels. The Egyptians shifted their weight out of the chariots to shove with one foot as they held tightly to reins and rails. Slowed, but not stopped, Pharaoh and his men were relentless even covered in sand. The Hebrews were only one hundred chariot lengths ahead of the advancing army. If the chariots made it across the reeds, the horses would fly over the smooth seabed.

Hur began to pray while he, too, focused on Pharaoh's men. "Yahweh, Your power and might are supreme, and though we cannot guess Your plan, we will not doubt Your goodness."

Tears stung Miriam's eyes as she buried her face in her husband's chest. "We will never doubt Yahweh's goodness." Oh, to remember that always.

"Can't these oxen go faster?" Taliah screamed, on the verge of hysteria.

Miriam reached for her hand, and Taliah desperately clutched Miriam's hand. "Remember, my girl, you wanted a God you couldn't understand to do the things we know are impossible." Taliah nodded, still trembling violently. Miriam squeezed her hand, infusing what courage she could. "Watch for the impossible. We serve such a God."

Hur leaned over to speak above the noise. "Pharaoh has reached the line of reeds."

Miriam looked, heart in her throat. It didn't matter now how fast the oxen went. They could never outrun Pharaoh's stallions. *Yahweh, deliver us!*

As the first chariots entered the seabed, another trumpet sounded, and the chariots slowed. Ramesses looked left and right, utterly perplexed that another trumpet signaled the halt. His face twisted with rage, screaming at the trumpeter nearby.

Yahweh's fading cloud suddenly swirled behind them, lifting sand and debris into a whirlwind, further confounding Egypt's advance.

The oxen continued their jog, and Miriam covered a joyful sob. *Thank You, Yahweh.* Like an annoying fly, He was pestering Pharaoh, toying with the mighty king. Hope surged until she saw the whirlwind die. She heard the snap of reins against war horses and saw chariots lurch forward again, resuming their pursuit.

They advanced at an alarming speed; Miriam could now make out the red-feathered headpieces on Pharaoh's horses. Trembling all over, she jangled the timbrel unconsciously. Egypt's archers were within easy range of the last third of the rushing Hebrews. Why hadn't they fired? Even Miriam realized the military error—or was it another of Yahweh's interventions?

Hur reached for her hand. He was trembling too. Faith was a battle, its battlefield the mind. Surely, this moment would determine victory or defeat in their struggle to trust the God they proclaimed as good.

"I see the shore in the distance!" Hur shouted.

Miriam glanced toward their destination and saw Israelites lining the shore ahead, waving their hands, encouraging their brethren to run faster. Many of the tribes had already made it. Perhaps it was Yahweh's plan that only some of the nation survive. Her eyes slid shut. *Let it be as You will, Yahweh.*

"Miriam! Miriam, look!" Hur shook her. "The chariot horses are bucking and rearing."

Skittish and unruly, several pairs of horses clogged the alleyway, making it impossible to keep the pace they'd set on the smooth seafloor.

An Egyptian cried, "Get away from the Hebrews! Their God is fighting for them." Ramesses drew his bow and shot the man at close range. The whole army slowed and then stopped in an attempt to gain control over the frenzy that spread like a plague through the horses.

Cheers rose among the Hebrews. Timbrels clanged in rhythm with the Israelites' hurried footsteps. The shore was so close, only a quarter of the seabed left to cross. Taliah squealed, and her elderly friends in the cart cheered. Even Eleazar pounded his fist in the air with a victory shout.

Focused on the tribes waiting on the shore, Miriam scanned the crowd for Moses and Aaron and finally spotted them on a cliff overlooking the seabed. She raised her hand to wave, and they waved back—but she realized their wide gestures weren't a friendly greeting. They signaled with revived panic. Looking over her shoulder again, Miriam saw the reason.

Pharaoh's army had resumed their pursuit.

Israel's few moments of victory were swallowed up in renewed terror. *Yahweh, please. Please stop them.* As her prayer settled into her heart, she felt an overwhelming assurance.

Yahweh would stop them, but He was waiting—waiting on the choices of men. He'd promised He would gain glory, but He was a God of mercy and was giving Pharaoh and every Egyptian soldier ample opportunity to turn back—just as He'd given Ramesses ten opportunities to let Israel go. Yahweh wasn't toying with Pharaoh as Miriam had imagined. He was offering him a viable way out.

As others saw the chase resume, some on the seabed ran blindly, clawing their way through the crowd. Flocks and herds scattered. But others encouraged calm, seeming to realize the victory was theirs before the battle was over.

Joshua urged his guards forward as the chariot drivers closed the distance between them. Moses had instructed him to run, not stand and fight. Pharaoh's army was gaining ground, only fifty chariot-lengths behind, but Ramesses no longer led his troops. Where could he be? Miriam wriggled out of Hur's arms and stood, steadying herself in the moving cart with a hand on her husband's shoulder.

"Sit down. You're going to fall!" Hur tugged at her sleeve.

Miriam plopped down beside him. "Ramesses's chariot and two others have turned back. They're racing to the opposite shore while the rest of his army continues to pursue us." She was dumbfounded. "Why would he do that?"

The hope in Hur's eyes sparkled. "Perhaps he fears Yahweh after all." He nodded toward the shore where the Israelites waited for them. "I think we're going to make it—and Yahweh will gain His glory."

Taliah shouted at Miriam. "They should have used their archers by now." Miriam laughed out loud. It seemed everyone but Pharaoh realized it. Had Yahweh dulled the mind of Egypt's king?

They were close enough to shore to hear the riotous voices of Israel's men, women, and children. "Focus on His glory! Focus on His glory!" The chant had become the welcoming cry as each Hebrew stepped onto freedom's shore.

"The wheels!" someone behind them shouted.

Hur and Miriam turned in time to see the lead chariot tumbling end over end, its horse and rider with it. A second chariot lost a wheel, launching it into the air. Another, and then another—sending soldiers and drivers skidding onto the seabed. Oncoming chariots, unable to avoid the wreckage, trampled their comrades under hooves and wheels. Horses reared, and Pharaoh's army spiraled again into chaos.

The last of Benjamin's tribe crossed the line of reeds on the opposite shore, emerging from between the walls of water. Hur and Miriam's cart arrived next, followed closely by Israel's rear guard.

Moses, whose arms had been lifted in praise, suddenly extended his staff over the sea. With a horrible crashing sound, the magnificent walls of deliverance became Yahweh's final blow to Pharaoh's army. The waves began their collapse nearest the Hebrews, cutting off the immediate threat to God's people. The water rolled, like two giant scrolls, toward the far shore, crushing the Egyptians with their horses and chariots.

Reverent awe anointed God's people. Only the lapping of waves joined one strong baritone voice: "I will sing to the Lord, for He is highly exalted," Moses sang from the cliff above. "Both horse and driver He has hurled into the sea." He repeated the chorus and then let more words pour out in verse. "The Lord is my strength and my defense; He has become my salvation. He is my God, and I will praise Him, my father's God, and I will exalt Him."

Tears streamed down Miriam's cheeks, remembering the frightened boy she'd sung for when he was Prince Mehy. Now, he led God's people in praise to Yahweh with a song springing from his own intimate encounter. "Eleazar," she said, "help me down."

Her nephew hurried to obey and then help Hur. By the time Miriam's feet touched the soil of true freedom, Moses's tune had worked its way into her heart. She joined her brother in song, banging her timbrel on beat, "I will sing to the Lord, for He is highly exalted. Both horse and driver He has hurled into the sea."

The joy of the moment set Miriam's feet into motion, and soon every woman with a timbrel was dancing and singing the chorus between the verses of Moses's heart of praise: "The Lord is a warrior; the Lord is His name. Pharaoh's chariots and his army He has hurled into the sea."

The celebration diminished only slightly as dead Egyptians began to wash ashore. Hur found Miriam and bolstered her with his strong arm around her waist, her legs shaking from the dance. He pressed his lips against her ear. "Look across the sea, my love, and know that Yahweh is good."

Perhaps a dozen chariots were poised on the opposite shore. They made no effort to collect their dead. The distance was too great to make out their faces, but it was abundantly clear when they turned toward Egypt.

Yahweh had gained His glory, and Miriam would glory in Yahweh.

Author's Note

I n this brief space, I hope to give you a glimpse into my research and thought process for writing *Miriam*. I trust you'll see more clearly the person of Miriam, the plagues she endured, and the God she came to know.

A Peek at the Prophetess

Though first introduced to us as the "sister who stood at a distance" when Moses was rescued by Pharaoh's daughter, Miriam is mentioned by name only six times in Scripture. Her influence over Israel before and after the Exodus, however, was profound.

- Exodus 15—Miriam, the prophetess, led women in song and dance after crossing the Sea of Reeds.
- Numbers 12—Miriam criticized Moses and was punished with leprosy from the Lord.
- Numbers 20—Miriam died in the wilderness after forty years of wandering.
- Deuteronomy 24—Miriam's punishment is alluded to as ample reason to obey the Lord.
- 1 Chronicles 6—Miriam is confirmed as daughter of Amram, sister of Aaron and Moses.
- Micah 6—Miriam's leadership over Israel is affirmed as God-given.

Miriam's relationship with God was surely unique in a time when El Shaddai had been silent since the days of the Patriarchs. She holds two "first" designations in Scripture. One as the first prophetess mentioned in God's Word and also as the first to practice dance as a form of worship. Scripture affirms that Miriam, though not perfect, was wholly committed to God from early childhood until the day she died in the wilderness.

PROVING THE PLAGUES

In preparing to write about the ten plagues, studying the scientific view was vital to develop Pharaoh's doubts. Many scholars—even biblical scholars—deny the Israelites were slaves in Egypt, deem the plagues impossible, and disallow the historical Exodus. For those folks, no evidence will suffice; however, I discovered a very interesting book, *The Miracles of Exodus: A Scientist's Discovery of the Extraordinary Natural Causes of the Biblical Stories,* by Colin Humphreys (a British physicist).

Sir Humphreys included fascinating information and detail in his studies. Some I agreed with, some I did not. However, his scientific explanations for the plagues and his rationale for their seasons and pacing were extremely helpful in developing a believable timeline. Did the Nile turn to blood—real, organic blood—or was it some type of slimy red algae? I personally believe it was blood (because the Bible says it was blood), but Pharaoh may have doubted it was blood and explained it away with a scientific explanation—as many do today.

Sir Humphreys readily admitted science too often sought to disprove faith, but his book consistently proved the Bible correct in its assertions. A refreshing and interesting read.

INTERPRETING "I AM"

I've lost count of how many times I read Exodus 1–15 while writing this novel, but one day Exodus 3 rocked my world. Moses had gone to check out the burning bush on Mount Horeb, and God had just revealed his name, *Yahweh.* The study note on Exodus 3:14 in *The Jewish Study Bible* gave a slightly different interpretation of I AM: "God first tells Moses its meaning: *Ehyeh-Asher-Ehyeh* . . . meaning 'My nature will become evident from My actions.'"

I've heard Yahweh defined as, "I AM that I AM," but this idea of

God's nature being proven by His actions formed the crux of Miriam's internal struggle. For eighty-six years, God had acted quietly, spoken only in dreams, and only to her. He was manageable if not predictable.

Then He suddenly begins shouting through plagues? What's up with that?

Based only on the first three plagues—before the distinction between Egypt and Goshen was made, when there was no clean water, frogs were hopping, gnats were biting—what would you have thought of Yahweh's nature? Would you have trusted Him, or would you have feared such a God? Only after His fierce majesty was displayed did Yahweh show His great love for the Israelites. That's what we find in the Bible we hold in our hands today. Only after we see God's fierce holiness through the Old Testament Law can we fully appreciate Jesus's great love through grace in the New Testament.

It is my prayer that you, dear reader, will come to know Yahweh—intimately, personally, and fully—and become, as Miriam was, captivated by a God you can't understand that will do things you know are impossible.

READERS GUIDE
(Beware, spoilers ahead.)

1. When Miriam is plagued by troubling dreams, her first response is fear that El Shaddai will inflict suffering on her family. What do these fears reveal about Miriam's concept of El Shaddai's character? In what ways were her fears realized? In what ways were they misperceptions? Do similar fears lurk in your mind? How can Miriam's experience ease your fears?

2. A plateau slave remarks to Miriam, "If this is what it means to be *chosen* by your God, I'd rather serve Anubis and take my chances in Egypt's afterlife." Do we know from Scripture that some Israelites embraced Egypt's foreign gods or is this content purely fiction? How is the slave's attitude similar to those embittered toward God in today's culture—and how can a Christ-follower respond?

3. When Moses returns to Egypt, he reveals El Shaddai's "secret name"—Yahweh—which means, "My nature will become evident by My actions." (*The Jewish Study Bible,* Oxford Press, 2003). How does this definition expand your understanding of God's name? What have you learned of His nature through His work in *your* life?

4. Why do you think Yahweh allowed the first three plagues to affect the Hebrews as well as the Egyptians—without giving any explanation? If you went to church and suddenly frogs appeared from every corner and crevice, covering the floor, the chairs/pews, and the altar after the sermon and during the final song—with no explanation from the leadership—what would you think? Would you immediately assume it was judgment for sin? What would be your response?

5. When Prince Kopshef killed Taliah's abba, Putiel, Moses said the prince hated Putiel because he was like a *mirror* to Kopshef—Putiel's righteous acts *reflecting* the exact opposite of Kopshef's worst traits. Are there people in your life who are *mirrors*? What traits do they reflect in you—good or bad—that you might not see without them in your life? Do you humbly learn from them, or does pride cause bitterness to harm the relationship?

6. On the day of Taliah's wedding, Miriam advises her about Eleazar, "Love him as he is, and let Yahweh change him." Was this good advice for biblical-era marriages? Is it good advice for married couples today? Why or why not?

7. Moses wouldn't have known how many plagues Yahweh would visit upon Egypt, but he knew from the time he journeyed from Midian that the last plague would cost Pharaoh his firstborn sons (Exodus 4:22–23). Do you think that knowledge helped, hindered, or had no effect on the individual experience of each plague? Do you think knowing the outcome of some of your hardships would help, hinder, or have no effect on your experiences?

8. When Miriam is on her way to treat Pharaoh's boils, she and Eleazar have a serious conversation about why Yahweh has allowed terrible things to happen to the people they love. Miriam says, "I don't deny Yahweh lets bad things happen. We simply disagree on *why*." Did this discussion clarify or muddy your views on why God allows bad things to happen to good people? Why?

9. When Eleazar is badly beaten by Kopshef, Miriam breaks down and asks Moses, "How can we know when Yahweh will protect us and when He'll welcome tragedy into our house? Why did He protect Eleazar from the hail and then allow this?" Many people give up praying for God's protection or healing, taking a fatalistic

view of God's will. What would you tell Miriam if she asked you, "Should we pray for protection? Should we pray for healing?" Why would you give such advice?

10. Miriam struggles with her perceived changes in God, but Moses insists that it's not Yahweh who has changed but rather Miriam's *knowledge* of Him. Miriam is willing to agree but is left with the very real complexities of how the new knowledge changes her daily relationship with God. As God's work in your life reveals new aspects of His nature and character, how do you wrestle with the sometimes confusing feelings that arise?

11. Taliah grew timid when she was faced with asking Masud's father for the third time to consider circumcision (to save Masud from the plague of firstborns), but Miriam used two reminders to displace Taliah's shyness. 1) She reminded her that life and death were at stake, and 2) that Taliah had been passionate about the children's education—could she be any less passionate about their eternity? How does Miriam's wisdom transfer to sharing your faith today? Share a time when you were too shy to voice your beliefs with someone who needed that Lifeline. Share a time when you overcame timidity with boldness.

12. Eleazar asks Moses and Miriam if Mosi—as an uncircumcised foreigner—can believe in Yahweh and enter paradise with Abraham in the afterlife. Did anything surprise you about Moses's or Miriam's answers? What similarities do you see between Mosi's situation and the thief's circumstance on the cross in Luke 23:39–43?

13. While Eleazar was worried about getting weapons from the Egyptians, Moses was planning for Israel's defense against desert tribes in the wilderness. Eleazar described this as the "difference between wavering doubt and steadfast faith." Is there a circumstance

in your life in which you're acting more like Eleazar (wavering doubt—focusing on the impossible immediate problem) or Moses (steadfast faith—focusing on the issues that will arise *after* God's faithfulness)?

14. What was most surprising about the (fictional representation of) preparation for the Exodus? Are there questions in your mind still left unexplored? What part of the journey seemed most daunting—the number of people, the terrain, limited provisions?

15. Though Yahweh had promised their deliverance, Israel still fled in terror when Pharaoh's army pursued them through the Red Sea. Miriam acknowledged that *"faith was a battle, its battlefield the mind."* In what ways did she fight fear, and how can you use some of her tactics on your own battlefield of the mind?

16. Throughout the story, God tests each character—and proves Himself—at the core of each of their identities: Miriam as a prophetess and leader of Israel, Eleazar as a military slave, and Taliah as someone who values her intellect above all else. At what point in the story did each of these characters realize Yahweh met them at the core of their personhood? What do you consider "the core of your identity"? In what ways has God tested you there? How has He proved His faithfulness to you there?

FEAR
IS THE MOST
FERTILE GROUND
FOR
FAITH

MESU ANDREWS

"Poetic and fiercely compelling, this is Mesu Andrews's finest yet."
—TOSCA LEE,
bestselling author of
The Legend of Sheba and Iscariot

THE
PHARAOH'S
DAUGHTER

A TREASURES OF THE NILE NOVEL

Based on extensive biblical and historical research, Mesu Andrews breathes new life into the story of Moses from the perspective of the Egyptian princess who found him. You will meet the brave midwives who protected the sons of the Hebrews, the talented young Miriam whose singing soothes the heart of a Pharaoh's grandson, and a boy becoming a man on the verge of choosing which deity he will follow.

WATERBROOK PRESS
www.waterbrookmultnomah.com